PRAISE FOR

A fascinating and helpful read about a woman caught in the web of another person's deceit, manipulation, crazy making, and abuse and how God gently opens her eyes and leads her step by step out of bondage and into freedom.

—Leslie Vernick, counselor, speaker, coach, and author of *The Emotionally Destructive Relationship*

Like an executive chef in a five-star restaurant, Ginny Yttrup serves up an exquisite story, breathtakingly rich, with layers of flavor and the choicest of ingredients. Her characters are precisely and artistically carved and set atop a decadent bed of circumstances that tug at both heart and soul, with a grace to match each flaw. A story simultaneously rare and well done!

—Cynthia Ruchti, author of the Carol nominated novel *They Almost Always Come Home*, and one of the authors of the devotional collection *His Grace is Sufficient...Decaf is Not*

From Ginny's understanding about life's challenges but also an abiding life with God, she offers us the sort of heroine I love: a drifting woman whose growing trust in God gives her courage to reexamine her approach to life and make gutsy decisions.

—Jan Johnson, author of *Enjoying the Presence of God* and editor of *Madame Guyon: An Autobiography*

Lost and Found by Ginny Yttrup is an exquisitely written book, lyrical and poetic, charming in its presentation. More important, the message goes deep and takes the reader along on a pilgrimage toward the Father's heart, which is ultimately the purpose of every human being on the face of the earth. Thank you, Ginny, for reminding us of that simple fact in such a lovely and refreshing way.

—KATHI MACIAS, speaker and author of more than thirty books, Golden Scrolls Novel of the Year Award, and Carol Award finalist

LOST AND FOUND

GINNY L. YTTRUP

SHELTERWOOD
PRESS

To my soul friends . . .

Laurie Payne Breining and James Warrick

*What's lost is nothing to what's found, and all the death that ever was,
set next to life, would scarcely fill a cup.*
FREDERICK BUECHNER FROM *GODRIC*

I am lost and hope never to find myself. God is.
JEANNE GUYON

*Whoever finds his life will lose it, and whoever
loses his life for my sake will find it.*
MATTHEW 10:39

CHAPTER ONE

Lose yourself and you will find yourself again.
In doing this you will begin to experience the new life.
JEANNE GUYON

*J*enna

I LOSE THINGS.

Oh, I don't mean to, despite Brigitte's accusations.

The latest items I've lost include a watch. Platinum. Diamond bezel. The one Brigitte loaned me until my own watch was repaired. I told her I'd keep it in the safe in our cedar-lined master closet. But...

I noticed the watch missing the same evening I went to the safe to remove my wedding ring to wear to dinner. The ring was a family heirloom passed from Brigitte to the only Bouvier heir, Brigitte's son, Gerard. I pulled the ring from its black velvet box

1

and slipped it onto my finger over the platinum band I wear every day. I looked down at it, and tiny, empty prongs mocked me.

The four-karat, marquise-cut diamond was missing.

I open the safe for what must be the hundredth time since last week and look again for the watch. I run my fingers over the shelves feeling for the loose diamond. But neither is there. I close the safe and sigh. The missing jewelry, I sense, is an outward manifestation of something inward.

Gerard hasn't noticed the lost items. There is, it seems, a benefit to his detachment after all. Nor has he noticed the most essential thing I've lost.

Myself.

What *isn't* lost is the irony: Brigitte owns all three missing items.

I walk from the closet and stand in front of the mirror in the master bedroom. Downstairs, I hear guests arriving. I take a deep breath and, out of habit, glance at my reflection. I don't allow my eyes to linger on the image reflected back to me. I turn with the intent of heading downstairs for the charity brunch Brigitte and Gerard are hosting this morning, but once I reach the first floor of the house, I turn toward the solarium rather than taking the final flight of stairs to the ballroom.

I slip into the solarium through the open double doors. I ease the doors shut, not wishing to draw attention to my presence. I need a few moments alone. Time to prepare myself for the event ahead—the stares of those who don't know me.

The averted glances of those who do.

I used to enjoy such events—raising money for a worthy cause. I sat on the boards of various charities and planned many events.

I built relationships. I found a place for myself. A purpose.

But that was before.

I walk to the middle of the room and stand in front of the floor-to-ceiling windows, which offer an expansive view of the city and the bay. I breathe deep and bow my head, releasing all thoughts of what is lost and focus instead on what is found.

Solitude is my companion and peace its offered gift.

Love swells within.

With eyes closed against the sunlight streaming in through the windows, I feel a flutter against my cheek. I lift my hand and tuck the loosed strands of my dark hair behind my ear. A breeze swirls.

Refreshing.

Restoring.

The aromas of honeysuckle and jasmine encircle me as the strains of a string quartet soar in crescendo. The wind catches the end of the chiffon scarf around my neck and it tickles my bare shoulder. My mind searches for words but none convey the stirring I sense. I wipe away the tears slipping to my chin.

Wind rushes.

Love calls.

Somewhere behind me a door clicks shut. I raise my head, open my eyes, and strain to focus against the light. White linen fabric drapes across decorative rods and pools on the floor on either side of the paned windows around the room. The linen billows in the breeze.

As my eyes focus, I step forward to close the windows, wondering who opened them. But then I see they are closed.

Latched tight.

The drapes settle.

My breath catches and my skin prickles.

"Jenna!"

I jump.

She hisses through clenched teeth. Her heels tap in military precision against inlaid marble as she comes up behind me. I turn from the windows to face her just as she reaches for me. Her acrylic nails dig into my upper arm.

"We. Have. Guests."

"Yes. I'll be right there. I'm sorry."

I chide myself for apologizing. Again.

"You'll come now!"

She pulls on my arm and I stumble. Once she has let go of me, I find my stride behind her. At seventy-six her gait is still swift. With each step she takes the red soles of her Christian Louboutin pumps flash against the white, gray, and black marble of the solarium floor. When she reaches the doors, she stops. I stumble again, trying not to bump into her. She turns on one heel and looks at me. Her gaze lands on the jagged scar that follows what was my jawline on the left side of my face, pulling my mouth into an awkward smirk. "You called Dr. Bernard, yes?"

Her French roots slip out in her phrasing. There are times her accent almost sings. Other times, like now, it drips with the attitude so often attributed to the French: disdain.

"No." I lift my chin intending to meet her gaze, but with just one glance my heart beats like the wings of a hummingbird and I end up staring at the floor.

"I'll call him myself. I've told you, he can fix…*that*."

"It isn't that simple." I force my gaze to meet hers.

"*Mais oui*, it is." Then her look moves to the red, crescent-shaped welts on my arm. "Slip your cardigan over your shoulders before you meet our guests." She opens the door and speaks to one of the staff in the hallway. "Hannah, find Jenna's cardigan and bring it to her." With that, she turns and walks out.

I wrap my arms around myself and exhale. I turn back toward the wall of windows and see the bay glistening in the distance.

I inhale deeply, trying to catch my breath—the scent of honeysuckle hangs in the air. Just as I turn to go, I notice the drape on the end window nearest the French doors stir and billow again. I smile and feel the right side of my mouth rise up to meet the left side.

"Jenna, your sweater." The staff dispensed with *Mrs. Bouvier* soon after I arrived—not out of familiarity, or even fondness, as I would have hoped, but instead upon *her* orders. Hannah reaches to place the sapphire sweater, the exact color of my eyes, over my shoulders, but stops.

"You'd better put it on." She holds the sweater out for me as I slip my arms into each sleeve. "You also better watch yourself and stop wandering off. You know your role here. Madame Bouvier's made that clear."

Hannah looks at my jaw. Do I imagine her sneer? She turns and walks out ahead of me. I hesitate at the open door. The quartet plays, glasses clink, conversation drones. I lower my gaze to the floor.

Yes. I know my role. Help me...

I make my way across the formal entry, and down the staircase to the lower level ballroom. The ballroom shares the same exposure as the solarium and opens to the gardens surrounding the mansion. The San Francisco Bay and the Golden Gate Bridge set a stunning backdrop.

The Georgian-style mansion was built in 1912 and is one of the crowning jewels of the Pacific Heights area. An invitation to a soiree at the Bouvier home is coveted in many circles. Even today's brunch, a benefit for the de Young Museum, is a gold star on the social credentials of those who paid to attend.

I walk into the ballroom and stop a moment to admire the scene. The room is set with round tables, covered in pale sage damask, with tall fluted vases burgeoning with trailing ivy and white spring blooms as centerpieces. The china is the finest antique Limoges paired with Baccarat crystal and antique French silver, each piece stamped with a boar's head. The staff floats among the guests serving flutes of *Domaine de la Bouvier* St. Helena 2004.

I take a glass offered by one of the servers and drain the flute of champagne, then return the glass to the tray and reach for another. I take a deep breath and exhale. My heart rate returns to somewhere near normal and I attempt to put the scene with

Brigitte out of my mind. I've become adept at denial, but now, it seems, there's a chink in the gear of that mechanism.

"There you are." Gerard places his hand on the small of my back and guides me to the head table. "We've been waiting on you. The committee chair wants to make a toast to the hosts before brunch is served. Stay close, Jenna." Gerard, with a slight nod of his head, signals my arrival to the waiting de Young trustee.

A knife clinking against a Baccarat flute calls the guests to attention. "Ladies and gentlemen, I'd like to take this opportunity to thank our gracious hosts, Madame Brigitte Bouvier and Mr. and Mrs. Gerard Bouvier…"

I raise my glass and sip, this time allowing the bubbles to play on my tongue.

Gerard's hand still on my back applies gentle pressure as he bends to my ear. "Smile, Jenna. You know you need to smile."

He nods as his guests applaud his charity. His smile engages everyone in the room. The smile demanded of me simply balances my facial features and makes me look more acceptable for the role I'm called to fill.

It is a role I aspired to—a role I longed for: Mrs. Gerard Bouvier. Wife of the famed vintner whose label, *Domaine de la Bouvier*, originated in Epernay, France in 1743. Gerard was groomed to oversee the Bouvier empire and Brigitte groomed me, the daughter of a native Californian vintner, to be Gerard's wife. I married Gerard on my twenty-first birthday—the day I could legally toast our union. He was forty-three. That was eleven years ago.

After the toast, Gerard guides me to the head table where we're seated with his mother, two members of the de Young Board of Trustees, including the vice president for Annual Support, Carolyn Harris, who organized this fund-raiser, her husband, Bryce, and my brother, Jason, and his date, whom he introduces as Andee Bell. Jason winks at me during his introduction of Andee. Should I know her?

Carolyn smiles. "Andee, it's a delight to meet you in person. You are a dear friend of the de Young."

Translation: Andee's a big donor.

"Thank you, Carolyn. I'm always thrilled when I can play a small part in something bigger than myself." Andee turns to me, "Jenna, so good to meet you. We'll talk. Jason tells me we have a lot in common."

I smile as I shuffle memories—has Jason mentioned Andee?

"Andee, good to see you again. I thought you and Jason might hit it off—it's not every day I get to enjoy the role of matchmaker." Gerard lifts his glass and salutes Jason and Andee.

I raise my glass and then empty it.

"Jenna, of course you know who Andee is?"

At Brigitte's question, a blush begins at the base of my neck and crawls up toward my face. I pull the chiffon scarf close to my neck, reach for my water glass, take a sip, and nod. "Yes, of course. Thank you so much for joining us, Andee."

I turn, make eye contact with one of the servers, and with an almost imperceptible nod, make known my desire for another glass of *Domanie de la Bouvier's* best. I turn back to the conversation at the table.

It seems I am the only one unaware of Andee's identity. Not unusual. I am often in the dark regarding important people and issues—as Brigitte is fond of reminding me.

As conversation flows around the table, I'm given a few moments to study Andee. Even seated, I can see she is taller than my 5' 4" frame. Her long, thin torso is enviable as are her dark chocolate eyes and thick blonde hair that cascades over her shoulders. Her porcelain skin is flawless and her small chin and delicate jawline are perfect.

Gerard reaches for my fingers—wrapping my hand in his. Startled, I realize I've been tracing the scar on my face. He whispers, "No need to draw attention to your imperfection. You're beautiful." His compliment confuses me but I let it go.

I lean close to him, "How do you know Andee?"

"Why? Jealous?" His tone teases but strikes a chord.

Brigitte, seated on the other side of Gerard, places her hand on his arm and whispers something to him. I'm grateful for the interruption so I don't have to respond to his question. There is truth in what he asks. Am I jealous of Andee? Yes, but not for the reason Gerard implied. What I envy is her flawless beauty and the confidence with which she carries herself.

I push back from the table, bumping it as I stand. Water sloshes over the rims of the glasses. "I'm sorry...excuse me for just a moment." I say this to no one in particular, and as I walk out of the ballroom, I can almost feel Brigitte's stare branding my back.

I take the hallway that leads to the elevator—less chance of running into household staff. I press the button and wait for the door to open. Once inside, I exhale, close my eyes, and let the back upholstered wall hold me up until the door opens on the landing of the third story of the house. I step out of the elevator, bend down, take off my patent pumps, and pad my way to the master bedroom. Once inside, I close the double doors and head to the hand-carved Louis XVI vanity. I collapse on the stool and rest my head atop my arms on the vanity. Hot tears spill. Envy hisses its condemnation.

She's gorgeous. You'll never be that beautiful again. You're worthless now.

I pick up the gold hand mirror from the vanity, hold it up to my face, and stare into the cracked glass. The abstract image staring back at me is Picasso-esque. Segments of my face reflect in geometric shapes. Sapphire eyes, lined in indigo, seem set at opposing angles. Full, glossed lips are askew. And the angry scar stretches wide.

"Shattered beauty..."

I set the broken mirror down, stand, and turn to the mirrored wall that runs the length of the room. *"I want to see your reflection no matter where you are in the room,"* he'd said when we remodeled the suite.

I smooth the fabric of my skirt over my slender hips, and turn to observe my profile. My sweater hugs my torso, and when I pull the scarf around my neck aside, the deep neckline of the sweater exposes my ample cleavage. My long, dark hair is swept up in a twist and sapphire and diamond earrings sparkle at my lobes. I close my eyes then open them. The scar remains and with it the strangling sense of shame.

I turn my back to the mirrored wall and recall the swirling breeze of just an hour or so ago—along with my fledgling awareness of late that, like the breeze swirling in the solarium, a longing for change swirls within me.

I recall the words spoken to my soul last week. *Stand back, Jenna.* I'd emptied the contents of my aching heart before Him, as I so often do. I cried out. I begged for an answer to the nagging question: How do I please Brigitte? How do I honor You in my relationship with her?

Stand back, Jenna.

I'm still grappling with the meaning. What does it mean to stand back from Brigitte? From my life? While I don't yet understand, there is a knowing that change is on the horizon. Change that somehow rests on my willingness to obey.

Still standing in front of the mirror, I dare myself to glance at my reflection again—to really see what's there. But, dizzy from the champagne, my balance is precarious, and I sidestep back to the stool at the vanity.

How soon I forgot my recent declaration to face the present rather than escape to the bliss of denial. That, I recall, is the chink in my self-protective mechanism: my decision to face reality.

My decision to stop drinking.

It is not a decision I made alone. On this, God was clear.

But the awareness was gentle. Tender even. Not an admonishment, but instead an encouragement. Why would I turn to a substance for courage when I could turn to Him?

I hang my head. Change is a slow, zigzagging road. One on which I will lose my way if I go it alone.

I reach for the pumps I dropped by the vanity and put each shoe on. I turn back to the mirror, lift my head, and for just a moment, I see myself as He sees me. But the image is fleeting. I pick up my compact, press matte powder under my eyes, on my nose, and a light dusting across my jawline. I gather the strands of hair loosed from the French twist with one hand, and open the drawer of the vanity with the other. I feel for a bobby pin, sure I have one or two more in the drawer. I reach further back and my hand lands on something hard, cold. I drop the strands of hair, pull the drawer out further, and there, in the back of the drawer, is Brigitte's watch.

I slip the watch over my wrist and fasten the clasp. I look at the watch and a shimmer of hope surfaces. At least one thing lost is now found. But then I look at my left hand and the single platinum band I wear.

How long will it be before Brigitte notices I'm not wearing the heirloom diamond?

What will that loss cost me?

I sigh.

I find the bobby pin I sought and tuck and pin the loose strands of hair back into the twist. I stand, take a deep breath to quell the spinning in my head, straighten the scarf around my neck, and return to the ballroom.

CHAPTER TWO

You seek the honor which comes from men, and you love to occupy
important positions. God wants to reduce you to childlikeness.
JEANNE GUYON

ndee

"I DON'T GET IT. Get you. You barely said two words to Gerard today. He's family, Jason, leverage the relationship. Make it work for you. Wasn't that the point of that marriage—a business merger?"

I lift the lid of the sleek ebony box on my glass-top coffee table and pull out one of the remotes. I point it at the floor-to-ceiling windows of the penthouse and the blinds slide open, revealing the twinkling lights of the nighttime cityscape.

Jason, who's sitting on the sectional facing the windows, reaches for me and pulls me down next to him. I sink into the buttery leather. He wraps his arms around me and nuzzles my neck. Then he whispers against my ear. "There are other things in life, Andee. Business isn't everything."

My shoulders tense and I pull away from him. "You really don't get it, do you?"

He sighs and straightens. "Yes, I get it. But you're stepping into territory you know nothing—"

"*What?* Look around you, Jason. No one handed me the money for this penthouse. I earned every penny of it myself. Have you forgotten? And I earned it advising others."

"Retract your claws, babe. I know who you are." A smile plays at the corners of his mouth. "What I'm saying is that you know nothing about my relationship with Gerard. Gerard and I are on equal footing and our relationship is just fine. We're friends. It isn't about business with us. Now, relax and enjoy the view you've worked so hard for."

"Don't patronize me."

"I'm doing no such thing." He sits up, puts his hands on my shoulders, and turns me until my back is to him. His fingers knead the muscles in my neck and shoulders. I lean into him. "You're knotted like a gnarled tree."

"I've earned those knots this week." I do a mental tally of the week's accomplishments, which include negotiations for syndication of my radio program in ten additional major markets, giving me a listening audience across thirty-four states, completion of ten blog posts, which I've banked for my recent foray into the blogosphere, a meeting with the editor-in-chief of *Urbanity* about writing a monthly financial column, and an offer from my publisher for my next book. The column for *Urbanity*, a local magazine, pays so little it isn't worth doing, but it's an avenue—a means to an end. I sigh.

"That's better."

I turn to face him. "Don't get used to it. You don't get ahead by relaxing."

Jason chuckles. "So I've heard, over and over and over."

"Well, don't forget it." I smile and wink at him. "So what's with your sister?"

"What do you mean?"

I laugh. "What do you mean, what do I mean? For years, I've heard talk of the beautiful and gracious Jenna Bouvier—even in circles where the gossip is vicious Jenna is lauded for her *kindness*." I realize my tone is sarcastic and check myself. "I mean, I'm sure she is kind, but she was aloof. She barely spoke to me. I expected more."

Jason shrugs. "I don't know." He pauses. "She seems more in her head these days. Distracted, maybe."

"I don't know what you thought we'd have in common."

"You're beginning to socialize in the same circles. Get to know her, Andee. As you said, she's well liked. I think you two could be friends. Besides, she's well-connected, she can open doors for you in this city."

I pull away from Jason again and stand up. "I open my own doors. You should know that by now. I'm making inroads into all the right circles. I told you about the offer from *Urbanity*. I don't need Jenna's help, or anyone's help, socially. The column in *Urbanity* alone assures that anyone worth knowing in this city will also know me. Anyway, from what I hear, Jenna doesn't socialize in those circles anymore, not since…well, you know."

He shakes his head. "I'm just saying…"

I cross my arms across my chest and stare down at him.

"I take it that's my cue to leave?"

"I have—"

"—work to do. I know." He stands and wraps me in his arms and whispers against my ear again. "I love your drive."

I plant a kiss on the tip of his nose. "I love that you love it."

After Jason leaves I go to the kitchen, take a bag of cat food from the pantry, and fill one of the stainless steel bowls that sits on the floor next to the pantry door. The *ping* of the pellets hitting the bowl alerts Sam that it's dinnertime. I wait by the bowl until I see him sauntering down the hallway.

Cool. Independent. Detached.

Sam's my idol.

He sits in front of the bowl, all seventeen pounds of him, as though he can't be bothered to eat.

"I'll leave you alone with your dinner." I bend and scratch the top of his head. He turns and his ice-blue eyes glare at me. "Sorry. I won't intrude, I promise." Before I'm out of the kitchen I hear Sam crunching his food.

I settle at my desk and pull a pile of papers off the top of the black leather in-box. I nudge the mouse on my desk and the 27-inch screen of my iMac comes to life. I click on the stamp icon and see 198 e-mails in my andee@andeebell.com in-box. Those arrived sometime between Cassidy's departure at 4:00 p.m. on Friday and now, 8:17 p.m. on Saturday. I'll leave those for Cass to respond to on Monday.

I rifle through the papers in front of me—the recent contract from my publisher. I refuse to hire an agent to handle my business negotiations. Why would I pay someone for something I can handle myself? I reach for a red pen and begin marking changes I still expect the publisher to make before I sign. I look at the advance offered. I cross through the figure in red and scrawl in its place the six-figure number that I'll demand. I won't do it for less.

I've attained financial freedom. I advise the CEOs of some of the top Fortune 500 companies. And because of my radio show, I'm now known across the country. "A household name..." I look at the number I've scrawled in red next to the advance and again think of the paltry stipend *Urbanity* offered for my column. But not everything is about money. I may be known across the country, but this city is where I will be someone.

Where I'll be accepted.

That's why I agreed to work with the Bouviers. Brigitte is a stepping-stone. She and Gerard are known in this community.

Though not natives, they made a splash when they arrived from France. They've made a name for themselves here.

As I continue to work, the silence of the penthouse irritates like a nagging gnat.

I stop, reach for the remote on my desk, swivel in my chair, and point it at the flat screen on my office wall. I turn up the volume. "Sam, where are you?" I turn back to my work.

The next time I glance at the computer screen, it's 10:49 p.m. I stand, reach for the ceiling and then bend at the waist a few times, I grab the remote, turn off the TV, and stack the papers on my desk. Then I wander out to the living room. I drop onto the sofa and pull my feet up under me and allow myself time to think through this morning's brunch.

What is with Jenna? It isn't just that she was "in her head," as Jason said—she was rude to me during brunch. But what about earlier...in the solarium? I'd told Jason I needed to use the bathroom and took a few minutes on my own to explore the Bouvier digs. When Jenna walked into the solarium, I thought I'd introduce myself and maybe apologize for wandering.

I shift on the sofa and stretch my legs out in front of me.

But, as I think about it now, *that's* when she was "in her head." She didn't even see me. So I stepped back, behind the yards of linen hanging from the windows, near the French doors that led to the balcony. I considered making a run for it undetected, but I couldn't pull myself away.

That look on her face—tension or angst or something. But then she seemed to transform before my eyes. From stressed to serene in sixty seconds or less. Now there's a trick I'd like to learn. And what about the tears that followed? Tears of what? She still seemed in that serene state. Until Brigitte intruded, Jenna seemed almost...what? I reach for one of the down pillows on the sofa and wrap my arms around it. I search for the right word or emotion to describe what I saw on Jenna's face.

Ethereal.

Yes, that was it. As though she'd been transported to another world.

Whatever she's taking, I want a dose!

As for Brigitte's exchange with Jenna? Ha! "Now, that was something! Anyone who'd pull that act with me would be sorry." Sam, who's sitting on the back of the sofa looks at me, disinterested. I reach forward and let my hand rest on his back. I feel the vibration of his purring begin. Why didn't Jenna stand up to Brigitte? What's wrong with her?

After a few minutes, I drop all thoughts of Jenna. There's time. I'll figure her out.

I get up and walk to the windows and look at the view of the East Bay. I guesstimate where Alameda Island and the naval base are in the sea of lights. The base closed in 1997—the same year I graduated from the University of San Francisco's business school —the closure changing the island forever. But for me the island— and all it represents—lives on just as it was when I was growing up. It represents my past. My present. My future.

I stretch my neck, putting ear to shoulder, and feel a satisfying pull. I turn my head and stretch the other way—my gaze never moving from the imagined locale of the island and the memories it holds. It's this view of the East Bay that sealed the deal on my decision to purchase the penthouse. It's this view—or, at least, the knowledge of the island's presence out there beyond the bay—that reminds me.

Drives me.

I square my shoulders, take a deep breath, and speak to the universe the empowering vow I made so long ago. "I will never forget..."

A dull ache—that void inside—nags. I place my hand on my chest and feel the beat of my heart—the assurance that I live. I am. Despite what happened there.

"I am. And I am all that I need." I push a niggling sense of doubt down—down into the void and attempt to seal it with the reminder of the sweet irony my view offers. It is the reverse of the view I grew up with. My life is here now, part of the skyline I stared at and dreamt of belonging to for so many years.

"Yes, I am. And I am exactly where I planned to be." I whisper.

Yet the void nags.

I turn from the view, grab for the remote still sitting on the coffee table, point it at the blinds, push the button, and watch as they close out the city below. I walk around the back of the sofa and reach for Sam and heft him into my arms. I pull him close to my chest and hold him there. When I reach to pet his neck, it is damp.

Damp, I'm disheartened to realize, with my own tears.

CHAPTER THREE

Let God be the Master over your heart. Be open to whatever He has to teach you, whether that word comes directly from Him, or through others.
JEANNE GUYON

enna

I STEP off the curb and wave. The cab cuts off another car, switches lanes, and pulls up alongside me. Cars honk and whiz past. I open the door and slide into the back seat. The inside of the cab smells like curry, and the back of the turbaned head in the driver's seat nods. "Where to, Mrs. Bouvier?"

I glance at the driver's identification displayed on the dash and smile. I reach over the back of the seat and place my hand on the driver's shoulder. "Ahsan?" Dark eyes smile back at me from the rearview mirror. The driver turns and looks at me over his shoulder.

"It is good to see you. Are you well?"

"Yes...I'm fine. I've just come from another doctor's appointment."

"Good news?"

I shrug my shoulders.

"Going home, then?"

"No, not yet." I need time. I glance at my watch. I won't be missed, I hope, for another hour or so. "Head to the park, Ahsan, and drop me at the tea garden, wait for me, and then take me home. All right?"

"Very good."

"Oh, Ahsan, take Lincoln Way out to the beach and then drive back in through the park."

"That is many more miles."

"Yes. Do you mind?"

I see the smile in his eyes as he glances back at me in the rearview mirror. "No, Mrs. Bouvier, as long as you do not mind."

I put the doctor's appointment out of my mind and focus on Ahsan. "How is your family? Any news on when they might join you?" Ahsan's father, wife, and children are still in Kolkata, India.

"I save and save. Someday soon, I hope, I will have enough for them to come."

"I read the *Urbanity* article about the mayor and some of the transportation officials trying to alter Proposition K, which would abolish the medallion list. How will that affect you?"

"It is very bad for the drivers. So many have waited ten, fifteen years, or more, to purchase available permits. Now their wait may have been in vain. And I, and others like me, will have no chance of ever owning a medallion. So much of our earnings go to leasing our medallions." He shakes his head. "It is very bad."

Ahsan and I discuss the implications of the Transit Reform bill and other city politics as he darts in and out of traffic—all the while I fight to keep my mind from drifting back to Dr. Kim's office. But as soon as we enter Golden Gate Park, a swath of over

a thousand acres that cuts through the urban bustle of San Francisco, I quiet, as does my mind. Ahsan seems to sense my shift in
mood and quiets as well. I drink in the beauty of the park and
ponder the impossible odds against which it exists—brought to
life in an environment others touted as a wasteland of vast sand
dunes exposed to sweeping winds. The skeptics assailed the inno-
vators with cries of cynicism: "Nothing will thrive there!"

They were wrong.

Instead, the barren environment, coupled with the sheer will
of the visionaries, yielded...life.

Growing, thriving, life.

I cling to this reality.

Ahsan pulls up in front of the Japanese Tea Garden and I
unbuckle my seatbelt and open the cab door. "Thank you, Ahsan.
I'll be just thirty minutes or so."

I exit the cab and stop at Ahsan's window. I tap. He rolls the
window down and I reach inside the cab and place my hand on
the arm he leans out the window. "Keep the meter running this
time. I've asked you to wait, which means I expect to pay for your
time." I pat his arm. "We need to get your family here."

The last time I asked him to wait for me, he did so, but turned
the meter off.

He nods and smiles. "Enjoy the garden, Mrs. Bouvier."

"Thank you. And Ahsan, it's Jenna." I tell him this each time I
see him. But he is not accustomed to equality and although I long
to level the ground between us, I recognize I can't transform his
thinking, which developed in a country where class systems
reigned for centuries.

Of course, we have our own class systems here.

I turn, take a few steps away from the curb, then stop in front
of the entrance to the garden. I close my eyes and listen. The
lilting melody from the strings of a dulcimer invite me to tran-
quility. I breathe in peace and exhale tension. I open my eyes,
reach for my wallet, and pull a large bill out. I cross a patch of

grass to where Skye sits under one of the giant Cyprus trees with her dulcimer on her lap, her nimble fingers strumming the strings. She tilts her head and smiles her welcome as she plays. Soon, the authorities will ask her to leave. But Skye always returns to the park. As do I. I bend and drop the bill in the tip jar at her feet and smile my thanks for the gift she offers as she plays.

"We'll catch up later."

Skye winks at me as I turn to go—her blonde curls bouncing in the breeze. A small crowd has gathered. Perhaps today Skye will earn enough to buy herself a decent meal. This is the sacrifice she makes to pursue what she sees as her purpose—a sacrifice most would scoff at. But for her, using the gift God's given her is more important than food or a place to live. Skye lives in the moment. She's shared her passion with me many times.

She's made an admirable choice.

And a courageous one.

How would it feel to know your purpose and have the courage to pursue it?

I head to the gate of the Tea Garden and pay the reduced entrance fee for San Francisco residents and then step into the embrace of the lush grounds. I wander the path that leads around the large pond and see my favorite bench, the one with the waterfall just behind it. I pick up my pace and reach the vacant bench before others claim it. I sit under the canopy of a vibrant red Japanese maple.

Here, among the throng of tourists, I am anonymous.

No expectations. No judgments. No role to fill.

Here, I'm free to just be.

I relax against the back of the bench and close my eyes. A child giggles. A couple walking by speaks in soft tones. A gull cries overhead. And in the background, the waterfall gurgles and soothes, and thousands of leaves rustle in the breeze.

Creation's symphony.

I think about Skye. We connected the moment we met. I was

on the planning committee for a garden luncheon to benefit the cancer society. Someone suggested we have live music, something simple to accompany lunch. I suggested Skye and assumed responsibility for contacting her. I didn't tell the other committee members that I didn't know her or have her contact information. Instead, I visited the Japanese Tea Garden every day for a week. It's where I'd heard her play for the first time and I prayed she'd show up again. When she did, I asked if she'd consider playing for the luncheon. She asked what the "gig" paid.

Skye is straightforward. No nonsense. No pretense. Her honesty, her transparency, drew me. Something about her freedom awakened an awareness of my own captivity. I longed to explore the fear that bound me and Skye asked all the right questions. Intuition lights her way through every conversation.

I didn't plan it. Instead, I spoke my first words of truth to Skye and, like a long line of dominos, the rest tumbled forward, out of my control. It was a truth I hadn't even revealed to myself until that moment.

A truth that set me on a new course.

I open my eyes again and see a man, just a few steps away, watching me. When he sees that I've noticed him, he looks beyond me to the waterfall. But I know the expression I caught on his face. I see it all too often, that combination of curiosity and pity. It is a reminder of the appointment I've just come from and the news Dr. Kim imparted.

It wasn't the news I'd hoped for.

Not so long ago, men's glances were appreciative, their stares suggestive. My beauty was admired and even envied. It offered a power I didn't hesitate to use. Because it was, I thought, the only power I had.

But now—

"Hey, girl. Lost in thought?"

I look up to see Skye, all five feet of her, standing in front of me. "Hi. I didn't see you."

She bends and gives me a hug, her worn denim jacket soft against my cheek.

"I hoped I'd see you today. Can you sit for a few minutes?"

"Yeah, Keiko at the front gate let me into the garden. She's taking a break and told me she'd watch my instrument out front. So I have fifteen minutes." Her smile reveals small, white teeth behind small, pink lips. Everything about Skye is small. Except her heart. "Was your appointment today?"

I nod and look back out at the pond. Talking about it seems pointless.

"Enough said?"

I nod again. "Hey, I have something for you." I reach for my purse and dig inside, feeling for the book I dropped in the bag before I left the house. But my searching fingers don't find it. I open the bag wider and rummage through it. "I know I put it in here."

"What is it?"

"That book we talked about last week." I take the purse and begin dumping the contents on the bench between us. "It was here, I know it." When my purse is empty and it's evident the book is gone, I sigh. "How could I lose it?"

"Don't worry about it. It'll turn up."

I shake my head. "I don't know." I look at her and see the smile she's trying to suppress. "Don't laugh."

"Who, me?" Her smile widens and she puts her arm around my shoulders and squeezes. "So, how was the blowout brunch at the Bouvier's house over the weekend?"

"Typical." I watch a swan glide past in the pond. "You know how sometimes God's presence is almost palpable?" I look at Skye and know she understands. "I felt that the morning of the brunch, in the solarium—like I could reach out and touch Him. But then..."

"But then?"

"But then, I lost it. That sense. It felt as though He was there one moment, and gone the next. I know He didn't go anywhere. It's just that I got distracted, I guess."

"What distracted you?"

"The usual."

"Madame B?"

I laugh. "I'm never quite sure what the *B* stands for when you say it that way." But when I look at Skye, I see she isn't laughing with me.

"You know exactly what it stands for."

"Yes, I guess I do."

Skye seems thoughtful before she speaks again. "The object of our adoration can either sustain us or sink us." She bends down and picks up one of the red leaves fallen from the Japanese maple.

"What do you mean? God isn't going to sink us."

She rubs the leaf between her fingers. "No, but He's not always the object of our adoration. Right?"

"You're suggesting I adore Brigitte?" I laugh. "Really?"

She shrugs. "To adore someone is to revere them—to worship them. Isn't that what you're doing, in a sense, when you give someone so much power in your life?"

I look around me. Swans and ducks swim in the koi pond surrounded by trained bonsai and multiple varieties of Japanese maples. Deep blue irises sway in the breeze. I try to take in Skye's meaning—something in it is true and right. But I can't quite grasp it.

I look back at her.

"Who are you serving, Jenna?"

I start to protest, but Skye leans over and puts her hand on my forearm. "Jenna, your awareness of God—your experience of Him —is a gift. A rare gift. Don't let anyone take His place in your life."

"Excuse me, Mrs. Bouvier..."

I look from Skye to Ahsan, who's coming down the path. He holds something in one hand.

"The book! It was in the cab?"

"Yes. It was there." Ahsan hands the book to me. "Mrs. Bouvier, it is time."

I take the book and then glance at my watch. "Oh, Ahsan, I have to go!" I hand the book to Skye, throw my purse over my shoulder, stand, and bend to give her a quick hug. Then I turn and head back to the main gate, Ahsan on my heels. But before we get very far, I hear Skye call my name. I stop and turn back.

"Who are you serving?"

I have to go.

Now.

Once buckled back inside the cab, I reach again for Ahsan's shoulder. "Thank you. How did you...how did you know?"

Dark eyes stare back at me from the mirror. "I just know. It is important you return on time. Yes?"

"Yes. Very important."

As we exit the park and Ahsan maneuvers through traffic, I sink back against the seat of the cab. If Brigitte is waiting for me, there will be questions to answer—and my answers never seem to satisfy. My shoulders slump as I consider the possibilities. I twist the leather strap of my purse and swallow the lump of anxiety lodged in my throat.

Skye's question nags at me. Who am I serving?

Defeat calls my name.

There is truth in what Skye implied.

Fatigue, so familiar, settles in as I picture Brigitte. I work so hard to please her, yet she's never happy.

Something Andee said at brunch the other morning plays at the edges of my mind. I work to recall it. She was talking across the table to Carolyn, who was lamenting about the difficulties of working with a disgruntled donor who is impossible to please. Ah, yes. Andee's offhanded quip seems significant now: "If you can't win, why try?"

If I can't win, why try?

Why?

Because, I know no other way.

Oh, Lord. What are You asking of me?

Stand back, Jenna.

The thought follows me into the house after Ahsan drops me at the curb.

Stand back.

CHAPTER FOUR

*There are some people who cause me great suffering. They are selfish
and full of compromise, strange ideas, and human reasoning.*
JEANNE GUYON

rigitte

"NOON TOMORROW, oui? Perfect. We look forward to hearing your
thoughts. *Merci,* Andee."

She hangs up the phone, turns to the computer on her desk,
and types the details into her calendar. An e-mail to Gerard
informing him of the lunch with Andee—and of his expected
presence at 12:30 p.m.—follows.

Fini.

She purses her lips. Ah, Gerard. Her son is vice president of
Domain de la Bouvier and its enterprises. Of course, it's only a
title. Gerard, like his father before him, is…what is the American
term? She taps her Montblanc pen on the edge of the desk. Ah yes,

Gerard is the *figurehead*. His charm is what makes him valuable, not his business acumen.

Or lack, thereof.

She remains acting president, the reins in her hands. As they should be. That will be one of the topics for discussion tomorrow, she's certain. *C'est la vie.* Gerard may suggest, again, that it's time to begin shifting power. No matter. It is not Gerard's time. Not until she says it is.

Better for him to stay with what he does best—connect with the community here and abroad. After all, it was Gerard's connections that led them to Andee Bell. Andee's financial savvy is renowned and her recommendations for additional tax shelters and investments for Domain de la Bouvier have proven profitable.

Brigitte smiles. Andee continues to impress.

There is just one concern: Andee's relationship with Jenna's brother, Jason. Of course, Andee has the relationship under control—one more reason to respect her—but Brigitte will watch to be certain. There is no room for partiality in business. How far will she be able to trust Andee?

Time will tell.

She leans back in her chair and considers tomorrow's lunch.

Gerard will be included in the initial discussions of Andee's suggestions for the company, but the decisions? They will be made without him.

How unfortunate that there is no one to step in once she's gone.

She turns to the credenza behind her and opens a file drawer. She removes the Bouvier trust and peruses the clauses dealing with heirs and beneficiaries.

Heirs...

As always, the word gnaws at her. Not heirs, but *heir*. There is only Gerard. There should be more. Gerard should have a child, or several children, by now.

She taps the pen against the desk, more insistent this time.

Another of Jenna's failings.

She glances at a picture on her desk—Gerard and his father just before his father's death—a massive heart attack just before his fifty-third birthday. The photo was taken in one of the family vineyards in Eperny and appeared on the cover of a wine journal that year. Gerard and his father shared such distinctive traits. One could never doubt that they were father and son.

She reaches for the photo and holds it so the lamp on her desk illuminates the faces. She looks at her husband's features and sees Gerard today. At fifty-four, Gerard's resemblance to his father is startling. She runs a finger over the image. "What would you think of how I've grown your business, *mon amour?*"

Growing the business, that had never been the problem. But where to go from here...?

She sets the picture back in place and shakes her head. She'd been so sure of Jenna. Such promising breeding stock...

Jenna. She glances at her watch. *She should be back by now.* She reaches for the phone and presses the intercom that connects to the kitchen. "Hannah, has Jenna returned?"

"No, Madame. Not yet."

"Merci, Hannah. Let me know when she arrives."

"Oh, Madame, I believe she's just come in the front door."

"Merci, *encore.*" She drops the phone in its cradle, turns back to the credenza, and returns the file to its drawer. She turns the key in the drawer, then takes the key and places it in the small safe under her desk. She stands and brushes a piece of lint from her wool slacks. *Eh bien,* no time like the present.

She leaves the office connected to her bedroom suite and heads down the stairs. On the landing above the entry, she pauses, listening, discerning Jenna's whereabouts. She hears the murmur of voices beneath her—Jenna and Hannah—then footsteps, indicating they head in separate directions.

Brigitte comes down the stairs from the landing. "Jenna?"

"Yes." Jenna stops in the hallway and turns toward her.

"*Ma chérie,* you're back. I was beginning to wonder… Let's take tea in the solarium." Brigitte reaches Jenna, places one hand on her cheek, and leans in and kisses her other cheek. "I want to hear all about your appointment. I'll advise Hannah. Take a few moments to freshen up and I'll meet you there."

"But…"

Brigitte's eyebrows lift. "But what, darling? Surely you have nothing else to do? Take a few minutes to yourself and then we'll catch up. It's been too long, amour, since we've had time together.

I want to hear what the doctor said. I need to know that you're well. That's all that matters, yes?"

Jenna nods. "I'll be right there."

Brigitte turns, hiding her smile. *Bien sûr, she would be right there.*

Anything less would be unacceptable.

CHAPTER FIVE

How happy you will be when you no longer live by your own strength but by God's.
JEANNE GUYON

ndee

LOOKING BACK IS a waste of time, and time is too precious to waste. So I have no use for my past, except when recalling it propels me into the future I've designed for myself. Then I discipline myself to remember.

I divide my history by sounds.

Michael Jacobs, my first crush, on his skateboard, wheels bumping across asphalt in front of our house. The lyrics of "We Are the World" coming from Stephanie Hall's open bedroom window next door. The annoying electronic rhythm of my little brothers' Mario Brothers Nintendo game that not even my closed bedroom door could block.

The before sounds.

My father, Charles Bell, puking in the shared bathroom of the apartment house. Tina Turner's "Private Dancer" coming through the floor from the apartment of the prostitute who lived below us. Our neighbors arguing and slamming doors as I tried to sleep each night.

The after sounds.

Before: the brown-shingled, craftsman-style, two-story house with the wrap-around porch, just a block from the water. An Alameda neighborhood of doctors, attorneys, businessmen, and their families. The security of my early childhood.

After: the peeling white exterior of a Victorian-style mansion turned low-rent apartment house. A neighborhood of sailors, prostitutes, and pathetic idiots. The bane of my adolescence.

The two addresses were just a few city blocks apart. Which meant that even after the move, I got to stay in the same school as the kids I'd known since kindergarten. Great. My mother, who fought for so little, did fight for that sense of stability for my brothers and me. *Gee, thanks Mom.* But the sounds . . . she couldn't stop those. Evidence of a permanent break between past and present. I'd prayed the move would take me to a new school, where I was unknown. But my prayers went unanswered.

Shocking.

It was during those formative years that I learned financial security is something to be grabbed by the throat and wrestled into submission. Security isn't determined by fate. It's determined by drive.

From those lessons came the mantra I'm known for: *Drive determines destiny.*

Jack Welch, CEO of General Electric between 1981 and 2001, estimated net worth $720 million said, "Control your own destiny or someone else will." $720 million speaks. So I tweaked Jack's quote and made it my life philosophy.

Fate has no place in my life or in the lives of those who follow me and seek real security. If you want something, you focus on the goal and knockout anything or anyone that gets in the way. The premise is that you must be willing to let go of anything or anyone holding you back. The discipline of your drive determines whether you'll attain the goal.

Simple.

I reach behind me and pull my hair off my neck, twist the length of it into a loose bun, and grab a pencil from my drawer and stick it in the bun to hold the hair in place. I refocus on the project in front of me—the next book I'm contracted to write. I type in the title of the first chapter: *The God of Your Finances: You* I shake my head and think back to my childhood prayers. *Why pray when you can act and determine your own outcomes?* Faith is fantastical thinking.

I deal in reality.

I scan the detailed outline I work from and begin the process of putting the outline into chapters—expanding ideas into a step-by-step format that will lead the reader, should they choose to follow the wisdom of my advice, to financial security.

My cell phone rings, disrupting my thoughts. Few people have this number—Cassidy, for work emergencies. My editor. And a new member of Andee's Cell Phone Club: Jason. I smile when I see his name on the screen. I pick up the phone. "Hey, what's up?"

"I have business to attend to in the valley this afternoon and wondered if you'd like to join me? I won't be long and we can have dinner at the winery. I thought maybe you'd like to meet my dad."

"Really?"

"Yeah."

Meeting Bill before my meeting with Brigitte and Gerard is opportune. Though I hate disrupting my work schedule, this seems like a smart change of plans. "I'd love to."

"Really? I thought you'd say no."

"Well, that's part of the mystique," I purr into the phone. "I'm unpredictable."

Jason chuckles. "I'll pick you up at 4:00."

"Great. See you then." I hang up the phone and glance at my watch. I look down at the Ralph Lauren chocolate wool slacks and matching silk blouse I dressed in this morning—perfect for business, dinner, or both, which is often my prerequisite for clothing. I pull the pencil out of my hair, shake my head, and calculate how much time I'll need to freshen up. I set the alarm on my phone for 3:45 and return my focus to the chapter I'm writing.

But my mind wanders to Jason. I need to check my feelings for him. Feelings—not a realm I deal in much. But there's a softening, of sorts, when it comes to him.

Jason was—is—a purposeful choice in a companion. His connection to Brigitte and Gerard proves handy. He's stable. Good-looking. Pleasant. And he's easy-going, which gives me control of the relationship. Drive is essential in all people, except, perhaps, in those I need under my influence. Jason's a sure bet. And that's the only kind I make.

I know he's ready for more intimacy in our relationship. Not physically. The man is a gentleman in that respect. But he says he wants emotional intimacy.

My response? "What you see is what you get, babe." Emotional intimacy? I shake my head and laugh. "Whatever." Maybe my meeting Bill will quell some need in him. Taking me home to daddy, and all that. It benefits me and that's what matters.

I look back to the chapter outline and rein in my thoughts. I only have another hour to work.

Jason opens the door of his BMW 650i Coupe and I slide into the supple leather passenger seat. As I reach for my seatbelt, he leans down and kisses me. His kiss is gentle and something stirs inside. Not passion. Passion, I understand. Instead, this is... tenderness. And I find it unnerving.

I pull away. "We'd better go."

"We're fine. We have the whole evening ahead of us."

I shift in my seat. "I don't want to keep your father waiting."

"Dad?" Jason chuckles. "He'd work straight through dinner and never miss us."

"Really?" I say. "My kind of guy."

Jason bends toward me again. "Careful. I might get jealous."

I reach my hand behind his neck and pull him toward me and place a placating peck on his lips. "Mmm, no need to worry."

"Well, that's good news." He stands. "He'd never miss us because he doesn't know we're coming. I'll call on the way. We spoke yesterday and he said he's working every evening this week but he'll stop for dinner. It's fall—the crush—remember? He'll grab a quick dinner with us and then get back to work."

He shuts the door and I watch him walk around the front of the car to the driver's side. His stride, like him, is relaxed. His casual attitude and boyish good looks are a definite draw. He opens the door and gets settled in the driver's seat. Once his belt is buckled he turns and smiles. "Thanks for coming."

"Sure." I wink at him. "It isn't everyday that a girl gets an invitation to go home and meet the parents. Or"—I catch my mistake—"parent, I should say." I glance at Jason's profile to see if my gaffe troubles him. But he seems unfazed.

"So, what does your dad know about me? Does he know who I am?"

"Who you are?"

"Yeah, you know, the celebrity stuff."

"Oh, that." Jason turns his gaze from the road and glances at me. I see laughter in his eyes.

"What?"

"Nothing." He smiles at me and then looks back at the road. "I told him I'm spending time with someone I want him to meet. That's all."

"That's all?"

"That's it, babe. I'll let you fill him in on 'who you are.'"

"You know, Jason, a lot of men would be proud to bring me home to Daddy."

He's quiet for a minute. "I am proud to introduce you to my dad, but not for the reasons you suggest."

"What do you mean?"

"It's not about what you do, Andee. It's about who you are—who you're becoming. Not the titles—financial advisor to the rich and famous, radio personality, author—but who you are on the inside. That's who I want to introduce to my dad."

"You can't separate the two."

"Really? I think you can. In fact, I think you have to."

I feel my pulse accelerating. "Forget it." I reach for the shoulder strap of the seatbelt and pull it away from my chest. "Tell me about your dad. What's he like? It sounds like he's a hands-on businessman?"

"My dad—"

I take a deep breath and sit back in my seat when I realize Jason's willing to change the subject.

"—is an enigma. He's driven, certainly, but not to the exclusion of all else. He works hard, he plays hard, and he loves hard. And hands-on? Yeah. He loves what he does. He's kept the company small—manageable—so he can be hands-on." Jason takes the steering wheel in his left hand and reaches for me with his right hand. He holds my hand and rubs my wrist with his thumb as he talks. "When my mom died, something in my dad died with her. But something new was also born."

"What do you mean?"

"Well, that's when Azul was conceived, during my mom's illness. Before, wine had been a hobby for my mom and dad. Something they enjoyed together. They'd tour wineries, wander through the vineyards of neighboring ranches, enjoy evenings dining under the stars and sipping their favorite labels, notating varieties and vintages. They'd dream of someday planting the acreage of their ranch and opening a winery of their own. But the joy was in the dream, not in the living out of the dream."

"What's the point of dreaming if you're not going to accomplish the dream?"

"Like I said, for the joy of it."

"The joy comes in seeing the dream to fruition."

"Not always."

I shake my head but decide not to debate him.

"But when my mom was diagnosed, a shift took place in my dad. That year, he began selling off the cattle that roamed the ranch and planted his first hundred acres of grapes. Chardonnay. And as long as my mom was able, he'd walk her out to the vineyards and they'd track the progress of the seedlings.

"For the better part of the year, he spoke of nothing but grapes and the winery he and my mother would open. As long as he kept the dream alive, he thought he could keep my mother alive."

"But it didn't work?"

"No. She died nineteen months after the initial diagnosis."

"But the dream lived on?"

"Yes, and though it didn't keep my mother alive, I think it kept Dad alive. It gave him purpose."

"So the vineyards, the drive to achieve the dream, kept him going." *Drive determines destiny.*

Jason nods.

"What about the label? *Azul.* Where did the name come from?"

"It's Spanish. It means blue."

"I know. But why that name?" My question is answered with silence and I wonder if he heard me. "Jason?" He stares at the road ahead. I reach out and place my hand on his arm. "Did you hear me?"

He turns, glances at me, and then turns his gaze back to the road. He clears his throat. "Yeah, I heard you. My mother was Mexican-American—the daughter of my father's ranch manager and his American wife." He's quiet for a moment and then says more to himself than to me "She was beautiful." His tone is wistful. "Her skin was the color of melted chocolate and her eyes were the color of a twilight sky."

"Azul."

Jason nods. "Yes. Jenna has her eyes."

I think back to meeting Jenna at the brunch and recall the intense color of her eyes—her beauty. Then I remember the scar, but that will be a topic for another time. I've heard the rumors but decide not to broach the subject now.

Jason continues his little jaunt into his past and the hour-and-twenty-minute drive zips by. As we enter the valley, I look out the passenger window and tick off the rows of vines as they fly past.

I listen as Jason talks while calculating the information he offers.

The car slows as we turn into a winding drive flanked on either side by low rock walls, and I hear the tone of Jason's voice change.

"Andee..." Jason pulls into a parking space outside the administration offices of the winery and puts the car in park. He turns toward me. "Azul is more than a business to my family. As you work with Brigitte, I want you to remember that."

Surprised by the passion I hear in his voice, I hold my response.

"You mentioned something the other night and I want to be clear with you. You made the assumption that Jenna and Gerard's marriage was a business merger." He shifts in his seat and looks out the front window for a moment. "That wasn't and isn't the case. At least not from our perspective. *Azul* is more than a business to my father, Andee."

I nod as I assimilate this bit of information.

"Do you understand?"

"Sure."

He pats my shoulder and turns and gets out of the car. As I wait for him to open my door, I have just one thought: *The game is getting interesting.*

CHAPTER SIX

You will not see things as He does until you have clearer light.
JEANNE GUYON

*J*enna

MEMORIES of my mother tug at the recesses of my mind, calling forward longings so familiar they are woven, I'm certain, into the fabric of my fate, likely having informed every choice I've made since her death. I remember lying next to her in bed when she was sick—curling into the warmth of her and twisting strands of her long, silken hair around my fingers. She'd turn her head and through cracked lips whisper, "Jenna Brooke, my little lamb."

As I climb the stairs to our suite, I feel the welcoming warmth of Brigitte's kiss lingering on my cheek and wonder at the concern I saw in her expression. I want to believe, need to believe, her love is genuine. Yet, I so often doubt her.

After my mother's death, I lived in a world of men—my father,

Jason, and the many men who tended the vineyards and worked in the winery. Then, when I was twelve, I met Brigitte at a vintners' dinner hosted by my father. I'd been allowed to greet guests with him as they arrived.

Brigitte's elegance sang like fine crystal and the song drew me. Her attention stirred the longings I'd attempted to bury with my mother when I was seven years old—longings for beauty, tenderness, and love. And later, the longing to embrace my impending womanhood. A daunting task without a woman to guide me through that delicate transition.

While my father taught me the wiles of winemaking and introduced me to a way of life known only to those who live amongst the vines, it was Brigitte who noticed and then nurtured my beauty—tending to me like one of those precious vines. Brigitte trained me and I grew into her vision of the woman Gerard needed. Like a plant reaching for the sun, I grasped for Brigitte's attention and determined I'd flourish and bear fruit for her.

I gave Brigitte the place in my heart left gaping upon the loss of my own mother.

As I reach my room, I recognize how I still grasp for and cling to Brigitte's approval.

I am ever the trained vine.

Was I what Gerard needed? Or was I, in some way, what she needed? Perhaps Brigitte's void was as great as my own.

Maybe it's my need that so often leaves me feeling crazy in Brigitte's presence. I think of Skye and tuck these thoughts away for our next conversation. I look forward, always, to the wisdom she imparts. I leave our times together with a deeper understanding of human nature—and a fledgling understanding of myself.

I wish I could hold onto that understanding, but my mind feels like a sieve—what's poured in, drains out, leaving just the sediment of what I've always known.

I enter the alcove off our master suite, where my desk and

laptop sit surrounded by shelves of books. I open the lid of the computer and watch as the screen lights up. I sit at the desk, rest my fingers on the keyboard, and open my mailbox and scan the list of e-mails. They'll have to wait. I open a new message and type a quick note to Skye, apologizing for my abrupt departure today and asking if I can buy her lunch soon. She'll pick up the e-mail either at the library or an Internet cafe. It may be today, or a week from today, but I'll hear from her.

I close the lid to the laptop. Brigitte waits.

I'm warmed by her concern.

Maybe, if I'm careful, our conversation will end well today. Maybe we'll find the footing we've shared in the past.

Is that what I want?

I remove the jacket I'm wearing and cross the room to the dressing area. As I hang the jacket, I notice the small crescent-shaped bruises on my upper arm. I rub my hand across the yellowing marks and recall the many times through the years that I've wished she'd actually hit me—wished she'd leave her mark in a visible, tangible way.

Yet, what do a few small bruises mean? In a moment of self-awareness, I recognize that the wounds she's inflicted are so much deeper than a surface bruise.

Though, I tell myself again, *she doesn't mean to hurt me.* Anyway maybe things will be different this time. After all, if I hadn't lingered in the solarium the morning of the brunch, if I'd fulfilled my role as hostess and instead greeted guests with Brigitte and Gerard, if I hadn't been so selfish and taken off on my own, then Brigitte wouldn't have become angry.

I think back to those moments in the solarium and recall the stirring breeze and the sense of love and peace that enveloped me.

A moment of pure joy. Yes, my focus shifted when Brigitte came in, but do I really allow her to stand in the way of my relationship with God, as Skye implied? I think of Skye's nickname for Brigitte—Madame B. Maybe I've misrepresented Brigitte to

Skye. Guilt surfaces. I shouldn't talk about her. It isn't fair. Brigitte was right to be upset the morning of the brunch. I shirked my duties—I can see that now.

I feel the flush of fever spread across my brow as a wave of nausea passes. Perhaps Brigitte is right and I should contact Dr. Bernard. Maybe it is time for another opinion. How foolish I've been to resist her efforts to help me.

Optimistic—yet again—that I can right what I've wronged, I head downstairs.

I find Brigitte waiting for me in the solarium, but instead of tea, there's a bottle of wine and two glasses on a tray on the glass table between the two settees, along with a plate of cheeses and fruit.

"I thought we were having tea," I say as Brigitte reaches for the bottle and begins to pour.

"I thought you might prefer a glass of wine. You know, if we were in France..."

She winks at me, her implication clear. She picks up a glass and hands it to me. I take the glass by the stem and twirl it. The straw-colored wine swirls around the bowl of the glass. I lift it to my nose and breathe in the bouquet. "Honeysuckle. And"—I lift the glass to my nose again—"a hint of orange."

I haven't told Brigitte of my decision to shirk denial and stop drinking. She won't understand, nor will she respect my choice.

"It's one of Domain de la Bouvier's new still wines. A chardonnay."

Perhaps I don't have to tell her. Maybe just a sip every now and then...

I feel the tension in my shoulders ease as I lift the glass to my lips "Mmm, the Los Carneros region. My dad's grapes?"

Brigitte smiles. "Ah... The vineyards are in your blood, chérie. You know, once you are well, maybe it's time we consider how to put that degree of yours to work."

She sets the bottle back on the tray and reaches for her glass, which I notice is only half as full as the one she's poured for me.

"And yes, they're your father's grapes, and the Bouvier label. It's one of the organic wines that Gerard and Jason were so eager to co-create." She shakes her head. "Organic. Ridiculous, really. Not cost efficient."

"No, but it's good for the environment. And for the points."

"Yes, but we only gain a point or two. And that is nothing but a ploy in my opinion. But your father is doing some organic farming anyway, as you know." She waves her hand. "It is just a fad."

I ignore Brigitte's disdain. I learned the benefits of organic farming as it relates to winemaking during my years of study at Cal Poly. Pesticides and herbicides hamper the vines' ability to absorb natural chemicals from the soil. Wines made with organic grapes display the distinctive flavor of the site where the grapes are grown. And both Jason and Gerard know that the point value is important to consumers—a grade of sorts—and is therefore reflected in sales.

I take another sip of the chardonnay and relish the hints of butterscotch and baked apples. One sip begs another.

"So, tell me. What did the doctor say?" Brigitte has set her glass back on the table. Her stature is relaxed but her gaze intent. Her eyes hold mine—as though she is working not to look at my jawline.

I take another drink of the wine and lean back against the settee. I feel heat rise to my face, but don't know if it's the affect of the wine or if the fever is spiking again. I recall my father's oft-stated belief: *"Wine is to be enjoyed, sipped, paired with food to enhance the flavors. But as soon as wine is used for its effect, it becomes a dangerous force."*

The thought chills me. I set my glass back on the table. I can't trust myself with even a sip. No, I must abstain altogether. I brace for Brigitte's response as I answer her question. "It wasn't good news."

She is quiet. A shadow of something—anger, perhaps—crosses her face. Or is it just my imagination? Whatever I thought I saw is replaced with tenderness.

"I am sorry. This explains your continued fatigue and illness. Oui?"

I nod, expecting her to chide me for not taking her advice and contacting Dr. Bernard sooner. But, again, I am surprised.

"Oh, you must be so disappointed."

I long to trust her care, but I'm wary. "Well…yes, I'd hoped that I could get"—I swipe a finger across the scar on my face—"this taken care of once and for all." I reach for my glass again—something to at least hold and focus on as I speak. "A home-care nurse will come tomorrow and insert a port and I'll wear a pump that will inject antibiotics every few hours around the clock. It's inconvenient, but less so than another hospital stay. After that…" I shrug.

Brigitte reaches for the plate of cheese and fruit and offers it to me. "You'd better eat something, darling. You need to keep up your strength."

I set the glass back down and eat a section of pear with some brie. Feeling emboldened by Brigitte's good mood, I ask about Dr. Bernard. "Maybe—I mean—I wonder if now is the time to get another opinion. I'll call"—I look at the floor—"Dr. Bernard, I guess? I'm sorry, I should have—"

She waves her hand again as though brushing off my apology. "Nonsense. Jenna, I am the one who is sorry. I've pushed you regarding Dr. Bernard. He is the best, in my opinion. But you have the right to make your own choice and I need to respect that. I allow my love for you to take over and I become"—she tips her head—"indelicate."

She leans toward me. "I'm accustomed, as you know, to business dealings. And in business, you get nowhere if you don't push.

That, however, is not the best practice in personal relationships, *non?*"

I scoot forward on the settee and attempt to grasp Brigitte's words and hold on to them. I don't recall ever hearing her apologize before. Maybe things are really changing. "I should have listened to you."

"*Bien sûr.* If you'd listened in the first place, you wouldn't have had the surgery at all." Brigitte reaches across the table for my hand. She gives it a squeeze. "You were beautiful, chérie. There was never a need to change anything. You simply couldn't see that."

My mind reels. "But...you said, many times, that... You suggested the surgery. It was...*your* idea."

Brigitte leans back into the settee and laughs. "Chérie, I said no such thing. That is crazy talk! But no mind, we must move forward and get you well. If you'd like, I'll call Dr. Bernard myself in the morning."

I nod through an all-too-familiar fog—and the haze has nothing to do with the wine this time.

"*Calme toi.* Have another glass—"

I hold up my hand. "No, thank you. I've had enough."

She takes my glass from the table and pours, topping it off, then sets it back in front of me.

As I watch her pour, anger, a raging river running just beneath the surface, spews forth. "Brigitte!" I slam my hand, palm down, on the glass-top table. The glasses slosh and the china plate of cheeses and fruit rattles. "I said, no!"

I'm not sure which of us is more startled. Surprise registers on Brigitte's face, but then it's masked by her own anger. My pulse quickens and I long to take back my outburst.

It is too late.

"How *dare* you—"

"Well, here are my two favorite ladies." Gerard walks into the solarium, stopping at the built-in bar along the back wall to take a wine glass from the cabinet.

Brigitte glares at me—an unspoken warning in her eyes.

Gerard walks over from the bar and bends and kisses his mother on the cheek and then takes the place next to me on the settee. He reaches for the bottle on the table. "The new chardonnay. What do you think?" He looks to me for an answer.

But before I can speak, Brigitte maneuvers. "Darling, Jenna was just heading upstairs. She isn't feeling well." She looks at me. "Please, Jenna, go."

Gerard places a hand on my knee. "You do look flushed. Go ahead—go upstairs and rest. I'll come up later and check on you."

I hesitate. I want to explain. I want to tell Gerard...what? That his mother poured more wine into my glass after I'd said, "No, thank you?" And I exploded? Even to me, it's ridiculous. I have no words to explain what happened.

But it is about more than a glass of wine.

The river of resentment running through me, a river forged over many years, is raging. A river so rugged and rushing that to explore its depths would prove a perilous journey, I fear.

I look at Brigitte and it is clear: I've been dismissed.

I stand, mumble an apology, and head to my room. How am I to still the raging torrent—both the one within myself and the one I saw stirring in Brigitte's eyes?

When I reach my room, I stop at the alcove and sit in the chair in front of the small antique desk. I lift the lid of my laptop and notice my hands shaking. I sit back, take a deep breath, and try to quell the fear rippling through me. *What will Brigitte do?*

I click the mouse and open my e-mail and see a response from Skye:

Jenna, if you're free tomorrow, I'll be at the outdoor labyrinth at Grace Cathedral at 11:00 a.m. There's someone I'd like you to meet. Lunch afterwards?

Peace,

Skye

As the afternoon sun drops low on the horizon, the natural light in the room softens and a pink glow suffuses the alcove. I lean forward in the chair and bow my head, resting my elbows on my knees.

Peace.

How hard I work to maintain peace. Yet, it eludes me.

My heart still beats a staccato rhythm but I take deep breaths, exhaling each in slow procession. A practice I learned from Skye. The intentional breathing brings me back to the present moment. And with each breath I take, I sense the presence of the Comforter, the Spirit of God. My soul stirs and I surrender the angst of the day. Tears slip down my cheeks and land on my hands clasped beneath my chin.

Oh Lord...

I wait for words to come, but none convey the depth of my need. Instead, I open my heart to my heavenly Father and allow His Spirit to search my soul.

Words are unnecessary.

The feeling of love that envelops me belies my understanding and the dam that's held my emotions in check since leaving Dr. Kim's office today breaks.

The torrent is unleashed.

When my tears are spent, I think of my mother again. I recall her oft-repeated words during her illness: *This is my cross to bear.* I was too young to understand their meaning at the time. But now, I assign meaning to the phrase. We, like Christ, are allowed crosses to bear—suffering to endure. But through that suffering we share in Christ's suffering and identify with Him in new and intimate ways.

I pick up my Bible sitting on my desk and turn to the concordance and look under the heading *Cross*. I think the verse I want is somewhere in Matthew. I see the reference and turn to Matthew 10:38: *"...and anyone who does not take his cross and follow me is not worthy of me."*

Oh Lord, how I long to be worthy...

My relationship with Brigitte is my cross to bear. I feel the weight of that knowledge like a wooden beam across my shoulders. But I will carry it.

Thank you, Lord, for the honor of sharing in your suffering. Strengthen me to bear this burden.

I sigh as guilt niggles at me. *Brigitte isn't always that bad. I'm the one, after all, who exploded. She did nothing but show her concern for me.*

I close my Bible, turn off my desk lamp, and then rest my head on my arms crossed on top of my desk. I want to go to bed, to the bliss of slumber, but the walk across the room to the bed seems mountainous. I stand and then make the trek to my bed, pull back the heavy spread, and climb in.

Confusion, my constant bedfellow, accompanies me.

Before the light of day has faded, I surrender myself to sleep.

GROGGY AND DISORIENTED, I look at the clock on my nightstand. 11:02 p.m. I stretch as Gerard ambles across the room. His gait is slow and unsure. It seems clear he's had more to drink than usual. I sit up, reach for the bedside lamp, and turn it on so he can make his way through the room without stumbling.

"Hey... I didn't want to wake you."

I lie back against the pillows. "It's okay."

He comes to my side of the bed and perches on the edge. His hand warms mine as he grasps it. "How are you feeling? I hear the infection..." He doesn't finish his sentence but instead looks to me to do so.

His dark good looks seem worn tonight. Is it the alcohol or is there more?

I nod my head. "The stubborn infection persists." I try to make light of it.

He squeezes my hand. "I'm sorry, Jen." The lids of his eyes droop.

I own the responsibility here, there's no need to burden Gerard with the consequences of my choice. I do however need to unburden myself about something else. "Did Brigitte say anything about...about anything else?"

"Just the usual business banter."

"You look tired."

"Yeah, I am. Maybe a little drunk too." He shrugs and smiles. His grin is lopsided, charming. The thrill I felt at sixteen when he first smiled at me returns. "How drunk?" I lift my eyebrows and smile.

He chuckles. "Why, what did you have in mind?"

His question is playful, tender even. This is the man, or at least the ideal, I fell in love with so long ago.

I reach out and place the palm of my hand on the side of his face and he closes his eyes. "Actually, I just need to tell you something and I've wanted to wait for...well, you know...the right time."

He opens his eyes, inquisitive.

"Oh"—I see the hope in his expression—"no, it's nothing. It's... it's just if you're a little drunk, it might be easier to hear?"

"Ah... Okay. Allow me to brace myself." He bends and takes off his Italian leather loafers, stands, walks to the dressing area, and disappears into his closet. He comes out a few moments later with his tie off, and the top button of his shirt undone. He walks around to his side of the bed and sprawls out on top of the blankets. He rolls to his side, faces me, and props himself up with his pillow.

"Okay, I'm ready."

"Well, I…uh…I lost something."

He raises his eyebrows. "And what, pray tell, was it this time?"

"It's not funny. It's…I noticed…I mean, I don't know what happened."

"Jen?"

I lean over and open the drawer of my nightstand and pull out the black velvet box I'd placed there for just this conversation.

I open the box and hand it to him. He takes it, opens the box, and stares. He looks up at me, the obvious question in his eyes.

"I don't know. I opened the safe the other night to put it on for dinner, and…it was just gone. It must have fallen out the last time I wore it and I didn't notice."

"My grandfather gave that diamond to my grandmother."

"I know. I'm sorry."

"Does she know?"

I shake my head.

He hands the box back to me and rolls onto his back and stares at the ceiling.

I feel like a child waiting for my punishment.

He sits up, throws his legs over the side of the bed, and heads to the bathroom. Before he disappears, he turns and says over his shoulder, "I'll take care of it."

He comes back a few minutes later and climbs into bed smelling of soap and toothpaste. He says nothing more, but instead of rolling over with his back to me as I expect, he puts his arm around me. I turn off my bedside lamp and settle into the crook of his shoulder. Within moments, the steady rhythm of his breathing tells me he's asleep.

I let out a long, shaky breath. Guilt nudges. I know I used the moment—waited until alcohol would soften the blow. But I didn't have courage for more. When issues involve Brigitte, I never know what side of the fence Gerard will choose.

I think back to my father's warning before my marriage. My father, a man who holds his thoughts close, spoke out a few weeks after our engagement. "Jenna, Gerard's a good man, but he's weak. You won't be marrying just him—you'll also marry Brigitte."

But I was twenty years old and idealistic. And Brigitte loved me, so what did it matter?

I shiver and reach for the blanket and pull it close. Now, eleven years later, I understand my father's concern. There was no "leaving and cleaving," nor will there ever be. Gerard is bound to Brigitte by ties I will never understand. He is driven to succeed in her eyes and will stop at nothing to please her.

She seems to have that effect on people.

But how long can Gerard strive for her approval? She refuses to loosen the reins of control and give him any real responsibility. I see it wearing on him. See him dealing with it, or not dealing with it, as he drinks more and shrugs off his desire to step into a position that would allow him to use his strengths.

I listen to the steady drum of his snoring and my heart softens. How I've longed for Gerard to stand up for me, to protect me from Brigitte's emotional assaults. How I've hoped for a depth of emotional intimacy with him—to share with him what is most important to me. Yet she is always there, between us, angling, manipulating, controlling.

Gerard knows nothing else.

I hesitate to make excuses for him, but I do understand Brigitte's pull. Like a magnet, if you draw close, her force is undeniable.

I think of his response to the lost diamond: *I'll take care of it.* I don't know what that means, but it won't involve telling Brigitte the truth. We shy away from honest engagements with her— instead, we say what we believe she wants to hear.

We keep the peace.

As I stare into the dark, what seems so elusive in the light of day, becomes clear.

Skye was right. Brigitte is the god we bow to. But, the dark reveals no plan for toppling the idol.

I roll to my side, wrap my arm around Gerard, and rest my head on his chest. The thrum of his beating heart matches my own and lulls me back to the edge of sleep—that place where, for a time, I can close my eyes and mind to the truth and believe, with my husband at my side, that this is where I want to be.

CHAPTER SEVEN

When you meet a person whose heart is turned toward God there is a
natural, or should I say supernatural, drawing between you.
JEANNE GUYON

*M*atthew

I LOCK my office door and hit the pavement, pounding the uphill
blocks to the cathedral. I want time to myself before Skye shows
up. My gut tells me something's up. It's already been that kind
of day.

"Pay"—I huff—"attention, buddy. You don't want to miss out." I
nod to a woman looking at me like I'm a derelict talking to
himself. I laugh. There's always a conversation going on in my
head and most of the time, it spills out my mouth.

After the third block a red light and traffic stops me. I turn,
bounce on the balls of my feet, and look back at the bay. It's fall—
the air is crisp and the view is clear. "Cool." I don't think I'll ever

get tired of the view. Or of the city. People, traffic, noise, people. "This is life!"

Still bouncing, I pump my fists in the air like Rocky Balboa after reaching the top of the steps of the Philadelphia Museum of Art.

"A classic movie!"

Someone else, a man this time, stares at me as he passes.

I turn back just as the light changes and pick up my pace again. As I walk, I think through my last appointment. Blake, early thirties, molested as a child by his priest and now coming out of a lifestyle of homosexuality. He's in therapy with one of my colleagues working to heal from a painful past that, many would say, led to a confusing and painful present. "Man, life is hard." I shake my head.

I think of the blog post I read this morning—one I read several mornings a week. I'm not one for staring at a computer screen, so I print the entries and read them with my morning coffee. The author of the blog, whoever it is, is the real deal—someone with a working knowledge of pain and a real relationship with Christ. The kind with skin on it. A relationship where you struggle, cry out, and then curl up in the lap of the Comforter. "That's real, baby."

I think of the verse from 1 Peter quoted in the post today: *"In this you greatly rejoice, though now for a little while you may have had to suffer grief in all kinds of trials."* I love that verse. *In this.* In our inheritance in Christ. That's the hope we Christians hold to. It's what keeps us focused on the finish line when we're dealing with the painful realities of life.

"But, man, if you don't have that…" I shake my head again.

Blake is exploring spirituality and the idea of returning to the church. His therapist suggested he start by getting to know Jesus. That's where I come in. Blake wasn't ready to walk back into a church—any church—so instead, his therapist recommended me, a counselor turned spiritual director. It's not a long stretch between the two. Blake is one of my directees, but he isn't a typical directee. Don't get me wrong, by typical, I don't mean normal.

I laugh. "There is no normal."

A passerby apparently agrees as she makes a wide arc around me.

No matter. We're unique. Every one of us. Created in the image of God. Meaning, we each reflect the Divine in some way. "Very cool."

I so often see similarities in those who seek Christian spiritual direction. The number-one similarity? Most are followers of Christ. So, in that respect, Blake isn't typical. But my job is to listen. To Blake. And to the Holy Spirit. Today, as Blake asked questions and I responded, I knew that I knew more than I know. Get it? I answered Blake's unasked questions. Well, not me, but God in me—through me.

And Blake got it! You could see the cogs spinnin' and the gears shiftin'. It's called dancing in the moment. And baby, that is one cool dance. "Totally cool!" I pump a fist in the air again and watch as the tourists crowding the sidewalk ahead of me part like the Red Sea.

Man, I want Blake to have the hope of Jesus. "How cool would that be?" I lift my hand and a passerby gives me a high five. "Yes!"

When I reach the cathedral, I climb the steps leading to the entrance, veer to the right, and head to the outdoor labyrinth. I grab a seat on the wall on the outside edge of the lab and remind myself to shift to inner dialogue mode.

I want to respect those who are practicing an ancient tradition by walking the labyrinth—those who may be listening for a voice other than mine. Imagine that. I smile, and sense I'm not smiling alone.

While I wait for Skye, I watch a handful of people walk the inlaid terrazzo stone circle. The labyrinth attracts those from many traditions. *Father God, do they know it's You they seek?* I notice the young woman sitting in the middle of the labyrinth in a posture of meditation. Legs crossed, palms open, hands resting on her knees, eyes closed. I close my eyes against the distractions in front of me—a discipline that helps me still my active mind and turn to prayer. I wait until the Holy Spirit forms His prayer in me for the young woman. I pray things I have no way of knowing.

"Matthew? Hey, Matthew…"

I feel a nudge on my shoulder and open my eyes.

"You're mumbling." Skye's eyes twinkle. "How long have you been sitting here?"

I look around her to the middle of the labyrinth—the girl I was praying for is gone. "Dude… I don't know, awhile, I think."

"Talking to yourself again?"

"No, I was… Wait, was I talking out loud?"

Skye laughs and says to the woman standing next to her. "He's a verbal processor. Very verbal!" She pauses, looks at me, and smiles. "But he's also a listener."

Listener. That's the title Skye gave me when I added spiritual director to my vocations. It fits. She gets what I do and why I do it. And if I'm a listener, then Skye is an intuitive. She reads people like no one else I know. We're connected as friends by our innate curiosity about people.

I look at the woman she's talking to but don't recognize her.

I stand and stretch out my hand. "Hi, I'm Matthew." She takes my hand and her smile reaches her eyes—the same deep blue as the bay on a sunny afternoon—and something inside me reacts. Hard to explain. But it's not what you might think. Honest.

I'm married. All in. All the time.

But there's something about this woman. Although, uh…she looks wiped out.

"Matthew, this is Jenna Bouvier. I've been wanting the two of you to meet."

"Bouvier? As in the rich San Francisco family that brews the bubbly?" As soon as the words are out of my mouth, I notice the chain of the Chanel bag looped over her shoulder and the exquisite cut of her slacks. Yeah, I said *Chanel* and *exquisite*. Tess, my wife, works in the fashion industry and she's trained me well. And if she were standing next to me, I'd have an elbow in my ribs about now. "Oh, uh, sorry."

"The bubbly isn't actually brewed, it's aged. In barrels. In caves." Jenna, still holding my outstretched hand, laughs. "Nice to meet you, Matthew." She gives my hand a squeeze and then lets go.

"Have a seat, ladies." I motion to the wall and Skye and Jenna sit. I take the place next to Skye, hoping she'll explain why she wanted Jenna and me to meet. My sense is that Jenna is the "what's up?" that I was waiting for today—the something, or rather some*one*, that God told me I wouldn't want to miss. Although, experience has taught me, I could be wrong. Dead wrong. But then, that's part of the adventure.

Either way, I'm paying attention.

Skye looks from me to Jenna, then she gets up. "We can't have a conversation like this." She takes off the jean jacket she's wearing, spreads it on the concrete in front of the wall, and then plops down in front of us. Her legs hide under her vintage patchwork skirt. Yeah, it's definitely vintage. Tess, remember?

"So, you two"—she points at me, then at Jenna—"share the same spiritual vibe." The silver ring on her index finger reflects the sunlight.

Jenna looks at me and then at Skye. "Spiritual vibe?"

Skye's golden eyes, catlike, shine. "Yeah, we carry the same Spirit within us, but I get a vibe from both of you. Like the Spirit speaks to both of you in the same way." She cocks her head to one side. "Or maybe you both interpret the Spirit's voice in the same way. I don't know. But there's some kind of connection here." Again she waggles her index finger between us. "I feel it."

I nod. "Cool."

Jenna looks at me. I can't read her, but I'd guess she's as curious as I am.

Then Skye laughs—deep and throaty—which is always surprising coming from such a petite thing. "Besides the vibe, you two have nothing in common." She shakes her head and laughs again. "But that's okay, 'cause you've got a foundation to build on."

"So…" Jenna seems hesitant. "You want us to get to know each other?"

She glances at me and I shrug. "I'm game."

"No. I mean, yes. Sort of. I was thinking you could work together." Skye looks at Jenna. "Like I said, Matthew's a listener—he's a spiritual director. He's a guide for those on a spiritual pilgrimage."

"Spiritual pilgrimage?" I roll that over in my brain. "Hey, I like that. You've never said that before."

"I just thought of it."

Jenna holds up her hand, like a traffic cop. "Wait, a spiritual director? Aren't spiritual directors Catholic or"—she waves toward the cathedral—"Episcopalian, or…something? Which is fine, but I'm not…"

She leaves her sentence hanging, so I jump in. "Yep. They're associated with some of the more liturgical traditions. But it's an ancient practice that more Christians, even those in the evangelical traditions, are embracing. Like me. I'm just a plain ol' nondenominational follower of Christ who believes God still speaks."

She nods. "I believe that too."

"Look, girl," Skye says, "you've got a lot going on in your life and you're searching for God in all your circumstances. Sometimes, we need someone to journey with us. Someone gifted to listen to us and with us—someone who will help illuminate the path. That's what Matthew does. Right?"

"Yep. That's basically what I do. Or more accurately, what God does through me."

Skye, shading her eyes, looks up, at the sun I'm guessing. Then she leans over and grabs my wrist and looks at my watch. She gets up and picks up her jacket and shakes it out.

"I have to run."

Jenna's eyes widen a fraction. "Run? What about lunch?"

"I got a gig—a paying gig—last minute. We're rehearsing in thirty minutes. Sorry. I'll leave you two to talk." She bends and kisses Jenna on the cheek. "Lunch next week?" And then she turns to leave. She holds her fingers in the symbol of peace as she says good-bye.

I turn and look at Jenna. "So…"

She smiles and her eyes light up like blue bulbs on a Christmas tree, erasing the wiped-out look I picked up on earlier. She's a dazzler. Even with that scar.

"What happened there?" I point to her jaw. As soon as I've asked, I can feel Tess's imaginary elbow in my ribs again. "Whoa, sorry. None of my business." I watch as her eyes shift from my face to the ground.

I know that look. I've sat across from it in my counseling office way too many times and seen it on the faces directees as well on occasion. Saw it on Blake's face this morning.

Shame.

"Uh, sorry, occupational hazard. I don't do pretense well. I'm used to going deep with people. But sometimes, it comes across as tactless."

She looks back at me and smiles. "Really?"

Her playful sarcasm surprises me. I chuckle. "Guess you already figured that out, huh?"

She nods. Her eyes meet mine and she seems to think about something. Then she nods. "I'm vain. Or"—her gaze drops to the ground again—"I was. My looks are, or were, very important to me. Too important. Anyway, I didn't like my jawline and chin. Someone told me they were too strong and suggested I have them fixed." She glances away, and then looks back at me. "So I had plastic surgery."

"Oh." Such honesty right off the bat. That's rare. "So how'd that work out for you?"

I watch as a slow smile spreads across her face. Then she starts to laugh. And she keeps laughing. Soon, tears are running down her cheeks. I laugh with her. Can't help it. Of course, I have no clue why we're laughing. When she catches her breath, she reaches into her purse, pulls out a tissue, and wipes her eyes.

"Oh my goodness. I'm"—she giggles again—"I'm sorry. I just... I've never told anyone like that. Just blurted it out. Most people don't know. I mean, people don't just ask. They look away. They pretend it's not there. They pretend I'm not there." She takes a deep breath and looks around like she's seeing the place for the first time. "It feels so good to just say it out loud. And to laugh. I don't remember the last time I laughed like that." She wipes her eyes again. "In answer to your question"—she chuckles again—"it didn't work out too well, obviously! Although, in a way, it's a gift. Vanity is no longer an issue—or an option, for that matter."

I'm not sure I agree with her, she's still a stunner. "Do you blame God?"

"Oh, no, not at all."

She seems surprised by the question. Like she's never considered it.

"I made a choice—a choice I knew was accompanied by risk. I made the choice for all the wrong reasons, but I believe plastic surgery is a valid choice for some people. So, I'm suffering the consequences of my choice. That's all." She shrugs.

"What happened? I mean, since I've already stuck my foot in my mouth, I might as well get the whole story."

She smiles. "You didn't stick your foot in your mouth, you offered me the freedom to talk—to speak truth. I appreciate that." She glances back toward the ground and then she looks back at me. "After the surgery—it's called a mentoplasty—I developed an infection. The infection eventually went to the bone. I've had subsequent surgeries to clean out the infected bone, but..."

"So is that what the pack is about?" I reach over and pull back the bottom edge of her jacket and point to the thing I noticed on her side at her waist.

She looks down. "You weren't supposed to see that. But yes, as of this morning, I have a new line to administer antibiotics."

"What about the person who suggested the surgery? I mean, why'd you let them influence you?"

She looks across the plaza to the cathedral. "I don't know. I'm still trying to figure that out."

I nod. "Well, bummer, dude. Sorry you're going through this."

She looks at me, one eyebrow raised. "Dude?"

"Yeah, well…" I shrug.

"Spiritual director? Really?" She shakes her head and her long dark hair falls forward. She brushes it back behind her ears. "I guess I would have expected someone more …well…something."

"Serious. Staunch. Holy?"

She laughs. "Maybe."

I close one eye and channel my best Popeye. "I yam what I yam." Then, more serious, I say, "Sorry to disappoint."

"I'm not disappointed." She tilts her head to one side. "I'm intrigued."

"For the record, if we work together, I don't usually call my directees Dude." I nod. "But"—I cock my head and look at her—"it seems like I already know you. Like an old friend or something. You know?"

She nods.

"Maybe Skye's right. Maybe there is a connection here."

"I'd like to find out."

"Yeah, me too." I reach into my shirt pocket and pull out one of my business cards. "Give me a call if you decide you want a spiritual director."

I watch as she opens her purse and puts the card into her wallet.

Intrigued? Heck yeah.

CHAPTER EIGHT

When you are living out of your own life, you act as though you are the central reference point.
JEANNE GUYON

ndee

I REACH INTO MY WALLET, extract a couple of bills, and pay the cabbie for the fare. I tip him well under the standard fifteen percent. He did nothing special to earn the standard. A waiting valet opens the cab door and I walk the few steps to the entrance of the restaurant. I glance at my watch. Noon. On the dot.

I glance at the hostess. "Bouvier party."

I'm led through the bar and down the grand staircase to the main dining room, reserved during the day for private parties. There, in the far corner of the dining room, Brigitte sits at a table alone. What does it cost to reserve the entire dining room for a party of three? In the past, we've met in the city offices of Domaine de la Bouvier with Brigitte, Gerard, and their CFO.

"Brigitte, hello." I sit in the seat the hostess pulls out for me, across from Brigitte. "What's the occasion?" I gesture to the empty dining room.

"It's good to indulge occasionally, *non*? I like the chef here, I like the ambiance, and now, I'll also enjoy the company."

As she's talked a waiter has filled my glass with sparkling wine. Brigitte lifts her glass and I follow.

"*La fortune soutir aux audacieux.*"

"I'll drink to that, I think."

Brigitte laughs. "Fortune smiles upon the audacious."

"I *will* drink to that." I feign a sip of the wine and then set the glass back on the table. I don't drink, which proves problematic when working for vintners. "Is Gerard joining us?"

"He is. But first, I thought we'd chat privately—one business-woman to another. I value your thoughts and I'd like to apprise you of a delicate matter. Oui?"

I nod. Schmoozing. That's the occasion. The private dining room, expensive wine, and gourmet lunch. I'm here to be schmoozed. *Go for it, lady.* While I admire Brigitte, I don't trust her. "Of course. I'm accustomed to delicate matters. I'm happy to offer whatever insights I can."

She assesses me from across the table. I watch her eyes as she takes in what I'm wearing, a designer knit suit and white silk blouse, the diamond studs at my ears, and the understated Cartier watch on my wrist. She's running a tally of some sort in her head, I'd guess. Not financial, but rather, she's sizing me up, wondering if I can be trusted to receive whatever she's going to dole out.

"I have been CEO of Domaine de la Bouvier for more than thirty years. I took over after my husband's death. In that time, I moved the operation of the company from France to the United States, I've purchased land, bored caves, restructured—"

I stifle a yawn. I've done my homework. I know what she's done. As she drones on about her accomplishments, I jump one step ahead of her and try to anticipate where this is headed.

"—and, as you know, our holdings in Eperny and now the Napa Valley are, shall we just say, vast."

I reach for my water glass. "Your accomplishments are admirable." Is she tooting her own horn?

"Yes. The point being, they are *my* accomplishments."

Ah, now we're getting to it. I nod. "Meaning?"

"Meaning, like the empire you're building, I built this company on my own and I have no intention of turning it over to anyone else. Not anytime soon, anyway." She lifts her wine glass again and tilts it toward me in a mock toast. She takes a sip and sets it back on the table.

I measure my words. "There is no place in business for familial sentimentality." She looks at me and I know I've gained another point.

"My philosophy exactly. However—"

"—Gerard doesn't agree."

She smiles, but there is no warmth in her steel eyes. "No, he doesn't. But I expected you would. Do we have an understanding?"

"We do. I'm also clear on who hired me. I work for you, Mrs. Bouvier."

"Please, it's Brigitte."

This time, I pick up my wine glass and toast her. "To Domaine de la Bouvier, may it continue to prosper under your leadership."

I lift the glass to my lips and pretend to take another sip. The smell of the wine makes my stomach roil as pictures of my father flash in my mind. I set the glass back down and reach for the plate of warm rolls. I peel back the white linen napkin covering the bread and offer a roll to Brigitte.

When she shakes her head, I take a roll and reach for the small crock of salted butter. Focused on buttering the roll, I take the moment to let my stomach settle and to process the information she's shared and how it will fit with the recommendations I'm here to make.

"Ah, darling, here you are." I look up and see Brigitte looking beyond me. I turn to see Gerard approaching. I reach for the napkin on my lap, wipe my hands, and then offer my hand to Gerard, who first shakes it, then bends to kiss it."

"You Frenchmen are quite the charmers," I say.

"We try. Good afternoon, Andee, Mother. May I join you?"

"Of course, darling, we've been waiting for you."

I notice him glance at his watch and see a flash of confusion cross his face.

"We were early," I say.

Gerard seats himself and the waiter, right behind him, fills his glass with wine. "One of ours, I assume?"

"Of course, Mr. Bouvier."

Gerard lifts his glass. "To business and the pleasure of lunching with beautiful women."

You've got to be kidding me. I lift my glass, but this time I don't even pretend to sip. Gerard, on the other hand, makes a show of twirling his glass, and sniffing the bouquet of the wine before tasting it. "Perfect." He takes another swallow of the wine before he speaks.

"Andee, Mother tells me you have some additional recommendations for us. I look forward to hearing them." He takes another drink of his wine before setting the glass down.

I lean forward and jump in. "With the current economic slump, many of the smaller wineries are struggling, as you know. Now's the time to add to your holdings and further diversify." I reach into my briefcase and pull out a file folder. I open the file and hand both Brigitte and Gerard copies of my recommendations.

"Azul?" Brigitte takes off her glasses and looks at me. "Bill and Jason have never entertained our offers. Do you know something we don't? Are they in trouble?"

"Maybe you haven't made the right offer." She watches me, searching my face for information, but I give nothing away.

Gerard jumps in. "Andee, you're aware of my friendship with Jason, not to mention our family ties. I think I'd know if they were ready to sell."

I shrug. "It's about timing and the right offer."

Brigitte purses her lips. "What do you have in mind?"

"I've worked the figures. Though, as I'm sure you know, it's about more than money. Azul holds deep sentimental value for the family. Keeping the name, the label, would be paramount."

"Of course." Gerard studies me. "That's never been an issue with us."

I reach into the file and hand each of them another packet of papers. The initial suggested proposals for each winery.

They look through the proposals. After a few minutes, Brigitte sets the packet down. "Andee, you realize, of course, that to acquire these companies will spread Domaine de la Bouvier thin. We aren't immune to the downturn in the economy."

My adrenaline surges as I propose my plan. "I realize that. But now, I believe, is the time for Domaine de la Bouvier to go public. Doing so will increase your capital reserves and make the acquisitions possible."

Brigitte leans back in her chair. She wears a smug smile. "I like it. Though there will be added expenses in the process."

I nod. "Of course."

Gerard reaches for his glass and drains it. He turns, pulls the bottle out of the ice bucket, and tops off Brigitte's glass. "Andee?"

"No, thank you. I'm working."

He fills his glass and places the bottle back in the bucket. "Let's put this aside for a moment. There's other business I want to discuss before we launch into these types of decisions. Andee, as you know, I will be taking over Domaine de la Bouvier at some point. It seems we should begin that shift sooner rather than later. Especially if we're considering going public and acquiring additional assets. Before that happens, we need to establish new leadership, alert the press, etc. This type of restructuring would be the natural outflow of new leadership."

I look at Brigitte. Her silence tells me all I need to know. I'm to take the fall here.

"I disagree." I see Gerard's chin lift as he braces for a battle. "Investors want stability. A shift in leadership before going public wouldn't be wise. The strength of Domaine de la Bouvier, beyond its holdings, is that it's a known entity. Both you and Brigitte are known in the community, here and in France. Your roles are established. Your product has proven itself. And with new leadership comes new possibilities. While a business needs to grow and flex with the times, during an economic crunch, your best bet is to remain steady."

Before Gerard has a chance to respond, Brigitte speaks up. "I'd like a meeting with Bill and Jason. If they're ready to sell, it's time to talk details."

I expect Gerard to interrupt. To reclaim the conversation. Instead, he signals for the waiter. "We're ready for lunch." His tone is tight. He picks up his glass, which the waiter refills, and leans back in his chair. Apparently, he's removed himself from the conversation.

The man is so weak it's disgusting. I turn my attention back to Brigitte. "As I said, timing is important for the Azul deal. I'd advise you to wait to meet. I'll let you know when the time is right."

"*You* would know, wouldn't you?" Gerard throws back another swallow of wine.

His implication is clear—that I have inside information. I'm walking a fine line here, I know. I feel the rush of potential, the thrill of an impending deal. A substantial deal.

As lunch is served, I breathe in satisfaction. Life continues to unfold just as I've planned.

∾

IT'S ALMOST 10:00 p.m. when I return home from the studio where I prerecorded several segments of my radio program. Wired and restless, I kick off my heels, feed Sam, and then go through the pile of mail Cassidy left on my desk. Included in the pile is the current issue of *Urbanity*. I take it to the sofa, stretch out, and I thumb through the magazine and read restaurant reviews, and skim articles addressing the arts, city issues, and a feature on the ecosystem of Golden Gate Park. Whatever. Nothing holds my attention for long, until I come to the *Buzz* page where five columns list five reviews each written by an individual reviewer: film, book, blog, album, and exhibit. The critiques are short enough to hold my meandering mind captive for the fifteen seconds it takes to scan each one.

The film is foreign—no thanks, I don't do subtitles.

The book, a memoir on ADHD, doesn't interest me, though, tonight, maybe I should consider reading it.

The exhibit is pretty mainstream for *Urbanity*—*The Van Gogh, Gaugin, Cezanne and Beyond* exhibit at the DeYoung. Been there, done that.

The album is retro '70s psychedelic folk. Really?

I land on the blog review.

"Illuminate me" is the cry of this blogger. On a spiritual journey to enlightenment, the city is a-Buzz wondering which local is penning, or keying rather, the anonymous blog www.iluminar.me. Known only as lightseeker@iluminar.me, the author chronicles her life of privilege—the angst (give us a break), the abuse (really? Do tell), and the spiritual (ho-hum). Here's what we know: She's infected (AIDS?), she's desperate (poor baby), and she's gearing up, we're guessing, for a revolt (yee-haw!). If you can get past the "christianese," this is a blog to watch. Join in the citywide fun and guess the blogger's identity. Will she reveal herself? Go to www.urbanitysf.com/blogger for contest details.

"I hope she has advertisers, cause this chick's blog is going to get some hits this week. Way to make your blog pay off, babe, whoever you are." I look again at the URL and go sit at my desk and key in the address. The blog header is a picture of the Golden Gate Bridge shrouded in fog, and below the picture is the title: *Iluminar*.

Spanish for *illuminate*.

The blog is nondescript otherwise. I scroll down. No advertisers. The reviewer referenced her life of privilege—maybe this blogger thinks she doesn't need the money? Stupid. What a waste. No links. No bio. Nothing. Just entry after entry and icons linking to her social networking pages, which I check. They're also set up under the pseudonym. I check the comments on a few entries. Yep, she has followers. Lot's of them, it looks like. The comments read like an ongoing conversation with lightseeker@iluminar.me responding to and reengaging her readers.

"This thing is a moneymaker and she's clueless."

Sam hisses in response.

I hit the archives, find her first entry, and begin reading. The entries are journal-like. Raw. Vulnerable. And yeah, they sort of read like a soap opera. But she writes well. Maybe it's her vulnerability, so rare in this city, that draws the reader in.

Draws *me* in.

I read several more entries. Christianese? Geez, no kidding. I expect to see judgment in her responses to those who challenge her beliefs, but there is none. She doesn't touch on any of the issues either—she's not using the blog as a platform for the usual fundamentalist stuff. Nor is she defensive about what she believes. Her responses to readers' questions and challenges are straightforward, compassionate even.

She's hitting a nerve. A felt need of some sort. I think about the blog I write and the many followers who comment and submit questions. In this economy, the advice I offer fills a need. But, I don't receive as many comments as this chick. And why, excuse me, is *Urbanity* featuring her when they could feature a blog like mine? After all, I'm one of their own now. "C'mon, people. Give your own writers a leg up."

I close the window and type in the address for *Urbanity* and find the contest information mentioned in the review. For the best guess, they're giving away an all-expenses paid weekend at *Auberge du Soliel* in Rutherford with spa credits, a bottle of wine, and dinner for two at the resort's famed restaurant. There's $1,000 additional cash prize if the blogger comes forward if she is identified.

I shake my head. "That's a chunk of change you're offering. Ridiculous."

I stare at the screen and think again of the entries I've just read. I can't stand it that, whoever this woman is, she's letting a prime financial opportunity slip through her fingers. So what if she's rich? I don't care if she's Oprah rich, J. K. Rowling rich, or the Queen of flippin' England rich. Why let an opportunity to make money pass you by? Especially one this easy. *Urbanity's* set her up. Why miss the opportunity?

I mouse over the history tab and click back to the blog site.

I leave a comment for lightseeker@iluminar.me:

Let me illuminate you. You're missing a nice financial opportunity with your blog. E-mail me for details at andee@andee-bell.com.

My e-mail address—my name—speaks for itself. I'm known for my financial advice. I'm not scamming her. Though I'd love to be the one to out her. I'm not, as a contributor to *Urbanity*, eligible for the contest, but why not see if I can lure her anyway? "We love a good game of cat and mouse, don't we, Sam?" I turn in my chair and see Sam, curled up in his bed on my office floor, snoring. "Such apathy, Sam."

I close the window on the blog, then get up from my desk, stretch my arms wide, twist my torso, and then bend and reach for my toes. I stand straight again and wander back to the living room. Rain pelts the windows and the lights below are streaked across the cityscape. I listen to the sound of the rain hitting the windows and then reach for the remote on the coffee table and close the blinds against the annoyance.

Enough of this. Time to get back to work. I go to the kitchen, take a small black ceramic cup from one of the glass-front cabinets, and fill it with fresh espresso from the built-in espresso maker above the granite countertop. I take it black and fully caffeinated, even at this hour of the night. I head back to the office, turn the flat screen to the usual: CNN. The voice of the anchor drones, but it is better than silence.

I need to make up for the time I lost this afternoon and evening.

I sit back at my computer and open the file containing my work in progress. I read through the draft of the chapter I finished earlier today. It's good. The language is fresh. The advice, stellar, of course. I open my outline file and read my notes for the next chapter, but I find my mind wandering back to the blog entries I read. *Who cares. Let it go, Andee. Focus.*

I read through my notes again and type and delete at least three beginning sentences of my next chapter. Frustrated, I rewrite the first sentence for a fourth time. It will have to do for now. I pound out a few paragraphs, but all the while the blog posts play on my mind.

I save my document and return to the blog. I need to put it to rest—to figure out what's bugging me.

I reread the first entries. Then I skip to the most recent entry —one I haven't read yet. It isn't so much the words she writes, but the conviction with which she writes them. Have I ever felt that sort of conviction about anything? I smile. Yes, *money!* But as I try to laugh it off, a gnawing emptiness nags.

She's just a Jesus freak. I close the blog, get up, and walk back to the kitchen, where I dump the remainder of the now-cold espresso down the drain of the sink. I refill the cup with fresh espresso and drink it as I walk back to my desk. *Gnawing empti-ness? Get over it.* I look around my office and out to the living area. I have everything I've ever dreamt of and more.

I sit back at my desk and determine to put all thoughts of blogs and emptiness, good grief, aside. Instead, I'll do what I do best.

Work.

CHAPTER NINE

His light pursues you, slowly unfolding more and more as you walk more deeply into it.
JEANNE GUYON

enna

I DECIDE to walk the blocks home after my meeting with Matthew. The sun is shining against an azure sky, and the walk will give me time to think through the feelings unearthed during my conversation with Matthew. And time to process what I've put off thinking about: my appointment yesterday with Dr. Kim.

His words come back to me. "There are still signs of infection." He glanced at my chart and then looked back at me. "We need to administer another round of intravenous antibiotics—just as we did in the hospital after the last surgery. Only this time we'll arrange for a home health-care provider to insert a port as soon as possible. We'll hit the infection hard. Once the infection clears, we'll look ahead to reconstruction. Understood?"

"Yes." I tried to assimilate the information.

"I'll insert an implant to build up the deteriorated section of your jaw and chin and correct this line." He ran his index finger along my jaw. "And then, for the scarring, we can graft skin. Once it heals, we'll use laser to smooth the skin."

I listened and nodded, but a war raged in my mind.

Dr. Kim stepped back and looked at me. "Mrs. Bouvier, you've been through a lot. The recurring infection and subsequent surgeries were unexpected, but now, if…when…the infection clears completely, we will begin restoring your appearance."

I shook Dr. Kim's hand. "Thank you. I appreciate all you've done."

"Do you have any questions?"

Questions churned in my mind, but I couldn't pin a single thought down. The other voice, the one raging within, distracted.

That voice—the voice of accusation—slithered into my mind during those first years of marriage, when I failed to become pregnant. Failed to produce what was expected of me—what I expected of and longed for myself. Since then, condemnation has been my constant companion, even though our infertility was no fault of my own. The voice strengthened following the first surgery, when the initial rounds of antibiotics, burning as they pumped through the IV and into my bloodstream, failed to eradicate the bacterial infection raging first in the incision beneath my chin and then, later, in my jawbone.

What have you done to yourself?

How could you be so stupid?

Why couldn't you be content?

You don't get anything right!

With each slur cast, my sense of shame deepened. And in the darkest moments, I hurled blame at others. If Brigitte hadn't made those comments about the "strength" of my chin and how "masculine" it looked…if she hadn't suggested the surgery in the first place…or if Gerard had defended me, for once, against his mother's attacks…

But casting blame just shamed me further.

Matthew asked if I blamed God. Absolutely not. I knew from the beginning, and still know, there was no one to blame but myself.

I walk around the tables on the sidewalk of an outdoor café, the aroma of bread baking and coffee brewing waft from the open door. Today, more than a year after the mentoplasty, that first fateful surgery following the choice I made to fix what wasn't perfect in my eyes—the voice still woos me. Now, when I look back at photos of myself before the surgery, I can't see the imperfection that seemed glaring to me before. Like an anorexic seeing fat where there is emaciation, I saw something in the mirror that was never there.

The insistent accusations are hard to ignore.

Why can't I rest in truth? Rest in my relationship with the One I know loves me most? There are moments of rest. Of joy. A sense of God's presence as sure as the scents coming from the café. Like in the solarium the other morning. In those moments, just maybe, I glimpse who I'm meant to be.

No. That's not it.

I glimpse who He is.

And all else fades and becomes extraneous.

Why can't I maintain that focus—that frame of mind?

How much time have I wasted over the years first serving my beauty, then lamenting over its loss? How many hours wasted on this obsession with self? It wasn't just the physical beauty—it's what it represented. My beauty, I know, is why Brigitte was drawn to me—why she chose me for Gerard. It is why Gerard acquiesced to his mother's plan. He still jokes about the "arranged marriage" but says, "Who can argue with her choice?" Maintaining my appearance, fixing the flaws I saw there, became imperative—it was necessary, in my mind, to please Brigitte.

And as Skye implied in the park yesterday, I strive to please Brigitte at any cost. *Who are you serving, Jenna?*

Who am I serving? Brigitte? Myself?

The question nags at me as I walk the remaining block to the house.

I slip in the front door unnoticed, then stand for a moment just inside the entry and watch as shards of light dance on the marble floor. The sun shinning in the upper windows and through the crystal prisms of the chandelier account for the show on the floor. I think of Skye's words this morning, *sometimes we need someone who will illuminate the path.* Choice words. God knew they'd catch my attention, just as the crystal prisms catch the light.

All is still.

Brigitte isn't here. I'd know.

How long have I prayed for illumination? For a light to lead me out of darkness? Skye has been an answer to that prayer. Is Matthew also part of God's answer?

I think of my blog. Even the URL is a prayer: www.iluminar.me. *Iluminar*—Spanish for illuminate—in deference to my mother who was the first to cast light into my world. I began writing the blog while fighting the infection following my surgery —while fighting the sense of shame and stupidity suffocating my soul. During those months, I was realizing, for the first time, the hold Brigitte has on me—the hold I've allowed. The surgery, once I was willing to admit it to myself, was done to please her. Yet, it didn't please. It—*I*—failed.

Miserably.

For the first time, I wondered what lengths I'd go to, to please her? In a sense, I'd sold my body. Would I sell my soul as well?

As the bacterial infection raged in my body, an emotional infection raged in my soul. The blog became an outlet for the infection—a place where the poison could drain.

I was desperate to begin understanding why I'd allowed Brigitte such power in my life. Why I'd surrendered my life. My life! To anyone other than God. For the first time, in the blog posts, I processed thoughts, feelings, and the fractures of self.

And then, I sent the entries into oblivion—into the sphere of the unknown—the cosmic World Wide Web, where no one would know me. Where I could just be. Where I could become. Somehow recording the entries in a journal wasn't enough.

I needed, wanted, longed, to be heard.

There was solace in the words I typed on the screen. They were real. I wrote my truth. My heart. My soul. I began a dialogue with God. Unabashed and raw. I opened my wounded body and soul to Him. And to a cloud of unknown witnesses.

I read articles and a book on blogging, I linked the blog with social networking pages I set up and like ants, followers came. First one, then a few, then hoards. My posts were shared over and over again. I began receiving comment after comment. And with the comments came conversations.

I found a place where I had a voice.

Where I was heard.

Where I was accepted.

A place where I could be real, unencumbered by roles, or the judgments of those who think they know me. Or, at least, it's become a place where the anonymous author of www.iluminar.me can be real.

Ironic.

It's all I'm ready for. I'm known as lightseeker@iluminar.me. That's enough.

Still standing in the entry, watching the light dance, I bend and slip off my shoes. I cross the marbled entry, hoping to avoid detection by the household staff—Brigitte's eyes and ears. I tiptoe up the stairs, down the hallway, and into our suite where I inch the door closed, turning the handle so it doesn't click. Once it's closed, I lean my back against it and let out a sigh.

I head to the alcove, drop my shoes by my desk, and sit down and open my laptop. As it loads, I think again about Matthew, and as I do, I'm aware of the right side of my face rising to meet the left. The smile comes as I recall the surge within when Skye introduced us. Matthew shook my hand, but it was my soul that was shaken. Something inside me came alive.

What did I feel? I think of Matthew's stature—about Gerard's height, I'd guess—maybe 6'2", maybe a bit taller—and in good physical shape, as though he's a runner or a hiker. His weathered good looks speak of time spent in the elements. His dark hair is a mass of curls. And the intensity of his gray eyes startle, until they soften with a smile.

But it isn't his looks that stir me. It's something beneath the surface—the core of who he is. He's goofy, but there's more there.

I shake my head. I don't even know him. I pick up a pen from my desk and twirl it in my fingers. Yet, it's like he said—it's as if we do know one another. As if we've always known one another. It was as if our souls recognized one another in some way.

Odd.

Before leaving the cathedral this afternoon, I scheduled an appointment next week to explore the idea of spiritual direction. As I told him, I'm intrigued. Our meeting energized me.

But now that I'm here, I feel the familiar sense of fatigue slipping in.

I place the pen on the desk and turn my attention back to my laptop. I open my browser and sign in to my blog site. I open the blog and click to begin a new entry. I think back to last night and the anger I felt with Brigitte and the way I reacted when she ignored what I'd said and refilled my glass. As I recall the anger and then the fear that followed, my fingers fly across the keyboard.

As I write I can drop the veil of pretense, a veil that distorts even my own vision, and explore what I feel and wait for, hope for: illumination.

I read back over the words I spewed on the page and then I edit. I cut any reference that links the blog to me. I remove Brigitte's name. Omit the sentence about the PICC line inserted today. What instigated the infection. The readers know the generalities and the heart of an anonymous life. In this way, I remain free to explore—to open my life not only to God, but also to the cloud of witnesses.

This afternoon, I am weary. The infection continues to wage a war within my system. It marches through my bloodstream, taking healthy cells hostage. But, I must remind myself, I am the one who invited the troops in. The battle is a consequence of my actions.

I am battle weary. But today it's more than physical exhaustion that I experience. Today, my soul is exhausted. Tired of the battle in my body, but also in my home. Tired of not getting it right. Tired of falling short.

I lose things, often, but I don't lose my temper. Is it the war still raging in my body? Or the war raging in my soul?

A torrent of anger I can no longer quell? Will I ever be free of either? I've become weak. I'm losing my self-control. Was my anger justified or had she misunderstood?

Yet, I know better, don't I? She didn't misunderstand. Her act was deliberate. A judgment? Perhaps. But there is knowing in my spirit. Though I discern her intent, I know not what to do with the discernment.

Illuminate me...

Lord, I long to be an instrument of Your love and peace. But

I'm operating on my own strength. And today, my strength wanes.

"My grace is sufficient for you, for my power is made perfect in weakness." (2 Cor. 12:9)

Before I click *publish*, I stand, stretch, and walk to the window. As I look out across rooftops to the glittering bay, I submit my concerns to Him. Do I write to glorify myself? To draw attention or seek sympathy? Or, is there value in the words I send into cyberspace. *Are they of You?* I'm never sure.

I bow my head and wait. Will I hear His still, small voice? After several minutes of silence, I whisper my prayer. "Oh Lord, fill me with more of You and less of me."

"Who, may I ask, are you talking to? And what is this?"

I feel the hair stand up on the back of my neck. I turn and see Brigitte standing in front of my computer, bending to read the screen. She holds her coat over her arm and her purse on the other arm.

"What is this?"

I walk to the desk and reach for the mouse, but before I can click and minimize the screen, Brigitte grabs my wrist.

"I asked you a question." The edge in her tone is sharp, cutting.

"It's just a blog."

"Whose blog?"

I jerk my wrist from her grasp. I take a step back and take a deep breath. "Does it matter?" My voice shakes, but I hold her gaze.

"Why so defensive, chérie? Hiding something?" She turns from the screen and faces me. "More spiritual gibberish, *n'est-ce pa*? No wonder you're defensive." She walks toward the window, looks out, then turns back. "What is your American saying? 'You're too heavenly minded to be any earthly good'? Very apropos, I'd say. You're wasting your time, if you ask me."

So saying, she turns and leaves—the sound of her steps lost in the plush carpet.

"I didn't ask you." I whisper.

I sit back down in front of the computer and look at the screen. My insides tremble like the leaves of fall, but all that's visible of the blog is the last paragraph and the Scripture reference. I'd scrolled down to that point as I edited. My shoulders slump as I lean my elbows on the desk.

As I reread what I've written, I can't help but do so through Brigitte's eyes. What would she think? What would she do?

I shudder.

I click *publish*, close everything, and lean back in my chair and consider. What am I feeling? When I'm with God, when I'm pouring out my heart, my soul, to Him, when I'm in His Word, when I'm seeking His light—I'm most alive.

When I'm with Brigitte, I cease to exist.

This incongruence dawns like the winter sun. Slow. Cold. Gray. I grasp for understanding but it flees. I can't hold on to it.

*Help me understand. Help me...be...*I search for the words hidden in the fog of my mind. *Help me be who...You want me to be.* That's it. But then I sense there is something more He's asking of me. *Help me to be who You want me to be.*

Knowing comes.

In all circumstances.

Even when I'm with Brigitte. That's what God's asking of me?

Knowledge is accompanied by a ripple of fear.

"How? How, do I do that?"

I can't begin to imagine.

Stand back...

CHAPTER TEN

Those who are living in the natural life have faults, but nothing is being done to change them.
JEANNE GUYON

rigitte

SHE SETS her purse on the credenza, drapes her jacket across the back of her chair, and presses the intercom button on the phone on her desk. "Hannah come to my office."

She puts on her glasses, reaches for a pen, and writes Jenna's name on the top sheet of a yellow legal pad. She underlines the name and begins scribbling notes until she's interrupted by a tap on the door.

"Come in."

"Good afternoon, Madame." Hannah stops in front of Brigitte's desk.

"The report, please, Hannah."

Hannah reaches into the pocket of her apron and pulls out a

small sheet of notebook paper and begins to read. "She took breakfast at 8:15 in the kitchen with Nicoletta. Coffee and toast. At 9:00, the home health-care nurse arrived. They took the elevator upstairs, where Jenna could lie down while the line was inserted. The nurse left about 9:45. At 10:25, I heard her call for a cab. She left about 10:40. She said she'd return sometime after lunch." Hannah glances at her watch. "She isn't back yet."

"Of course she's back. She's in her room now. Really, Hannah, can just anyone walk into this house unnoticed?" She taps her pen against the edge of the desk. "Never mind. Where did she go?"

"She didn't say, Madame. She was dressed casually."

"Did you see the cab? Get the number?"

"No. Not this time." Hannah shifts her weight from one foot to the other.

"La méfiance est mère de la sûreté."

"I'm sorry, Madame. I don't understand."

"It is simple, Hannah. *Mistrust is the mother of security.*

A simple principle—one you must learn. If you do not, I will be forced to replace you. Oui?"

"Yes, Madame."

Brigitte scrawls a few more notes on the pad of paper. "Have a seat." She motions to one of the chairs across the desk from her. She leans back in her chair, removes her glasses, and looks at Hannah. "I'm concerned about Jenna. Her welfare. The infection is, I believe, taking a toll. She isn't acting herself."

Hannah nods.

"I'd like to make certain that it is only the illness that's influencing her and not something else." She pushes back from her desk, stands, and walks around to the front of the desk where she perches on the edge, near Hannah. She lowers her voice. "She spends an inordinate amount of time at her computer. I'd like to know why."

Hannah nods.

"You understand, oui?"

"Yes, Madame. Give me a few days."

She leans forward and places her hand on Hannah's shoulder. "Merci."

After dismissing Hannah, she sits back at her desk. She must keep Jenna in check. The insolence she's demonstrated in the last couple of days will not be tolerated. What is prompting the change? Perhaps it is the illness. Or perhaps it is something more. Or someone more.

She picks up the phone and punches in a number, her acrylic nails clicking on the number pad. "Marcus? Yes, hello. I'm fine, thank you. You? Mm-hm. And how's Estelle? Good to hear. Listen, Marcus, you'll be having guests this weekend. Oui. Gerard and Jenna are taking a few days away. I told them I'd alert you so the chateau's ready and you have the kitchen stocked. Of course, I knew you would. What's that? Oh, yes, they'll arrive tomorrow evening and stay through the middle of next week. They'll let you know for sure once they arrive. Yes. Merci, Marcus."

Satisfied, she hangs up the phone then jots another series of notes on the pad before she turns to her keyboard.

Gerard,

I'd like you to spend a few days in the valley to make initial contact with the wineries on Andee's list. Don't play our hand, of course. Just get a read on things. Do what you do best, darling. I've contacted Marcus—he and Estelle know you're coming and the chateau will be ready. Take Jenna with you— perhaps a dose of the valley will be healing. I told Marcus the two of you will arrive tomorrow evening. Let's meet in the morning, 8:00 AM, to go over details.

She sends the e-mail.

Yes, it will be good to get Jenna away for a few days.

CHAPTER ELEVEN

What we call the "death of will" is the passing of your will into His will.
JEANNE GUYON

M atthew

OPPOSITES ATTRACT. Bummer, right? Wouldn't it be easier to be in relationship with someone who views life through the same set of lenses? Man, it sure seems like it'd be easier. Take Tess and me. She's quiet. I'm, well, not. She appreciates culture. I love a good baseball game and a paper tray of nachos—you know, slathered in the bright orange goo. She's passionate about fashion. I'm passionate about the worn flannel shirt I've had since my freshman year of college.

Surface issues. No big deal.

I appreciate what Tess adds to my life—a little class, for one thing. But she also tones me down, which isn't a bad thing. I'm exuberant if I'm nothing else. And sometimes that overwhelms people. I've learned from Tess to give thought to the words that shoot out of my mouth before I pull the trigger. Okay, I still pull the trigger too soon sometimes. But now, I'm at least aware that I need to apologize afterwards. Tess has made me a better counselor. A better spiritual director. A better man.

It's when you and your spouse veer in opposite directions on the deeper issues that it's like hitting a patch of ice and spinning out of control. The thing to do then is take your hands off the wheel and surrender. Trying to force things back under your control just makes matters worse.

Trust me.

When I counsel couples, clients look to me for the answers. They expect that I have it all together. I have the book knowledge, but applying that knowledge in everyday life is challenging. Joining two flawed lives into one harmonious unit? That's work. Even for me.

Or as Tess might say, especially for me.

As a spiritual director, clients are looking to God for the answers and I'm just along for the ride. Sure, some people confuse my role—think of me as a go-between, a priest of sorts, but when that happens, I make it clear. I'm just an observer of their process.

A listener. An interpreter of sorts. As a spiritual director, I'm, as Skye put it, a fellow pilgrim on the journey and I'm as much in need of grace as the next guy.

Tess and I hit our patch of ice about a year into our marriage as we discovered that our fundamental priorities differ. Big time. Weird that we didn't see it when we were dating. Back to the lenses—those rose-colored lenses distort our vision when we're in the throes of emotional love.

For instance, when Tess said she didn't want children, I thought, yeah right, who doesn't want kids? She's just not ready. Instead, what Tess meant was she doesn't want children.

Period.

Ever.

She has her reasons, and they're valid for her. But man, I've looked forward forever to the day when I'd have a little dude or dudette holding my hand and exploring the world alongside me. I want to nurture, and love, and share what's most important to me with a little sponge who'll soak it all up. I want to offer them the love of God, to be a picture of the Father as a father. I want to toss a ball, sit at ballet recitals, and put Band-Aids on boo-boos.

God put those desires in me. They're in my wiring. Yet, it doesn't seem He's wired Tess that way.

So, for a time, I encouraged her. I shared my view. Often. Okay, I even tried to bribe her. Not good. Don't try that. And I hounded her. The more I hounded, the more she hid. It took awhile before I got that I was asking her to be someone she isn't. I was disrespecting who she is. I was saying, I don't like the way God wired you and I want to rewire you.

Not only was I disrespecting Tess—I was disrespecting the God who created her.

Heavy sigh.

If I loved her—and man, I do—then I had to surrender.

Not to her.

To God.

I had to take my hands off the wheel and let the car spin and pray for God to bring it, me, under His loving authority.

I am not a hands-off kind of guy, you know? So this wasn't and isn't easy. But easy isn't always better.

But see, that's the beauty of opposites attracting. In the process, when we surrender our will, God molds us and transforms us. And as a husband, when I sacrifice for my wife, I'm loving her in a way that resembles Christ's love for us. I become more Christlike.

Awesome!

Dude, painful.

But awesome!

The printer finishes sputtering and spits out the last several www.iluminar.me entries. I gather them up, grab my Bible off the desk, and pad, barefoot, to the other side of the kitchen where Mr. Coffee has also finished his sputtering. I grab my San Francisco Giants mug, fill it, add creamer, and head for the recliner in the living room. I plop the Bible and blog entries on the TV tray next to my chair.

Yeah, the recliner and TV tray were definite concessions on Tess's part. We're keeping our eyes peeled for an affordable side table to replace the tray. I sit in the chair, kick my feet up, and take my first sip of coffee.

"Ahh... Good stuff."

"Morning, babe." Tess's velvet voice warms me. She walks by my chair on her way to the kitchen and I lift my hand for a high five. She slaps me five, grabs my hand, and then bends to kiss my open palm. When she straightens, she tosses her head and her long, auburn hair falls across her shoulders. She winks one of her gorgeous green eyes at me.

"Yowza! You look great." I look her up and down. "Let me guess, Tommy? No, wait. Michael?"

"Oh, you're good. It's Michael."

Michael Kors, in case you're wondering. The sheath, another name for the straight, sleeveless dress she's wearing, shows off her sleek figure. "Busy day?"

"Yeah, and I'm running late." She turns her back to me and bends at the knee. "Can you zip me?"

I reach for the zipper and pull it up the last inch or so to the top of her dress.

"Thanks." She turns and looks at the stuff piled on the tray. She doesn't say anything, but I know she doesn't get my morning ritual.

Another patch of ice.

She comes back through with a thermal mug of coffee and her briefcase slung over her shoulder. "I looked her up last night." She points to the printouts on the tray. "I read several of her posts. I can see why you're addicted. I'm dying to know what happens between her and the witch she lives with." She bends, kisses me, and heads for the front door, where she grabs her jacket off the coat rack. "See ya... Oh, hey, I'm making lasagna tonight."

"Yeah? What's the occasion?"

"You're the occasion."

"Love ya, babe." After the front door closes, I say to God, "Cool. Thanks." Not for the lasagna—though that's cool too—but because Tess decided to read the blog.

Tess and I met—and married—young. She is my first and only love. But we've grown in different directions. It happens. We're each unique creations. Where my fledgling relationship with God shot off like a rocket in my mid-twenties, hers was a slow sizzle that fizzled.

Man, nothing hurts me more.

Deeper than my desire for kids is my longing to share the wonder of God with my wife. But again, we're wired different. I'm a feeler, all emotion and passion. She's a thinker who analyzes the facts, and for her, they haven't added up. Yet.

In our early years, my exuberance for God pushed Tess away. From me. Maybe even from God. Now, I hold my feelings close. Like a great poker hand, I don't announce it to the table. I let the cards tell their own story.

And I pray.

Lots.

I pick up the pile of papers off the tray and begin reading. Like Tess, I'm curious to see how Lightseeker will respond to the woman whose emotional abuse she endures. In my professional opinion, the behavior is destructive. And that's just one issue this gal is facing. But there's a new strength in her—and baby, it's not her own.

If her story draws people like Tess, great! Because, as they read, they will see the heart of God in every post. Funny, but her posts are so real, so transparent, that I feel like I know this woman. I'm going to sound like a sissy, even to myself, but this woman stirs my soul—my passion.

I set the pages aside before I've even finished the first post and, as I often do, I pray for Lightseeker.

\

CHAPTER TWELVE

Be assured that God does not invade the unwilling soul...
JEANNE GUYON

ndee

THE MOST IMPORTANT thing I learned from my adolescence was to trust my gut. My instinct developed along with my father's drinking habit. From my small room in the apartment, I could hear the ice clinking and then crackling in the glass as he poured his first drink of the day. The third time I heard the clink and crackle, I knew it was time to leave—whether it was 10:00 a.m. or 10:00 p.m.

I downshift as I reach the Golden Gate Bridge and a clot of traffic. Thursday is the new Friday and it seems everyone is headed out of the city for a long weekend.

Was the ice trick instinct? Maybe not. Maybe that was learned behavior. But the times I knew I needed to leave the apartment before I heard the ice and didn't? Those were the times that taught me to trust my gut.

I learned to move, ghostlike, and slip out the front door, undetected. I knew it was better to spend a day at the library or a night on the street rather than under my father's drunken hand.

I also learned another important skill during those years: bluffing. On the rare occasion that he caught me leaving, I mastered the art of the bluff. "Oh, I'm meeting Mr. Mallory at school to help him grade math tests. I'm his aid this semester." Or "I'm spending the night at Stephanie's. Her parents are out of town and she's afraid to stay alone." Whatever. Just say anything to appease him—to get out.

I weave back into the fast lane and put my foot on the accelerator. The Porsche 911 GT2 RS responds and shoots past the slower traffic.

Heeding my instinct and bluffing are the two skills that serve me best in the business world. I get the last laugh. Whatever cosmic game was being played with my life in those years, I wound up the winner.

I think back to my lunch with Gerard and Brigitte and my suggestion that Bill and Jason might be ready to entertain an offer for Azul. A bluff based on what my gut tells me. Sure Jason gave me his speech about what Azul means to the family, but I watched Bill the evening we met. As we discussed the economy and the impact on local wineries, his foot tapped under the table. His eyes shifted when Jason spoke of the strength of Azul's financial foundation. The vein in his neck bulged.

Maybe Bill's hiding something from Jason. Or maybe he just had indigestion. Time will tell. But I also heard the passion in both Bill and Jason as they spoke of soil, vines, varieties, crop yield, aging, blends, blah, blah, blah.

These two are artisans. What they are not is businessmen.

"Hey, *move* it!" I slam my palm on the horn until the idiot in front of me has the sense to move out of the fast lane.

So I'll wait and watch. Opportunities present themselves to those who are patient and attentive. And I smell an opportunity with Azul. I wouldn't do anything to hurt Jason. But if Azul's in trouble, and my gut says it is, then brokering a sale for them would be in their best interest, of course. And why not keep it in the family? It makes sense that Jenna's family by marriage would bail out her family of origin.

And for some reason, Brigitte wants Azul. I'd stake my life on it.

As long as it's legal, all's fair in business.

I think of the weekend ahead. A fortuitous invitation from Gerard and Jenna for Jason and I to join them at the Bouvier chateau, as they call it. "It's Napa people, not Nice." Whatever. The timing is perfect. If Gerard says anything to Jason about Azul being on my list of recommended acquirements, I'll be there to cover myself. For every good bluff, there needs to be an equally good cover—just in case.

A car changes lanes ahead of me and cuts me off. "What the—!" I switch lanes, pass him, and glare.

My heart pounds and my neck and shoulders ache. I'm accustomed to stress—it comes with the job, but this evening, it seems to have the upper hand. I pull the seat belt strap away from my chest and roll my shoulders. As I do, a memory smacks me. My dad at the wheel of our station wagon with his window rolled down and his head hanging out as he yelled at another driver who'd cut him off. As he swore, his spittle blew back, hitting me in the face. We careened down the highway, him swerving, as he blasted the guy in the next car. I'd slouched behind him in the backseat, terrified. Afraid we were going to crash. Afraid of what my father might do. Or of what the other driver might do to my father.

I shake my head. What's with all this angst? I'm nothing like him. The very thought disgusts me. But it's also a reality check. What's eating at me? Why can't I shake this feeling of doom? The thought that around the next corner it's all going to fall apart, everything I've worked so hard to construct.

Will I ever reach a point where I can rest? Will the demons that taunt me ever lay off? How much money will it take for that to happen?

How much money will it take to fill the emptiness?

Drive determines destiny. At the rate I'm driving myself my destiny may be my demise.

I shudder.

I glance at the clock on the dash. 5:34 p.m. I'm supposed to meet Jason, who worked in the valley today, at the chateau at 6:30 p.m.

I have plenty of time. "What's the rush, Andee? Ease up."

I flip my signal and maneuver to the slow lane. I turn on the radio and search for something in the easy listening genre rather than the talk radio I prefer. I loosen my grip on the wheel and stretch my fingers.

The music grates and the tension remains. I flip the radio off.

Security is what I'm after. Any moron could look at my childhood and understand why financial security is important to me.

I don't need a shrink to figure that out. So why don't I feel secure?

I think, as I have a dozen times this week, about the author of the blog highlighted in *Urbanity*. I, like all the other suckers who read the blog, am hooked. I may not agree with the way this woman is handling her life—I'd boot the biddy who's treating her like dirt—but, even in the midst of it, she is sure. Secure. She believes God is for her. Not against her.

I know better.

I thrum my fingers on the steering wheel.

Whatever.

This weekend will be good. The way my mind is jack-rabbiting down senseless trails, it's obvious I need a break.

A little vacation.

I reach for the radio, turn it back on, and tune it back to KGO *Newstalk* but just as I get involved in the topic, my phone rings and cuts the radio. I click the phone button on the console. "Hello."

"Hi, hey I have a message for you that I thought might be important." Cassidy's voice reverberates through the interior of the car.

"Okay, who called?"

"Bill Durand. He left his cell number."

"Bill Durand? Really? What's his number?"

Cass repeats his number and I file it in my mind.

"One more thing, he asked that you call him when you have a few minutes alone."

"Got it. Thanks, Cass."

I hang up and smile. Instinct? I won't know for sure until I talk to him, but everything in me says there's only one reason Jason's dad would call me. He's in need of a little financial advice.

I flick the voice activation button on the console and speak Bill's number. He answers on the first ring.

"Bill Durand."

"Bill, it's Andee Bell."

"Andee, thanks for getting back to me. Sounds like you're on the road?"

"Yes, I'm meeting Jason in the valley for the weekend. Gerard and Jenna invited us to stay with them."

"Jason mentioned that. Listen, I hope this doesn't put you in an awkward spot, but I wondered if you'd have some time to meet and discuss a business matter. I could use some input."

"Sure, Bill, I'd be happy to meet. What works for you?"

"Well, Jason said he and Gerard have a few appointments tomorrow—looking at some wineries that Brigitte is interested in acquiring. Jason's always interested in seeing what other vintners are up to, so he's going along. Any chance you and I could grab a cup of coffee together while they're tied up?"

"I don't see why not. I'll tell Jenna I have a meeting."

"Great. Shouldn't take long."

We discuss a time and place to meet.

"Like I said, I don't want to put you in an awkward spot, but it might be better, at this point, if neither Jason nor Jenna knows we're meeting. I'd like to get your input before—"

"No problem. Confidentiality is my policy. Has to be with what I do. I'll look forward to talking."

"Thanks, Andee. See you tomorrow."

I punch the phone button on the console and laugh. "Instinct? You better believe it!"

So much for vacationing.

CHAPTER THIRTEEN

Seasons form and mature you. Each is needed just as a year must have different seasons.
JEANNE GUYON

$\mathcal{J}$ enna

I LIE in bed trying not to stir, trying to let Gerard sleep. I turn my head on my pillow and through the tall west-facing windows I watch the sky turn from the ink of night to the blush of dawn. I long to greet the morning in the vineyard. I listen to Gerard's steady breathing and decide I can slip out of bed without waking him. I ease the covers off and inch my way to the edge of the bed. Once out, I find a fleece sweatshirt of Gerard's in the closet, pull it over my pajamas, and step into my shearling-lined boots.

I brush my teeth and my hair, put my cell phone in my pocket, and make my way down to the kitchen for coffee.

I place my mug under the spigot of the built-in coffeemaker

and press the coffee icon on the panel. With my steaming mug in hand, I step out the back door, cross the drive, and step over the low rock wall that surrounds the vineyard. The fall morning is crisp and musky, the organic scent of earth and vines like a welcome embrace. I sit on the wall facing the vineyard and sip my coffee. The deep magentas, ambers, and russets of the leaves on the vines are a fiery display of the Master's creativity. Since childhood, the peace of late fall following the activity of the crush has been my favorite season to be amongst the vines.

I'm awed. Silenced. By the glory before me. The sun peeks over the mountains at the end of the valley, casting the light of a new day. I warm my hands on the mug and raise my gaze heavenward in an act of worship.

The valley takes me back to my childhood. It's here that I'm most at home.

I'm grateful for the time alone before Gerard, Jason, and Andee wake and the activity of the day begins. Andee... Is Jason serious about his relationship with her? She's beautiful, but there's an edge to her. She isn't lacking in confidence, that's for sure. She is bold, in control, and...what? Something's nagged since spending the evening with her and Jason after they arrived last night. There's something under the surface that I can't put my finger on.

I struggled last night to find common ground with Andee. Maybe I'll get some time alone with Jason. I'd like to understand what he's drawn to in her.

I put thoughts of Andee aside, take the last swallow of my coffee, and then leave the mug sitting on the rock wall. I want to walk and spend some time with God amidst the beauty of His creation.

I choose a row and amble between the vines. I stop now and then to watch a rabbit shoot between the stalks or to watch as a vine seems to loose its reluctant hold on a fall leaf that spirals to the ground. Though I'm alone, I'm aware of the Presence walking and watching with me. I smile at the thought and sense His delight.

I stop and look at the vines on my left. They are new vines, grafted this past spring. They won't bear fruit until next year.

I think back to my days at Cal Poly in the school of horticulture and crop science. I graduated with a concentration in viticulture and winemaking, of course. Though I've never used the degree, the knowledge has served me well with both Gerard and Brigitte.

The process of grafting, attaching a new vine, even a new grape variety, to an old stock always fascinated me. I rub a finger along the crown where the new vine was attached and a thought breezes through my mind. *I am the vine; you are the branches.* I think back to what I know of vines and branches. It is the vine or the stalk that nourishes the branches. I look at the visual before me and sense the Spirit's whisper.

There's more...

I tip my head. *What do You want me to see?*

I wander further down the row and see vine after vine after vine. I lift my head and look around me—rows of grapes scale the earth for as far as I can see. I think of the passage from John and Jesus' metaphor of vine and branches. It was, I remember, one of my mother's favorite parts of Scripture. I reach into my pocket and pull out my phone. I open the Bible app and scroll to the book of John, searching for the passage. I read words I've read a hundred times before.

"I am the vine; you are the branches. If a man remains in me and I in him, he will bear much fruit; apart from me you can do nothing. If anyone does not remain in me, he is like a branch that is thrown away and withers; such branches are picked up, thrown into the fire and burned."

I look back at the row of vines with the new branches grafted to them and think of the process of grafting. How the crown of the stalk is cut to expose the heart of the vine. Likewise, the new branch is cut, also exposing its heart. The two hearts are placed together and the nourishment from the stalk, or the vine, feeds the branch.

None of this is new information to me, but for the first time, I see it with eyes of understanding. And understanding turns to longing…to be grafted to Jesus—for our hearts to beat in unison. To remain so close to Him that I'm nourished and strengthened daily. "Oh, how I need Your strength." I whisper.

I drop my phone back into my pocket and turn to walk back to the house, but as I go I have the sense that my business in the vineyard isn't finished. That God has something more He wants me to see. I stop again and look around. I wait. Then I reach for my phone again and return to the passage in John. This time I read from the beginning:

> "I am the true vine and my Father is the gardener. He cuts off every branch in me that bears no fruit, while every branch that does bear fruit he prunes so that it will be even more fruitful. You are already clean because of the word I have spoken to you. Remain in me, and I will remain in you. No branch can bear fruit by itself; it must remain in the vine. Neither can you bear fruit unless you remain in me."

I still as a sense of knowing settles in my soul. A season of pruning is at hand.

As clarity dawns, I shudder. What will God cut from my life? Then ashamed, I'm reminded that pruning brings health and fruit. I turn in a slow circle and look again at the thousands of acres stretched before me—acres of healthy, fruit-bearing vines. And fear is replaced with desire. *Yes, Lord. Cut away the dead branches and prune any that You know will bear fruit for Your glory.*

As I walk back toward the house and take in, again, the

vibrant fall colors, I know it's nearing the end of a season. Soon, all will seem barren and stripped. The branches will be cut and pruned.

A cold, gray season of dormancy lies just ahead.

I shiver and pull the fleece close.

WHEN I WALK in the back door, Jason is standing at the coffeemaker as coffee streams into his mug. "Good morning, you're up early."

"Yeah, it's in the genes. Out for a walk?"

"Just wandering through the vineyard. It's a beautiful morning."

Jason looks from me out the window above the sink. "Looks like it."

I take my mug to the sink and rinse it. Then turn back to Jason. "I'm glad you and Andee joined us. I've wanted to get to know her."

He chuckles. "Yeah? So what do you think?"

I hesitate. "I don't know. She's beautiful."

"That she is, but beauty's only skin deep. We both know that."

I nod and laugh. "I do now."

Jason leans against the granite counter and sips his coffee.

"Are you in love with her?" I ask.

He looks out the window behind me again and seems thoughtful. "I'm drawn to her."

"What draws you?"

He laughs again. "The challenge."

"Jason..."

He sets his cup on the counter and raises both hands in a sign of surrender. "I know. I know." He sticks his hands in the front pockets. "There's something behind all those walls she's worked so hard to build. I want to find out what it is—who she is. I want to get beyond the walls, because I think there's more there." He shrugs. "Crazy?"

"No. But..."

"I'm sure to get hurt?"

I nod.

"I don't know, Jen, sometimes I see something in her. I can't explain it, but—"

"I know, I saw it too. I was thinking about her while I walked. She's wistful, or... I don't know. Something doesn't fit with the persona she presents."

"Exactly. You know me, I've always loved a good puzzle."

I nod and note the unsettling of my spirit. "Jason, be careful."

Andee walks, or staggers, into the kitchen and yawns. She looks from Jason to me. "You're up? Coffee?"

Jason turns, grabs a mug from the cabinet behind him, sets it under the spigot, and taps the coffee icon. Once the cup is full, he hands it to her. She takes a sip. "Ugh. Got anything"—she lifts the cup to her nose and sniffs—"stronger?"

Jason laughs. "We could add a shot of something if you'd like."

Andee sneers at him. "Espresso. Do you have any espresso?"

Jason directs a smile at me. "She's not a morning person."

I laugh. "I see that."

Jason takes her cup, sets it on the counter, grabs a clean one, and starts over.

"I'm a morning person. I'm just not a"—she glances at the digital clock on the coffeemaker—"barely post-dawn person."

Jason hands her the fresh cup. "What are you doing up?"

"I thought I'd write. Knock out a chapter or two before breakfast."

Ah yes. She's a writer. "What are you working on, Andee?"

"Another financial book, this one empowering women." She sips the espresso. "Now, *this* is worth drinking." She leans against the counter next to Jason and seems to almost relax.

"Do you enjoy writing?"

"Enjoy it?" She runs one hand through her mane of hair. "Huh, I've never thought about it. I enjoy the advances and the royalties." She laughs. "But the writing itself is too solitary for my taste."

Jason grins. "Not enough action."

Andee looks up at Jason and, for the first time, I see a flash of vulnerability in her eyes, but it passes. "You've got it."

"What *do* you enjoy?" I take my mug out of the sink and head to the coffeemaker for a second cup.

"Twenty questions? Okay, I'll play. What do I enjoy?"

As she thinks, I notice her navy satin pajamas and matching robe and the way her blonde hair shines like gold against the dark satin. I look down at the too-big fleece and shearling boots I'm wearing over cotton striped pajamas and wish I'd given a little more thought to what I put on before.

"I enjoy financial security. I enjoy determining my own destiny—setting goals and attaining them. I enjoy advising others how to do the same."

I nod.

Jason laughs. "I think what Jenna may be asking is what you do for fun—hobbies, you know." I watch as any opening in Andee's fortress closes. Her defenses engage.

"My fun is my work." Her tone is tight. "Speaking of which, I need to get to it. Thanks for the coffee. What time is breakfast?"

I glance at the note Estelle left on the fridge. "Looks like breakfast is at 9:00."

"Great." She turns to walk out, but then stops and turns back. "By the way, I have a meeting with a client this afternoon." She looks at Jason. "You'll be gone, right?"

"Yeah, I'll be with Gerard for a few hours."

"Great. You don't mind do you, Jenna? Thought I'd save myself a trip since I'm here."

"No problem."

Thank heaven. I had no idea what Andee and I would do with time alone together.

CHAPTER FOURTEEN

Pride, a sense of self-importance, and self-reliance must give way to childlikeness and simplicity.
JEANNE GUYON

ndee

THE CHATEAU IS all old-world French charm, good grief, and my guest suite is no exception. But I'll give the Bouviers this—they've spared no expense on this place. Brigitte's designer didn't miss a detail.

I close the heavy oak door to the bedroom and cross the rich wood floor to the desk in front of the window. I'm glad Jenna had the foresight to offer me a room with a desk. There are also three guest cottages on the property for when the Bouviers entertain large groups. I sit in the upholstered chair at the desk and lift the lid of my laptop.

Fun? Hobbies? Give me a break. Sure, I decided last night that I'd relax more. And I will, but that doesn't mean I need to take up knitting. I scroll through the list of new e-mails, open, read, and respond to a few that are important, and then open my manuscript file. I reread the last chapter I worked on, make a few edits, and then check my outline to see what comes next. My chapters advise readers on topics like checking and savings accounts, credit cards and FICO scores, retirement savings, etc. It's unbelievable to me how many women know nothing about the basics of finances. I shake my head.

As I peruse my outline, I get an idea. How about a final chapter on enjoying money. How to spend what you've earned and saved. Fun? I can have fun. And I'll show others how to do it too, in a fiscally responsible way.

I begin to jot notes for the new chapter but stop short.

I think about how I've spent money. I purchased the penthouse and the Porsche. I wear designer clothes and own a few pieces of jewelry. I try to recall if I enjoyed purchasing the things I own? No.

I didn't buy them for enjoyment. I bought them as symbols of success. To show I walk my talk. I know how to make money.

So what have I enjoyed outside of my business?

Not much.

No, wait. I enjoy Jason. Or I could, if I'd let myself.

I save the open file on my computer and open my browser and type in the now-familiar blog address. I scroll through the archives until I find the post I'm looking for and I read:

Reality is a place I've avoided. It's stark. Uncomfortable. Painful. If I live there, I have to feel, and stretch, and grow.

I've preferred the land of Denial. It's a dark, furtive place.

Yet a place of seeming ease.

But, I was wooed to Reality. My ticket paid for, at great price, by another. One whose call I could no longer resist. And Reality isn't a place one visits. No. Reality is a place of no return. But within its borders lies every good and perfect gift.

I slam the lid of the laptop shut before I've finished reading the post. It's ridiculous. I stand, pace the length of the room a few times, then untie the belt of my robe, slip it off, and throw it onto the bed. I'll shower and get ready for breakfast and the day ahead.

I go to the antique armoire where I've hung my clothes, choose a pair of slacks and a cotton blouse—business casual. Appropriate for the day, including my meeting with Bill.

That's reality.

Anyway, who is she to talk about real? What a joke! She isn't even willing to identify herself.

Still holding the clothes, I walk to the desk, reach for a pen, and scribble a few thoughts about the meeting with Bill. Then I head for the bathroom attached to the guest suite. But a nagging question follows me into the shower: *What am I denying by working so hard?*

BILL'S EMBRACE IS QUICK. "Good to see you again, Andee. Thanks for meeting me."

Bill's rugged good looks are a glimpse of what's to come for Jason. Nice to know he'll age well if I keep him around for very long. "No problem. I've been looking forward to it since you called last night."

"I thought it best we meet here"—he gestures to the little French cafe that appeals to valley tourists—"rather than my office. Just in case Jason and Gerard dropped by, or Jenna, for that matter. They wouldn't think to come here." He looks at the floor for a moment. "I'm not . . . I don't usually keep things from them, and I won't for long, just thought I'd—"

"Bill, no need to explain. It's business, right? It's what we do."

He nods as he reaches to pull a chair out for me at the bistro table he's chosen in a corner of the cafe. "Coffee?"

"Espresso."

"I'll be right back." He walks to the counter and places the order. He returns with a cup of coffee for himself and my espresso and sits across from me.

"So Bill, how can I be of help?"

He stirs his coffee and is silent for a minute. Then he clears his throat. "When Maria was dying"—he looks from his coffee cup to me—"Jason and Jenna's mom…"

I nod, letting him know I've heard the story.

"Well, that's when I started planting the vineyards. It took a chunk of change, but I sold off the cattle and reinvested the money into the vineyards, which helped. And we'd done well ranching and had money in savings.

"But as Maria's condition worsened, the medical bills mounted. Even with insurance."

I nod again. I'm tracking with him and am pretty sure I know where he's headed.

"I was pretty driven back then, not only did we plant but we bored a cave, set up a small processing plant—the whole nine yards. I put my energy into the vineyard rather than dealing with losing Maria." He clears his throat again. His pain, even after all these years, is etched in his features. "The grief was…well, it overwhelmed me. The vineyard became my outlet, so I kept expanding. I did too much, too soon—financially—and started to have cash flow issues."

"So you took out a loan?"

"Yup. The valley's smaller than it seems. We're all connected in one way or another, or at least we were back then. We had a friend, Duke, another vintner, who was advising me along the way and he could see what was happening. He pulled me aside one day and asked if I needed cash."

"How much?"

"Five hundred thousand. We set up a monthly payment plan, with interest. He hand-wrote a note that we signed. And that was that. About a year later, he knew I was still struggling—waiting for the first crop yield—and he came to me and told me not to worry about the payments. Said I could pay him in five years, ten years, whenever it worked for me." He folds the paper napkin he's holding into quarters. "For him, the amount was a drop in the bucket."

I lean back in my chair and cross my legs. "What happened?"

"I went to him five years later with a check for the full amount plus interest. I handed it to him and, wouldn't you know it, he tore the thing up. Said he was happy he could help and that he'd tear up the note too." He smiles. "I argued with him, of course. But he was a stubborn 'ol coot—said he'd made a wise relational investment and wanted to leave it at that."

He looks past me and out the window of the cafe. "Duke died last year." He shakes his head. "Still miss him. He was a good man. And a good friend."

"Bill, I'm not seeing the problem."

"Oh, right. Well, last month, I got a call from…" He reaches into his back pocket, pulls out his wallet, and takes out a business card and hands it to me. "Said he was Duke's attorney and is working for Duke's daughter, Kelly Whitmore. They'd come across the note in some of Duke's papers and the daughter is demanding payment, including twenty-six years of interest."

"What was the interest rate you'd agreed on?"

"Nine percent, which was good for the times. Prime was between 11.75 and 13 percent in '84."

"Ouch."

"Ouch is right. You know, Andee, we're a small company. I've kept it that way. We make a good product, and because we don't produce much, our label's in demand. We get a pretty penny per bottle. But, I don't have that kind of cash sitting around."

I do the math in my head and figure out what he owes. "So he didn't tear up the note?"

"Guess not. Knowing Duke, he just forgot."

"Do you have a copy of the note?"

"Likely have it somewhere."

I nod.

"Any suggestions?"

I'm not a miracle worker, if that's what he's asking. "What are your plans for Azul? Down the road?"

"Keep it in the family. Jason's taking more and more responsibility. I'd love to see Jenna step in too. She's smart as a whip and has a keen understanding of the process." He shrugs. "We'll see." He leans back in his seat and sighs. "You know, I'm not getting any younger." He chuckles. "I've loved this business, but if I can get this money thing ironed out, then it's time for me to step back and let Jason run with it."

"What will you do?"

He smiles and there's a spark in his eyes. "Oh, I'll find something. I'm not about to be put out to pasture. It's time to relax, have some fun. Maybe travel some."

"Well, let's see what we can come up with. Are you comfortable having me give him a call?" I point to the business card of the attorney that I laid on the table.

"Sure. But, I don't want any favors. I intend to pay you for your time."

I shake my head. "Let me just make a call. Give this some thought. I don't want your money, Bill. Jason's special to me. If I can help in any way, I'm happy to do so—for both your sakes."

He slides the business card toward me.

"And this is between us. If you want to tell Jason at some point —that's your business."

He holds out his hand across the table. I take it and he shakes my hand and then gives it a squeeze.

"Andee, I'm sure appreciative."

"My pleasure."

~

AS I DRIVE BACK to the chateau, I wonder, as I often do, at the business deals that are made with the equivalent of a handshake. Handwriting a note for $500,000? Not asking to witness the note being torn up? Idiocy. Yet Bill, like Jason, is likable. Trusting. But, I'm reminded again, these two aren't businessmen. Can I forgive them for that?

I think of Jason and how the information Bill imparted impacts him. I'm surprised by the sympathy I feel for both Bill and Jason. Normally, I have no sympathy for idiots. I chuckle. "You're getting soft, Andee."

I pull onto Highway 29 and head back toward St. Helena and the Bouvier chateau. As I drive, what strikes me is that Bill and Jason are good men. Solid. Trusting and trustworthy.

They are men who fall outside my realm of experience.

The road ahead of me blurs as I wipe away unexpected tears.

"Oh man, I *am* getting soft." I sniff. No, wait, maybe it's hormones. I vote for hormones. I wipe my eyes again and a thought plants itself in my mind: *Jason's a keeper. Hang on to him.*

"A keeper? What is he, a trout?"

Anyway, since when did I want a keeper?

I try to put the thought out of my mind and refocus on Bill's issue. But as I turn into the winding drive that leads to the chateau, all I can think about is Jason. I pull up to the house, turn off the ignition, throw my keys into my purse, get out, and slam the car door. Hard.

CHAPTER FIFTEEN

True, sometimes this natural place of rest is so different from what you have been used to that you will still feel twinges of fear or anxiety. But when you experience what it is like to be a creation of God, you will see what simplicity and innocence, and enlargement is waiting for you.
JEANNE GUYON

enna

ON SUNDAY AFTERNOON, Gerard and I stand in the driveway of the chateau and wave good-bye to both Andee and Jason as they head back to the city, each in their separate car. As we stand there, the afternoon sun hanging in the sky, Gerard drapes his arm around my shoulders. When we can no longer see their cars on the winding drive, Gerard glances at me. "Have a few minutes?"

I look up at him and see that the etched lines furrowing his brow have softened a bit. He looks relaxed, refreshed, and his eyes are clear. The valley is good for him. The time away from Brigitte,

I think, is even more so. I haven't seen him have a drink, not even wine with dinner last night, since we arrived.

I slip my arm around his waist and give him a squeeze. "For you, I have all the time in the world."

"I want to show you something."

He takes my hand and leads me behind the house where the old ranch truck is parked. He opens the passenger door for me. "Hop in."

"Where are we going?"

"You'll see."

He climbs in the driver's side, starts the truck, and soon we're bumping across one of the dirt roads that runs alongside part of the vineyard. We ride in companionable silence and I'm reminded of the year before we married—the year before we lived with Brigitte. It was the one time in our relationship that we were left alone—to form a bond, to fall in love—or at least develop an abiding tenderness for one another.

In many ways, ours was an arranged marriage—though I don't think either of us was aware of it at the time. Brigitte, clever as always, made us think it was our idea. She'd chosen me for Gerard —as his wife, and the mother of her grandchildren. She succeeded on one count, but only one.

Some things even Brigitte cannot control.

That is the one solace I've found in infertility.

After years of trying to become pregnant and then failed attempts at in vitro fertilization, I let go of my hope, and even my need to produce to please Brigitte. Letting go of my hope for children was heart wrenching. A soul-wound that perhaps only other infertile couples understand. Letting go of my need to produce for Brigitte's sake was terrifying. But we couldn't comply.

Gerard asked me, after initial tests showed our inability to conceive was due to his low sperm count, to keep that informa-tion to myself. "We're in this together, Jen. Can we take the fall together?" In other words, he couldn't bear revealing the truth to his mother, who would consider it another failure on his part.

I complied.

It is one of many untruths I've agreed to over the years to maintain peace between Gerard and his mother.

Then I had the plastic surgery and the ensuing complications put an end, in Brigitte's mind, to any further attempts to conceive for the time being. She assumes, of course, that our failure to produce a Bouvier heir is my failure and mine alone.

I look over at Gerard and feel the familiar ache for him. I would have loved for him to have a child. Someone of his own to love and guide. Parenting might have given him a sense of purpose, something Brigitte robbed him of long ago.

I look back to the road and see how far we've gone. Just as I'm ready to ask again where we're going, he turns onto one of the roads that crosses the vineyard. There are several outbuildings that house equipment scattered throughout the vineyard and Gerard stops at the first one on the road. He pulls in alongside the old building. This one is small and stands alone. Like many of the buildings, it was built of stone by Chinese laborers more than a century ago.

Gerard puts the truck in park, turns off the ignition, and then looks at me. There is a glint in his eyes and he smiles.

"What?" I look from him to the building next to us. "What do you want to show me all the way out here? What are you up to?"

"You'll see."

He comes around the front of the truck, opens my door, and helps me out of the truck. Then he leads me to the side door of the old building and searches his key ring for the key. He inserts the key into what I notice looks like a new handle and lock set. Before he opens the door, he turns to me. "Close your eyes."

"What?"

"You heard me. Close your eyes."

"Oh, Gerard..." I do as he tells me but I feel silly. I hear the door creak open and then Gerard guides. He stops a few steps inside.

"Wait there just a minute. Don't peek."

I hear him take a few steps and then hear what sounds like switches being flipped. As I stand there, I realize the inside of the building is warm and smells of wax and polish. It isn't cold and musty as I'd expected.

"Okay, open your eyes."

I open my eyes, and—

"Oh. Oh, Gerard. Oh, how…" I turn in slow circles and take it in. "How did you…?" I'm staggered by the simple beauty surrounding me. Soft golden light illuminates the interior. I look up and see two iron fixtures hanging from the beamed ceiling, each bearing six waxen candles. The fixtures are electric, but give the impression of candles lit above.

The light spills over gleaming rough-hewn plank floors, stained in a dark patina and polished to a rich hue. At the front of the room is what looks like an altar. There are two free-standing iron candelabras on a small raised platform, flanking a large rustic iron cross hanging on the rock wall behind the altar. There is a small chest that looks like it's old-world Mexican made of pine with iron hardware. Draped over the chest is a woven Mexican blanket and a single pillar candle sets atop the chest. There is also a chalice and decanter next to the candle. In front of the chest is a red velvet kneeling bench.

"Stay there." Gerard turns and walks back outside. I hear something banging against one of the outside walls and then the room is dancing with prisms of colored light. There are two stained glass windows, one on either side of the cross behind the candelabras. The pieces of colored glass depict vines laden with bunches of grapes.

"I am the vine; you are the branches…"

The two windows match and must be covered by shutters on the outside.

"Oh, Gerard..."

He comes back in and stands next to me. "It's a prayer chapel. For you."

"I...I see. But...why? How?"

He doesn't answer. Instead, he walks to the altar, opens the top drawer of the chest, and pulls out a lighter. He lights each of the twelve candles in each candelabra. Soon, the flickering flames dance along with the prisms of colored light.

Gerard turns back and reaches his hand out to me. I go and join him at the altar where he kneels in front of me.

"What are you—?"

He puts one finger to his lips. "Shh."

He reaches for my left hand and holds it in his hands. He bends and kisses the back of my hand and then he reaches into the front pocket of his pants. He slides a ring onto the ring finger of my left hand. Over my wedding band, he's placed a large diamond solitaire.

"Oh, you found it! Where?"

"No. I didn't find it. I re-created it. It's a different diamond in the same setting." He bends, turns my hand over and kisses my open palm. "Jenna Maria Durand Bouvier, will you marry me... again? Here? Now?"

I'm speechless.

He stands and embraces me and pulls me close. He whispers into my ear, "You deserve so much more than I've given you. So much more. You are good and pure and giving. And you've dealt with"—he clears his throat—"so much."

He leans back from me and looks at my face. He lifts his hand and traces one finger along my scarred jawline. "My beautiful Jen. I am sorry for all I lack. The courage to stand up for you. The strength to protect you—"

I place my index finger on his lips and quiet him. He wears the look of defeat. He gave up long ago. But when we are away, alone, I see glimpses of who he could be—who he was intended to be. He is charming, generous, and caring. He is intelligent and wise. When we are away, he reengages with me, with life.

When we return home, back to Brigitte, he detaches again. It is, I think, the way he survives. He doesn't have the strength to stand up to Brigitte. And there is a gaping gorge between who Gerard is and who Brigitte demands he be.

Standing here, in this small chapel Gerard has created for me, I wonder if God is asking me to lead the way for my husband. Am I to stand back from Brigitte, to stop entering the chaos she creates in our lives? Am I to be the first to stand up to her?

"You haven't answered my question." Gerard's tone is tentative, uncertain.

I look into his eyes. "Yes." Would I do it all over again? It's not a question I ask myself. That would be pointless. But there is also no point in hurting my husband now. So I stand on my toes and reach to kiss him. I don't know that I'm in love with Gerard, or that I ever was. But I do care for him deeply. He is my only experience with a man—with love. I've imagined romantic love as the passion found in the Song of Songs and the sacrifice mentioned in Ephesians.

I thought I'd share a partnership with my husband. That he'd defend and protect me and that I'd help and comfort him. But that is not the relationship we share. However, in these moments alone, away from the claws of control, I glimpse what it could be like.

If only these moments weren't so fleeting.

Marrying Gerard made sense to me when I was young. I was familiar with his world, both that of winemaker and of affluence —Brigitte had schooled me in the world of affluence—she groomed me for the role. And although Gerard was much older, he felt familiar. I'd tagged along with my father for so many years, spent time with him, his ranch hands, and his friends, that Gerard felt like a fit.

He steps back from me and takes my hands in his. "I promise

to love, honor, and pro…" He falters and drops his gaze to the floor. Then he begins again. "In sickness and in health…" He touches his forefinger to my chin. "I love you, Jenna."

My eyes well. "I know you do." *To the best of your ability.*

He pulls me close and holds me in his embrace. We stand that way for several minutes.

Then he whispers in my ear. "I have reservations for us—dinner, alone."

"Mmm…perfect."

And in this singular moment, life seems perfect. I am content. At peace. But then, a ripple of fear causes me to shiver in Gerard's embrace.

Jenna, a season of pruning is ahead. Remain in Me.

As we lie in bed together, I turn from Gerard's embrace, roll onto my stomach, and lean up on my elbows to look at him bathed in the glow of his bedside lamp. I continue the conversation that began as he held me. "You have so much to offer, Gerard. You are knowledgeable, wise, and intuitive. You are knowledgeable about winemaking, and of business. More than that—you have a strong sense about both. I know you don't believe that, but it's true. My dad and Jason see it too. We see in you what you don't see in yourself."

I long to encourage him, to help him see himself as God sees him, so full of promise.

"What good does it do to see it, Jenna? I can't use those skills. Until she decides to loosen her grip on the reins, I have no opportunity to do more than I'm already doing." He shakes his head. "You know how things are."

It is the closest Gerard has ever come to acknowledging the truth of his mother's control. We are, I know, venturing into territory he has marked with a *No Trespassing* sign.

"You were created for more, Gerard. Maybe it isn't with Domaine de la Bouvier. Maybe it's time to venture out on your own. Take the knowledge and skills and the gifts God's given you and follow Him." I feel my passion rising. Hopeful, prayerful, that he'll listen. I long to offer him strength and courage. "His strength, through you, Gerard. You could do it."

A look of longing passes between us. But then he shakes his head. "It isn't like that for me. I don't have your faith, your conviction. It is what it is, Jen. Let it go."

"But..."

"Let it go." His tone is firmer this time.

I roll onto my back again and pull the covers up to my chin.

The warmth and intimacy we've enjoyed is replaced with the cold reality that tomorrow we return to life as usual.

Life with Brigitte.

"I wish..." But I leave the sentence hanging and Gerard doesn't encourage me to finish the statement. There is much we both wish for but those wishes will go unrealized, I'm learning, unless one of us risks making major changes.

And I will have to be the one to take the risk.

Gerard reaches and turns off the lamp on his nightstand. He rolls over, turning his back to me. I reach out and place my hand on his back and rub the valley between his shoulder blades.

I fight sleep, wanting to prolong the night. Morning will arrive too soon. But then I remember the prayer chapel. Gerard's gift to me. I will go there before the sun rises. I'll light the candles and kneel before God and beg for His mercies before returning to the city.

CHAPTER SIXTEEN

If you insist on controlling your own life, your Lord will not force you to give up your control.

JEANNE GUYON

ndee

AFTER THE WEEKEND IN NAPA, I return to a pile of work. I should know better than to take a couple of days off. I dive in on Sunday evening and don't let up until Wednesday night, when Jason calls and I decide to answer.

"Hey, I've been worried about you. You haven't returned my calls or texts."

"Yeah, sorry." *Someone has to work to cover your father's backside, and yours, by the way.* "Catching up on work."

"You okay?" His tone, his concern, irritates me.

"Of course. I'm a big girl, Jason. I'm used to taking care of myself."

"I know you are. But I need to know you're okay."

"Oh." I don't know what to say to that. "Sorry. Like I said, I've been busy."

I expect anger, or at least agitation, from him, but instead, he laughs. "Well, it's good to know you're alive and well."

"Oh, yeah, well, that I am. How about you?" I get up from my desk and walk to the kitchen where I bend, reach for Sam's food dish, and take it into the pantry and fill it while Jason talks.

Before we hang up, Jason says, "How about dinner tomorrow night?"

"Sounds great." I'd intended to say no, but, oh, he is charming. "And hey, Jason, sorry, I don't mean to... You know?"

"I know, Andee. I'll see you tomorrow."

With that, he hangs up. No reprimands. No hurt feelings. "He's a pushover," I say to Sam. "No backbone whatsoever." But even as I say it, I know it isn't true. I've seen Jason stand up for what's important to him. But he doesn't demand his own way. Instead he offers something else...

"What is it?" I ask Sam. He flicks his tail, takes the last piece of food from his dish, and then saunters away. "You're a big help."

Jason does seem to know. Sometimes he seems to know more about me than I know about myself.

And he accepts me.

Why?

"Because he *is* a pushover."

From the living room, Sam mews his agreement to my reasoning. I walk out to where he's sprawled on the sofa and scratch him behind the ears.

"Oh well, who cares right? He's good for a free meal." I look back toward my office and the remaining piles on my desk. But instead of going back to work, I sigh, and sit down next to Sam.

I reach over and heft him onto my lap, where he settles in and kneads my legs with his paws.

"Well, look at you." Sam closes his eyes and begins to purr. "You're all the man I need." I bury my hand in Sam's fur and question the agitation I feel regarding Jason. My work provides ample agitation for my life. I don't need more.

I think about my meeting in Napa with Bill and, as I have so many times since we talked, I consider the perfect solution for his financial situation.

Well, almost perfect.

I'm not employed by Azul. I'm just a friend. An acquaintance of Bill's. That's all. I won't accept any payment from Azul and, therefore, I'm not ethically bound in any way. I consider the details again.

And again, I hesitate.

I weigh the pros and cons of the plan and realize there is one thing, or person rather, standing in the way.

I lift Sam off my lap, go back to my desk, and pick up the phone. I dial Jason's number and wait. The call goes to voicemail. Perfect.

"Hey, it's Andee. Listen, about dinner tomorrow, I think we'll have to hold off a few more days. I'm buried and taking off tomorrow night was wishful thinking. I'll give you a call at the end of the week."

I hang up the phone satisfied. "Keep your eyes on the goal, Andee." Love, or even infatuation, isn't part of my master plan. It's time to take a step back and refocus. I reach for the mouse and wait as the screen lights up on my desk. There is work to be done. I open my in-box and scan the contents. I have e-mails from some of the top executives in the country, along with those of smaller companies that I've handpicked to work with for various reasons, including an e-mail from Brigitte. I open it and read:

Andee,

We are moving forward on your suggestion to take Domaine de la Bouvier public. Research is underway and a decision will be forthcoming soon. I'd like to schedule another meeting for next week. Thursday, 2:00 p.m., at the Bouvier offices. Will that work for you?

On a personal note, I'd also like to invite you to join me for dinner at our home that evening. It will be an intimate party of friends including the mayor and a few other interesting locals you might enjoy.

Regards,

Brigitte

I check my calendar and hit *reply*.

Brigitte,

Thursday, 2:00 p.m., at the Bouvier offices is fine. And I'll look forward to dinner at your home that evening. Thank you for your kind invitation.

A. Bell

Brigitte's invitation didn't mention Jason as my date for dinner. Did she mean to exclude him? Is she sending a veiled message? Perhaps it was just an oversight. I'll wait and see. But I have no intention of mentioning the dinner to Jason. I'll follow Brigitte's lead.

I look again through the list of waiting e-mails and see I've received another post from www.iluminar.me. I subscribed to the blog, but now I press *delete* before reading the entry. Let the rest of the city follow her little drama, I'm not interested in her brand of spirituality.

Been there.

Done that.

Then I notice I have an e-mail from lightseeker@iluminar.me. It looks like a reply to my e-mail regarding her blog. "Ah . . . maybe you want to make a little money after all." I open the e-mail and read:

Dear Andee,

Thank you so much for your interest in my blog. I'm aware of the opportunity, through advertisers, for financial gain.

However, that isn't my purpose for the blog. But again, thank you for your interest.

The e-mail is, of course, unsigned. I shake my head. "What a fool." I read the note again and then hit *reply*.

Lightseeker,

If you aren't interested in financial gain, what is your purpose?

A. Bell

I let my irritation take over. There's no point engaging her. She's a fool. But then, I open my trash folder and search for the new post I just deleted. Let's see what she's whining about now. I'm just curious, I tell myself.

I find the post, open it, and begin reading. But just as I begin, the computer pings, letting me know another e-mail has come in. I click on the stamp icon and see that Lightseeker has already responded. This should be interesting.

Andee,

What is my purpose? That's a question I'm wrestling with.

I don't know the answer. What is your purpose?

Ha! She's serious? I thought we were talking blogs, but it seems she's moved on to life purposes. What is my purpose? Isn't that obvious? I click *reply* and begin to type, but then I stop. What am I doing? Who cares? I don't need to respond to her. She's desperate for relationships—that's obvious. "Maybe if you lived somewhere other than cyberspace you'd have real relationships."

I delete my response and close the mail folder. Then I delete the post I'd begun reading.

I have more important things to do.

CHAPTER SEVENTEEN

Spiritual union between two believers is a very real experience although it is not easily explained.
JEANNE GUYON

*M*atthew

FIVE DIRECTEES TODAY. Cool. Blake is the first on my schedule. I feel his pain—a reminder that leads me to pray for him each day. My last appointment of the day is Jenna Bouvier. I've waited for this one. Holy anticipation is what I call it. I'm curious to see what God's doing with the bubbly heiress. Bubbly as in champagne, not as in personality. Though, I'm sure she's bubbly enough.

Never mind.

I round the corner to my office. I walk the nine blocks to work. Always. Rain or shine, snow or sleet. Just like the postal service. Although, here in the city, I'd have to say rain or shine, fog or fog. The walk is another ritual. It centers me—gives me time to pray. Out loud. Whereas when I pray out loud on a city bus or cable car, well, people get a little edgy. The walk also burns energy. And man, if there's one thing I need to burn, it's energy.

My morning walk and talk is my time to pray through my own stuff.

This morning's walk and talk was all about Tess.

It often is.

This is how I prepare to set myself aside and be present—to the Spirit and to the directee sitting across from me. It sharpens my focus. On Him and on the directee.

Without the walk and talk, dude, it's not pretty.

I turn the key in the lock of my office and enter what, for many, I know, is a sanctuary of sorts. A safe place, I pray. A place where my directees hang with and hear from their God. I work to keep the environment tranquil, and for me, that's definite work. I stash my piles in the console cabinet that conceals a cluttered desk when its doors are closed. Tess found it for me. She's familiar with my piles.

Tess also found a couple of overstuffed chairs and a small matching sofa for the room. She put a fountain on a side table to help mute the street noise outside my door. The fountain looks like a pile of rocks and reminds me of the altars the Israelites built in the wilderness reminding them of places where God met their needs.

Tess may not get what I do or why I do it, but she supports me anyway. Before I added spiritual directing to my counseling practice, Tess and I talked about it a lot. Okay, *I* talked a lot and she listened a lot. The change didn't make sense to her. She didn't and doesn't understand my relationship with God or why others would seek a companion for their spiritual journey. But, bottom line, she respects my desires and supported the change.

That's one of the awesome things I thank God for.

The last block of my morning walk is the time I make a mental shift and think about the schedule of the day and the clients or directees I'll see. Before they each arrive for their appointments, I pray for them.

I unzip the jacket I wore over my standard work shirt—oxford style. Today's selection is charcoal, the color of my eyes according to Tess. I hook the jacket over the coat rack by the door and then cross the room and open the console, revealing my desk.

I pull a chair up to the desk, reach for my Bible, read a passage, and pray through it for Blake before he arrives.

By afternoon, I've already seen the Spirit move in miraculous ways. Sure, the Spirit's work is often subtle, sometimes slow, at least in my impatient opinion, and often unrecognizable. But then you'll have a day when, in His perfect timing, all those slow, subtle workings add up to one big bang. Kaboom, baby! All of a sudden, sitting before you, is a miracle.

It happened with Blake this morning when he recognized, after a gut-wrenching, lifelong search for love, what he longs for most is available. Today, he took the step of faith into the arms of Jesus.

Man! There are no words for the honor of observing, participating even, in a moment like that. It's stayed with me all day and heightened my earlier sense of Holy anticipation as I've prayed for Jenna Bouvier.

I hear a tap on my office door and then the door cracks open and Jenna pokes her head in.

"Hey, c'mon in." I have a sign hanging outside the door that says *Available* on one side and *Unavailable* on the other side. It lets people know they're welcome to come in when I'm available and to wait otherwise. But the first time around, clients and directees are sometimes hesitant. "Any trouble finding the place?"

She steps inside the office and the space feels like it shrinks. "No, no problem." She reaches out her hand.

"Good." I take her hand and shake it. "Have a seat." I motion to the overstuffed chairs separated by a small cube that acts as a coffee table. On the cube is an unlit candle. I wait to see which chair she'll choose as her own and then I take the one across from her. I reach into the pocket of my shirt for the book of matches I keep there. I strike a match and light the candle. "The flame represents God. I find it's a powerful visual reminder of His presence."

She nods as she watches the flame flicker.

"We're not alone here."

She looks at me and, man, the intensity in her eyes slams into me. I struggle to maintain eye contact with her. What's the deal? I hand the issue to God so I can remain present to Jenna.

I clear my throat. "Typically, I'll begin our sessions with a time of silence. It's a time for prayer, reflection, listening, or what I call soul settling. You may take as much time as you need. You tell me when you're ready to begin. Got it?"

She nods and her lopsided features do their balancing act as she smiles.

"Okay. We went through our beliefs, traditions, and the practice of spiritual direction when we met. Do you have any other questions that have come up?"

"I don't think so. I've looked forward to the time."

"Me too." I lean forward. "So, let's get started." I watch as she bows her head and closes her eyes. Her features relax and a visible peace settles over her.

I want to watch her. Hard to explain. It isn't her—it's something more. But out of respect for her, I bow my head and close my eyes too. I spend the time of silence surrendering the session to God.

After a few minutes, she says, "I'm ready."

I open my eyes, lift my head, and signal for her to take the lead.

"Oh, okay." She looks at the floor for a few seconds then looks back at me. "Do you think, I mean, I'm wondering if… Does God manifest Himself to us in physical ways?"

"Give me an example." I scoot back in my chair and relax.

"Sometimes, when I'm praying, or just"—she looks at the floor again—"just being with God." When she looks back at me her eyebrows are raised—the perfect question mark on her words.

I nod my understanding.

"Sometimes, I sense His presence in a physical way. A breeze, for example. I feel it."

I see color rise to her cheeks and her gaze, so intense before, is now uncertain—shifting. She is testing the waters. Will I tell her she's crazy or affirm her? So begins the dance. Can I be trusted? She needs to know.

"Think of the last time you felt that presence. Describe what it felt like." I lean forward again.

"It felt like"—she closes her eyes—"a cool sea breeze—refreshing, rejuvenating. It felt like a caress." She opens her eyes and looks at me. "Like…a kiss." She whispers.

"And what did you feel?"

"I felt total peace. And love. Complete love."

"Can you hang with that feeling?

"Hang with it?"

"You know, rest in it. Stay with that feeling for a few minutes."

"I can try."

"Good. Bask in it if you can."

We sit silent for a few minutes. Jenna stares at the flame flickering between us and I see its reflection in her eyes. But more than that, I see Him reflected in her. I break the silence. "How does that feeling of complete love compare to other experiences you've had with God?"

She thinks for a minute. "Yes."

"Yes?"

She smiles. "Yes, God manifests Himself to us in physical ways. Sometimes, anyway. My experiences with God, when I'm focused on Him rather than myself, are marked by that sense of a deep and abiding love. Complete love."

I don't say anything. I let her sit with her realization for a minute. And I sit with mine: My journey with Jenna, I know, is as much for my benefit as it is for hers. Though I don't know why yet. It happens sometimes with a directee—although I try to set myself aside and focus on them—the Spirit nudges me in the midst of a session and says, *Pay attention, buddy, I have something for you, too, in this relationship.*

"So...do you experience God like that? Have you felt His presence that way?"

"A tangible experience?"

She nods.

I shake my head. "Nah..." I recognize the wistfulness behind my answer. How cool would it be to see and feel God like that? "But that doesn't make your experience any less real."

"But why...?"

"But why...what?" A blush creeps up her neck to her cheeks again.

"Why do I"—she looks down, uncertain again—"experience Him that way?"

"Because that's how He's chosen to reveal Himself to you. Cool, huh?"

"Yes." She leans back in her chair and her shoulders slump a little. "I just wish I could rest in His love all the time. Keep that confidence, you know?"

"What blows it for you?"

"Circumstances, I think."

"Would you like to explain or share an example?"

She shifts in her seat and then shrugs. Her face becomes blank —unreadable. I won't press her. She'll share more when she's ready.

"Circumstances shouldn't matter. I should be content in all things—like Paul. Thriving in less than ideal conditions."

I hold back. This is the hardest part of spiritual direction for me. Paying attention to the rhythms, allowing silence when I sense the need for it. Not talking when I very much want to talk. But I wait.

"Like the park."

When she doesn't explain, I dig a little. "The park?"

"Golden Gate. Critics said nothing could thrive there. The conditions wouldn't support growth. The battering wind, the sand dunes, rock outcroppings. But they were wrong."

"So despite your circumstances or living conditions, you're determined to thrive."

"I didn't mention my living conditions."

"No, you didn't." But those words were not my own either.

"I'm just saying that the Bible tells us to be content in all circumstances, to give thanks for all things, and that God will cause all things to work together for good for those that love Him and are called according to His purpose. Right? So despite circumstances, or conditions, people, like the park, can be content and thrive when they're in relationship with God."

"You find encouragement in the metaphor of the park then?"

I see her shoulders relax again. "Yes."

"What is God saying to you through the metaphor?"

"Just what I said. Be content in all circumstances, or as you said, conditions."

"Did all the vegetation planted in the park thrive?" I try to avoid leading questions, but this one is out of my mouth before I can catch it.

Her chin juts forward and her answer is quick. "Only the vegetation with the strength to endure."

She's given the metaphor a lot of thought. I go back to her stated desire, "So, you want to rest in God's love. Is our conversation shedding light on how that might occur?"

"I need to persevere, I think." Then she sighs. "But..."

I wait and say nothing. But what comes to mind is a recent

post from Lightseeker about her reliance on her own strength. I see that same reliance in Jenna. Or, I think I do. That's not a judgment, just an observation. Believe me, I get it.

"...that isn't working. I'm"—her eyes fill with tears—"so weary. So tired." She wipes her eyes with the back of her hand. "Tired of trying so hard and not succeeding."

I reach for the box of tissues I keep nearby and hand it to her and she wipes her eyes again.

"I just want, more than anything, I want to please God. I want to do what He wants me to do. To handle things the way He'd have me handle them."

I lean forward again. "Jenna, what happens when you dump your weariness on God? When you turn to Him and say, 'I just can't do it anymore?'"

She hesitates. "I...I don't do that." She shakes her head.

"I don't turn to God during those times. Because I think I *should* be able to handle whatever is going on."

Energy courses through me and it takes every ounce of self-control to stay in my seat. I want to stand up and high-five her and say, "Yeah, baby! Now we're getting somewhere!" I can feel and see the Spirit working. Instead, oh man and it's hard, I just nod. I give her time to process the awareness. "How would it feel to turn to God when you've hit that wall—when you're in that place of weariness?"

She is silent and stares, again, at the flame of the candle. I watch as tears fill her eyes and fall down her cheeks. She covers her face with her hands and cries. Her sobs fill the space between us.

"I'm sorry." She says after several moments. She reaches for more tissue and wipes her eyes and blows her nose.

"There's no need to apologize. This is a place to be real. To feel. To express. To just be. A place to let the Spirit move you, even if He moves you to tears."

She looks at me and the pain I read in her eyes cuts me to the core. She is dealing with more than she is saying. "Can you tell me what you're feeling?"

"Relief...and guilt. Of course God wants to carry my burdens —wants me to rely on His strength rather than my own. I just...I forget. I think I have to be strong. To endure. To persevere. But... it's Him through me that will strengthen me. I feel bad, guilty, for not seeing that sooner. I regret withholding a part of myself from God. I've known I rely on myself too much. But I didn't see it as withholding myself from Him. But now, I see it and I'm sorry."

"Guilt is condemning, Jenna. There is no condemnation in Christ."

She looks at me and those crystal blue eyes sparkle. "Right. That's right. Oh, Matthew, isn't God amazing?"

This time, I do lean forward and put my hand in the air. She responds by slapping me five and giving me one of those dazzler smiles of hers.

WHEN I WALK her to the office door after the session ends, she turns before leaving and places her hand on my arm.

"Thank you, Matthew. This time was a gift."

"I'm glad."

She turns and walks out the door. When she reaches the curb in front of the office, I call out to her. "Hey, dude..." She turns and looks back at me, and the wind catches her long dark hair and it swirls around her face. "See ya next time."

She laughs, reaches up and catches her hair, and pulls it back from her face. She waves and then turns back to hail a cab.

I watch her get into the cab. I stand in the doorway for a long time after she's gone.

Today was a game changer for me.

Hard to explain.

I know, I say that a lot. But when you're dealing with God,

man, there's just so much that's beyond explanation. I feel it in my gut though—today was significant for reasons I don't yet get. I turn, step back into my office, and close the door. I know I have some unfinished business. With God. We need to talk through the issue I handed Him just after Jenna arrived.

The issue being my reaction. To her? I'm not sure. But something in me stirred when she came in the door. I need to know what it was.

For her sake.

And my own.

CHAPTER EIGHTEEN

You see, most people would rather suffer anything than allow themselves to be dethroned in the kingdom of their own heart.
JEANNE GUYON

rigitte

"MUST I attach a tracking device to you? I've called several times. It would be helpful if you'd answer."

After leaving the message, she slams the phone down then taps her acrylic nails on the desktop. She picks up the phone again and presses the intercom to the kitchen. "Hannah, please come see me upstairs."

A few minutes later, there's a knock on her office door.

"Come in."

Hannah enters and stands in front of the desk. "Madame?"

"Where is Jenna?"

"I don't know. She said she had an appointment and left a

couple of hours ago. She took a cab. She didn't say when she would return."

"She isn't answering her phone."

"I'll let you know when she comes back."

"Have you taken care of the task I assigned you last week? Jenna's computer?"

"Not yet. She took the laptop with her to the valley over the weekend. I checked it this afternoon, but everything is protected with a password."

"Figure it out. Soon. *Chose promise, chose due.*"

"Madame?"

"Nothing!" As though a servant would understand the importance of keeping one's promises. She looks back at her desk and begins shuffling through a file folder.

"Is that all?"

"Yes, Hannah. Go."

When the office door closes again, Brigitte closes the file folder and drops it back on her desk. Where *is* she? She gets up from her desk, crosses the room, opens the door, and steps into the hallway where she listens before walking down the hall and crossing to Gerard and Jenna's suite. She opens the door and heads for Jenna's laptop sitting on the desk in the alcove. She lifts the lid and the screen lights up. A small box appears on the screen requesting a password.

She slaps the lid closed and riffles through a small stack of papers beside the laptop. Nothing significant. She opens Jenna's calendar and scans the date. There's a note jotted in Jenna's handwriting that says "M—3:00."

M? What or who is she hiding?

"Mother?"

She turns. "Gerard, what are you doing here?" She glances at her watch.

"I guess I could ask you the same thing. Looking for something?"

"I'm concerned about Jenna. No one seems to know where she is. She left without telling anyone where she was going." She takes a few steps away from the desk toward Gerard. "Do you know where she is?"

He hesitates. "She mentioned having an appointment this afternoon. She is an adult, mother."

Her eyes narrow. "It's common courtesy to alert others to your plans. You didn't answer my question. What are you doing here?"

"My afternoon meeting ended early. I decided to come home rather than go back to the offices." He walks past her and heads toward the dressing area.

"Gerard…"

He stops and turns back toward her.

"You'd better keep track of your wife."

"What are you implying?"

"Il n'est pire aveugle que celui qui ne veut pas voir." There are none so blind as those who will not see.

Gerard shakes his head. "I am not blind, Mother. Jenna isn't hiding anything."

She shrugs and walks out.

Gerard starts to follow her and then stops. He seems to think better of it. But then, shaking his head, he crosses the room and heads down the hallway. "Mother, I asked you a question."

She stops at the door to her room, her hand on the door handle, and looks back at him. "I don't care for your tone, Gerard."

He takes a deep breath, "You don't need to concern yourself with Jenna."

She drops her hand from the handle of the door and takes a few steps toward him. "It isn't your place to tell me what or with whom I concern myself."

"She is my wife."

"Oui. And if you want to keep it that way, I suggest you keep an eye on her." She heads back to her room, opens the door, and then shuts it behind her—dismissing him. She leans against the closed door and lets out a sigh.

It seems her weekend getaway for Gerard and Jenna didn't have the hoped for effect. Whatever is stirring this new defiance in Jenna is now rubbing off on Gerard. Well, she won't stand for it. She turns around and opens the door to her room again and leans out, catching Gerard just before he walks back into his own suite. "Gerard, I'd like to speak to you in the solarium. We'll have a drink there before dinner. Meet me downstairs in fifteen minutes."

"Mother—"

She closes her door before he can protest.

CHAPTER NINETEEN

The Lord is always near you as you seek His will simply and sincerely.
He will support you and comfort you in times of trouble.
JEANNE GUYON

enna

AFTER MY APPOINTMENT WITH MATTHEW, I want time to process, time to think and pray through our conversation and the emotions it evoked. I ask the cab driver to take me to the park and drop me off near the main gate of the botanical gardens.

I look at my watch and my stomach twists into a knot. For the first time in eleven years of living under Brigitte's roof, I told no one where I was going or when I'd return. Fear now strangles the sense of freedom I felt when I left. But I take a deep breath, exit the cab, and let the fall sun warm my shoulders as I stand on the sidewalk in front of the entrance to the gardens.

All around me, swaying in the breeze, are the giants of the

park—the eucalyptus, Monterey cypress, and Canary Island pine trees, among others. These, as I recall from my science studies at Cal Poly, are known as overstory trees—those that tower above the other vegetation. It's these giants in the park that buffet the understory crops from the winds of the coastal region.

I head into the Botanical Garden, show my driver's license as proof of San Francisco residency to the volunteer at the admissions booth, and enter the gardens free of charge. I wander the paths nearest the main entrance, through the Garden of Fragrance and then around one edge of the Great Meadow. The scents of fresh-cut grass, soil, fertilizer, and the perfume of fall blossoms embrace me. As I wander, I think through what I said to Matthew about the park—about the metaphor it represents to me—thriving against all odds. There are even plants here, I know, that thrive though they are now extinct in their indigenous environments.

I think of Brigitte and how I feel on the verge of extinction when I'm with her.

Though I've found comfort in the metaphor of the park, today, as I explained it to Matthew, I felt...what? I think back to my desire to make him understand. My need to make him understand.

Defensive. That's what I felt.

But why?

Matthew's question comes back to me now. *Did all the vegetation planted in the park thrive?* And my answer... *Only the vegetation with the strength to endure.* My answer had nothing to do with the park and everything to do with me. I am determined to endure. To persevere. To thrive against all odds.

But instead, I'm weary. Exhausted. Nearing extinction.

I stop and look out across the meadow and a new thought, a gentle breeze, stirs in my mind.

You're not thriving, Jenna.

My immediate response to the thought is an apology to God. *Oh Lord, I'm so sorry. I'll try harder.* But even as I pray the words in the silence of my soul, I know I can't try any harder. I have nothing left to give.

The meadow before me blurs into a smear of green and I wipe the tears from my eyes.

The new thought stirs again. *You're not thriving.* But this time I realize the thought isn't an accusation, nor does it require an apology. It is simply truth—a truth I've avoided.

A truth I have no idea what to do with.

Stand back...

Stand back? The familiar thought irritates. Stand back from what? If I knew, I'd do it. Why didn't I talk that through with Matthew today? Now it will have to wait until our next appointment.

I think again of the park. What about the metaphor I've leaned on for so long? How do I differ from the park? I turn and head for the garden bookstore, which has a wide selection of horticulture-related books. But as I enter the store, the knot in my stomach tightens. I glance at my watch again—5:05 p.m.

I make my way to one of the shelves, glance at a couple of books, and then decide on one about the trees of the park and another on the history of the park. I head for the cashier, pay, and then dash out of the bookstore and then the park, and back to the waiting cab.

When I slip in the front door of the house, I hear voices echoing across the marble floor. They're coming from the solarium. Brigitte and Gerard. I bend and take off my shoes, as has become my habit when trying to sneak in unnoticed. I creep across the entry and up the stairs, holding the bag of books close so it doesn't rustle.

Is it possible my absence has gone unnoticed? No. I know better. But at least they won't know how long I was gone.

I tiptoe into the bedroom, set the books on my desk, sit in the desk chair, and bend to put my shoes back on. I sit back up, exhale, and lean back in the chair. I rub my jaw, attempting to alleviate the ache there.

Maybe I'm not thriving because of the infection. Maybe that's all it is.

No. It's more than that. The antibiotics have done their job. And I've floundered for much too long—much longer than the infection attacking my body.

I reach for the bag on my desk and pull the two books out.

I crumple the bag and put it in the wastebasket beneath my desk. As I do, the voices in the solarium escalate. I still and listen. Even through the closed bedroom door, I hear Gerard yelling.

At Brigitte?

He would never...

I stand, walk to the bedroom door, and crack it open, but all is quiet. Was it my imagination? I stand there a little longer but hear nothing more.

I sit back down at my desk and pick up one of the books I purchased and begin thumbing through it. I land on a section dealing with species selection:

> The selection of tree species for the replacement of the park's evergreen forest canopy and windbreak has changed over the years. The spread of the fungal disease pine pitch canker (*Fusarium subglutinans*) into the Bay Area and southern part of San Francisco has resulted in a suspension—

The double doors to the bedroom fling open and slam against the wall. "Come! Hurry! It's Mr. Bouvier."

Startled by Hannah's abrupt entrance and the fear in her voice and on her face, I drop the book, jump to my feet, heart pounding, and head for the door. "What? Hannah, what is it?" As I reach the door, I hear Brigitte yelling downstairs.

"Hannah! Did you call? Did you call an ambulance?"

"Yes, Madame!" Hannah yells back down the stairs. She grabs my arm and pulls me behind her as she heads to the stairs.

"Hannah? What's happened?" Breathless, suffocated by fear, the words come out in a hoarse whisper and I'm not sure Hannah's even heard me.

Again from downstairs, I hear Brigitte. This time she wails. "Non! Gerard! Non! *S'il te plait!* Gerard, please!"

We take the stairs two at a time. At the landing, I push past Hannah and fly down the remaining stairs and through the hallway to the solarium where I see Gerard slumped over on one of the settees. A wine glass lies broken at his feet and a splash of red wine stains his white shirt. Brigitte stands bent over him, her hands on either side of his face.

"Gerard! *Gerard!*"

"What happened?"

She doesn't respond.

"Brigitte?!" I sit on the settee next to Gerard and reach for his wrist. I lift his arm and try to feel for his pulse. Brigitte has quieted, stepped back, and I feel her eyes on me. Watching. Waiting.

"Well?"

"I...I don't"—I move my fingers on his wrist. Searching. Hoping—"I can't...feel—"

I press my ear to his chest, hoping, praying. Nothing. Nor does he seem to be breathing. *Oh, Lord...* "What happened?"

"This! This is your fault!" Brigitte spits the words at me. "It's all your fault! If you hadn't planted thoughts in his mind, pushed him, told him he could do more. If you—"

"Stop! Help me!" I stand and move the coffee table out of the way. "We need to lay him down on the floor." I reach for Gerard's legs and lift them. Brigitte doesn't move. "Help me! Hannah, help us! Hannah!"

She is standing at the front door watching for the ambulance, but I hear her coming back down the hallway. The hollow echo of her steps brings a sense of foreboding.

When she gets there, she takes Gerard's shoulders, but he is too heavy for us.

She looks to Brigitte. "Madame, you must help!"

Brigitte, dazed, steps to Gerard's side and helps us lower him from the settee to the floor. Once he's on the floor, I kneel next to him, remove his tie, and begin to loosen the collar of his shirt. My fingers shake as I undo the buttons down the front of his shirt. I hear Brigitte tell Hannah to direct the ambulance to the back entrance, where they won't have to deal with the front steps. Then she kneels at Gerard's head.

"Hannah, get someone else to watch for the ambulance. I need you!" I shout. I look at Brigitte, but she doesn't argue.

I pull Gerard's shirt back, though the weight of him makes it difficult. "CPR. We need to begin CPR." I place my hand on his chest, hoping, praying, that this time I'll feel his heart beating. But again, nothing. *Oh God, oh Lord, help . . . help him! Help me!*

I think of Gerard's father. *Oh Lord...*

"*Do* something!" Brigitte sounds both demanding and desperate.

I try to remember the steps of CPR—the training I've had, along with the rest of the household staff, at Brigitte's insistence, each year since our marriage. But stress robs me of clarity. I lean back on my heels and take a deep breath. Think! Then I lean down, open Gerard's mouth, and make sure the airway is clear. I pinch his nose and cover his mouth with my own. His lips are gray and cool and a flash of memory catches me—the warmth of his lips as he kissed me in the valley just days ago.

No, wait! This isn't right! The CPR guidelines changed. Compressions first. *Oh Lord, help us!* I move to Gerard's chest, my hands still trembling, and place the heel of my palm on the pressure point about an inch and a half above his sternum. I begin the quick pumping—100 compressions a minute. "One, two, three, four…"

Oh, God. What is happening. This can't be happening. Help us!

I glance at Brigitte, who still kneels at Gerard's head. She stares straight ahead, no longer seeming connected to what's taking place. Perhaps she, too, is remembering Gerard's father.

I reach for Gerard's nose again, pinch it shut, give two quick breaths, and begin the process all over again. I shout for Hannah again and this time, she comes back into the solarium and kneels next to Gerard's side. "I need you to check his femoral pulse as I do the compressions."

I begin pumping his chest again. "Can you feel it? Am I doing it right?"

Hannah nods. "Keep going."

I pump and breathe and pump and breathe.

Over and over again.

"Ma'am." I feel someone next to me. "Ma'am, please, we'll take over."

"Jenna, move!" Brigitte is now standing back from Gerard.

I lean back on my heels again, and push myself up off the floor.

I step back from Gerard. From this vantage point, I can really see him. And what I see seems surreal. He is ashen and still.

Lifeless.

How can this be happening?

I stand near Brigitte, though not too near. I feel her rage seething.

"If you weren't so selfish, this never would have happened." She hisses, *"C'est ta faute!"*

I look at her, guilt slicing my conscience. Is she right? Am I in some way responsible? But how? Tears choke me.

Please save him. Please. But with each minute that passes, hope wanes.

I feel the change in Brigitte before I see it. I turn to look at her, but her expression is unreadable. She wears a mask of control. "He is gone." And then she turns and walks away.

Gone? How...? I continue to watch the paramedics work, but it's as though I'm someone else. Somewhere else. Nothing makes sense.

Gone?

And then I see the knowing look that passes between the paramedics, though they continue to work on him as they load him into the ambulance.

Gerard is gone.

Forever.

CHAPTER TWENTY

I want you to know that I sympathize deeply with your trials. I present
you before the Lord with all my heart.
JEANNE GUYON

$\mathcal{M}$atthew

WHEN I WALK through the living room on Friday morning, I
notice Tess has already printed the blog post and placed it on my
tray along with the morning paper. Cool. She's still reading it. I
make my way to the kitchen, pour my cup o' Joe, open the fridge,
and pull out the toffee-nut creamer. Don't say it. I know.

I head back to the living room and plop myself in the recliner,
where I sit for a long time drinking my coffee and thinking about
my meeting with Jenna yesterday afternoon. This morning, I'll
call Tim and schedule an appointment to see him. Tim is my spiritual direction mentor and supervisor. It's important as a director
to have a supervisor, someone to process with, someone who is

invested in my walk with God and holding me accountable for the work I do with directees.

After my reactions to Jenna yesterday, I need to place myself under Tim's authority and talk through what I'm feeling. Or not feeling. I'm not sure. I just know something's up and I need to pay attention.

I pick up my Bible and turn to the Psalms and pray David's words:

> Search me, O God, and know my heart; test me and know my anxious thoughts. See if there is any offensive way in me, and lead me in the way everlasting.

I pray these words a lot and then practice letting go and allowing the Spirit to elbow me rather than obsessing over my own conscience, a habit I learned kept me nose to nose with myself when I'd much rather be nose to nose with God.

When I set my Bible aside and reach for the blog post, something catches my attention on the front lower section of the *Chronicle* and I pick up the paper instead. As I read, a pit forms in my stomach.

> Gerard Bouvier, vice president and sole heir of the family-owned Domaine de la Bouvier, was pronounced dead on arrival at the UCSF Medical Center last night. It is believed Bouvier suffered a massive heart attack at his home yesterday evening. Bouvier was 54 years old and is survived by his wife, Jenna Durand Bouvier, and his mother, Brigitte Bouvier.

The obituary continues, listing Gerard Bouvier's accomplishments, civic involvements, etc. I skim the rest of the article and then read the opening paragraph again—my eyes rest on the name, *Jenna Durand Bouvier*.

"Oh, Father God…" But then I realize I have no words to pray.

Nothing.

I bow my head in silence, knowing the Spirit will pray the words I can't. I don't know how long I sit, but after awhile, I lift my head, wipe my eyes, and go to my desk where my cell phone was plugged in overnight. I reach for the phone, scroll through the contacts, and find the cell phone number Jenna gave me yesterday.

I dial the number, and hear her voice: *"This is Jenna Bouvier, please leave a message and I'll return your call."* I clear my throat before the beep and then leave my message.

"Hey, Jenna, it's Matthew MacGregor. Uh, I know we don't know each other well, but I saw the paper this morning and"—I run my hand over the stubble on my chin—"I just want you to know that I'm here if you need anything. If you need to, you know, talk, or pray, or..." I sigh, "Or if you just need a place to be for awhile, call me. Leave a message at my office, or call my cell. I'll fit you into my schedule."

I leave her the cell phone number and then say, "I'm praying for His strength through you, His comfort for you." I hesitate, not wanting to hang up, but realize there's nothing left to say.

I walk back to the living room and sit in the recliner. I set my phone on the tray and pick up the paper again. Just as I do, the phone rings. I pick it up and see Jenna's name on the screen.

"Hey, Jenna?"

"Matthew..."

Her voice is almost inaudible.

She speaks up a little. "Thank you for your call. I didn't know...I mean, it's crazy, but...I wanted to talk to you. I don't talk about, I mean...there aren't many people who understand...my relationship with God. And I need to understand. I could talk to Skye, but—"

"She's hard to reach."

"Yes."

"Would you like to meet?"

"Yes." The word is barely a whisper. "Yes, please."

"Name the time."

"I...uhm...I don't know. There's so much..."

I wait.

"Maybe this afternoon. Late afternoon?"

"Four o'clock? My office?"

"Okay. If I can't get away—"

"Just call me. No problem."

"Thank you, Matthew."

"I'm praying for you."

"Thank you. I'll see you later."

I hang up the phone. What must it feel like to lose your spouse? I think of Tess and punch in her number.

"This is Tess." Her tone is all business and I know she didn't look at the screen of her phone before she answered.

"Hey, babe."

Her tone softens. "Matthew, hey, what's up?"

"Nothing. Just wanted to tell you that I love you."

"Oh, honey, I love you too." There's a smile in her voice. "Hey, are you okay?"

"Yeah, I'm okay. Just thinking about you. Oh, hey, I have a client appointment at four this afternoon, so I may be later than usual."

"Okay. It's just leftovers tonight anyway."

"Why don't I call you after my appointment and we can meet for dinner. I'd love to take my beautiful wife out."

"Really? Okay, that sounds great. I'll stay at the office until I hear from you and then swing by and pick you up."

"Cool. See ya, babe."

I hang up the phone and give God thanks for my wife and pray a prayer of protection over her. Then, I pray again for Jenna Bouvier. I reach for the post Tess printed and I read:

Remain in Me . . . These words knock on my conscious

moment by moment. As my health wanes, I hear *Remain in Me*. As I struggle, I hear *Remain in Me*. As I fight against my circumstances, as I wonder how to please those impossible to please, the words again swell in my soul: *Remain in Me*.

"I am the vine; you are the branches. If you remain in me and I in you, you will bear much fruit."

But other words also swirl and with them come a ripple of fear: Every branch that does not bear fruit He prunes. . . .

A season of pruning encroaches, I know. How much will He prune? What will He cut away? How much can I bear?

Remain in Me . . .

Is Jenna familiar with www.illuminar.me? She'd relate to Lightseeker, I think. They share the same transparency and intensity of focus. I pray Jenna will remain in God during what I imagine will be dark days ahead.

I read through Lightseeker's post again. I feel her fear. But there is no fear in perfect love—nothing to fear from the hand of an all-loving God. But we must each learn that for ourselves. I say a prayer for Lightseeker and another for Jenna.

Then I pick up the phone and call Tim.

HER EYES ARE SWOLLEN and red, her complexion pale. Where there was emotion in her voice when we talked on the phone this morning, now, sitting across from me, she seems numb.

I light the candle and we sit in silence. She is silent for so long that I wonder if maybe she's fallen asleep. I raise my head from its bowed position and sneak a peek at her. Her head is bowed and I can't tell whether she's awake or asleep. If she's asleep, it's what she needs. I bow my head again and continue my dialogue with God on Jenna's behalf.

"I'm ready…"

I look up and see her wheels spinning.

She searches my face, then looks around the room. "I don't understand. I just can't…believe…I don't…I don't know what to do. Or why this happened." She looks at me. "Why did this happen?"

"I don't know, Jenna. But I can tell you this—death was never part of God's original plan. That's why, I think, it's so jarring and painful. We know He's conquered death for all time, but in the here and now, that doesn't lessen the sting."

"But He could have prevented it."

I nod.

"It's started…" She looks past me and her eyes fill with tears.

"What's started?"

"The pruning."

"Pruning?"

She nods.

I want to ask her if she reads Lightseeker's blog. But I hold back and listen, first for the Spirit and then to Jenna as she speaks again.

"In the vineyards, the canes, or branches, are pruned from the vine. Usually, the pruning is done in the winter months. The timing depends on the variety of grapes."

She looks at me to see if I'm tracking with her.

I nod my encouragement to continue.

"We spent last weekend in the valley and while I was walking in the vineyard, I felt like God told me a season of pruning was ahead. He told me to—"

"—remain in Him." I interrupt. I can't help it.

She looks at me and I see her swallow. Her facial expression is now wary, cautious.

"I'm sorry, Jenna. I didn't meant to interrupt you. I was just, you know, thinking of the passage from the book of John."

"Right. That's what I read last Saturday while I was in the vineyard."

Maybe it's just a coincidence. But my heart feels like it's beating overtime. I take a slow, deep breath. "So you think that your husband's death is…" I admit it, I'm baffled. But she finishes my thought.

"Is God's pruning."

I read confusion in her eyes. "Tell me the purpose of pruning—in a vineyard."

She hesitates. "In laymen's terms, it promotes a healthy yield of fruit."

"Just like in the passage from John." I reach for my Bible and open it to John 15. "'…so every branch that does bear fruit he prunes so that it will be even more fruitful.' How does your husband's death fit into the pruning metaphor?"

Her eyes fill with tears again. "I don't know."

"I read a blog called www.iluminar.me." I watch for a reaction, but she reveals nothing. "The entry I read this morning was based on this passage. The author felt fear at the thought of what God might prune from her life." Her eyes are wide. She doesn't speak or nod, but she is hanging on my every word. "After I read it, what came to me is that perfect love drives out fear." I flip the pages in my Bible and turn to 1 John 4:18: "'There is no fear in love. But perfect love drives out fear, because fear has to do with punishment. The one who fears is not made perfect in love.'"

Her mouth forms the word *oh*, but no sound comes out.

"The pruning you're talking about sounds punishing to me. Maybe I'm misunderstanding…"

"No…that's"—she takes a deep breath—"that's what I felt. I just hadn't . . . identified it. But…if Gerard's death isn't a pruning of sorts, if it isn't God cutting away something from me, then why?"

She stands up and begins pacing. "I need to know why. I need to understand."

"Some things are beyond our understanding."

She shakes her head. "No, I *have* to understand."

I hesitate. I don't like sounding like the Bible Answer Man, but... "'Trust in the Lord with all your heart and lean not on your own understanding...' Sometimes, we're just called to trust rather than understand."

I can't read her face as she stands over me, but I watch as her shoulders seem to relax. Then she drops back into her chair and breathes what sounds like a sigh of relief.

"Just trust? I don't have to...figure it out? I don't have to understand?" She leans back in her chair, arms hanging over the sides. "You mean I don't have to work so hard?" She almost cracks a smile.

"No. You don't have to figure it all out. You can trust Him. Cool, right? You can trust His love, His goodness, His sovereignty."

She is thoughtful for a few minutes. "But if I can't figure it out, if I don't understand whatever it is, then I can't fix it."

"Ah, that's the crux of it, huh?"

She nods. "And I certainly can't fix what happened"—tears fill her eyes and spill onto her cheeks—"last night."

I reach for the box of tissues and hand it to her.

"Jenna, I'm so, so sorry."

"I don't know"—she gulps back a sob—"what I'm going to do."

I lean forward, *Oh Lord, give me Your words for Jenna.* "Did you and your husband ever dance together?"

She sniffles, wipes her nose, and nods. "Not often, but occasionally at a social function, a charity ball, or at a wedding. Gerard was a wonderful dancer."

"Could you relax in his arms and let him lead? Just follow his steps?"

She ponders this, then she nods again. "Yes…but I had to learn to let him lead. Once I did, dancing with him became a joy."

"Yeah, I bet." I give her a minute to sit with that image. "Jenna, God's asking you to dance." I reach out my hand like I'm going to lead her onto the dance floor. She reaches across the space between us and takes my hand. "He's asking you to relax in His embrace and allow Him to lead."

Her eyes are locked on mine and my heart thunders in my chest. "Just follow Him, step by step."

Her mouth forms the word *oh* again and her eyes are wet with tears.

"It's that simple?"

I give her hand a gentle squeeze and then let it go. "It's that simple. But that doesn't mean it's easy."

After Jenna leaves, I sit in my chair for a long time and stare at the flame still flickering in front of me. Jenna Bouvier is Lightseeker. I don't have proof of that, but I know. And Lightseeker is my spiritual counterpart, or at least, that's how I've thought of her. No wonder I've reacted to Jenna the way I have. But Lightseeker was safe. Anonymous. Untouchable. Jenna on the other hand…

I stare at the flame until it burns out. I process my feelings. I surrender my heart to God. And I pray. I pray until my prayers are interrupted by the vibrating phone in my back pocket. I lift my head, reach for the phone, and glance at the screen.

Tess.

Oh, man, I forgot the time.

Forgot about dinner.

I forgot about her.

CHAPTER TWENTY-ONE

No matter what insight or revelation you have, it is nothing compared to
your total need of God.
JEANNE GUYON

ndee

GERARD BOUVIER'S death was a city headline maker. It began with
an abbreviated obit in the *Chronicle* the morning after he dropped
dead. It hit the noontime news shows, and was the lead story on
the local evening news. A follow-up obituary hit the paper two
days after his death, and included a statement by "the family" that
the memorial service will be an invitation-only event.

That's one invitation I could do without.

I rarely miss the morning *Chronicle*, but the morning after
Gerard's death, I had a meeting and forfeited my espresso and
paper-reading time. Instead, I grabbed an espresso on the run and
decided the local news could wait.

Bad choice.

During my meeting, my cell phone rang over and over. Though it was silenced, the screen flashing with Jason's name annoyed.

I had two unheard messages from the night before and he'd called several times during the meeting. *What's the deal? Getting needy, lover boy?*

I picked up my phone from the conference table where I was meeting with yet another CEO and dropped it into my briefcase. No reason to let it distract me. At the end of the meeting, Mr. CEO went all philosophical on me droning on about how the death of a friend makes you reevaluate your priorities. Blah, blah, blah…

"You knew him too, didn't you?"

Okay, I admit, I tuned him out for a few minutes—I was focused on the business discussion we'd just had. That is my job, after all.

I sifted through the portions of the conversation I had heard and tried to figure out who he was talking about.

"Gerard Bouvier. Aren't you seeing his brother-in-law or something?"

I tried to make the connections. "Gerard? What about him?"

"Oh no, I'm sorry. You haven't heard?"

"Heard what?"

"He died last night. Massive heart attack."

"What? Are you kidding me?" I'm sure my mouth was hanging open like some gasping fish. I reached back into my briefcase, grabbed for my phone, and scrolled through my missed calls again. I had five messages from Jason since the night before. And I'd been playing hard to get.

Okay, sometimes, I'm a total idiot.

"Will you excuse me?" I didn't wait for his response. Instead, I gathered up my things while listening to Jason's voicemails.

"Andee…" He was quiet for a minute and then continued. *"Please call me. I need to talk to you."*

I'm such an idiot.

"Andee, please call me. Something's happened. I need to talk to you."

Then came the morning calls. *"It's me again. Andee, Gerard died last night. I...I want to talk to you."* His voice cracked on the last word.

Okay, a total and complete idiot!

I didn't listen to the other messages. I got the gist of it. I called him before I was even out of the building. I'd witnessed the friendship between Jason and Gerard the weekend we spent in Napa. Last weekend. Could it really be just a few days ago? And now...

The reality was, is, hard to grasp. Their friendship was hard for me to grasp too. Friends are a luxury I haven't made time for. Or something like that. But I knew Gerard's death would be hard for Jason in ways I couldn't understand.

But hearing the emotion in his voice rocked me in unexpected ways, and I wanted to be there for Jason. I wanted to try to understand. I tried not to overanalyze my feelings.

Feelings?

"Get a grip, Andee."

As I dress for Gerard's funeral—funeral, memorial, whatever—

I put thoughts of Jason aside and think through the practical aspects of the day. I don't like this kind of thing, but this service is the place to be seen today. Anyone who is anyone in this city was sure they wrangled an invitation. Not only was I invited to attend but I will be seated, at Brigitte's request, in the section reserved for family and close friends.

"You've come a long way, baby," I tell myself. "This will be one of the social events of the year," I say to Sam who's sprawled across the chair in my dressing area. It will be somber, of course. But nonetheless, it will be a media circus, despite Brigitte's invitation-only decree.

I respect her control. When you're visible, you need to protect yourself from the public, while also making sure you're visible to the public. It's a balancing act.

Brigitte.

I think again of her call to me the afternoon after Gerard passed. I laugh. "That woman is a piece of work." My respect for her has grown as we've worked together. She is a model for my philosophy: *Drive determines destiny.* She is single-minded and bent on her goals.

But something about her call bothered me.

I reach into the velvet-lined drawer in my closet where I keep my jewelry and remove a pair of pearl studs and a pearl bracelet. The perfect accessories for the designer black suit I'm wearing. I put the jewelry on and then stand in front of the mirror.

"Classic."

Sam mews his agreement.

What was it about her call that continues to agitate me? Brigitte is a businesswoman and there was business to attend to. That's all.

Just as I have all week, I put the thought aside.

WHEN I ARRIVE at the cathedral, I'm ushered to a seat in the row just behind the family. Brigitte, Jenna, Jason, Bill, and Max, the family attorney, sit together. Jason asked me to attend with him, but I declined, telling him he needed to be focused on supporting his sister. Plus, I wanted distance—the opportunity to observe rather than participate. I lean forward and place my hand on Jason's shoulder and whisper to him. "How are you holding up?"

He turns, puts his hand on mine, and mouths, "Okay."

I squeeze his shoulder and then sit back. I will acknowledge Brigitte and Jenna after the service. And Bill, of course.

I pick up my handbag, stand, and move to the end of the pew

so others don't need to step over me as they're seated. From here, I can see Jenna and Brigitte's profiles—it's a better seat.

Others are ushered to the pew including a tall, dark-haired man and his fashion-plate date. Oh, make that wife—I notice matching gold bands. His dark, mussed curls, his lopsided grin, and toothpaste ad perfect teeth are heart stoppers. His impeccable attire doesn't seem to match his persona though. The fashion plate dresses him, I'd bet. They sit just behind Jenna and Brigitte. The heart-stopper leans forward, places his hand on Jenna's shoulder, and whispers something in her ear. She turns in her seat, and hugs him across the top of the pew.

There is an intimacy between them that's unmistakable. Unless she's blind, the fashion plate sees it too. And so, I notice, does Brigitte. I see her glance and then turn and watch the embrace. She stares at the couple for a moment and then nods at them, but I don't get the sense that she knows them.

Who. Is. That? Inquiring minds want to know!

This event is becoming more interesting all the time.

Soon, another woman is ushered to our aisle. Her gauze skirt and denim jacket are so inappropriate. She looks like a flippin' flower child. The hunk and the fashion plate scoot down and make room for her. They seem to know her. She, too, leans forward and she kisses Jenna on the cheek. Again, Jenna turns and hugs the flower child. They embrace for a long time, the flower child whispering in Jenna's ear the entire time. When they part, I see the flower child checking out Brigitte.

Brigitte's disdain is palpable. Ha!

Jenna's friends. And definitely not friends chosen by Brigitte. Maybe Jenna isn't as passive as I thought.

I focus my attention, for now, on the family.

Jenna sits close to Jason, who has his arm around her shoulders. And Bill sits on the other side of Jason. He reaches over and whispers to Jenna and seems to reassure her.

Brigitte seems statue-like. An appropriate expression of

bereavement in place, but I notice her eyes shifting, looking, watching. Max is seated on Brigitte's left at the end of the pew. There's a comfortable distance between he and Brigitte. Jenna sits on Brigitte's right but there is enough space between Brigitte and Jenna for another person to be seated between them. They offer one another nothing—no warmth or comfort.

Brigitte, it occurs to me, is an island.

And for some reason, the thought agitates me.

I think again of Brigitte's call last week, just one day after Gerard's death. Yes, his death will impact Domaine de la Bouvier in some ways, but her business and financial concern seemed misplaced so soon after her son's death.

There's a disparity between who I thought Brigitte was and who that call revealed her to be.

This is the source of my agitation. Regarding Brigitte, the columns in my head aren't adding up and I don't want to work the numbers to find out why. But I have to. It's what I do.

I begin a mental tally. For each characteristic I've attributed to Brigitte, I negate it with another characteristic I've seen. I add. I subtract. I come up with a bottom line. The sum of who she is.

A sum that is far from appealing.

Perhaps it's the setting—a service to memorialize a man who was still in his prime when he dropped dead—that makes me introspective. But today I can't help comparing myself to Brigitte. In a Dickensian moment, I wonder if I'm being given a glimpse into my own future.

If so, I don't like what I see.

I glance at her again, surrounded by the wealthy, powerful, and beautiful. Yet, she is alone. There have been no hugs or words of assurance for Brigitte. And being alone, I sense, is what she fears most. That is why she called just after Gerard's death. To manipulate. To control. To ensure she'd never be all alone.

I am privy to the vast Bouvier financial holdings. Yet, money didn't prevent Gerard's death. Or his father's death.

The hand of control only reaches so far, Brigitte.

I think again of the way Brigitte models my philosophy. I consider the words: *Drive determines destiny.* I think back to my college English classes and, for the first time, it occurs to me that drive, in the context I use it, is a noun. Drive meaning ambition. But when drive is used as a transitive verb, it's attached to an object. And now I see the object of Brigitte's drive is fear.

The thought disgusts me.

I shift in my seat and put my chin to my chest to ease the tension in my neck and shoulders, then I lift my chin and do the stretch again.

This whole line of thinking is ridiculous.

This is why I like numbers. Absolutes. Plug in a variable, and you can still count on the outcome. But when you're dealing with emotions, the outcome is a crapshoot. Those aren't odds I deal in.

There are similarities between Brigitte and myself. But so what? I can learn from her mistakes. And adjust my own life, right?

I look at Jason again and remember the sense that I should hang on to him. Well, maybe I will. It doesn't have to be an emotional decision—it can be a practical decision. Okay, the fact that he's financially destitute and doesn't even know it poses a problem. Can I get over it?

Maybe. There's no doubt I have enough money for the both of us. There are, I imagine, benefits to having a kept man.

I settle in for the duration of the service satisfied that the time has proven productive.

CHAPTER TWENTY-TWO

Oh, Love! You are the pure, total, simple truth which is expressed not by me, but by You through me.

JEANNE GUYON

enna

A WEEK after Gerard's services, Brigitte still hasn't spoken to me beyond the absolute necessities, like the pleasantries spoken before and after the services when others were watching. Otherwise, she's communicated through Hannah and the other household staff. I am accustomed to following her lead, so I haven't made any attempts to initiate a conversation either. It's evident she still blames me for Gerard's death. But as time passes, questions nag.

Does Brigitte expect me to continue living with her?

How were things left in Gerard's trust?

Will I be provided for?

Does she know Gerard asked me, more than once, to care for her should anything happen to him?

Does honoring Gerard's wishes mean that I have to live with Brigitte?

These are the questions that plague me as I lie awake at night. During the day, I vacillate between denial, grief, and acceptance. There are both tears and moments without feeling.

But at night, my mind and my heart race.

Though I'm attempting to participate in the dance Matthew suggested and allow God to lead, so far He seems to be standing still.

So I wait.

EIGHT DAYS after the memorial service, Brigitte taps on the door of my suite.

"Come in," I call from the sofa near the window.

She comes in and stands in front of me. "I think it would be good for you to get away for a few days. To get out of the house. Take some time to regroup, oui? I've called Marcus. He and Estelle are expecting you. When you come back"—she waves her hand in the air, like she's brushing away something distasteful—"we'll deal with the trust."

She turns to leave.

The idea of the valley is appealing, but…"Wait, Brigitte. What will you do?"

"What do you mean?"

"While I'm gone. What will you do? Will you be okay?"

She sighs and her eyes speak of her weariness. "I'll be fine. I have business to attend to. You focus on yourself."

It is so like her to act as though nothing has transpired between us. To move forward without a backward glance. An apology. An acknowledgment of any sort. These are the times that leave me feeling crazy. Doesn't she remember blaming me for Gerard's death?

Once she's gone, I get up from my desk and head to my closet.

I will pack now and leave this afternoon. An idea took root just days after Gerard's death, and now I will implement it. The music has begun playing, and my Partner is reaching for my hand.

He will lead.

I pack a few items of clothing—most of what I need is already there in my closet at the chateau. Then I go to the back of my closet and reach for the sealed dress box that I keep on an upper shelf.

I search for the matching shoes, and then open the safe and take out a small turquoise-colored ring box. I place the box in an inside pocket of my suitcase, and close the suitcase.

I am grateful for Brigitte's suggestion and the sense of purpose I feel.

Before I leave, I sit back at my desk and write a quick e-mail to Skye letting her know where I'll be. And I type another to Matthew:

Dear Matthew,

I am heading to the valley for a few days where I will carry through with the idea I shared with you. Just wanted you to know.

Following His lead,

Jenna

I send the e-mails, shut down the laptop, and pack it to take with me. Then I go downstairs and tell Hannah that I'm leaving. Less then forty minutes after Brigitte's suggestion, I'm on the road.

My first morning in the valley I wake long before dawn, roll over in bed, and reach for Gerard. I experience his death all over again when I realize he isn't there. I lie there, alone, yet not alone. I sense God's presence—His nearness—as I have since the night Gerard died. The dark room seems alive with Him, as though the walls are inhaling and exhaling.

This is the day that I have made, rejoice and be glad in it, Jenna.

Yes, this is the day.

I get out of bed and get ready to go.

I PARK the old ranch truck in front of the cave entrance, reach for the bag I packed, and get out. I stand by the truck for a moment. The air is cool and the scent earthy, organic. The rolling acres of vines appear as mere shadows. Above me a silver moon is slung low and a million stars twinkle their welcome—a heavenly host here as witnesses. The hush of predawn stills the fluttering of my heart and prepares me for what's to come.

I thought of doing this in the prayer chapel, but the memories my time with Gerard there are still so fresh—the grief still raw. Instead, I opted for the cave.

A new place for a new beginning.

I pull the flashlight from my bag and shine it in the direction of the cave—the beam of light illuminates the massive oak door fitted to the mouth of the cave. I look heavenward again and smile in anticipation.

He is here.

And He waits for me.

For these moments, I will set my grief aside.

I walk to the cave and shine the flashlight on the small panel next to the door. I key in the alarm code and hear the faint electronic whir of the alarm disarming, followed by the click of the lock releasing. The heavy door glides open with just a push. Just inside the entrance is another panel—this one a series of switches that light the cave. I touch just one switch and small lights come to life along the bottom of the cave walls, illuminating the path ahead. I make my way into the cavern and head for the alcove bored into the side of the cave, just a hundred yards or so from the entrance. It is a space used for private tastings or small parties. Beyond here are hundreds of barrels filled with aging wines and champagnes. I point the flashlight along the back wall of the alcove and see the three large, wrought-iron candelabras standing guard. I switch the flashlight off, drop it into my bag, and reach for the lighter I brought. I click the lighter on and let the flickering flame lead me to the candleholders.

One by one, I light the dozen tapers in each stand. Behind the candelabras hangs a large mirror in which the three-dozen flames are reflected, bathing the alcove in a warm hue. I stand back and watch the shadows dance on the wall of the cave. In the center of the alcove, just as I requested when I called ahead yesterday, is a small table covered with a white linen cloth and two chairs. There are three candles in the center of the table. I light the outside two and leave the one in the middle to be lit later. There is also a decanter of red wine, a glass, and a round of sourdough covered with a white linen napkin on the table.

I slip my coat off and drape it across the back of one of the chairs. Then I smooth the ivory satin, ankle-length dress I'm wearing—the one in the sealed box I brought with me. My mother's wedding dress. I'd wanted to wear it when I married Gerard, but Brigitte had insisted on a gown created for me by the French designer, Monique Lhuillier. It was beautiful, but held no meaning for me. I turn back to the mirror and study my reflection. The glimmering light disguises my scar and I can almost believe it isn't there. Instead, the pearls at my lobes and neck shimmer, as do the seed pearls sewn on the bodice of the simple dress.

I am pleased, for once, with what I see reflected back to me.

Though I know it doesn't matter. I am here for One who doesn't notice the outward appearance but instead looks at the heart. And through the unfathomable work of grace, I know He sees a pure heart, virginal, and white as snow. I still struggle to grasp the magnitude of such a gift.

I turn back to the table and reach into my bag, then pull out my Bible and the small turquoise box and place both on the table.

I shiver in the musty chill of the cave and wrap my arms around myself.

My whisper breaks the silence. "Is this silly?"

You are My beloved.

I open my Bible to the Song of Songs. "'I am my beloved's and my beloved is mine.'" I leave the Bible open on the table, reach for my coat, and fan it out on the floor in front of the candelabras.

I walk back to the table, close the Bible, and take it and the little box back to my coat. I kneel on the coat and set the Bible and box on the coat as well.

In the flickering glow of the cave, I bow my head. But before making the vow that's woven itself into my mind and heart since Gerard's death, I think of Matthew.

I see the ease of his smile and hear the exuberance of his tone. I think of his passion. His love. His strength. And all he represents to me. Matthew embodies my deepest desire—the Spirit of the One I love.

"Lord, I want no other. No one but You." I shiver again. "I give myself to You now and for all eternity."

I pick up my Bible and turn to the verses I have marked for this moment and read aloud:

"Do not be afraid; you will not suffer shame. Do not fear disgrace; you will not be humiliated. You will forget the shame of your youth and remember no more the reproach of your widowhood. For your Maker is your husband—the Lord Almighty is his name."

I claim God's words to the Israelites for myself today.

Cold, I wrap my arms around myself again and consider picking up my coat and putting it back on, but decide to wait until I'm finished and stand again. Instead, embracing myself, I bow my head again.

I wait. Silent. Wondering. Will the Spirit speak to my soul on this day?

As I wait, I'm aware of a warm sensation beginning in my chest. It spreads inward and then outward, from chest to neck, shoulders, and then down my arms. Soon, every part of my body is flushed with a radiant heat, from fingertips to toes. I unwrap my arms from around my torso and let them rest at my sides. I lift my head and open my eyes. But there is no explanation for the warmth that envelops me like...

I smile. Like the embrace of a lover on a cold winter morn.

I lean my head back, inhale, and raise my arms heavenward.

I offer myself body and soul to my Beloved.

Loving.

Desiring.

Trusting.

"I will have no other god before You." My vow echoes through the chambers of the cave and in the recesses of my soul. "You are my Husband."

I bend and reach for the little turquoise box. I open it and smile. Inside is a simple platinum band inlaid with small baguette diamonds. It has none of the flash of the four-karat Bouvier heirloom or its recent replacement. But it is, I'm certain, the ring my Beloved has chosen for me.

I think back...

Was it just three days ago? The day before Gerard's funeral, I'd gone to find something appropriate to wear—a dark-colored suit or dress. I didn't care. It seemed so insignificant. I'd taken a cab to Union Square and wandered, dazed. People on the streets or even the stores themselves went unnoticed. It was the first time I'd had been alone since the night of Gerard's death. I ambled on Post

Street headed nowhere in particular. My mind was empty—my heart cold. As I neared the corner, I felt a nagging sense that I was to stop and look back.

Curious, I turned and saw nothing but a few tourists window-shopping. I looked up to see what store they stood in front of. Tiffany's. I turned back and continued to the corner. But the nagging sense followed me. When I reached the corner, I turned back again.

Why would I go to Tiffany's? I have a safe full of jewelry. But I wandered back nonetheless. I stood in front of the square display windows gazing at diamonds, emeralds, and sapphires glittering under the jeweler's lights.

Just as I turned to go, I noticed the band, elegant in its simplicity, and was drawn to it. As I looked at it, an idea formed. And then I knew.

This was to be my ring.

Our ring.

Symbolic of a new union.

I look down at the marquis diamond and platinum band on my left hand. The diamond hasn't left my finger since . . . Not even to go into the safe. But now, I slide the rings off my finger and place them on the ring finger on my right hand. I open the Tiffany's ring box, but hesitate. Is it too soon for such a public display of my widowhood? What will Brigitte say?

No. Now is the time. God made that clear. Gerard is no longer my husband. I put all thoughts of Brigitte's judgment out of my mind. "I will have no other god before You."

I pull the band from the box and slip it onto my ring finger of my left hand.

I smile. "Thank You." The tiny diamonds sparkle in the candle-light. "I am Yours."

I love you, Jenna. The words dance through my mind and rever-berate in my soul.

I close the ring box, pick up my Bible, and stand back up, my knees stiff from kneeling. I walk the few steps back to the table and place the box and Bible back beside the three candles. I take one of the lit tapers and light the middle candle—the unity candle. Another gesture symbolic of the covenant I've made today.

I reach for the decanter and pour some of the red wine into the wine glass and I uncover the bread. Then I open my Bible to 1 Corinthians 11 and read aloud.

"The Lord Jesus, on the night he was betrayed, took bread, and when he had given thanks, he broke it and said, 'This is my body, which is for you; do this in remembrance of me.'"

I bow my head to give thanks, but find that nothing in the language of humanity suffices to express the gratitude I feel. Instead, in silence, I offer Him access to my heart—a heart, I pray, that is fully surrendered to Him. Then I pick up the round of sourdough, break off a small piece, and place it in my mouth.

His body, broken for me.

I glance back to the Bible.

"In the same way, after supper he took the cup, saying, 'This cup is the new covenant in my blood; do this, whenever you drink it, in remembrance of me.'"

I sip the wine and swallow it despite the lump in my throat.

I wipe the tears slipping down my cheeks.

His blood, shed for me.

This is the new covenant. Our covenant, my Beloved.

Joy, the emotion so elusive in my marriage to Gerard, swells within. And with it comes waves of gratitude. I linger at the table awash with love. Perfect love. I close my eyes and sway to the rhythm of an imagined chorus—the morning stars singing together and all the angels shouting for joy.

I dance in the embrace of my Beloved.

CHAPTER TWENTY-THREE

Do not think so much of yourself that you are not concerned with others.
JEANNE GUYON

rigitte

HER NAILS CLICKING on the keys, she types in the e-mail address: andee@andeebell.com.

> It is imperative that we meet in the next two days. Please call or e-mail with a time that works for you. We'll meet alone at my home office.
>
> Brigitte

She thinks back to the dinner party she had planned. But that was before. She reaches for her calendar, counts forward three months, an appropriate time of bereavement, and chooses a date to reschedule the party. She senses Andee's desire, need even, to rub shoulders with the elite of the city.

She will see that it happens.

She will have Andee in her back pocket, as they say. But she will have to be patient.

She pushes the calendar aside, picks up her phone, and leaves a message for Andee. The same message contained within the e-mail.

Patience isn't one of her virtues. C'est la vie.

Now that Jenna's gone for a few days, there are things she must discuss with Andee. First and foremost, the deal with Azul. Andee need not know all the specifics of her plan. Just those specifics that relate to Andee's participation in her plan. Again she smiles—thin lips stretched tight.

Her plan is in everyone's best interest, of course. Even Jenna's, if she knows what is good for her.

Jenna.

Her hand tightens on the receiver of the phone she still holds.

She thinks back to her conversation with Gerard the night he... She sighs. It's clear the whole fiasco was Jenna's fault. If she hadn't encouraged Gerard to "acknowledge his strengths and use them," as he'd said, or given him the idea that he might step out on his own and start his own business.

"Who have you been speaking to, Gerard?"

He'd stood tall, her handsome son. *"Jenna and I have talked about it and, Mother, if you're not ready to relinquish the leadership of the company, then I think it's time I pursued other ventures."*

Other ventures? Ridiculous! He is... He *was* her son. She knew what was best for him. But no, Jenna had to stick her nose into things that didn't concern her. If she hadn't encouraged him, he wouldn't have dared argue with her, and he'd still be alive.

And now? Jenna is all she has left. Fine. So be it.

She checks her e-mail to see if Andee has responded. Nothing yet. She glances at her watch and dials Andee's number again. She must make her understand the urgency of their meeting.

CHAPTER TWENTY-FOUR

As your will is lost in God's will you still have purposes, but these purposes are God's desires within you and have nothing to do with you.

JEANNE GUYON

ndee

I SCROLL through my e-mail and search for the most recent www.iluminar.me post. Did I miss it? The last one in my e-mail folder is one I read, when? Over a week ago?

"What's up, Lightseeker? So I said I was done with you. You didn't let that hurt your feelings, did you?"

I click on my Internet server and type in the URL www.iluminar.me and check the blog site to see if anything new has been posted. Nothing. I click back to my e-mail folder and do a search for the e-mail exchange I had with Lightseeker. "Maybe you've run off to discover your life's purpose. Good luck with that." Sarcasm reverberates between my office walls.

I open a new message and type:

Lightseeker,

Dropping off the face of the earth doesn't bode well for your blog. Your readers will lose interest if you don't post consistently. From one blogger to another, take my advice and get back in the saddle before you lose your audience.

BTW, sorry I didn't respond to your last e-mail. Life gets busy, right? In answer to your question, my purpose is, of course, to secure financial freedom for myself and those I advise.

A. Bell

After my little foray into introspection during Gerard's memorial service, I came to a couple of conclusions: First, it's time to invest in my relationship with Jason. It's a sound investment. Sure, I have feelings for him, but a choice like this must be based on something more stable than mere emotion. Jason is intelligent, dependable, trustworthy, and well connected. He's also a looker. I smile. I'm attracted to him in all the right ways. Having a partner is practical. And someday, my biological clock might begin ticking. Although, I think mine is defunct. But should that change, Jason and I would produce stunning offspring.

Second, Gerard's death led me to reconsider my spirituality— or lack thereof. While financial security is important, it isn't an ironclad guarantee against things like death. Even Brigitte couldn't control that. As I observed Brigitte, I realized one needs to insure the things one cannot control—like life. And I'm not talking about a whole-life or term policy. I'm talking eternal insurance. So, I will investigate religion again, and will begin by paying closer attention to Lightseeker's blog.

Again, a practical decision.

Which is why it's annoying that she's provided nothing new to read. I click the mouse and scroll through the blog again.

Whatever.

I'll wait for her to respond to my e-mail.

I look at the time on the upper right corner of my computer screen. Four hours since Brigitte's e-mails and phone calls. I will not be at her beck and call. But I supposed I've let her stew long enough. I pick up the phone and punch in her number. I listen to her voicemail message and wait for the tone.

"Brigitte, it's Andee Bell. I'm available tomorrow after 3:00 p.m. or after 11:00 a.m. the following day. Let me know which time you prefer. You may call or e-mail me, as usual. See you soon."

Just as I hang up, my doorbell rings. The only one who rings unannounced is the building doorman, everyone else has to buzz me from the lobby. I cross the living room to the front door and open it.

"Delivery, Ms. Bell. It's heavy, may I set it somewhere for you?"

"Who's it from?"

He looks at the mailing label. "Azul Winery."

"Okay, take it to the kitchen, if you don't mind." I point the way.

He heads for the kitchen, and leaves the box on the island.

"Thanks, Jack."

"No problem, Ms. Bell. I'll see myself out."

I look at the box, reach in a drawer for a knife, and slice it open. Inside, are two cases of Azul's finest. Great. Just what I need. There's also an envelope. I tear open the envelope, which reveals a thank-you card. Inside, Bill has scrawled a note:

Andee,

I appreciate your expertise and your efforts on behalf of Azul. Thank you for the meeting in Napa. I'll look forward to hearing from you.

Bill

I consider the note and how it could be interpreted, and then I tear it up. No need for anyone to come across it and link me with Bill or Azul. The wine? I stash the cases in the back of the pantry until I can figure out what to do with them.

Note to self: Don't let Jason snoop around in the pantry. It's Bill's place to reveal he's sought my advice.

I head back to my desk, where I'll work for the next hour on the information I'll present to Brigitte when we meet. She has an agenda and I assume it will include more questions regarding Azul. This time, I'll give her what she wants. That is, of course, after she's agreed to my stipulation.

Before I dive into the Azul details, I check my e-mail again. There's a response from Brigitte, we'll meet at 3:30 tomorrow afternoon. And there's a response from Lightseeker. "Ah, there you are." I open the message.

Andee,

Again, thank you for your interest in my blog and your concern. It's nice to know you missed my posts. I had a personal crisis last week that prevented my blogging, but I anticipate posting another entry soon.

Thank you, too, for your response to my question. May I ask another? How did you determine your purpose?

"Hey, I didn't say I missed your blog, I just said you're going to lose readers." I scan her e-mail again and then reread her question. So, what? Now we're pen pals? Okay, I'm game. I hit *reply*:

Lightseeker,

I'm sorry for your crisis, but perhaps it will lend itself to some...

THE WORD *JUICY* comes to mind, but even I know it's a bit insensitive if she's had a real crisis.

...profound blog entries.

I stop and think about her question. How did I determine my purpose? Uh, I grew up in utter humiliation and vowed I'd never live that way again?

Regarding purpose: My life circumstances clarified my purpose. My advice is to look at your circumstances and determine what about your situation you want to keep, and what you'd like to change. Perhaps your purpose will reveal itself in the process.

My turn: Why are you so passionate about religion?

A. Bell

This chick isn't very self-aware. Anyone who reads her blog knows her purpose is wound up in her beliefs or her religion or whatever. But she can't see it? What's with that? I may think her purpose is hokey, but to each his own.

Then I reconsider. Okay, maybe it's not hokey. It's just... Whatever. I have work to do.

I close my mail folder and turn my attention back to Azul and Brigitte.

CHAPTER TWENTY-FIVE

An external religion, with its rules and forms, has taken the place of an
inward experience with Christ.
JEANNE GUYON

enna

I SIT at the large antique desk in the den of the chateau—the vineyard sprawling before me—my fingers on the keys of my laptop.
Guilt pricks my conscience as I read Andee's e-mail. She assumes
she's writing to a stranger. Her first e-mail a few weeks ago startled me. It was the first time someone I knew responded to my
blog. I responded back, not giving myself time to think about it. I
thought that would be the end of it.

But then she replied and her question about my purpose hit
me, and I answered with the truth, almost forgetting I was
responding to someone I knew. When I didn't hear back from her,
I was relieved.

Today's e-mail from her caught me off guard. What could I say that was truthful but wouldn't reveal my identity? Which made me wonder again at the dichotomy of wanting to share truth but instead, hiding behind a lie. Or at least an omission. My blog is where I'm most transparent and free to be myself. Yet, I'm not myself at all. I'm anonymous.

The parallel to my life isn't lost on me.

I chose my words to Andee with care. To say there'd been a death in the family might tip her off. A personal crisis was true, and yet...

Drawing Andee in by asking questions was foolish. Yet, having spent some time with her now, I long to engage her on another level. To break through that self-protective barrier that's so evident. There is a vulnerable, and I'd guess, wounded soul, beneath the polished exterior.

I understand now why Jason is drawn to her, though I am concerned for him—for his heart.

But as far as the blog, I can't reveal my identity. If Brigitte were to discover... Well, it just isn't an option. I press *send* and my e-mail to Andee is off to her. Then I reach for the lid of my laptop to close it. As I do, the light from the fixture above catches the diamonds in the band on my left hand and sends small dots of light dancing across the wall. I reach for the ring and twist it around my finger, finding comfort in its meaning.

You are my Husband. I will have no other god before you.

I get up from the desk and wander to the kitchen, but a niggling sense of unrest follows me. I ignore it and place a mug under the spigot of the coffeemaker. I add a little cream and stir the coffee as I consider Andee's advice: *Look at your circumstances and determine what about your situation you want to keep, and what you'd like to change.*

Oh, if she only knew. How many times in the last eleven years have I wished to change my circumstances? Too many to count. And now? If I could change anything, I'd bring Gerard back.

Or would I?

The thought has nagged me since reading Andee's e-mail for the first time this morning. It has nagged every time I've read it since. If I had the power to change anything, would I wish Gerard back to life? The answer, I'm ashamed to admit, is no. Though I grieve him and know I will miss him, there is a new freedom that came with his death.

I feel the scarlet of shame creeping up my neck and face.

"Oh, Lord, forgive me. I'm so sorry." I cover my face and wait for the tears to come, but they don't. I take my hands away from my face and take a deep breath.

There was a hopelessness to Gerard's existence. Not because he was without eternal hope—he believed—but because he didn't live out of that hope while he was alive. Instead, without meaning to, he placed his hope in his mother. His hope, his loyalty, his very life. His death ends the pain of watching him, day-by-day, slip further away into the comfort of detachment or the seeming solace of alcohol.

Now he is at peace. Finally.

But it isn't just that.

There's Brigitte, of course. And with Gerard's death comes the hope of escaping her clutches.

When I married Gerard, he lived with Brigitte and it was understood that, as a couple, we, too, would live with her. Gerard explained that since his father's death it had been his role to care for his mother. Although she never allowed him to care for her. She took care of everything, including herself. I didn't question the decision. At twenty-one, I was enamored with Brigitte, the home in the city, and the life I'd idealized.

Reality proved a poor substitute for what I'd imagined and when, a few years after our marriage, I spoke with Gerard about buying our own home, his unwillingness, or perhaps his inability to "leave and cleave" became evident. I recalled my father's warning, but by then it was too late.

Back to Andee's question: What would I change? What *wouldn't* I change? But foremost, I'd walk away from Brigitte.

I dream of it.

I fantasize about it.

When Gerard died, I began to hope. But I'm still bound to her. I must honor Gerard's request that I care for her. I must love her, as God calls me to love everyone, even my enemies.

Brigitte is my cross to bear. I've understood this for many years.

Understood... Matthew's words come back to me—King Solomon's words from Proverbs: *Trust in the Lord with all your heart and lean not on your own understanding.* For the first time, I wonder if I've misunderstood Jesus' decree that *anyone who does not take up their cross and follow me is not worthy of me?* But what else could it mean? I'm to bear my circumstances, and in doing so I share in the sufferings of Christ, right?

Stand back, Jenna.

The words breeze through my mind and soul. And again, for what seems like the hundredth time, I ask, "Stand back from what?" Agitation marks my question. "Stand back from my own understanding?" The words are out of my mouth before I've even thought them. Where did they come from?

Were they from God?

Lord, have I misunderstood? With my prayer comes a hope that brings me to tears. And with the hope a sense of relief so intense that it points to the depth of my emotional fatigue with Brigitte.

But how can I care for Brigitte, love her as God calls me to love her, *and* walk away? It doesn't make sense. I reach for my calendar and on the small square where I've noted my next appointment with Matthew, I write the initial B. Maybe this will be the topic of my next session.

In the meantime, I will enjoy my moments of freedom, here, now, while I'm away. Just as Gerard and I used to do. Tomorrow, I will return to Pacific Heights, and to Brigitte.

I dump my now-cold coffee in the sink and determine to think about something else.

I head back to the den and my computer. I sit at the desk again and open the laptop and return to Andee's note and her question for me: *Why are you so passionate about religion?* I am still for several moments before I lift my fingers to the keys. In those moments, I pray. *Lord, give me Your words for Andee. May she sense Your love and grace.*

Dear Andee,

I'm not passionate about religion. I'm passionate about a relationship—my relationship with Jesus.

I stop typing and consider what I know about Andee—or at least what I think I've observed. She's self-sufficient, controlled, and intelligent. She makes choices based on logic, or thoughts, rather than feelings. And she's . . . I close my eyes and wait. I sense the Spirit leading my thoughts. She's...afraid.

Ah. Perhaps the wounding I sensed in her has something to do with her fear.

I return to the e-mail and feel my passion stirring. It's when I'm engaged in an exchange with a reader that I feel most alive. These are the times when I sense the Spirit's presence in me, through me, around me. I catch my breath and whisper, "Thank You," and then continue my note to Andee.

Religion is about rules and rituals and expectations. Religion comes with judgment. Jesus is about total acceptance and unconditional love. One of my favorite verses says that in Jesus there is no condemnation.

If you read my blog, then you know I'm imperfect, struggling to find my way, and often afraid. Yet, Jesus loves me.

Oh, I could go on and on, but this feels like enough. My instinct with Andee tells me to keep things short and to the point. I leave the e-mail unsigned as usual and press *send*. I let the condemning thought about my anonymity go.

"Father, lead me..."

I trust, or try to trust, that He will show me the time and the way in which to reveal myself. If that is His desire for me.

CHAPTER TWENTY-SIX

The only perfect fellowship is the union of spirits in God. This union not only exists in heaven, but also on earth as the resurrecting power of life begins to transform the believer.

JEANNE GUYON

*M*atthew

ON SATURDAY MORNING, I roll over in bed, look through the crack between the blind and our window, and see that the sun is shining. Looks like an awesome fall day. I glance at Tess. "Breakfast?" She knows what I mean.

"Mmm, absolutely." She throws the covers back and leaps out of bed. "I get the bathroom!" Then she lunges toward our one small bathroom.

But my legs are longer than hers. I jump up, follow her, and then wrestle her for position in the hallway. "Oh, no you don't!"

I beat her to the bathroom, open the door, and then I surprise her by bowing, and making a sweeping gesture. "It's all yours, m'lady. But hurry, I'm hungry."

She laughs. "Just give me time to wash my face and brush my teeth."

While she does that, I go to our closet, reach for sweats, a T-shirt, and my favorite flannel shirt. I step into tennis shoes, bend to tie them, and then take my turn in the bathroom. Within twenty minutes we're on the street and heading for our favorite neighborhood cafe where the grub is good and the coffee cups bottomless.

We walk and talk, ribbing each other along the way.

"You know, I only let you wear that outfit because we never see anyone we know at this place."

I eye her flawless designer—though purchased at a discount—olive-colored yoga pants and matching jacket. "And I only let you wear that outfit because I'm above what other people think."

She swats at me and laughs. "Yeah, right."

We cover the three blocks to the cafe in record time and claim our favorite table by the window. Before our napkins are even on our laps our coffee cups are full. Cool. I reach for the half and half and the sugar.

"You're going to get fat, babe."

"Yeah, but I'm not a real man like you. I can't take it black." I wink at her.

She leans across the table and takes my face in her hands and gives me a lingering kiss. "You're man enough for me."

"Well, that's a relief." I smile and then pick up the menu. I try something different each time we come.

"So, what'll it be this time?" Our waitress, coffeepot in one hand and an empty plate in the other, swings by our table and waits while I decide.

"How about the San Fran Scramble, with grilled potatoes, and OJ."

"Good choice. And the usual for you?"

Tess nods.

The usual is one poached egg and a piece of dry wheat toast. Why bother?

Our coffee time, while we wait for our food, is our catch-up time. We cover the week's happenings and make small talk. If we need to go deeper, we do that over breakfast. If not, we share the *Chronicle*, passing sections across the table to one another.

Tess sets her coffee cup down, pulls her long auburn hair into a ponytail, and takes a thing out of her pocket and secures it around her hair. She always seems to have one of those ponytail things with her.

"What happened to Lightseeker's blog this week?" She picks her coffee cup back up and takes a sip.

I set my cup down and…fumble. "Uh… What do you mean?"

She eyes me. "What do you mean, what do I mean? You read her blog every single time she posts. You're telling me you didn't miss it this week?"

"Oh, that. Yeah… I don't know. Makes you wonder, huh?"

"I hope she's okay."

I nod. "Yeah, me too." I pick up my coffee and take another sip. "Hey, can I ask you something?"

She nods.

"Why are you reading that thing? I mean, I know why I read it, but I'm just wondering what you're drawn to." I expect her to be defensive.

Instead, she smiles. "This is kind of deep for coffee talk."

"Need some protein to fortify you first?"

"No, I think I can handle it."

She looks at the table for a minute and then looks back to me.

"I think it's her honesty. She doesn't have it all together— doesn't have all the answers, you know? She's searching. Looking for illumination. It's like she's on a journey and she's letting the rest of us come along."

"So, how does that differ from when I try to talk to you about faith? I mean"—I lift my eyebrows and smile—"except for the obvious. I do have all the answers."

She wads up her napkin and throws it at me.

"Hey!" I catch it and pretend to take aim at her and she ducks. "Ha! Gotcha."

She laughs. "Actually, that is sort of the reason. I feel like you do have all the answers or, no offense, at least you think you do."

"Ouch, really?"

"Really."

I give this some thought and then concede. "Yeah, I can see that. Sorry." I've thought if I could reason with Tess, answer all her questions, appeal to that logical side of her, then maybe...

"That's okay. I know you're passionate." She laughs. "To say the least. And, I wasn't ready to hear it. I'm still not sure I'm ready. Somehow, I feel pressured when it comes from you."

I nod. And for once, I keep my mouth shut. But dude, inside I'm hurting. For Tess. For myself. I want her to know His love. I want to share the things of God—the depth of His love—with her. I want that fellowship together.

We're quiet until our orders arrive a couple of minutes later.

"What do you have going on over there?" Tess looks at my plate.

"This, my dear, is the San Fran Scramble. Three eggs, Jack cheese, spinach, onions, and the kicker—hunks of grilled authentic San Francisco sourdough bread. Want a bite?" I stack my fork with a bite, but she shakes her head and holds up her hand. "What? You're missing out."

"Yeah, on about a thousand calories."

"It'll put a little meat on your bones."

"Great, just what I need."

She takes a bite of her dry toast and reaches for the *Chronicle*. "Want a section?"

"Nah, not yet. I'm going to focus on my calorie intake."

"Enjoy." She lifts the paper and is hidden behind it. Then she puts it back down. "Oh, I meant to tell you something."

"What?" I stop. Major fumble—talking with my mouth full.

"Nice save." She smiles. "Well, at first I wasn't going to say anything because I thought it was just gossip, but then I remembered something."

Gossip is one of the things Tess dislikes most about her industry. She says the cutthroat backstabbing is ridiculous. So I'm curious about what she's going to tell me.

"I decided that maybe it would be helpful to you. So, for what it's worth . . ." She folds the paper back up and sets it aside. "Several days after we attended the memorial service for Gerard Bouvier, a gal at work was talking about Gerard's mother, Brigitte Bouvier. The gal, Caroline, you've met her, right?"

"Caroline, the malnourished blonde?"

"Matthew…"

"Sorry, yep, I've met her."

"Anyway, she was a personal shopper for one of our competitors before coming to us and Brigitte Bouvier was one of her customers. Evidently, she placed an order for her and something she'd requested was backordered. It happens sometimes. Anyway, she said the woman was verbally abusive to her on several occasions—blamed her, belittled her—that kind of thing. Then, she finally called Caroline's manager and had her fired. She said she'd take her business elsewhere unless they fired her."

"Sounds like a major case of entitlement."

Tess picks up her coffee cup again. "Yeah. In fact, I remember the incident, because when Caroline applied with us, she'd told me the story and I called her former manager to verify it. Her manager told me that was exactly how it happened, and that Caroline was a wonderful employee, but that the customer in question was too well known in the city to ignore, as were her expenditures. I didn't hear the customer's name until last week."

I give Tess my deer-in-the-headlights stare.

"I know. You can't talk about it. But..." She's thoughtful again. "But Jenna's one of your clients and"—she shrugs—"I don't know, it's weird, but I just felt compelled to tell you."

I stash Tess's information away for later. "Thanks, babe. I appreciate it."

She returns to the *Chronicle* while I consider again the trust it takes between spouses when one of them works in a capacity that requires confidentiality. When I received the invitation to Gerard Bouvier's memorial service, it was addressed to Mr. and Mrs. Matthew MacGregor. I called Jenna and told her that I would come alone if that was more comfortable for her. She insisted that Tess was welcome to attend with me. The lines blur more easily with spiritual direction than they do in counseling. And I was happy to have Tess's company at the service. Besides, I needed her to dress me.

Tess understands the rules of confidentiality and she respects them.

And, I remind myself again, she trusts me.

Later in the day, I think through Tess's words about Brigitte Bouvier. Jenna hasn't spoken about her mother-in-law so, given what I know from her, I might not give much thought to the information Tess passed along. But what I know from Lightseeker's posts is something different altogether. She's inferred that she's involved in a relationship with a woman that is, at the least, controlling.

At the worst, abusive.

If Lightseeker and Jenna are one in the same, and I'm pretty sure they are, then man, I pray the relationship with her mother-in-law will come up in our conversations. Maybe that's why Tess felt compelled to tell me—maybe the Holy Spirit nudged her, so that I would pray.

And dude, I will pray.

CHAPTER TWENTY-SEVEN

God wants to teach you that there is a silence through which He operates.
JEANNE GUYON

enna

WHEN I RETURN to the house in the city, I'm followed by what feels like an oppressive fog. The thought of life with Brigitte weighs on me like an anvil—crushing my spirit. I slip into the house from the garage and make it all the way to the stairs before I'm noticed.

Hannah comes around the corner. "You're back."

"Yes."

"I'll notify Madame."

"That won't be necessary, Hannah." I head up the stairs assuming she'll notify Brigitte anyway. I enter our suite, my suite, and cross the room. I stop at the vanity, too tired to take another step. I sit on the stool in front of the vanity and rest my forehead on my crossed arms.

I felt fine in the valley. Well even. The antibiotic pump was removed the day before Gerard died. Time, I realize, will now be marked by his death. And though the emotional trauma of his death drained me, I knew my body had responded to the antibiotics. The low-grade fever subsided and the nausea and lethargy were gone.

But now, here, I'm spent.

I lift my head and stare at nothing. My heart feels like a rock and each breath a chore. But there's something more. Something's different. Is it just that Gerard is gone? I look around the room and notice the...

Silence.

All is still.

Like death itself.

I shiver. Then I look at the vanity and notice the hand mirror.

I let my mind wander back. Gerard had brought me home from the hospital after the second surgery—the surgery to clean out the infection in my jawbone—the surgery that left me with the angry scar across my chin and jawline.

I walked into the house with my head hung low and my hair hanging forward, covering part of my face. I looked at no one. I was still weak, still sick. I made my way to the elevator and up to our suite without encountering Brigitte, for which I was grateful. But when I entered our bedroom, she was there, waiting for me.

"Ma chérie, you're home."

Startled, I looked up. I watched her expression change, saw the disgust written across her features. She chose me for my beauty. To produce perfect Bouvier heirs, or something. I never understood her reasoning. Yet, my beauty wasn't enough. And as I stood there, watching her, I knew even that was lost.

Had she forgotten the surgery was her suggestion?

"What have you done to yourself?" Her words were measured and weighted. "You're ruined."

Her words, machete-like, shredded me.

"You're worthless."

Fighting tears, I made my way past her, made my way to the vanity, where I reached for the stool. I didn't have the strength to take another step. I dropped onto the stool and felt her eyes still on me.

She swung the machete a final time. "How could you be so stupid?" She turned and left.

The word *stupid* echoed in the empty room just as it would echo in my soul for months and months afterward.

I picked up the hand mirror sitting on the vanity and lifted it to my face. The jagged red scar accused. *How could you be so stupid? How could you be so stupid? How could you...*

I stood, the mirror still in my hand. I walked toward the door that Brigitte had closed behind her, anger roiling inside me. I lifted the mirror and I hurled it at the door. At Brigitte, who was, of course, long gone.

The mirror crashed against the door and dropped to the floor. But in my weakened state, there wasn't much power in my throw and the only damage were the cracks in the mirror itself. I picked the mirror up, walked back, and dropped it in the wastebasket next to the vanity. I knew one of the maids would empty the trash the next morning.

But then, a few days later, the mirror reappeared.

I found it sitting, face-up, on the vanity, the cracked glass incriminating me. So, I threw it away again. But this time, I took the elevator downstairs, walked through the kitchen, and dumped the mirror in the outdoor garbage can.

That would be that.

But no.

That evening, as I lay in bed resting, Brigitte walked into the room. She didn't knock. She walked past me to the vanity, something in her hand. When she reached the vanity, she turned toward me and held up the mirror.

"I believe this belongs to you." She set it on the vanity. "You must keep it, chérie, as a reminder of what you've done to yourself. See that it stays here."

Now, sitting at the vanity, I pick up the hand mirror, walk into the bathroom, and close the door. I lift the mirror in my hand above the granite countertop and I bring it down hard against the edge of the granite. I hear the mirror splinter in hundreds of satisfying pieces. I lift the mirror again and smash it down. Again and again, I pound the mirror on the granite. Until both the mirror and the outside casing are destroyed.

Breathless, I lean against the counter. Then I use a damp cloth to wipe up the shards of glass and metal from the countertop and the floor, being careful not to cut myself, and put them into a trash bag along with the now-broken handle of the mirror. I take the trash bag and stuff it in a drawer to dispose of later.

The oppression lifts just a bit.

I go in search of Brigitte. I let the anger of the memory invoked propel me. I find her in her sitting room, dozing on her sofa, a stack of papers on her lap. "Brigitte?"

She startles and looks at me dazed. "Oh…"

"I'm back. We need to talk through a few things."

She sits up straighter, shuffles the papers on her lap, and then stands. "Such as?"

I've caught her off guard and can see the anger now flashing in her eyes. Her lips are pursed tight as she waits for my response.

I take a deep breath. "Such as what to do with Gerard's things —his clothes, and"—I wave my hand in the air—"other things. We also need to talk about his trust. And…the future." I feel myself cowering under her stare.

"Yes, we will talk. But for now, leave Gerard's things alone. I have, as I'm sure you can imagine, many things to take care of with the business since Gerard…" She sniffs. "Then, we will discuss the future. In the meantime, I don't expect that anything should change, n'est-ce pas? We'll go along as we always have." She walks past me to her desk and lays the file folder down. Then she turns back. "Was that all?"

"Um…yes, I guess so."

"Good." She looks at her watch. "We'll have dinner in the dining room this evening. I'll see you at 6:00."

I nod, duly dismissed. "Fine." I turn to go, but guilt turns me back. "A you okay? You look tired."

"Tired? Well, yes, I suppose I am a bit tired. But is it any surprise? While you were off vacationing in the valley, someone had to take care of things."

I start to protest, to remind her that it was her idea. But it's pointless.

I shake my head as I return to my room, the all-too-familiar confusion swirling in my mind. When I walk back into my suite, I notice that one of the household staff has brought my bags up from the car. My laptop sits on my desk, its bag just beneath the desk. My Bible and other books are stacked alongside the laptop.

But I notice something else…again.

The silence.

And with it comes a gnawing loneliness.

I walk to the desk, and rest my hand on the stack of books and look out the window. Fall is loosening its hold and winter, cold and gray, is marching in.

I wrap my arms around myself and shiver again. *Lord, meet me here. Assure me of Your presence.*

I wait.

Expectant.

Hopeful.

But all I hear in response is…

Cold.

Hard.

Silence.

CHAPTER TWENTY-EIGHT

Within yourself there is only darkness, but in God there is only light.
JEANNE GUYON

ndee

RELIGION? Lightseeker pegged that right. Rules, rituals, expectations, and judgment. At least, that's my memory of religion from the church we attended when I was young.

Sure they talked about Jesus. About love and acceptance and all that grace stuff. But as soon as our lives spiraled southward, as soon as my dad's drinking became evident, my mom got a visit from a few men from the church telling her that my dad was a bad influence. A "stumbling block" they said. I remember, because for months afterward, my mother would cry and mumble the words *stumbling block*. Of course, she didn't question them. Didn't stand up for herself. For us.

After that, no one from the church came around again.

I need some eternal insurance, not religion. But a relationship?

Can't I just sign a contract or something? I glance at the clock on the screen of my computer. Time to get ready…

I get up from my desk and cross the living room to my bedroom. I'll change and freshen up for Jason, who's coming for dinner tonight. I've planned an intimate little dinner for two—well, three, if I count Sam. And if I don't count him, there will be no living with him for days. He's taken a liking to Jason.

I go into my closet and reach for the outfit I've planned to wear—chestnut velvet lounging pants with a matching pullover—all lined in chestnut satin. I slip into brown satin flats and choose simple, large gold hoops for my ears. Casual elegance, of course. Perfect for an evening at home. I go to the bathroom where I brush out my long blond hair until it shines, dab a bit of dark brown shadow on the lids of my brown eyes, and a bit of gloss on my lips.

I look at my reflection in the mirror and like what I see. "Perfect."

I go to the kitchen and set the small round table that sits in the corner. The corner is comprised of two floor-to-ceiling windows affording a stunning view. I set candles in the center of the table, use two place settings of china, two settings of sterling, and linen napkins. I include a water and wine glass at each setting for balance, although, tonight, I may tell Jason that I don't actually drink.

Then I open the fridge and take out the cartons delivered earlier and follow the warming instructions. I called my favorite restaurant and they agreed to deliver. Just for me. Smart people. I told them they'd need to include directions. I don't cook. At all.

Things are going well until I realize I forgot to pick up a bottle of wine. Shoot. Then I remember the stash in the pantry. Perfect.

I go to the pantry, take a bottle out of one of the cases, and then shove the cases under the back corner shelf. I remind myself to get rid of the cases of wine as soon as possible.

When Jason arrives, the appropriate dishes are on the range

and in the oven. When he buzzes from downstairs, I pour him a glass of wine and meet him at the door with it.

"Hi there." I lean into him, kiss him, and then hand him the glass.

He takes the glass and then steps back and looks at me. "You are gorgeous," he says.

I smile. "I know."

He chuckles.

"It's good to see you smile. It's been awhile."

Gerard's death hit him hard. He nods and then takes a sip of his wine. "One of ours?"

"Of course. I buy the best. C'mon, follow me to the kitchen." When we reach the kitchen, Sam is poised in one of the chairs at the table, claiming his place. He mews in protest when I try to move him. Instead, I scoot another chair up to the table and scoot the chair he's sitting in around the side of the table. "There, satisfied?"

"So now I see who really rules." Jason goes to scratch behind Sam's ears.

"Oh no, I still rule. I just let him think he does."

"Right. Wow, something smells good. You've been holding out on me, I didn't know you could cook."

"Ha! I can't, I don't, and I won't. And don't you forget it. But I can fake it well. I reach into the trash under the sink and pull out one of the cartons."

"Ah, takeout."

"Yes, but not just any takeout. I am not your average consumer, you know."

"Believe me, I know." He smiles and comes up behind me and puts his arms around me. He kisses my neck and I count to ten. I don't stand still well. But by the time I reach five, I realize I'm counting slower and slower. By seven, I stop and lean back into him. I close my eyes.

"Andee?" Jason whispers.

"Hmm…"

"Are you okay?"

I pull away from him and turn around. "What do you mean?"

"You're so relaxed."

I look at him, not sure if I should feel embarrassed or complimented. "Yeah, kinda weird, huh?"

"Kinda nice." He leans in for a kiss.

And I let him.

When dinner is ready, Jason replaces one of the wine glasses on the table with the one I'd handed him at the door. He's taken a few sips. He reaches for the wine bottle on the island. "May I pour you a glass?"

About that…"

He waits, bottle in hand.

"I"—I wipe my palms on a kitchen towel—"It's just that…"

"Andee?"

I take a deep breath and chide myself for even caring what he thinks. "Listen, I don't drink. Never have. Socially, I'll take a sip if I have to, but otherwise"—I shake my head—"nada. Nothing."

He cocks his head to one side, looks at me for a minute, and then sets the bottle back on the island. "Okay. But why did you feel like you had to keep that from me?"

"You're a winemaker?"

He laughs. "Well, yes, but it's not like you to be someone other than who you are."

I shrug. "It's not a big deal."

"Does it bother you that I drink?"

I shrug again. "You're a winemaker."

"Does it bother you that I drink?"

"It's not a big deal."

He smiles. "I think there's an echo in here."

"Okay"—I wipe my palms again, this time on my pants—"my dad was an alcoholic. And not the jolly type, if you know what I mean."

He looks at me and I see compassion in his eyes. "Hey, don't feel sorry for me or anything. I'm just saying…"

He turns back toward the table, reaches for both wine glasses, and takes them to the sink. He empties his, rinses it, and leaves it in the sink. He turns back to me. "I think that's done." He points to the pot boiling over on the gas range.

"Oh, no!" I run to the range, turn off the gas, and lift the lid and look in the pot. "I think it's okay." I turn back around. "I told you, I don't cook."

He smiles that charming smile of his and shrugs. "It's not a big deal."

He mimics me in jest and I feel my heart skip a beat. *Get a grip, Andee, this isn't a romantic comedy. Good grief.*

When we sit down to dinner, Jason raises his water glass in a toast. "To water." He smiles.

I lift my glass and clink his. "I'll drink to that—at least for tonight. But wine is your future, buddy, so don't turn your back on it so fast."

"Maybe."

"Maybe? What do you mean, maybe?"

"I'm not married to the winery, or to anything for that matter. I trust God has a plan for my life—it may or may not include the winery."

I nod. *That's for sure, considering the mess your father's in.*

He takes a bite of his gnocchi with creamed herb sauce, at least that's what the carton said it was.

"Mmm, perfect."

"If you're good, maybe I'll share my recipe."

He laughs and then leans back in his chair and looks out the windows. "Wow. This view never gets old, does it?"

"No."

Then he looks back at me. "So, you've never told me about your childhood. Your dad, or anything else."

"Yeah, well, it wasn't exactly noteworthy."

"I'd still like to hear about it."

I shake my head. "Nothing to tell." But as I say it, I know that's not true. "At least nothing interesting."

"So, bore me."

"Why?"

"Because it's part of who you are, who you've become, and I want to know you—all of you."

Is he just curious, like a bystander at a train wreck? Or does he really care? I think I know the answer, but . . . "Okay, so it wasn't the ideal childhood, but I've used it—let it shape me. I am successful today because of where I came from. It could have gone the other way. I could be a doormat, like my mother, or a drunk like my father, but I made better choices."

"How did it shape you?"

"It made me strong. It clarified my goals. It helped me define my life philosophy."

Jason leans forward, the candles on the table flickering between us, a million city lights twinkling below, and Sam curled on his chair at the table. "Tell me something I don't know."

I watch him across the table. Do I ruin this perfect moment? Do I tell him? Do I ever tell anyone? Or do I leave the past buried, where it belongs? Before I can even make a decision, my eyes fill with tears and I feel them slipping down my cheeks. I look down at the table, but it's too late, Jason's seen the tears.

"Great," I groan. Then I scoot my chair back, get up, and turn my back to him. I go to the sink in the kitchen and reach for a paper towel to wipe my eyes.

As I stand there, I feel Jason behind me. He puts his hands on my shoulders and turns me around to face him. He says nothing. He just stands there, hands on my shoulders, and waits. I try to pull away, but his hands are heavy—holding me there.

Trapped.

I lift my arms and grab his forearms and fling them off my shoulders. My heart beats like a hammer and I feel a scream rising in my throat. Panic grips me. Words hiss through my clenched teeth. "Get away from me!" Tears blur my vision and I turn to run. I have to get away from him!

"Andee! Wait."

He follows me through the kitchen, to the living room, and catches me at the front door. He doesn't touch me this time—instead, he jumps in front of me and puts his back against the front door, blocking my exit. He holds his hands up in the air so I can see them. "I won't touch you. I'm sorry. But I can't let you go. Not like this."

I shake my head in frustration and my hair whips my face. I try to push past Jason, to push him away from the door, but he's too big, too strong.

"Andee...please."

"Okay! You want to know? I'll tell you!" I step back and realize I'm yelling, but I can't help it. "He raped me! Okay? There! Now you know. You know it all! Now, get out!" I choke back a sob.

He takes a step toward me and I reach out and shove him hard. "Get *out!*"

But he just stands there. "Your father?"

I shove him again. But still he stands there, between the door and me.

"Andee..."

His tone is so gentle it hurts. "Just go."

"Andee, I want to stay. I don't want to leave you alone."

I don't respond. Instead, I turn and walk away. I can't fight him. I lie on the sofa, knees curled to my chest, and tears still falling. Soon, Jason is kneeling in front of me, wiping my tears with a tissue. He sets the box of tissues on the sofa in front of me and leaves it there. He watches me for a few minutes and then sits down on the floor, turns his back to me, and leans against the sofa in front of me. He stretches his long legs out and crosses them at the ankle as though he intends to stay put. Then he turns his head, and over his shoulder he says, "Andee, I love you."

You love me? What is wrong with you? I reach for one of the pillows on the sofa and hold it tight in one arm and reach for a tissue with my other hand. I've kept a lifetime of tears dammed up, and now they flow? *Give me a break.*

By the time the tears stop, I'm exhausted. Just on the fringe of sleep, I reach for Jason and put my hand on his shoulder. He reaches back and takes my hand in his and holds it there, over his shoulder. His thumb rubs my hand—his stroke gentle.

I fall asleep like that, with my hand in Jason's, and him sitting on the floor, leaning against the sofa in front of me.

WHEN I WAKE, I'm covered with a blanket—the angora throw I keep draped across the back of the leather sofa, and Jason is slumped at the other end of the sofa, his head leaning at an odd angle against one of the sofa cushions.

I lift my head, confused for a moment, and then I remember...
Great.

I lift the blanket and move it aside and then get up, without, I hope, waking Jason. Once standing and sure he's still asleep, I walk to the bathroom where I remove my smeared makeup, wash my face, and brush my teeth. Then I return to the living room.

I nudge Jason on the shoulder. "Hey, wake up. You're going to have a terrible neck ache." I nudge him again, "Jason, wake up."

He stirs, rubs the back of one hand across his eyes, and then focuses on me. "Are you okay?"

"I'm fine."

I see the doubt in his expression.

"Really. But you need to get up—you need to go. Get some decent sleep."

"I'll stay—"

"No, Jason. I'm fine. I need some sleep too. I have to work tomorrow. I have meetings."

He stands, turns his head from left to right, and then reaches up for his kinked neck. "Okay. I'll call you in the morning. May I…" He reaches out his arms to give me a hug.

I give him a quick hug and then step back.

He watches me. "Call me if you need anything. Anytime. Or if you want me to come back."

"I'm fine."

He nods and then heads for the door.

Once he's gone, I go to the kitchen and make myself a cup of espresso. I don't want to sleep. Don't want to go where my dreams may take me tonight. I take the espresso and go to my desk. I sit, reach for the mouse, and watch as the computer screen comes to life. I stare at the screen for a long time, my eyelids swollen and heavy.

I sip the espresso as memories play like a horror movie.

The night it happened, my brothers had gone their separate ways—to different friends' houses. We'd all learned not to hang around unless we had to. I went to Stephanie's, but she wasn't there. So I wandered the streets until I was too cold to stay out any longer.

I thought, hoped, I could sneak back into the apartment. Hoped he'd passed out. And I almost made it.

But just before I reached my bedroom, he grabbed me from behind and shoved me into my room…

I shudder. This is the first time I've recalled the details. I mean, why bother, right? But tonight, I can't seem to help it.

I tried to fight him. I screamed for help. Screamed for my mother. But she didn't come. Even though she was in the bedroom next door.

No one came.

In our complex, a scream heard in the middle of the night wasn't uncommon.

I get up from my desk and go to the living room and stand at the window. I look beyond the bay toward Alameda. Toward my past. And I allow the most disturbing memory to take form...

I didn't smell alcohol on my father's breath that night. The words he hissed into my ear weren't slurred nor did he stumble when he pushed me into my room and onto my bed.

He wasn't drunk.

No, the rape took place during one of his attempts at sobriety.

Maybe, somehow, I could have excused it or at least made sense of it in some way if he'd been drunk. But no.

My father may have won the battle that night—I wasn't strong enough to fight him off. But it never happened again. I saw to that. The next time, I was ready for him and told him I'd slit his throat if he touched me. I held a knife at the base of his neck, and...

He believed me.

I took care of myself.

I still do.

I turn from the window, closing the door on the memories. The past is best buried, where it's always been.

And where, from now on, it will stay.

CHAPTER TWENTY-NINE

You do not experience any major results because you are not always ready to receive them.
JEANNE GUYON

*M*atthew

"REMEMBER when we talked about the park, during our first meeting?"

I nod. *Buckle your seat belt, buddy. We're takin' off.* Her question comes as I'm lighting the candle. No time of silence today.

"I left here that day and went there—to the park. I wandered around the botanical gardens for a while and was awed, again, by the different species that thrive there. Then I went to the book-store and bought a couple of horticulture books. I went home and had just picked one up to read when"—she shakes her head —"when Gerard had his heart attack."

I nod again, not wanting to interrupt her thought process.

"Anyway, I had some new thoughts in the park that day—

thoughts I didn't consider again until last night, after coming back to…" She looks down at her lap, then back to me. "After returning from the valley."

I nod for her to continue, but she is silent. I wait and watch as her eyes widen and fill with tears.

She takes a breath. "I'm not like the park, I'm not thriving."

I see the shadow of shame cross her face again, and man, I hate that. I wait for the Spirit's lead and I'm taken back to the question I asked her during our first session. "Jenna, did all the vegetation planted in the park thrive?"

This time, she shakes her head. "No."

"Why not?"

"The conditions were too harsh for some. Through the years, as they replanted the trees of the park, they chose varieties that endured the harsh conditions. Those trees became the overstory —the covering that protected the understory—the smaller, less resilient plants. They needed a protector in order to thrive."

"And you're also living in harsh conditions." I pose it as a statement, not a question.

Her nod is almost imperceptible. "But that's where the metaphor breaks down."

"How?"

"I'm not a plant." She smiles, the first since she arrived tonight, though her lashes are still wet with tears.

I chuckle. "Thanks for the info."

"Any time." She smiles again and then looks down at her lap. She sighs.

She's working hard and I know it's intense for her. The humor gives her a moment of relief.

"It breaks down because I should be thriving regardless of my circumstances. Like I said last time."

"Why?"

"Because…"

She doesn't offer the pat answer she gave last time. Then I see her shoulders droop. "I don't know. I thought it was because I should be content in all circumstances. But maybe, as you suggested, I'm leaning on my own understanding. It seems like everything that used to make sense to me, doesn't make sense anymore. I'm so confused."

"What else isn't making sense?"

"All those verses about taking up your cross."

Jesus' words in Matthew and Luke. Tough words. Vital words.

"For so long, I've thought my circumstances, the harsh conditions, were my cross to bear, you know? But what if"—her brow furrows as she orders her thoughts—"what if I misunderstood?"

Was that hope I saw flash in her eyes?

I reach for my Bible and turn to Matthew 10. "Mind if I read a few verses?" I look at her and she shakes her head—she doesn't mind. I start with verse 38.

"'Anyone who does not take his cross and follow me is not worthy of me.'"

She leans back in her chair. "Exactly. That's one of them."

"Okay, let's back up a few verses—read it in context." I look back to the Bible on my lap, and take a deep breath to steady myself. Because, man, God is working. Here and now. These are the exact verses God led me to after Tess told me about Jenna's mother-in-law. And now, just a few days later… Awesome!

I pick up the passage at verse 34.

"'Do not suppose that I have come to bring peace to the earth. I did not come to bring peace, but a sword. For I have come to turn…'"

Whoa. I look at her and then look back at the Bible and continue.

"'…a man against his father, a daughter against her mother, a daughter-in-law against her mother-in-law—a man's enemies will be the members of his own household.'"

I look up. The tears are running again. I keep reading.

"'Anyone who loves his father or mother more than me is not

worthy of me; anyone who loves his son or daughter more than me is not worthy of me; and anyone who does not take his cross and follow me is not worthy of me. Whoever finds his life will lose it, and whoever loses his life for my sake will find it.'"

I stop there and look back to Jenna.

"What did you hear in that passage?"

She sits very still, tears still streaking her face. "That Jesus didn't come to bring peace. That sometimes He's divisive. That even the members of our family may become our enemies?"

"What else?" I can see her cogs still spinnin' but then she looks away and shrugs.

"I...I don't know."

Give her time.

"But Jesus also said that we're to love our enemies."

I see the confusion on her face. *Lord, confusion isn't of You. Bind the enemy.*

"So...that seems like a contradiction. I mean, I know it isn't, but I don't understand."

I open my mouth to explain, but man, I feel the Spirit holding me back. He's got a bit in my mouth and dude, He's pulling tight on the reins.

So I wait.

Then she whispers, "'Trust in the Lord with all your heart and lean not on your own understanding...'"

"What does that mean to you in this circumstance?"

"To wait. To trust Him. He'll make it clear...in His time. Not mine."

Her wisdom is not her own.

"You okay with that?"

"I am." She looks down at her hands resting in her lap and then back at me. Those big baby blues stare me down. "I don't think I'm ready for more."

I respect her honesty.

I respect her.

After she's gone, I wonder about her harsh conditions. She hasn't shared them with me, but she did admit to them today. Man, I'm bummed for her, but also, in a weird sort of way, I'm also excited. I bow my head and pray. "Lord, infuse her with courage. Surround her. Prepare her. Shield her." In my mind, I see a battalion preparing for war. I let the image inform my prayers. "Strengthen her, Father—Your strength, through Jenna. This is Your battle, Lord."

I pray for a long time.

When I say "Amen," I'm filled with a sense of anticipation.

God is working.

And I'm stoked!

CHAPTER THIRTY

Let me urge you to allow your spirit to be enlarged by grace. If you do
not yield, your spirit will shrivel and hinder the openness you should
have toward everyone...
JEANNE GUYON

ndee

AT 7:12 A.M., I drain another cup of espresso, and get up from my
desk to go shower and dress for the day. I glance at my calendar
first. A lunch meeting, and then my meeting with Brigitte at 3:30.
I need to make a final decision before this afternoon on how I'll
handle the Azul deal with Brigitte.

I stretch, trying to loosen muscles that haven't rested, but
instead spent most of the night hunched over a desk. Just as I turn
to head to the bedroom, my cell phone, sitting on my desk, rings.

I turn back and look at the screen.

Jason.

I listen as the ringtone plays again. And again.

Then I turn and head for the shower.

By the time I reach the bedroom, my home line is ringing.

I grab my robe, walk into the bathroom, shut the door, lock it, and turn the shower on full blast. I stand under the steaming water and clear my mind. Then I refocus on my goals. *Drive determines destiny, Andee. Don't lose sight of what's important to you.* By the time I turn the shower off, I'm clear on what I'll present to Brigitte.

In fact, I'm clear on a lot of things.

After I dry my hair, cover the circles under my eyes with concealer, apply the rest of my makeup, and dress, I return to the office where I turn my cell phone to silent and turn the ringer off on my home phone. When the intercom at my front door buzzes, I ignore it. Instead, I pick up my phone, and call the doorman.

"It's Andee Bell. Please tell whoever is here to see me that I'm working. I won't be accepting visitors."

"Yes, Ms. Bell. I'll relay the message. But the gentleman seems concerned."

"I'm fine. Thank him for his concern."

I hang up.

There is work to do.

At 3:30, I climb the stone steps to the Bouvier residence and ring the bell. A maid answers the door and escorts me up the stairs to Brigitte's home office, where Brigitte greets me.

"Andee, right on time. Please, have a seat." She motions to a round table in the corner of the office. "Coffee or tea?" There is a sterling coffee and tea service set on her antique French desk.

"No, thank you." I pull a file folder and a yellow legal pad from my briefcase and set it on the table in front of me. I'm here for business, not a flippin' tea party. But Brigitte turns to the desk and pours herself a cup of tea and then leans against the desk while sipping said tea.

She lifts her cup and says, "Mariage Fères—a French tea. Just a hint of vanilla."

I look at my watch. "I'm on a tight schedule this afternoon."

She raises a manicured eyebrow and clicks her nails on her china teacup. "Well, I'd hate to keep you."

What is this? She's the one who called the meeting. Her son isn't even cold yet and she wants to socialize? You're a piece of work, lady. I take a pen from my briefcase, and sit poised for business.

"I was under the impression this was urgent?"

She looks at me and her eyes narrow.

I better watch myself. I have a stake in this meeting too. "I want to devote all the time I have this afternoon to your interests."

"Merci, Andee." Her tone is as tight as her smile. "Let's get to it then." She takes a leather portfolio from her desk, reaches for her trademark Montblanc pen, and sits across from me. "I want information on Azul."

"I thought you might." Now we're on the same page. I open the file folder and pull out a sheet of information I've prepared. Before I hand it to her, I say, "There will be a stipulation we need to agree on first."

She eyes the sheet that I've laid facedown on the table.

"Such as?"

I lean back in my chair, and wait until I see her shift in her seat. She is anxious. Perfect.

Time to reveal what I'll require from her before sharing the details of the plan.

CHAPTER THIRTY-ONE

*Do not torment yourself because you do not always feel that you trust
Him or feel His presence with you.*
JEANNE GUYON

enna

AFTER LEAVING MATTHEW'S OFFICE, I check my phone and notice I
have a message from Jason. I listen to the message while sitting in
the cab.

"Hey, Jenna..." He sounds tired. "I know you have enough on
your plate right now, but I wonder if you'd have time to grab a
cup of coffee. I could use a listening ear. Call me." I glance at my
watch and call him back. He answers on the first ring.

"Jenna..."

"Hi, what's up? Are you okay?"

He hesitates. "Yeah, just tired and puzzled. I could use a female
perspective."

"Okay, do you have time to meet now? I'm out—just leaving an appointment."

"Sure. Starbucks on Fillmore?"

"Okay, I'll see you there in fifteen minutes."

"Thanks, Jen."

I hang up. Is it Andee that Jason wants to talk about? I lean forward and tell the driver to drop me on Fillmore rather than at the house.

As the cab flies over the city hills, I think about Jason. Five years older than I, Jason was on the cusp of his teens when our mother died. He entered high school just a year later. He was a kind big brother and I adored him, but by the time I reached high school, he was off to college. Our lives didn't intersect much. It wasn't until we reached adulthood that we became friends.

Jason is comfortable with himself in a way I've never experienced. He was neither drawn nor intimidated by the Bouvier wealth or affluence, as I was. He enjoys simplicity, but seems to fit in wherever he is. His group of friends is a diverse bunch.

We grew up attending a small Baptist church in Napa. My parents were married there, we were both dedicated there, and my mother's memorial service was held there. Jason is still involved and spends most weekends in the valley just so he can attend church.

I miss the little church—the hymns, communion, and the fellowship of other believers. I still attend with Jason, when I can, but Brigitte never approved of the church. Or any church for that matter.

It occurs to me that church is just one more thing I've sacrificed for Brigitte.

But Jason and I were both set on a solid foundation at the little Baptist church—my foundation in Christ has sustained me through adulthood and through the trials of life. It has done the same for Jason. So, even though I heard the fatigue in his voice, know he's still grieving Gerard, as am I, I know he will be okay.

It is more difficult, for some reason, to claim that same knowledge for myself.

As the cab pulls up to the Starbucks, I whisper another prayer for Jason. He is waiting for me on the sidewalk. I get out and reach to give him a hug. I notice the bags under his eyes and the way his jaw is set. I pull back from him. "You look beat."

"It was a long night. C'mon, I'll buy you a cup of coffee."

We walk into Starbucks and Jason motions to an empty table in a corner. I go sit at the table while he gets our coffee. While I wait, I savor the rich aroma of coffee and relax to the hum of people chatting.

When Jason returns, he sets a cup in front of me and sits across from me.

"How are you, Jen?"

Ever the big brother. "I thought we were here to talk about you."

"We are. But first, I want to know that you're okay. Or at least as okay as you can be under the circumstances."

"I'm okay. It's hard. There are so many unanswered questions about the future, but"—I shrug—"it will all fall into place, right?"

"Right."

"So, what's going on?"

Jason sighs and his shoulders slump. "It's Andee."

"I wondered."

"I had dinner with her last night and she shared something from her past. A trauma she experienced. I don't think she'd ever talked about it. I don't know that she's ever told anyone else." He picks up his cup and takes a swallow of his coffee. "Jen, it was intense."

"How'd you handle it with her?"

He tells me about the rest of the evening, how she fell asleep, and that she asked him to leave once she woke.

"She was in good hands, Jason. I can't think of anything else you could have done."

"Yeah, I actually felt like maybe we formed a bond through it, you know? I've never seen her that vulnerable and I hoped she could experience God's love and mercy through me. But…"

"But?"

"When I called her this morning, she didn't answer. I left messages on both her cell phone and home line. Then I got concerned, so I went to her building, but she wouldn't see me."

"Sounds like she let her guard down and maybe regrets it now."

"Yeah, but why?"

"I don't know."

He leans an elbow on the table and rests his forehead in his hand. Then he looks back at me, "Are you sure I didn't blow it somehow?"

God, grant me wisdom. But I don't sense His lead. Instead, I just say what comes to mind. "I don't think it's about you, Jason. If she's waited this long to tell someone, then, I don't know, maybe the wound is just too deep. Too hard for her to deal with." I shrug. "I'm just guessing."

He nods. "I just hoped I could help. I've known there was something under the surface, you know? I hoped that if she'd let me in…"

"Maybe you just need to give her time. Drop her a note or text and tell her you're available when she's ready."

"Yeah, maybe." He leans back in his chair and sighs. "Thanks."

We chat awhile longer and then Jason asks if I've talked to Dad.

"He's called a few times since Gerard's service. Why?"

"I don't know—he seems distracted. Just wondered if he's said anything to you?"

I shake my head. "No, he hasn't."

"Maybe it's nothing."

As we stand to leave, Jason puts a hand on my shoulder. "You mentioned the future. Have you made any plans?"

Now it's my turn to sigh. "No. I'm waiting on Brigitte. We need to talk through Gerard's trust. Hopefully, that will happen in the next few days. I need to know how to plan, financially, and otherwise."

"What do you mean financially? Aren't you set?"

I shrug. "I don't know for sure. You know, Gerard received a good salary from Domaine de la Bouvier, but nothing like what you might imagine considering our lifestyle. Keeping up with Brigitte hasn't been easy. Gerard grew up with extravagance and that's how he lived his adult life. He always knew that one day, when Brigitte was gone, the company and her vast estate would go to him."

"Gerard did enjoy the finer things in life."

"Our personal accounts are almost empty. Just before he died, he gave me an incredible gift—did he tell you about it?"

It's Jason's turn to nod and there's a sparkle in his eyes. "The prayer chapel? He showed it to me the weekend we were in Napa with the two of you. It's beautiful."

"It is beautiful and it was so thoughtful, but it was expensive. On top of that, I'd lost the diamond out of my wedding ring—the Bouvier heirloom diamond. And after checking our accounts, I realized that rather than reporting the loss to the insurance company, he replaced it with our personal funds. The diamond was under Brigitte's policy, and I'm sure Gerard didn't want to tell her."

"Speaking of Brigitte, you won't stay with her, will you?"

"Why do you say that?"

"Why would you stay with her?"

"Because Gerard asked me to take care of her if anything ever happened to him. I feel responsible. Plus, it's hard to explain, but Brigitte's been a significant part of my life since I was thirteen years old. I can't just walk away. She's alone now. I don't want to stay, but... I don't know what else to do."

We get to the door and Jason holds it open for me. Once we're outside, he turns and faces me, his expression serious. "Jen, she's not your responsibility. She..." He shakes his head. "Never mind. You need to think of yourself now. Make a wise choice for yourself. Promise?"

"That sounds so selfish."

"Selfish? Taking care of yourself isn't selfish, Jen. It's stewardship—it's taking care of the life God's given you."

His words are new to me—something I've never considered. I nod, but say nothing. I'll have to think through what he's said.

He gives me a hug. "I'm here for you—for anything you need. And so is Dad. You know that, right?"

"Right. Thanks, Jason. You know, Andee's a lucky woman, whether she recognizes it or not."

"Thanks."

Once Jason and I part, I decide to walk the rest of the way home. As I do, I consider Jason's thoughts about Brigitte. He may not see that I'm responsible for her, but I feel a deep sense of responsibility. *Is my feeling of responsibility from You, Lord?*

I wait, hoping I'll get a sense from God. An answer maybe. But just like in Starbucks when I prayed for wisdom, I hear nothing from God. That's okay. I don't believe in the vending machine version of God—I put in a request and He spits out an answer. It doesn't work that way. Instead, as I told Matthew earlier, I believe He'll reveal Himself in time—His time.

But still, all I've heard is silence. And it isn't the silence between two souls so comfortable with one another that words aren't necessary.

No.

This silence is different.

I twist the band on my left ring finger as I walk—my reminder that whether I sense Him or not, He is present. He is my Companion, my Protector, my Husband.

I shift my thoughts to Andee and say a silent prayer for her—for comfort and healing. God knows her needs. I wonder about e-mailing her again. Or rather, I wonder about Lightseeker e-mailing her again. Or do I wait? See if she contacts me? *What should I do, Lord?*

But I receive no answer. The silence echoes in my soul like the tapping of my heels on the concrete sidewalk.

God isn't speaking, it seems.

I ignore the ripple of fear the ongoing silence evokes.

CHAPTER THIRTY-TWO

The things you assume to be your virtues, God may see as faults.
JEANNE GUYON

rigitte

As SOON AS Andee is gone, she returns to her desk and picks up the phone. She dials information and asks for the listing she wants. She waits, tapping her pen on the edge of her desk, while the operator searches for the number. It doesn't take long.

"Thank you," she says, and then hangs up and dials the number she's been given.

"Kelly Whitmore, please. This is Brigitte Bouvier calling." She reaches for a notepad.

"This is Kelly."

"Hello, Kelly, how are you?"

"Brigitte, I'm well, thank you. But I was so sorry to hear of your loss."

"Yes, it's a difficult time, as you know. How long has your father been gone now?" She taps her pen against the desk again. The pleasantries require such patience.

"Almost six months."

"Such a loss. Duke was a good man. He is missed in the valley, as I'm sure you know."

"Yes, just as Gerard will be missed. What can I do for you, Brigitte?"

She clears her throat. "Kelly, I have a business deal I'd like to discuss with you. I'd like to meet at your earliest convenience. I'd prefer we speak in person. I'm happy to come to your office."

"Well, you've piqued my curiosity. How about tomorrow morning at 9:15?"

She jots the time on her notepad. "Perfect, I'll see you then. Merci, Kelly."

AT 9:00 A.M. she parks her Bentley Continental outside the offices of Whitmore and Whitmore Wines. Though Kelly is young —midthirties, she'd guess—she's earned a reputation as a strong businesswoman. She was running Whitmore and Whitmore long before Duke died and is proving she'll far exceed her father's vision for the business.

The timing of this meeting is fortuitous. Duke never would have agreed to the offer she's about to make.

She reaches to the passenger seat for her Chanel Black Caviar briefcase and exits her car. She enters the building through the large etched-glass front doors and stops at the reception desk.

"Brigitte Bouvier for Kelly Whitmore." She brushes invisible lint from her suit jacket as she waits.

"Brigitte." Kelly extends her hand.

"Hello, Kelly. Nice to see you again." She notices Kelly's

designer suit and the large diamond on her right hand. "You're looking well."

They exchange the usual small talk on the way to Kelly's office. But once inside, with the door closed, the tone changes.

Kelly sits behind her large glass and chrome desk, offering Brigitte a seat opposite her. Her choice is intentional, Brigitte assumes. And she respects her for it. She is young, bold, and she holds the power here. She won't let Brigitte forget it. Kelly reminds her of herself.

"You said you have a deal you'd like to discuss?"

"I do. It's come to my attention that you're holding a demand note for Azul." She sees a flicker of surprise in Kelly's eyes, but Kelly is quick to conceal it.

"How did you happen upon that information?"

"Does it matter?" There's no reason to reveal her source. That was Andee's stipulation—a wise one, of course.

"No, I don't suppose it does."

"I'd like to buy the note. I'm prepared to offer you a generous return, of course."

Kelly swivels her chair and opens the credenza behind her desk. She pulls out a file folder, turns back to Brigitte, and opens the file. "You're aware of the amount owed?"

"I am."

"What kind of return are we talking about?"

"I'll pay one hundred and fifty percent of the amount currently owed."

Kelly nods. "Are you also aware that Bill Durand says my father cancelled this note? Told him he'd tear it up?"

"I'd heard that." How foolish Durand had been, not to have that cancellation in writing and witnessed.

"But there is no record of that discussion, nor, as you can see, was the note ever destroyed. Durand is lying."

"Obviously."

Kelly leans back in her chair and eyes Brigitte. She smiles and then laughs. "I'd love to know why you want it, but I won't ask. That's your business."

"Oui. And I'd like your word that this transaction will remain anonymous. If you accept, I'll have my attorney contact you to take care of the details."

Kelly nods, closes the file, and stands. She reaches across her desk to shake Brigitte's hand. "Your secret is safe with me. I accept your offer."

"You'd be foolish not to." Brigitte stands and takes her hand.

"I'm no fool, Mrs. Bouvier."

"No, you've proven that. In fact"—she looks Kelly up and down —"you remind me a bit of myself."

"Thank you. I consider that a high compliment."

"As you should."

They laugh together as Kelly walks her to the door.

She walks to her car, satisfaction knit into a tight smile. Soon, she will implement the next phase of her plan. Her meeting with Andee yesterday proved fruitful. She was glad to see that Andee didn't allow her personal relationship with Jason to interfere with business.

She considers again the stipulation Andee demanded. Complete anonymity. As Andee reminded her, it is in both their best interests. They each know too much. Brigitte has a flash of doubt. Did she reveal too much to Andee with her call just after Gerard's passing? Will Andee use her knowledge against her? No. That is the brilliance of Andee's plan—neither of them will reveal the details because both have too much to lose.

It's perfect. Her respect for Andee has grown over the last twenty-four hours. She lives up to her philosophy—she doesn't let anything or anyone stand in the way of her goals—not even her relationship with Jason Durand.

The only Durand she'll have to deal with now is Jenna. And this little business transaction ensures that Jenna Durand Bouvier will remain a Bouvier.

What choice will she have?

The end, as the Americans are so fond of saying, justifies the means.

Her laughter fills the interior of the Bentley as she pulls out of the parking lot.

CHAPTER THIRTY-THREE

The external actions of a person's life proceed from the inward man.
When you live in your old self, you have a strong will and many desires,
with ups and downs of all sorts.
JEANNE GUYON

ndee

I GUN the Porsche around the final curves in the road before turning off on the winding drive that leads to Azul. As I pull into a parking space, I reach for the radio and turn off the talk of KGO that filled the void in the car, and my mind, as I drove.

I called Bill last night and set this appointment, making sure it was set for a time Jason wouldn't be at the winery. All I revealed to Bill was that I had news after speaking with Kelly Whitmore's attorney.

Sorry, Bill, the news isn't good.

I could have delivered the news over the phone, but a personal visit makes me look good. Facts are facts.

I reach for my briefcase, get out of the car, and set the alarm.

I take a deep breath to clear my mind. *Don't overthink this, Andee. It's business. That's all. If Bill had been wiser in his business dealings, this wouldn't be happening. You're just delivering news of his consequences.*

Anyway, I remind myself, I don't know what Brigitte will do with the demand note. Maybe she'll leave well enough alone. Maybe she's just bailing out a family friend. *Yeah, right.*

As I walk toward the winery offices, I run through the plan one more time. There's just one risk: Brigitte. Can I trust her? No. But I have some collateral—she doesn't want her involvement known at this point either.

We'll see...

In any event, I don't work for Azul. I took nothing from them in return for my services. Just listened to Bill and, as far as he's concerned, made a helpful phone call to check out the situation.

I pull open the heavy oak door of the winery tasting room, take an immediate left, and follow a hallway that opens into the winery offices. Bill stands at a coffeepot in the reception area, pouring himself a cup of coffee.

"Andee, good to see you." He sets his cup down and reaches to shake my hand. "May I offer you a cup?"

I look at the weak brew and shake my head. "No, thanks." Has he spoken to Jason in the last thirty-six hours? Does he know? I put the thought out of my mind.

"Well, then, follow me and we'll have a seat in my office."

"Great."

We round a corner and enter Bill's office, where he motions me to a brown distressed-leather chair. He sits on the matching sofa. In front of the corner arrangement is a large cowhide-covered ottoman scattered with wine magazines. The office's decor is what I expected: warm, comfortable, relaxed. Just like Bill. Just like Jason.

I scoot forward in the large chair. *Don't get comfortable, Andee.*

This isn't a social call. "Well, Bill, I'm afraid I have some potentially bad news."

"I was afraid of that." He leans forward, elbows on his knees.

"I spoke with the Whitmore's attorney, as I told you on the phone, and he told me that sometime within the last week, Kelly sold your note to an anonymous investor who offered her substantially more than the value of the note."

He takes in the information, nods. "So what does that mean for Azul?"

"I don't know for sure. That's why I said it's potentially bad news. It could mean that whoever bought the note will demand payment immediately. If you can't pay, then they will ultimately force Azul into bankruptcy."

He shakes his head.

"Or maybe whoever purchased the note just wants to protect you—help you out. If Kelly made it known that she was holding such a note, then it's possible someone you know stepped forward on your behalf and wants to remain anonymous."

"Can't think who'd do something like that. But I suppose it's possible."

"Time will tell."

"That it will." He leans back. He seems relaxed considering the information he's just heard. "It's all in God's hands."

God's hands? Actually, it's in Brigitte's hands. I just nod. "Sorry I couldn't be more help, Bill."

"Andee, you did what you could and I appreciate it."

I stand to leave, making the excuse that I have another meeting to get to.

Bill stands and shakes my hand again. "Thanks again, Andee. Hope to see you soon."

Not likely.

After the meeting with Bill, I drive back to the city and go straight to the studio, where I tape several radio segments. From the studio, I head over to Silicon Valley for a meeting. After that meeting, I return calls, including one to a cable producer interested in producing the *Andee Bell Show*. Once back at my office, I make a long list of things that need my attention in the next few weeks: Web site revamp, manuscript edits, book tour, promotional events, media requests. The list goes on and on.

I prioritize and determine what I need to do myself, and what I can pass off to Cassidy. I look at the list again and add: hire a publicist and call a real estate broker.

It's time I build my staff and invest in an office building.

I have a busy year ahead of me.

It has to be.

I open my e-mail. Cass has already gone through the andee@andeebell.com folder and responded to what she could. The remainder I'll deal with. Then I open my personal e-mail folder and see an e-mail from Jason.

"Well, I might as well get this over with." Sam, who's curled himself around my desk lamp, looks at me and hisses.

I open Jason's e-mail and read:

Dear Andee,

I'm concerned about you. I understand if you need some space. Know that I love you and I'm here for you when you're ready.

Jason

I don't let myself think or feel. I just act.

Dear Jason,

My intent isn't to hurt you, but I told you in the beginning that I don't have time for personal relationships and I'm not being fair to either of us. I need to remain focused on my goals and give full attention to my business endeavors.

I'm sorry. I wish you well . . .

Andee

Jason deserves more than that. But that's all I can give him.

"He'll get over it," I say to Sam. "And so will you."

With that done, I dive into work. I work through the afternoon and into the evening. I suffocate any thought or feeling that surfaces with work.

I won't let up.

I can't let up.

CHAPTER THIRTY-FOUR

Remember the present moment is where we meet God.
JEANNE GUYON

*J*enna

I WAKE WITH A START. Heartbeat pounding in my ears. The room is
still dark. I turn my head and glance at the clock next to my bed:
4:13 a.m. Something is wrong, but I can't recall what it is, though I
feel the weight of it sitting on my chest. Groggy, I sit up and reach
for the bedside lamp.

All is silent.

And then I remember.

I lean back against my pillow, stare at the ceiling, and twist the
band on my left ring finger. God, my present companion for so
many years, is silent. I'm alone. Abandoned. But as soon as that
thought enters my consciousness, I discard it. "You are here,

whether I sense You or not, whether I hear You or not. You are always with me. You will never forsake me."

As I whisper my prayer, my assurance, tears slip down my cheeks.

The ache of loneliness is a constant companion now.

I reach for the Bible on my nightstand and turn to familiar passages of comfort. But the words are empty, meaningless. I put the Bible down and cry out. *Oh Lord, how I long to hear from You— long for Your embrace. Your comfort. I don't understand... Help me to walk in faith, to trust You. Make my path straight, Lord. Lead me. I am lost.*

I allow my mind to wander—to think ahead. Although Gerard assured me through the years that he'd provided for me in his trust, I don't know that he told me the truth. Where confronting Brigitte was concerned, I could never trust Gerard to stand up for me, and any change he made in his trust would have resulted in a confrontation.

A breeze of unease stirs.

Brigitte will provide for me, I'm certain. But at what cost?

"You won't stay with her, right?"

Jason's words dig deep. Do I have a choice? I can't even begin to imagine leaving. Where would I go? What would I do? What would she do if I tried to leave?

Anxiety moves in like a nagging neighbor. Pestering and provoking.

There is no rest.

I cannot look ahead. Instead, I must trust God moment by moment.

I throw back the covers and get out of bed. As I stand, a wave of nausea swells, forcing me to sit back on the edge of the bed. I take deep breaths, willing it to pass. With each breath, my sense of dread deepens. The infection. *Oh, Lord, will it never end?*

I accept the consequences of my actions. But I'm tired of fighting. I lie back down and think about the surgery, and for the first time in many months, a new thought occurs to me. What if the surgery had been successful? What if I'd come out of it looking, in my eyes, in Brigitte's eyes, perfect? That is, after all, what I was striving for, wasn't it?

Perfection in Brigitte's eyes? I shake my head and say for at least the hundredth time, "Oh Lord, I'm so sorry."

But if the surgery had been successful, would Brigitte have been pleased? Would I have then been perfect in her eyes? No, of course not. She is impossible to please. Again, I think of Andee's words the morning of the brunch: "If you can't win, why try?"

Why, indeed?

Is the infection God's punishment? No. Instead, He's used the natural consequences and worked them for good. This is new thinking. I get out of bed again, my movements slow this time, and I go to the vanity and sit on the stool and look in the mirror. For the first time, I see the scar as a gift—a reminder of the lessons God is weaving in me. He is stripping me of the lies I've believed and replacing them with His truth.

There is no punishment.

No condemnation.

Only grace.

I run my index finger along the scar and look at myself in the mirror again. This morning, for the first time since the surgery that left the scar on my jawline, I don't see the scar. Instead, I see me—God's creation. The scar isn't important. It doesn't define me. It isn't who I am. "Thank You." I whisper.

God is still silent, but He is present. I can find Him, I determine, His goodness, in all things, if I just look.

When I stand, the nausea returns with a force that drives me to the bathroom and to my knees. As my stomach empties and I gasp for breath, I beg for mercy. "No more, Lord. No more, please…" I lie on the bathroom floor, my face against cold tile. Where is the good in this?

Ah, how fleeting my determination.

After awhile, I get off the floor, brush my teeth, and shower.

I step into the spacious enclosure, sit on the granite bench, and let the hot water wash over me until I feel well enough to stand. After my shower, I wrap myself in my robe, run a comb through my wet hair, and then go sit at my desk in the alcove. I check my e-mail and then open my blog and begin a new post.

> Loneliness calls my name. It woos me to believe nothing can fill the cavernous void in my soul. Tendrils of fear wrap around my heart. But I pry fear loose and toss it aside. For I've known perfect love and though my senses betray me, love remains. So I wait. I listen. Confident I will hear the voice of my Lover again.

> There is no fear in perfect love . . .

I write to reassure myself.

I write to remind myself of truth.

I write because I've learned, I am not alone in my feelings. Once I publish the post, others will respond. They, too, feel the pull. The longings. They hear the hisses of the enemy.

Together, we stand.

I lean back in my seat, fingers resting on the keyboard. Fatigue batters me. I close my eyes and whisper a prayer for all those who wake alone this morning—those who wake sick, and tired. I ask God for comfort and strength for each of them, and for myself.

Then I finish the blog and publish it.

I get up from the desk and walk back to my bed. I slip out of my robe, drape it across the foot of the bed, and climb between the sheets. I pull the blanket to my chin and drift into sleep.

CHAPTER THIRTY-FIVE

Offenses will happen while we live in the flesh.
JEANNE GUYON

rigitte

SHE LOOKS at the URL Hannah's written on a scrap of paper, types it into her search engine, and begins to read.

The more she reads, the more her anger flares.

She reads for almost an hour before slamming the lid of her laptop closed. "That little, traitorous…" She picks up the phone and presses the intercom to the kitchen. "Hannah, come back to my office. Now!"

She paces in front of her desk while she waits for Hannah. "What is taking her so long?"

When Hannah taps on her door, she opens it and pulls Hannah inside. "I want everything. I want her e-mails. I want every document on her computer. Do you understand? And I want it now!"

"But Madame—"

"No buts, Hannah. If you want to keep your job, you'll deliver what I need."

"Fine, Madame. I will hire someone. I don't have the knowledge. As I told you, I got this information because she left her computer on while she slept. If I hadn't taken her coffee upstairs, and—"

"Do whatever it takes, and do it now!"

"Yes, Madame."

"Go!"

After Hannah's gone, she returns to her laptop and rereads some of her posts. But the posts, she suspects, are just the beginning of her hidden life. She types www.illumar.me into the search bar. Once the blog has loaded, she scans the list of comments. Another search leads to other links including a link to *Urbanity*. The magazine? She clicks on the link and reads of the contest *Urbanity*'s holding to unveil the identity of the blogger who calls herself Lightseeker.

Again, she slams the laptop shut. Her heels wear a path in the carpet in front of her desk as she rehearses what she'll say to Jenna. "Oh, no, you don't! You will not make a mockery of my name! Isn't it enough that I must endure the humiliation of your infertility, along with the shame of that hideous scar across your face?"

She spits the words as if Jenna were standing in front of her.

But then something occurs to her and she quiets. *Of course Jenna won't make a mockery of her name. She can see to that. Just as she's always seen to things with Jenna.* She returns to her desk and reaches for a notepad. She will make a plan. Wait for complete access to Jenna's computer. Wait to see what else reveals itself.

No, she won't confront Jenna. Not yet.

She will wait.

She thinks again of Azul—and smiles. Ah yes, Jenna will do as she instructs. There is no doubt. She's seen to that. She will reveal all to Jenna, when the time is right.

And she will know when the time is exactly right.

Until then, a couple of days away will be best. She'll go to the valley, give Jenna a little space, freedom to roam as she's prone to do, and Hannah some time to complete her task.

CHAPTER THIRTY-SIX

I love you in the love of the one who humbled Himself on account of love.
JEANNE GUYON

$\mathcal{M}$atthew

SATURDAY MORNING, I wake and reach for Tess, but then remember she's gone. A long work weekend in the fashion capital, New York City. She asked me to go with her this time, but funds are tight so we decided against it.

I sit up in bed, run a hand through my hair, and then feel the scruff on my face and neck. But hey, it's a weekend and Tess is gone, so there's no need to shave. "Bonus!" I get out of bed, grab my favorite flannel out of the closet, throw it on over my T-shirt and boxers, and then grab a pair of socks. I pad my way to the kitchen, where I . . . well, you know the routine.

Once I'm settled in my recliner, I bend, put the socks on, and then lean back and sip my brew. "Mmm . . . good stuff." I reach for my cell phone and text Tess:

Good morning, gorgeous! Or should I say good afternoon?
Slept late here—nothing worth waking up for when you're
gone. Lovin' you, always.

Then I reach for the printed blog and begin reading. Jenna's
words continue to resonate—I feel her longings, her need for
God. Man, her passion equals my own. I've even started
commenting on her blog. Sending my own thoughts her way. At
first, I hoped she'd reveal herself to me. But she hasn't.

Instead, we're now also connecting via e-mail. She knows it's
me, but she doesn't know that I know it's her. Or maybe she does
know and I don't know. But the conversations back and forth are
rich. And don't worry, I've shared them with Tess, though, I
haven't revealed that I know Lightseeker.

But I have shared that with Tim.

In fact, I've talked my relationship with Jenna up and down
and inside out with Tim. Even submitted to his authority and
asked if I need to step back, refer her to another spiritual director.
But we both feel clear on the boundaries of the relationship and if
Tim thought there was an issue, dude, believe you me, he'd tell
me. The man does not hold back. It's what I like best about him.

Anyway, this morning, as I read of Lightseeker's loneliness and
her longings for God, my heart hurts for her. Maybe she's going
through what St. John of the Cross made known as a *dark night of
the soul*. A season when God is silent. A time when it's easy to
believe He's left you altogether. But He never leaves. That's a
promise. And she knows it.

I respect her choice to walk in faith. But I continue to pray
for her. She's lost so much—her health, her looks—at least in
her mind—and now her husband. And I have to wonder if she
isn't losing herself in her relationship with her mother-in-law.
One of the things I tell my counseling clients is that when you
try to please others, you will always fail and you will always lose
yourself. Dude. Those aren't good odds. I don't often use the

word *always*. But that's how much I believe the truth of that statement.

And unless Jenna makes some changes, I fear she will lose herself and the beautiful purpose God intends for her.

Now she's also lost that sweet communion with God. At least for a time.

How much more, Lord? I trust God's work in Jenna's life. But it can be hard to watch. Though, I know—and I mean I *really* know —that God will work all for good in her life because she loves Him and is called according to His purpose. That's just truth.

As an observer of her life, that God-given purpose seems so clear. All you have to do is read the way she interacts with her readers—she loves them with a love from above. She cares about them. And she walks alongside them, sharing her heart, her aches, her journey.

Well, okay, she sort of does. It's all under a pseudonym. But I'm praying that changes too. That she will claim who she is as God's child.

I slam back the rest of my coffee and then go and pour myself cup number two. I drink it while walking laps around the kitchen and living room. I need to burn some energy. I take my cup, rinse it, and put it in the dishwasher, because I'm nothing if I'm not well trained. Then I peel off the flannel and head for the shower.

When I make my way outside, the day is gray and cold. I walk several blocks and then decide it's the perfect day for a game of bus roulette. So I catch the first bus I see. I don't look where it's going. I just hop on for the ride and I'll hop off when something looks good. I've found some cool places this way. All it requires is a spirit of adventure—no problem there—a little time, and a few bucks in my pocket.

The bus winds its way through the city streets until we hit Columbus. I sit through several stops until we come into North Beach. *Good grub in North Beach,* I think. So I get off. As I do, I'm greeted by the scent of garlic and baking bread. "Mamma mia!

That smells good!" I say to a passerby. I walk a block before I find what looks like the perfect piece of pizza pie. I pat my stomach as I eat. "What Tess doesn't know…" I say with my mouth full.

After the pizza, I hop back on another bus. This one is almost empty. I sit across the aisle from the one guy on the bus. "Hey, how's it going?"

He looks at me, gets up, and moves to another seat.

Okay, I can take a hint.

After awhile, the route the bus takes begins to look familiar. We're heading toward the Pacific on Lincoln. Soon, I see signs for Golden Gate Park. Cool. I hop off at the stop near the botanical gardens and decide I'll cut through the gardens and head for the Japanese Tea Garden to see if Skye's playing today. If not, some of those little tea cookies will make a decent dessert.

It's turning out to be a multicultural day. Maybe I'll have dinner in Chinatown. "Great idea, buddy." I'd high-five myself if I could. I make my way through the garden, seeing it through different eyes this time—Jenna's eyes. I notice odd little plants and even stop and read a few placards. I look up at the towering trees, the overstory, as she calls them, and see them now as the protectors of the garden.

I walk around the large meadow and exit on the other side of the gardens. I cross the street and round the corner to the tea garden. No Skye. Bummer. Oh well, cookies it is. As I head for the entrance, a cab pulls up to the curb and a woman gets out. A familiar woman. I watch as Jenna stands on the sidewalk and looks up at the trees towering overhead. I see her shoulders rise as she takes a deep breath and then lower as she seems to relax.

"Hey, dude."

She looks toward me and gives me one of those dazzlers of hers and waves. I wait as she makes her way to me. "I should have known I'd run into you here." I come alongside her, put an arm around her shoulders, and give her a quick squeeze.

"What are you doing here?" She looks around. "Is Tess with you?"

"Nah, she's at a fashion thing in New York and I, well, have I ever told you about bus roulette? You'll have to try it sometime."

She shakes her head and laughs. "I can only imagine."

"So may I buy you a cup of tea?"

She doesn't hesitate. "Sure, if I can show you my favorite bench."

"Bench?"

She nods as she laughs. "C'mon."

Oh man, it's good to hear her laugh. To sense her joy even in the midst of the pain she's experiencing. It's one of the things I respect most about her. Her joy is in Him, not her circumstances. I feel that familiar soul connect as we head into the garden.

"There it is." She points to a bench facing the pond. "Run, quick, grab it before someone else does! Go!"

She pushes me forward and I jog to the bench and stake our claim. I lean back, stretch my legs out, cross them at the ankle, and rest one arm across the back of the bench. She comes and sits at the other end of the bench and seems to relax. I look out at the pond. "Cool. Nice view."

"It's the best view."

"You're the expert." We sit in companionable silence for a couple of minutes. But then, hey, why be silent when you can talk, right? "So what brought you here today?"

She shrugs. "I had the day to myself, which is unusual. I didn't feel too well this morning, so I went back to bed. When I woke, one of the staff…"

She looks at me and seems to cringe. Embarrassed, I think.

"Hey, I could have staff too, if I wanted. But who wants pesky people around all the time doing your chores for you, right?"

She laughs again. "Right. Anyway, Hannah told me that my mother-in-law had decided to go to the valley for a couple of days. So I'm free!"

"Are you usually bound and gagged?"

She smiles at my joke and then shrugs. "It feels that way sometimes."

"Why?"

She looks out across the pond and seems to weigh her words. "My mother-in-law can be…challenging, I guess."

"Challenging?"

She is quiet and keeps looking at the pond. Then she turns on the bench so she's facing me and her eyes tell the story. "I don't . . . talk about it . . . much. I mean, just to Skye."

"What does Skye say?"

"Skye says she's abusive…emotionally, you know?"

I nod. "What do you say?"

She cocks her head to one side. "Are you playing counselor now?"

I hold up my hands. "Nope. Not me." Then I'm serious. "We're just two friends sitting on a bench having a conversation about life. I don't mean to press you. But, I care."

"You're not pressing me." She sighs. "It's just a hard topic. I feel like I betray her when I talk about her."

"Well, maybe instead you could just talk about your feelings— how you feel when you're with her."

"I feel"—she looks up at the huge eucalyptus and cypress trees swaying above—"unprotected. Nonexistent. Extinct."

"Dude… I whisper.

She looks at me again and I see the tears swimming in her eyes. "A little crazy, huh?"

I shake my head. "No, not crazy. Intense."

She laughs through her tears. "Maybe I need a counselor instead of a spiritual director."

"Maybe. How long have you felt like that?"

She looks back out and I watch her eyes track with the swans on the other side of the pond.

"It feels like forever. Brigitte came into my life when I was just thirteen. She filled a void for me, I think, after my mother died. It's hard because sometimes she seems so loving and thoughtful. She seems to care, but then . . . she changes. She'll say something and then deny it. I don't know. I just feel crazy most of the time."

"Yeah, there's a term for that. It's called crazy-making."

"Really?"

"Yep. You know, I can give you the name of a counselor, a colleague of mine." I hold up my hand. "Not because you're crazy. You're not. But he could help you navigate the relationship. If you're interested..."

"Okay, maybe."

As we sit there, a young family walks the path and stops in front of us. The dad bends and takes the hand of his little girl, she's maybe three or four, and she's a looker—all auburn curls, just like Tess. The dad points to something in the water and she squeals and laughs.

I watch the scene and feel the familiar longing, then I feel Jenna's eyes on me. I look at her and try to smile but fail.

"You'd make a great dad, Matthew."

"Thanks."

"Do you and Tess plan—" Her eyes go wide. "Oh, I'm so sorry, I know better than to ask that kind of question."

I look at her and reach for her shoulder and give it a squeeze. "Nah, it's fine." I clear my throat. "I'd like to have kids—dreamt of it for years—but it's not Tess's dream." I shrug. "So, whaddya gonna do, right?"

She nods.

"What about you? You and Gerard never had children?"

"No. We spent a lot of years trying. But...we couldn't. We maybe would have adopted, but then I had the surgery and... Anyway, I don't think his mother would have approved. Now, it's too late."

We sit in silence for a few minutes and watch the family in

front of us, each feeling our own pain. But there's something comforting about feeling it together.

Maybe too comforting.

I jump to my feet and look down at her. "Hey, how about that tea?"

CHAPTER THIRTY-SEVEN

So God imparts His grace both through believers and between them.
Their one common center is God.

JEANNE GUYON

enna

"LISTEN…"

Matthew leans forward. "What?"

I lift my finger to my lips, "Shh…" I point in the direction of the garden entrance.

Matthew turns his head toward the entrance then turns back to me. "Skye."

We each finish our tea and set our cups down, then Matthew grabs the last almond cookies and puts them in the pocket of his jacket. His third order of cookies, I might add.

"Mmm… A little lint with your cookies is always good."

He grins at me. "Exactly."

We stand and he follows me out the exit. Skye sits with her dulcimer under her usual tree. We stand, shoulder to shoulder, with the small crowd that's gathered and listen to her play. I reach for my jacket and pull it close as the gray afternoon threatens rain.

Soon, the first drops fall and the crowd scatters. I reach into my bag and pull out my cell phone and a compact umbrella. I hand the umbrella to Matthew and motion for him to cover Skye and her dulcimer. "I'll call a cab. Want a ride?"

"Sure."

"Ask Skye if she needs a ride. She can join us."

Matthew takes the umbrella and holds it over Skye as she finishes playing her last song. I pull up the hood of my jacket and scroll through the contacts on my phone until I find Ahsan's number.

"Ahsan, it's Jenna Bouvier. Are you anywhere near the park?"

He tells me he just dropped his last fare and can be here in less than ten minutes.

"Perfect. We're at the tea garden. Thanks, Ahsan."

I hang up and join Skye and Matthew under the umbrella. Rain pelts us as we help Skye put her instrument into its case and then we huddle together and wait for Ahsan. Once he arrives, he puts Skye's dulcimer in the trunk, and Skye and I get in the backseat of the cab while Matthew climbs in up front.

I lean forward and put my hand on Ahsan's shoulder. "Skye, Matthew, I'd like you to meet my friend, Ahsan. And Ahsan, these are my friends, Skye and Matthew."

Matthew reaches out his hand and shakes Ahsan's. "Nice to meet you, man."

"Nice to meet both of you." Ahsan turns and reaches for Skye's hand and shakes it too.

Seated behind Ahsan, I can't see his face. But he turns back around and looks at me in the rearview mirror. "Mrs. Bouvier, I am very sorry. I read in the paper of your loss."

"Thank you, Ahsan."

"Where may I take you now?"

"Chinatown!" Matthew says.

"What?"

Skye laughs. "Leave it to Matthew."

"C'mon. You're home alone for the weekend, I'm home alone for the weekend, and Skye, your gig just got rained out. Let's hang together over chow mein."

I look at my watch and am surprised to see how long Matthew and I spent in the tea garden. But he's right, where else do I have to go?

"You treating?" Skye eyes Matthew.

He reaches into his back pocket, pulls out his wallet, and looks inside. "Uh..."

I laugh. "It's my treat."

"Then, I'm in." Skye's grin says it all.

"Me, too."

I laugh at them both. "Ahsan, you have to come too!"

"Mrs. Bouvier, your invitation is very kind—"

"Mrs. Bouvier? I bet she'd let you call her Jenna, or you could even call her dude—she answers to both, right?" Matthew turns around, looks at me, and winks.

I laugh again and it feels so good. "I've been telling Ahsan for years to call me Jenna. Ahsan, please join us."

"But Mrs. Jenna, I must work."

"I know. But I'll ask you to wait anyway, and pay for your time, because that's such a help to me, so you might as well wait inside rather than outside. Right?"

His smile is broad and his white teeth flash in the rearview mirror. "Such wisdom you offer."

"Good, it's settled. Hit it, Ahsan, the chow mein is calling!" Matthew reaches for his seat belt and buckles in.

~

OVER OUR EARLY dinner of chow mein and at least ten other dishes that Matthew ordered, we share life. Ahsan talks of his family in India, and Skye tells us of the friend who's taken her in. And we talk about God. We share a common passion—our love for Jesus unites us. The conversation, the time together around the table, ignites in me a desire for more. When I reach for my wallet to pay our bill, I do so with reluctance.

I hate for the evening to come to an end.

"Is Madame B still doling out an allowance?"

I don't answer Skye. I just take the bills from my wallet and place them with the check.

"Madame B?" Matthew looks at me.

Skye raises one eyebrow. "I'll leave the interpretation to you."

"Ahh…"

I look at Skye, embarrassed by her question—embarrassed by the truth she speaks. "Yes, so far, she's still giving me the monthly amount."

"So, she controls your spending?" Matthew sounds surprised.

Ahsan says nothing, but he takes it all in.

"Yes. She paid Gerard a salary, of course, so we had some discretionary funds, but not as much as you'd think." I look down at the table and feel my face redden. "She's always given me an allowance. Some cash. The rest is deposited into an account with my name and her name on it. I use a debit card so she can track my purchases. If I take cash from the account, she asks for receipts. I've learned what are acceptable expenditures in her eyes, and what are not. In some ways, it's a generous arrangement."

"And now that Gerard is gone?"

Leave it to Matthew to cut to the heart of the issue. "I don't know. We haven't discussed it yet."

Skye reaches over and pats my arm. "Either way, Jen, God provides and He'll do so for you."

Ahsan leans forward and looks at me. "Mrs. Jenna, because you keep your eyes on Jesus, you have run the race well. But now, the course changes."

Matthew and Skye nod, but I wonder at his meaning.

Our waiter comes, takes our bill, and the conversation shifts as we stand, put on our coats, and ready ourselves to leave. Once back in the cab, Ahsan looks to me. "Where to now?"

We determine our route—Skye gets dropped off first, then Ahsan will drop me off, and Matthew's stop is last. I'll pay Ahsan enough to get Matthew home. But when Ahsan pulls up into the Pacific Heights neighborhood, Matthew changes the plan and gets out with me.

Ahsan joins us on the sidewalk and I pay him, then Matthew reaches for his wallet and chips in. I lean over and give Ahsan a hug. "Thanks for joining us tonight. I continue to pray for your family."

"Thank you, Mrs. Jenna."

After Ahsan pulls away, I turn and look at Matthew, and then I look up to the house. Our presence won't go unnoticed.

"You being watched?"

"Maybe." I look up to the sky and see a patch of dim stars between the clouds. The rain has stopped and the air smells clean, fresh. "Beautiful."

Matthew gazes at the stars with me for a few minutes and then looks back at me. "Hey, Lightseeker, want to take a walk?"

I look from the stars to him. "You know."

"Yeah, but I didn't know if you knew that I knew, so I thought it was time I let you know that I know. You know?"

I laugh again. "I suspected." I glance back at the house. "Let's walk."

As we walk, the moon shrouded by clouds and the patch of stars visible overhead, I turn to Matthew. "You're the only one who knows."

"How does it feel to be known?"

I take a deep breath and exhale. Then I stop, look up at the stars again, stretch my arms out, and turn round and round. I lean my head back and watch the stars circle with me. Joy bubbles forth into laughter. "It feels wonderful!" I stop and look at Matthew. "It feels like freedom."

"It's just the beginning, Jenna."

I nod. I don't fully understand, but I want to believe him.

By the time we walk around the block and end up back in front of the house, I realize how tired I am. "I'd better go, but thank you for a wonderful afternoon and evening. I don't remember the last time I spent a day with friends—at least, my friends. I need more of that."

"We all do. One of the ways God speaks to us is through the body of Christ. We need to spend time hanging with other believers."

I nod. "I've missed that. Hey, how are you getting home?"

"I'll walk awhile and then catch a bus. I need to burn a few calories"—he pats his stomach—"It's been a full day."

"Okay. Thanks, again, Matthew." I turn to go, but he reaches for my arm and pulls me back. "Dude, wait. I have something for you." He reaches into his jacket pocket and pulls out two almond cookies. "Dessert!"

I laugh and then reach for the cookies. "Gee, thanks." I give him a quick hug. "Good night, my friend."

"Good night, Lightseeker."

I climb the steps to the front entrance, and with each step I take, the fatigue weighs on me. When I reach the front door, I turn and wave to Matthew, who's waited to make sure I get in.

As I reach into my purse for my key, the front door opens.

Hannah.

I glance back at Matthew and then step inside.

CHAPTER THIRTY-EIGHT

*I beg you to renounce your own wisdom and self-leadings. Yield yourself
up to God. Let Him become your wisdom. You will then find the place of
rest that you need so badly.*

JEANNE GUYON

ndee

I SLAM THE RECEIVER DOWN. "IDIOTS!" I stand, take a deep breath,
and then stretch, turning my neck from one side to the other, and
then from chin to chest and back. The conference call with the
executive producers of one of the network morning shows didn't
go well.

"You get what you pay for, people. And if you're not willing to
pay well, you don't get me. Your loss."

I go to the kitchen, reach for an espresso cup, and hold it
under the maker's spout. As I do, I notice my hand shaking. I set
the cup down, put my hand across my chest, and feel my heart

racing. Okay, I get it—I've had enough already. "Oh, happy Monday!"

I go back to my office, grab my purse and briefcase, and head for the front door. I'll be a few minutes early for my meeting with the commercial broker who's showing me office space and buildings today. If he's any good, he'll be early himself.

I step into the elevator, push *L*, and watch as the numbers flash —30, 29, 28... I glance at my watch and tap my foot. "Anytime today..." When the doors open in the lobby, I step out, glare at the doorman, and dare him to say *good morning*. But he knows better. Instead, he tips his cap to me and opens the door.

Smart man.

I head for the curb with the doorman in tow who whistles for a cab. Once inside the cab, I give the driver the address on Market Street and then lean back against the seat—the filthy seat. "Don't you ever clean this thing?"

Dark eyes stare me down from the rearview mirror as he raises a hand and taps the cardboard pine tree hanging from the mirror.

"Yeah, that helps." *Whatever.*

I reach for my phone, check my e-mail, scroll through my calendar, and then text a reminder to Cassidy telling her I'll be out when she arrives at the office today. The cab pulls to the curb, I take the appropriate bills out of my wallet, pay the driver, and get out. I stiff him on the tip.

I navigate my way through the business suit-clad crowd on the sidewalk until I reach the broker's office. I push through the glass entry doors and announce myself to the receptionist.

And then I wait.

And wait.

When Mr. Broker saunters into the reception area, I share my mood with him. "Are you interested in making a sale? If not, I'm happy to find someone who is. Do you know who I am?"

His condescending smile doesn't help.

He holds out his hand. "Ms. Bell, I do apologize. I'm so happy to be working with you."

I ignore his hand and cross my arms. "May we go?"

"Of course. We'll walk to the first site if that's agreeable?"

"Fine." I curse the Jimmy Choo stilettos I chose for the day.

By 2:00 p.m., after a mediocre lunch where we went through the list of sites he'd shown me, I escape to the restroom and call Cass. "Hey, I'm done with this bozo. He hasn't shown me a single space that will work. Two things: Find a new broker, and then find a massage therapist who will come to the penthouse this afternoon."

"A massage therapist?"

Why does she sound confused? "Yes, Cassidy, massage therapist. Do I need to spell it for you?"

"No. I'm sorry."

And so you should be.

"What kind of massage?"

Oh, for heaven's sake! Just *do* it. "I don't know. The kind that will make me feel better. Just find someone good and get an appointment for this afternoon."

I hang up. *How hard is it, Cass?* Okay, granted, I've never had a massage or asked Cassidy to find a therapist for me, but there's a first time for everything. I reach for my shoulder and knead the muscle.

I need to do something to relieve this tension. Then something occurs to me and I pick up the phone again.

"Cass, make sure the massage therapist is a woman."

I drop the phone back into my briefcase, touch up my lipstick, and head back to fire Mr. Broker. The most productive moment of my day.

When I walk back into the penthouse, I kick my heels off at the front door, pick them up, and head for the office where Cassidy is sitting at my desk going through mail. She looks over her shoulder at me. "Massage at 4:00 p.m.—deep tissue—her name is Lauren."

"Deep tissue? Is that painful?"

"Depends."

Depends on what?

JUST BEFORE 4:00, Cass buzzes the massage chick up to the penthouse. She lets her in and has her set up in my bedroom. Cass comes out of the room with an intake form and a release for me to sign.

"A release? What's she going to do to me?"

"It's standard procedure, Andee. Fill it out. I'm taking off."

"Fine."

A few minutes later, I hear someone say, "Hello? I'm ready for you."

I walk into the living room and see a petite brunette dressed in black yoga pants and a T-shirt, her long hair pulled into a loose twist.

"Hi, I'm Lauren."

I'd guess Lauren is old enough to be my mother, but she's still beautiful and looks strong. "I'm Andee."

We talk through my problem areas, as she calls them. I tell her that my neck and shoulders need the most work.

"Are you under a lot of stress?"

I laugh. "Uh, yeah, you could say that."

"We often hold our stress in our neck and shoulders. Come on in and we'll get started."

I walk into my bedroom and in ten short minutes, she's transformed it. She's closed the drapes, turned down the lights, lit candles, and there's soft music playing in the background. Her table is set up near the foot of my bed and it's covered in soft white linens, and there's a white chenille robe draped over the end of the table.

"What's that smell?"

She smiles. "Lavender and vanilla. Your assistant said you didn't have any allergies so I took the liberty of using scented candles. Lavender and vanilla are soothing aromas."

"Okay. Soothing is good."

She gives me some instructions, tells me to change into the robe, and to let her know when I'm ready for her to come back in. I tell her to just wait and I go into the adjoining bathroom, change out of my clothes, put on the robe, and return to the bedroom.

"That was fast."

"I don't have time to waste."

She's instructs me how to lie on the table, and I settle in.

"Sometimes, Andee, massage can evoke an emotional response —especially when we're working areas where we hold stress or painful emotions."

"I just need you to work out the knots." *An emotional reaction? Get a grip, lady.*

"Okay. Let's get started."

She has me lie faceup and covers my eyes with a mask that also smells like lavender. Then she wraps each of my feet in hot, damp towels. A good start after walking the streets in the stilettos. She also drapes hot towels over my shoulders.

Okay, so why haven't I done this before?

Soon her warm hands begin to work at the base of my neck and up into my scalp. She massages my head, and then moves to my face, where she kneads my temples and works down to my jawline.

The sensation is amazing and I begin to relax. Maybe I can hire her to be on call at all hours, whenever I need her. We could set up a massage room in the new office building. Well, when I find a building, that is.

"Relax," she whispers. "You're tensing your neck muscles."

You think that's tense? I breathe in and then exhale in an attempt to clear my mind. *Don't think about office buildings, Andee.*

Or work.

Her hands return to the base of my neck and she removes the hot towels and then begins to work warm lotion into my skin. She works around to the front of my lower neck and using slow circular motions, she works the areas between my collarbone and shoulders.

Don't think about anything.

Then she places her hands under my shoulders, almost lifting them off the table, and she begins a deep kneading of the muscles from underneath. I feel the ache of tension begin to release as she works the knotted ligaments.

And with the ache come more thoughts.

Don't go there. Don't think about him.

"Just rest. Relax..."

Jason... I shouldn't have...

Her strong fingers press into my skin, probing, as though she's looking for something specific and won't stop until she finds it. I swallow and feel the lump forming in my throat as her hands move to the outer edges of my shoulders, still kneading and probing.

I let Jason go...

I take a deep breath.

How could I...

I swallow again.

How could I betray him?

I feel the first tears sliding out from under the mask.

"It's okay." She speaks in a whisper. "Release the emotion with the tension. Let it all go."

"I...I can't..."

"Just let it go. Relax."

Her hands are warm on my shoulders as she attempts to soothe me with her voice.

"No. No more." I pull the mask off my eyes and bolt upright. "*No!*" Sitting up on the table, I pull the sheet close to cover myself. "I'm done."

She puts her hand on my forearm, but says nothing.

I reach for her hand and throw it off. The force of it causes her to stumble back. "I said I'm done!" I swing my legs over the side of the table, wrap the sheet around me, and stand up. "Get your things, now." I go into my dressing area, where I grab my own robe from my closet. I drop the sheet and slip into the robe. My hands shake as I tie the belt tight.

I bend, pick up the sheet, and return to the bedroom, where I throw the sheet across her table. "Get"—my voice shakes like my hands—"your things and show yourself out." I push the words through clenched teeth. "Now!" Then I walk back into the bathroom and slam the door behind me. I sit on the edge of the large jetted tub, wrap my arms around myself, and let the tears come.

There's no stopping them now.

CHAPTER THIRTY-NINE

Self-love hides in many places, and God alone can find them all out.
JEANNE GUYON

rigitte

SHE REACHES into the pocket of her St. John cardigan and removes her vibrating cell phone. She looks at the name on the screen, then answers. "Yes, Hannah…"

"Madame, I got the information you requested. Access to Jenna's computer."

"You did?"

"Yes, I downloaded the information to a flash drive and I've just e-mailed it to you along with her passwords."

"Fine."

"There is something else, Madame…"

She walks to the large bay window in the living room and looks out over the vineyard as she listens.

"Jenna was gone most of Saturday. She left late in the morning in a cab. I don't know where she went. But when she returned, after dark, she was with a man."

"A man?"

"Yes, Madame."

"Who? What man?"

"I don't know."

"Fine, Hannah. Merci. Job well done." She smiles.

She walks to the antique desk where her laptop sets and looks for the new files Hannah is e-mailing. "Ah... There you are." She turns away from the desk and goes to the small bar on the other side of the living area and takes a crystal flute from one of the shelves above, then she reaches for the bottle of *Domaine de la Bouvier Reserve Pinot Noir Brut* that Estelle has chilling in a bucket on the countertop. She pops the cork, and laughs at the sound of it. She fills the flute and then lifts the glass in the air. "To me."

She takes a sip of the champagne and then, glass in hand, heads back to the desk, where she sits for an evening of reading.

CHAPTER FORTY

If you ever saw how deeply corrupt you really were, all your courage to reform yourself would run away in terror.
JEANNE GUYON

ndee

WHEN I EMERGE from the bathroom, eyes swollen and tears spent, at least for the moment, I walk through the bedroom and notice the massage chick left her card and a note tucked into the mirror of my dresser. "Your bill, I assume?"

I pull the card and note from the frame of the mirror and read: *Andee, today was on me. Call anytime, I'd love to work with you.*

"Thanks for nothing." I crumple the note and stuff it, along with her card, into the pocket of my robe. I go to the living room and stand in front of the plate-glass windows and watch as lights begin to flicker across the city and bay. I look toward Alameda Island and anger, like a herd of charging elephants, crashes through the walls I've constructed.

The view of the island that I determined would remind me where I came from and where I'd never be again, now just agitates. Since the night I told Jason of the rape, the anger has pawed and snorted, and kicked up dust.

Tonight, the stampede rages.

If I hadn't gone home that night...

If I'd been stronger, screamed louder, pushed harder...

I pound my fists against the thick glass.

Idiot!

Since that fateful night, I determined I'd live strong, scream loud, push hard, demand cooperation, and control circumstances. I'd bully my way through life. And I'd protect myself along the way. Nothing. No one. Would take me down again.

Now, I realize, the one I've bullied the most is myself.

Hot tears run down my cheeks and I pound the glass again and again.

I pushed away what I wanted, what I needed most. I'm an idiot!

I think again of that moment of realization at Gerard's funeral—the moment of recognizing Brigitte's aloneness. Why didn't I learn? No, I was given a glimpse of my future and instead of turning from it and changing, I ran headlong into it.

I turned my anger on myself and sabotaged my life. But not just my own, oh no, I took Jason and his family down with me.

What is wrong with me?

And now, I'm alone.

Who, tonight, is more alone than me?

No one.

I've seen to that.

Brigitte still has Jenna. Under her thumb? Yes, but at least she is a living, breathing presence in her life.

I think of Jason again and the anger turns to an unbearable ache. The lump in my throat burns and my heart shatters like glass. This is the exact pain I've worked so hard to avoid. Yet, the path I forged was a direct route to destruction.

"Idiot!"

Sam hisses from the sofa behind me.

I turn, look at him, and hiss back. "Shut up!" Then I crumple to my knees, my robe spread around me, and I cry. I sob. I fall from my knees and lay facedown on the floor, I turn my head, lay my cheek against the carpet, and soak it with my tears. I pound my fists on the floor and then pull handfuls of the long shag carpet, yanking as hard as I can.

The aching void within screams for attention.

And my soul bleeds.

Nice going, Andee.

After awhile, I quiet.

I lie on the floor and soon I feel Sam's tail brush against my face and then his rough tongue on my cheek as he licks my remaining tears. I roll over on my back and he climbs onto my chest and kneads me with his paws. Then he lies down on my chest and licks my chin.

"Sam, get a grip," I mumble.

He looks at me with those ice blue eyes and begins to purr.

"Seriously, we both really need to get a grip." I bury my hand in his fur and we lie that way until I feel the strength to pull myself up off the floor.

"Way to have a pity party, huh?"

But I know it was more than that. Like a red flag waving, the anger, the tears, the ache of loneliness, they all warn me there are things I need to pay attention to. Finally.

I wander first to the bathroom, where I wash my swollen face. Then to the kitchen, where I start for the espresso maker, but think better of it. Maybe this is my first change. Maybe I need something a little less stimulating. I search my kitchen cabinets and find a box of green antioxidant tea. "That'll do."

I put a mug under the instant hot water spout at my sink, fill it, open the box of tea, and drop a bag into the mug. Then I go sit at my desk. I play with the string on the tea bag, lifting the bag in and out of the water, while I rest my other hand on the computer mouse and watch the screen light up. I pull the tea bag out of the water, wrap the string around it, and squeeze the remaining water into the mug. Then I toss the bag in the wastebasket under my desk. I lift the cup to my lips, take a sip, and then spit the tea in an arc of spray across my computer screen and desk. "What is that?" I look into the mug and sniff. "Antioxidant? This'll kill me!" I stomp to the kitchen, dump the contents of the mug down the drain, and head for the espresso maker.

I come back to my desk with a steaming cup of espresso—and a rag to mop up the mess. *There's always tomorrow.* I settle back in, sip my espresso, and stare at the screen on my desk for a long time. Thoughts of Jason continue to nag. I take a deep breath, and this time I force myself to stay with the thoughts.

I recall the thought that came to me like a voice from the cosmos that afternoon in Napa: *Jason's a keeper. Hang onto him.*

A voice from the cosmos? Or could it have been the voice of God? Like Lightseeker hears? "Yeah, right."

But maybe…

What does it matter now? I didn't listen. Hang onto him? No, I betrayed him. I lean my elbows on the desk and put my head in my hands and sigh.

Lightseeker.

I think of her e-mails to me—her willingness to engage. Maybe I'm not alone. Okay, sure, I don't know her, it's not like a real friend, but hey, besides Sam, she may be all I have left.

I lift my head and rest my hand on the mouse again. I move the cursor on the screen to the icon that opens my Internet browser.

I tap the icon and then type in the familiar URL: www.ilumi-nar.me. I read her last post:

Loneliness calls my name. It woos me to believe nothing can fill the cavernous void in my soul…

CHAPTER FORTY-ONE

The turmoil you experience is your resistance to what God is seeking to accomplish.
JEANNE GUYON

enna

I TURN MY HEAD, careful not to move too fast, and look at the clock on my nightstand. Even the slightest movement causes the waves of nausea to swell again. 9:18 a.m. My stomach roils and gurgles. I've kept nothing down since Sunday morning. I've spent more time on the bathroom floor than in bed in the last twenty-four hours.

I hear Hannah tap on my door and then let herself in. She comes to my bed and sets a glass of clear juice on the nightstand. She looks at me and her face reflects what I already know. I'm a mess.

"Sip the juice."

"I…can't."

"You sip the juice or you'll end up dehydrated." She places her hand on my forehead, her touch brusque. "No fever." She goes to the bathroom to wash her hands, muttering something about eating in Chinatown.

"It isn't…food poisoning."

"Whatever it is, Madame has decided to stay away a few more days. She doesn't want to catch it."

"It's the infection…Hannah. The same…old thing."

"Then you best call Dr. Bernard."

I don't have the strength to argue. Anyway, it's time for another opinion. Dr. Kim hasn't helped me.

"I'll be back. Drink the juice."

Once she's gone, I pull the sheet over my head longing only to fall back to the escape of sleep.

THE NEXT TIME I look at the clock it's almost 3:00 p.m. I lift my head, wait, and realize my stomach has settled. I sit up, lean back against my pillow, and reach for the glass of juice Hannah left. When I pick it up, it's cold—she's replaced it with a fresh glass while I slept. "Bless you, Hannah." While Hannah's disdain for me is clear, she still does her job.

I take a few sips of the clear liquid and then gulp the rest. Hannah was right, I'm nearing dehydration and now my body is begging for liquid. The juice gurgles in my stomach, reminding me to take it slow.

I get out of bed, shower, and dress in soft sweat pants and a long-sleeved T-shirt. I pull on socks, and then step into my slippers and venture out of my room for the first time in almost two days. Feeling weak, I take the elevator downstairs, thinking I'll sit outside for a few minutes of fresh air. But when I pass the kitchen, the aroma of something cooking overwhelms me. My stomach lurches and I make a quick U-turn and head back to my bedroom.

Each time the infection returns, it's worse—though never anything like this. I dread what's to come—more doctor's appointments, blood work, antibiotics, surgery, hospitalization. I wear each possibility like a lead jacket as I make my way back to bed.

How much more, Lord?

At dinnertime, Hannah brings me a mug of hot chicken broth and another glass of juice. I sit on the sofa in the alcove and sip both. By evening, I feel strong enough to sit at my desk for a while and check my e-mail and respond to blog comments.

Readers can either make direct comments on the blog for all to see, or e-mail me at lightseeker@iluminar.me. I also have a private e-mail address. I'm surprised when I open my private e-mail folder to find a note from Brigitte. I glance at the time on my computer and realize she's just sent it.

Ma chérie,

Hannah tells me you're ill. I've given her Dr. Bernard's number. She will call in the morning and schedule an appointment. I will wrap up business here tomorrow and return to the city on Wednesday morning.

Take care,

B.

Another day alone. I am grateful for the time, but wonder at her note. It seems her tone has softened. Is she really staying away due to business? There is no trusting her.

I move on to my other e-mail folder and see several new e-mails from readers. As I begin reading through their comments and questions, my computer dings, telling me a new e-mail has come in.

I glance at the list and see it's from Andee.

Oh Lord, lead me...

Jason called a few days ago and told me that Andee had ended their relationship. I open the e-mail.

Lightseeker,

I have a couple of questions about your last post. But I'm uncomfortable not knowing who I'm dealing with. Want to share your identity? I'm a public figure and need to know I can trust you not to reveal our e-mail exchanges.

A. Bell

Oh Lord, now what? I sit in silence for several minutes hoping I'll hear from God, or experience a sense of direction, or something. Anything. But nothing comes. So I decide to just be honest with her.

Dear Andee,

I am aware of your public status and understand your concern. I assure you that any exchange we have will remain confidential. However, I cannot reveal my identity at this time. I'm sorry. I ask for your understanding. Because of the personal nature of my posts, I need to protect myself from those who would disapprove. I'd like to continue our exchange and ask that you trust me—and if not me, maybe you can trust that God has brought us together.

I reread the e-mail before sending it and feel a pit form in my stomach. Will my insistence on remaining anonymous drive her away? No more than my identity would drive her away. Because of her relationship with Jason, I'm certain I'm one of the last people she'd open up to. So for her sake, I tell myself, I need to remain anonymous.

But then there's also her relationship with Brigitte. And in that instance, my anonymity is all about my own protection.

No, I don't have a choice.

I press *send*.

It's in Your hands, Lord.

I continue going through my e-mail and come across a note from Matthew.

Hey Jenna,

Your secret life is safe with me. Enjoyed the time together Saturday. Look forward to seeing you soon.

Matthew

I smile and recall the sense of freedom, the soaring joy, that accompanied Matthew's admission that he knew who I was—really knew. Somehow, he assimilated the parts of me and came up with the whole. And he accepted the whole.

Could that happen with others?

I allow myself to consider the thought—to dream of freedom. But then I think of Brigitte. No, I've shared too much in my blog.

I can never reveal my identity.

She can never know.

For the first time, a question occurs to me: *Is it Brigitte who keeps me bound? Or is it myself?* The familiar swirl of confusion accompanies the question.

I get up from my desk and go to the window. The city lights cast a pink glow in the night sky. *Lord, lead me...*

Again, I'm met with silence.

CHAPTER FORTY-TWO

So you can see how tragically you will be imprisoned if you cling to the old self.

JEANNE GUYON

ndee

"TRUST HER? YEAH, RIGHT." I get up from my desk and walk circles around my office. "Why should I trust her?"

Sam mews.

"You're a big help."

Trust her, or trust that God brought us together? I don't think a few e-mails constitutes a divine intervention. Good grief.

I walk back to my desk and read her e-mail again. She needs to protect herself? Listen lady, I can tell you something about protecting yourself—it doesn't work. Then it hits me. If it doesn't work, then why am I protecting myself with her?

"That's different." I walk away from the desk again. "Right? *Right?* I'd love an answer here."

But I'm met with maddening silence.

So what am I expecting? The voice of God to agree with me?

I make another loop around my office and find myself wanting to sit down and e-mail her back. To begin a relationship that's real. Honest. I laugh. Like I'd even know where to begin.

But it isn't just her I want to trust.

It isn't religion—it's a relationship.

I want to trust God.

I want, I need, the perfect love she writes of.

Is it possible?

I go back to my desk, sit down, and read her e-mail again. So, maybe I trust her? What's the worst that could happen?

"She could sell your e-mails to the tabloids. That's what. Think it through, Andee. Don't be an idiot." I can see the headlines now: *Financial Guru Seeks Market Advice from Jesus.* And then, of course, I'd be abducted by aliens. As I laugh, bitterness bites at me.

What am I doing?

I close the e-mail, click back to my desktop, and instead open my personal financial portfolio. I look at the balances in my accounts. Stocks, 401Ks, money markets, on and on it goes. I have more money than I could spend in ten lifetimes.

I have everything I've strived for. Why would I need anything else? Or anyone else?

I stare at the figures on the screen. My fingers shake as they claw at the mouse, clicking to reach the bottom line.

The figure is staggering.

Yet, I feel the familiar tremor. The tremor I've refused to acknowledge. The tremor I've demanded bow to my control. I feel the tremor of...

Fear.

You'll never have enough, Andee. You'll lose it all. You'll have nothing. You'll be nothing.

You are nothing.

What's driven me? Ambition? No.

I'm driven by fear.

Fear owns me.

I lean my elbows on my desk and put my head in my hands as the realization dawns: *I am no different than Brigitte.* The same disgust I felt for Brigitte at Gerard's memorial service, now rises like bile in my throat.

Fear has dictated my every choice. And tonight, fear has me flat on my back.

I've achieved all I set out to. There's nothing left to strive for.

Nothing to live for.

Nothing.

And no one.

Head still in my hands, hot tears run down my face and pool on my desk. I move my hands from my forehead to my scalp and grab fistfuls of my hair and pull until I can stand the pain no longer. But physical pain is a weak manifestation of the pain writhing within.

I jerk my head up and get to my feet. I walk away from the desk, walk away from the office, and want to walk away from myself.

I go to the bedroom and without turning on any lights, I make my way to the nightstand next to my bed. I feel for the handle on the drawer and pull it open. I reach inside and feel around until my hand lands on cold, hard, metal. I wrap my fingers around the grip and pull it from the drawer.

I stagger back to the living room, heart pounding, blood rushing.

I look at the gun in my hand, feel the weight of it, and then lift it to my face—the metal is cool against my hot cheek.

I set the gun on the glass coffee table and walk to the windows. I stare out at the city I've clamored to own. I've demanded the respect of those I've deemed important. Yet—I take a deep, shaking breath—I have no respect for myself.

I loathe who I've become.

A scream rises in my throat and my skin crawls. I reach for the thick robe I wear and rip it off my shoulders. I wrap my arms around myself and dig my nails into the flesh of my arms. I dig until the crawling stops. I dig until I feel the sweet release of pain. Until I feel the warm trickle of blood.

But it isn't enough.

Hatred rages.

I turn back, take the few steps to the coffee table, and reach for the gun.

And I lift it to my head.

CHAPTER FORTY-THREE

I present you before the Lord with all my heart.
JEANNE GUYON

enna

I SPEND the evening shifting between the sofa in the alcove, my bed, and my desk. I can't settle anywhere, and just when I think I might, I'm drawn back to my computer, hoping for a response from Andee.

But I hear nothing more from her.

As the final curtain is drawn on the nighttime hours, I stand in front of the window in the alcove, looking out on a city that never sleeps. A people riddled by restlessness. Tonight, I share their angst. Sirens, the sonorous backdrop of the city, wail in the distance.

The darkness wrapped around my soul portends evil.

I shudder, cross my arms across my chest, and turn away from the window.

Lord, I know You're here, though I don't sense You. I know You've defeated evil for all time.

I stand for a long time. Silent. But with my soul open to God, trusting that His Spirit prays what I cannot. What I know not.

I usher in the midnight hour, wide awake after having slept most of the day. I check my e-mail one more time, then shut down my laptop. I reach for the Bible sitting on my desk and lay on the sofa with it open on my lap. I thumb through the thin pages and read stories as familiar as my own history—Adam and Eve, Noah, Abraham. I scan the pages, looking for hope. I try to immerse myself in the story of Moses and the rebellious Israelites, but everything I read feels stale, lifeless.

Finally sleepy, I flip through the last pages of Deuteronomy, my eyes scanning passages, but taking little in. Then I land on a passage that stirs something. It is the first stirring I've sensed for many days. I sit up and read aloud God's words to the Israelites:

"This day I call the heavens and the earth as witnesses against you that I have set before you life and death, blessings and curses. Now choose life, so that you and your children may live."

But what does it mean?

Lord, what do You want me to see?

I receive no response.

Frustrated, I close the Bible, set it aside, and get up. The sense I felt was nothing more than my own wishful thinking. I go back to the window and stare into the inky night. But as I stand there, a knowing settles over me.

I am to pray the words.

A shiver of fear crawls up my spine. *Why, Lord?*

He reveals nothing.

I am to pray.

Pray without ceasing.

I bow my head and repeat the words. *Choose life. Choose life.*

Choose life. The words become a chant. A mantra. I repeat them as I walk away from the window. I whisper them as I slip into my pajamas. They course through my mind like a raging river as I brush my teeth. They nag at me as I climb into bed. And in the wee hours of the morning, they lull me into a fitful sleep.

Choose life.
Choose life.
Choose life.

CHAPTER FORTY-FOUR

The loss of all the things of the earthly life will be deep and long.
JEANNE GUYON

ndee

CONSCIOUSNESS COMES ONE ACHING, throbbing, moment at a time. Before I open my eyes, I know something is wrong, but can't recall what. I shiver and reach to pull the blanket close, but find none. I roll from my back to my side and realize I'm lying on something hard and unforgiving. The floor? I open my eyes, startled by the hues of pink, orange, and gray splashed across the expanse of sky visible through the windows in front of me.

I lift my head, but it pounds me back down. I cover my eyes with my hands as memories of the night before flood my mind. When I dare to open my eyes again, I see Sam curled near me, his body wrapped around the gun on the floor next to me, as though protecting me from…myself.

"Oh, God!"

The exclamation isn't an expletive, but rather a recognition.

I force myself to sit up and take stock. I feel like I've been through a battle. My sinuses are swollen, my mouth and throat are dry, my head and teeth ache, and worst of all, every single muscle in my body is screaming. "Oh, please tell me I don't have to call the massage chick again."

The plea, I realize, is my first honest prayer.

Stiff, I struggle to get up. I roll over onto my hands and knees. But before I push myself up, I reach for Sam and run my hand through the fur on his back. He stretches, stands, and arches his back. His blue eyes accuse.

"I know. I'm sorry."

I push myself up, then bend and take the gun off the floor.

I take a slow walk to my bedroom, where I replace the revolver in my nightstand drawer. I look at the bedside clock and make a decision. I reach for the phone on the nightstand and dial Cassidy's number.

She answers after the first ring. "Morning, Andee."

"Hey, Cass. Take the day off."

"What?"

"We're taking the day off. Don't come in. Do something fun. Oh, but first, call and reschedule my appointments for the day."

She's quiet. "Are you okay? Are you sick? You know it's Tuesday, right?"

"I'm fine. I know it's Tuesday. And we're both taking a paid day off."

"Is this Andee Bell?"

"Very funny, Cass. Have a nice day. I'll see you tomorrow."

I hang up and go into the bathroom, turn on the shower, and then take off my robe and hang it back in the closet. When I come out of the closet, I catch a glimpse of myself in the mirror and I see long, red scabs on my arms. The marks left by my own nails.

I lower my head and look at the floor—the realization of what I almost did sobers me. I lift my arm and place my hand over my chest and feel the beating of my heart. I'm still here, but the ache, the desperation, also remains.

It's time to make a few changes.

I step into the shower followed by the realization that change won't come without a fight. A fight with myself.

"I'll need help…"

I whisper not to myself.

But to God.

CHAPTER FORTY-FIVE

Let all your old ideas go as God directs.
JEANNE GUYON

*M*atthew

ON TUESDAY AFTERNOON, between counseling clients, I listen to my messages. One is from Jenna asking if we can meet at the outdoor labyrinth at Grace Cathedral tomorrow morning, rather than in my office. I check my schedule and see I have some extra time. Cool. This is one of the freedoms spiritual direction affords. I'd always rather meet outdoors. She says to drop her an e-mail or call with my response. I check my watch—my next client will be on my doorstep any second, so rather than call, I shoot off a quick e-mail.

Jenna,

Can't wait for tomorrow! See you at the lab at 9:00.

Expectantly,

Matthew

~

WEDNESDAY DAWNS BRILLIANT, baby. Crisp and clear. I pound the blocks from home to the office, and then from the office to the cathedral. My walk and talk with God is rich. Life is good. No complaints.

Well, maybe just one.

Tess came home from New York more enthused than ever about fashion and her career. I'm happy for her. Dude, I really am. But I want more with my wife and as I walk, I feel resentment toward her desires. And I go down the *What-about-me-and-my-desires?* road. Warning: That road is one big ol' dead end! And I know it. But I walk it again anyway.

Head down, arms swinging, I hash it out with God.

"How much longer? I pray and pray for Tess, and nothing changes. Her heart doesn't change. Her desires don't change. Kids? Still no. You? Still no. Yeah, it's cool she's reading the blog, but c'mon—she needs You."

I round a corner and broadside a guy with a briefcase. I lift up my hands and step back from him. "Sorry, man."

I catch my breath, and then pick up the pace again. "Not only does she need You, but I need her to surrender to You. I want that for her—for us. You say You'll give me the desires of my heart. This is my desire. Aren't I faithful to You? Don't You love Tess? I want more—more of You—with Tess. I want that intimacy with my wife. I want to see in her eyes what I see in…"

To feel with her what I feel when…

My pace slows.

"Oh man"—I rake my hand through my hair—"that's it. That's what I've felt all along."

A woman passes, staring at me like there's something wrong with me. "What? Never seen anyone talking to themselves before?"

She steps off the curb and crosses the street.

"Take it back inside, buddy. You're scaring the locals." I stop, stand still for a minute, and figure out where I am. I look at my watch—still time before I need to be at the lab. Better take an extra lap or two around the block and finish this.

I take it slow, my steps intentional. I work it out in my head. Tim and I have talked about this—it isn't new information—but I'm just getting it. Really getting it. I suck in my breath and then give the desire of my heart to God.

Father, I want with Tess what I share with Jenna. I want my soul to be knit to the soul of my wife in the way that only happens when Your Spirit is present in both people. I want, man, I long for, spiritual intimacy with my wife. I want to share the desires of my heart, my life, with her.

I'm drawn to Jenna, the same way I was drawn to Lightseeker, I'm drawn to Lightseeker, because I'm drawn to You. You in her. It's You I see in her eyes. It's You I see in those dazzler smiles of hers. It's Your heart I hear in her words.

It's You.

It's all about You.

I stop on a corner and bend at the waist, hands on my knees. I swallow the lump in my throat and then wipe my arm across my eyes—drying my eyes with my sleeve. I stand straight again. "Dude." I shake my head.

I get it. Lord, I get it. Tess is Yours. You love her more than I do. I give her to You. I surrender. She's Yours.

A cab careens around the corner and water splashes from the gutter and sprays the legs of my pants with specks of gray water and dirt. "Not cool." I look down at my pants and shake my head again.

Yeah, Lord, even if it doesn't go my way. I trust You. I trust You with Tess. And I trust You with my desires. I trust You.

I nod. "Yeah, I trust You."

~

BY THE TIME I reach the lab, I need a few minutes to regroup, and I'm glad to see Jenna hasn't arrived yet.

I take my place on the rock wall, the same spot where I sat with her the day we met, and I confess to God, who already knows, that I'm in a vulnerable spot. The air is clean, the day a beauty, but my heart is feeling bruised—tender—like I could use a manifestation of Jesus in the flesh.

A friend to lean on.

I remind myself, as I see Jenna come across the plaza, that she can't be that friend. Today, she's a client. I'm the director—she's the directee. *Lord, I'm Your broken vessel—Your cracked pot—and I need Your strength through my weakness today. This is about You, not me.*

I watch as Jenna approaches and notice her gait is slower than usual. I stand up and put my arm around her shoulders and give her a squeeze. "Hey, you feeling okay?"

She nods. "Better than I was." She smiles. "I had a bout of something. I thought the infection was back. Or . . . maybe it is." She runs her finger along the scar on her jaw. "But I'm hoping it was just a virus or something. It makes sense that my immunities would be down."

"Yeah, makes sense."

"I slept all day yesterday then was wide awake last night. But I think I was supposed to be—to pray, though, I'm not sure why." She shrugs. "Anyway, I'm relieved to feel better today."

I put my hand in the air for a high five.

She gives me five and then grabs hold of my hand and hangs onto it. "I'm still a little tired, but I'll get my strength back." She squeezes my hand and then lets it go. "How are you?"

"Only minor complaints." This is her time. "Have a seat."

I motion to the wall. She sits at an angle, and I do the same, so we're facing one another. There are a few people wandering around the cathedral plaza, but for the most part, we're alone.

"Well, we don't have a candle so we'll let the sky speak of God's presence. Cool?"

"That's why I wanted to meet here."

She looks up and her face mirrors His glory, the deep blue of the sky reflected in her eyes. And man, in this moment, I know I'm gazing at one of His most beautiful creations. And I'm awed.

Not by her.

By Him.

And in His presence, my desires wane. I know that He is enough. All I need. This is her time, but He's spoken to me, as He so often does, through her. And today, not through her words, just through her being. I clear my throat. "So how about a few minutes of silence?"

She nods and we both bow our heads, and as we do, our foreheads bump together. "Whoa, sorry."

She laughs. And we both scoot back an inch or so and try again. After a few minutes, I feel her hand on my arm.

"I'm ready."

I lift my head and wait while she gathers her thoughts. Her face grows serious and I see that look of pain in her eyes. She looks away—across the plaza—and then back at me and takes the plunge.

"I received an e-mail from a reader on Monday. Or, I should say, Lightseeker received an e-mail." She smiles that shy smile of hers, the one that surfaces when she's feeling vulnerable.

"Good ol' Lightseeker."

She nods and goes on. "She, the reader, asked my identity. She said she needed to know who I am so she could trust me. But…I couldn't tell her. I feel dishonest."

"What's God saying to you about it?"

"He's still not speaking. Although, it's not like it was. I sense Him again. It's like He's sitting with me, but just quiet."

"How's that feel?"

"Better. I wonder if"—she stops and looks at the sky again —"He's teaching me something?"

"You're a willing student."

"I am?"

I nudge her shin with my foot. "Really?"

She shrugs. "I don't know. I hope so. But for so long, I've heard from God. But now, I'm wondering if I haven't interpreted much of what He's said through my own understanding. You know? I wonder if His silence is an opportunity? A time to stand back…" She looks at me, eyes wide.

I nod. I get it—the phrase she heard so often but didn't understand. "Stand back from…?"

"My understanding. Maybe He's asking me to just trust, without understanding. Without trying to make sense of things. Without hearing from Him."

Man, do I get that. "How does that feel?"

"Terrifying…and liberating." She smiles. "Sort of a paradox, I guess."

I think back to where she began the conversation. "So, God hasn't weighed in on whether or not He wants you to reveal your identity—at least to this reader?"

"Not really. But I can't. It's too complicated. She's someone I know, someone who works with Brigitte. And you've read my blog. I can't ever reveal myself—I can't risk Brigitte knowing…"

"Madame B." I raise my eyebrows as I say it. "Sounds like maybe you're leaning on your own understanding of the situation."

She leans back—away from me. Her body language tells me she's not ready to consider that possibility with this situation.

"You don't understand..."

"Hey, that wasn't a judgment, just an observation."

She's silent for a long time, and I give her the space for the silence. I don't press forward. I wait and watch. And I see a storm brewing in her eyes. *Jesus, calm the storm...*

"So, maybe I think I understand what would happen if Brigitte were ever to find out, but maybe I don't. Maybe it would turn out differently than I think?"

"Maybe. Let me ask you something." I lean forward. "Do you trust Brigitte?"

"No." The word is as firm as the shake of her head. "Not at all."

"Do you trust God?"

The question stops her. I see the shift in her thinking. She nods and I watch as tears fill her baby blues.

"I'm acting on my lack of trust in Brigitte rather than my trust in God." She twists the ring on her left ring finger. "My lack of trust is bigger than my trust."

"Help my unbelief." I quote the father in the Gospels who asked Jesus if he could save his son.

She nods and wipes a tear from her cheek.

"But...how could I ever..." Then she shakes her head. "I'm trying to figure it out again based on my own understanding."

I don't say anything.

"Instead, He's asking me to let go..."

"What does letting go look like in this circumstance?"

"I...I don't know. I guess I just wait?"

"Waiting on God while walking with God."

"What if..." Her eyes, so easy to read, reveal the fear she feels. "What if He's asking me to take up my cross and follow Him? What if..." She shakes her head. "I can't."

"Jenna, do you trust Him?"

"I'm...trying."

∾

AFTER MY TIME WITH JENNA, I walk back to my office. But it's a slow walk. A listening walk this time. It isn't my turn to ask questions. It isn't my turn to talk. It is a walk of reflection and revelation. The storm I saw brewing in Jenna is just the beginning. A hurricane is coming—gathering force, swirling, strengthening. I don't know what that means, but I sense something life-changing on the horizon.

For Jenna.

And for me.

And He's speaking to me, telling me to prepare myself:

Pray.

Fast.

Focus.

By the time I reach the office, there's a chill in the air. Before I step inside, I look up at the sky and see a bank of angry, dark clouds gathering above the bay.

Get ready, Matthew. I'm taking her into the eye of the storm. And you're going with her. But I am there.

I stand for a long time looking at the coming clouds and thinking about what I've heard. Then I nod my head in agreement with God. "Okay. Game on."

I turn from the clouds, walk into my office, and close my door against the brewing storm.

At least for now.

CHAPTER FORTY-SIX

Superficial relationships weaken the spirit... Instead of the sweetness of mutual edification, there is only the clashing of broken gears grinding against each other.
JEANNE GUYON

rigitte

SHE GETS INTO HER BENTLEY, sinks into the cream-colored leather driver's seat, and pulls the seatbelt over her shoulder. She leans her head out the open window. "Marcus, make sure those weeds along the fence line are taken care of today." She points to the rock wall separating the driveway from the vineyard.

Marcus squints, trying to find the weeds she speaks of. "Yes, Madame. Drive safely."

She rolls up her window and heads down the long drive. She's aware of the smooth asphalt under her tires. So much more pleasing than the annoying crunch of gravel as it was before she had it paved.

Her time in the valley was productive. She considers her accomplishments. She interviewed and retained an attorney, who will act as a representative in the Azul deal should she choose to demand payment of the note. He will work as a private contractor and therefore, Domaine de la Bouvier will remain the anonymous note holder for as long as she chooses. She was pleased with Max's recommendation.

Yesterday, Max drove to the valley and they spent the afternoon going through Gerard's trust one more time. She is now prepared to meet with Jenna. All is in place. She will offer Jenna a generous settlement. There will be, of course, a few stipulations, but if Jenna is wise, she'll concede.

Concede? She laughs. No concession should be necessary. If Jenna's wise, she'll see the offer for what it is—a lifetime of provision and affluence. Should she act like a fool, well then there is the demand note. Her insurance policy.

There are still issues to consider, however. Troubling issues.

Who was the man Hannah reported Jenna was with Saturday evening? Was it Matthew MacGregor? They share an intimacy that was evident both at Gerard's service and in the e-mails they exchange. He is, she is certain, the one influencing Jenna's behavior. Which means, the relationship must end.

A spiritual director? Such nonsense anyway.

She will continue to watch the e-mails between them.

Her thin lips stretch into a smile. Yes, now that she has access to Jenna's e-mail accounts, nothing will get past her. She tested her access on Monday evening by sending Jenna that ridiculous e-mail, then signing into her account.

She thinks of the e-mail she read late last night. Another from Matthew. It's left her baffled. Her grip tightens on the steering wheel, making the prominent blue veins in her hands bulge.

She glances at the clock on the dash—Jenna is with Matthew now.

At a lab?

Why?

Hannah reported that Jenna was feeling better. There was no fever—therefore, no infection. At least that is the assumption. She makes a mental note to see that Jenna gets in to see Dr. Bernard anyway. If the infection is indeed gone, then it is time to have that scar taken care of. It is such an embarrassment.

So, if Jenna is well, why is she at a lab and why has Matthew gone with her?

What is she hiding?

Well, she will figure it out soon enough.

Then there is the other issue revealed in Jenna's e-mails: Andee Bell.

Andee asked for Lightseeker's identity. *Lightseeker.* She shakes her head. *Such foolishness.* Jenna seemed firm in her desire to remain anonymous. *Good thing, chérie, or you'll find yourself in an indelicate situation. There will be no revealing yourself. Ever!* Her anger seethes as it has so many times since reading Jenna's ridiculous posts.

But anger won't serve her well. No, she must remain calm and clear. There is no truth in the gibberish Jenna writes. It's obvious her perspective is skewed. In fact, the posts have her concerned about Jenna's mental stability.

Andee... Can she be trusted? The e-mail exchanges between Jenna and Andee are revealing a weakness in Andee, one she hadn't seen before. Knowing another's weakness is always advantageous. She smiles. But she will have to monitor their relationship.

And it will also have to come to an end.

Perhaps it has already taken care of itself. There has been no response to Jenna since Andee's request for her identity. If she's smart, she won't choose to trust Lightseeker.

Know who you're dealing with—in business and in life. A simple rule.

As she winds her way through Sonoma and then across the

marshes before Vallejo, she considers Jenna again. By the time she married Gerard, she was certain of Jenna. She was pliable. Teachable. And she saw to it that few others influenced her. There was her father, of course, but he was consumed with his own grief and his business. Which left Jenna, of course, receptive to her attentions.

But in recent years, she's loosened the reins a bit. Let up. Grown complacent where Jenna was concerned. She can see that now. An oversight on her part. But one she must rectify. She's made the necessary adjustments now. Jenna will follow along, as she always has.

They will return to the relationship they had—mutually beneficial and satisfying. She lets out a small, tight sigh. Is it perfect? No. Gerard should still be alive. There should be grandchildren. Jenna should no longer be necessary.

But she is all that's left.

And one must never look back. Instead, one moves on. Looks forward. Makes the best of all circumstances.

Life is simple for those who understand how to work together.

Oui, Jenna is off course.

But she can change that.

CHAPTER FORTY-SEVEN

There is no greater revelation than realizing that you can do nothing of yourself.
JEANNE GUYON

*A*ndee

ON WEDNESDAY MORNING, while Cass is calling new brokers, I pour myself a cup of decaf. I had my one allotted espresso after getting up this morning. I lift the cup to my nose, sniff, and then take a sip. A definite improvement on the green tea.

I walk back into the office, where Cass sits at my desk talking to a broker. I motion for her to take it into the kitchen, and she gets up and takes the cordless phone and her notes with her.

"This is ridiculous," I say to Sam. "We need space." His disinterest is evidenced by his lack of response. "Yeah, what do you care?" I sit at the desk, reach for my cell phone, and then think better of it. The call I need to make is private. I lean back in my chair and look at Cass through the door leading to the kitchen. I pick up my phone and head for my bedroom, where I can make the call behind a closed door.

I sit on the end of my bed and first dial the Domaine de la Bouvier San Francisco office. I'm told Brigitte is returning from the valley today and won't be in the office until tomorrow. I leave a message with the receptionist, then glance at my watch—maybe she's already home. I dial her home office number and reach her voicemail. I leave a message there too. Then I dial her cell phone, which she answers.

"Andee, I was just thinking about you."

I hear a slight echo and know she's in her car. "I just spoke with your receptionist who said you're on your way in from the valley."

"Yes. I just crossed over the Marin County line. I always feel better once I'm back in civilization."

Her laugh agitates me. "Brigitte, listen, I'd like to set a meeting as soon as you're free."

"Regarding?"

"A proposition that's come up—I think you'll find it interesting. I'll share the details when we meet."

"Fine. I'll be back in the office tomorrow morning. What time works for you?"

"How about 10:00?"

"Very good. I'll look forward to seeing you, Andee."

I hang up the phone and lie back on the bed and look at the ceiling. I spent all day Tuesday, the day I told Cass I was taking off, thinking through the offer I'll make Brigitte.

It will cost me.

A lot.

I ignore the knot in my stomach that forms each time I think of the amount I'll offer her. But I'm determined to right my wrong. So it has to be an offer she can't refuse.

I close my eyes and put my hand on my pounding forehead. Caffeine withdrawal. Great. How will I ever get through a meeting with Brigitte without the benefit of caffeine? "C'mon Andee, you've pushed through more than this to get to where you are. You can push through this." *Maybe.*

I sit back up on the bed just as Cass taps on my door.

"Andee?"

"Come in, Cass."

She opens the door and takes a step into my bedroom. "You okay?"

"Never better." I pull myself up off the bed and stand.

"Could have fooled me. Are you sure you don't want . . ."

"Cassidy"—I point my finger at her—"I told you. No more. And the next time you offer me a cup, I'll fire you."

She laughs.

"I'm glad you find this so amusing."

"It's just that I always thought drive determined your destiny, not caffeine."

I look at her, eyebrows raised, and then push past her and head back to the office. "Oh my gosh, what if you're right?" I say over my shoulder. "Maybe just one more cup . . ." I bypass the office and head for the kitchen, but Cass cuts me off at the pass.

"No. No more. You can do this." She pushes me back to the office. "It'll be great. Really. It's already helping. You're becoming the kinder, gentler, Andee Bell."

I turn around and glare at her.

"Okay, not really. You're still a—"

"Watch it."

She smiles. "Hey, I'm going to meet with this broker and see some of his inventory. I'll save you another wasted morning." She takes her jacket off the back of my desk chair, and grabs her purse. "Okay?"

"Okay. And . . . thank you."

"Thank you?" She feigns an expression of shock.

"Get out of here!"

THE DOMAINE DE LA BOUVIER offices in the city are nondescript—a suite on an upper floor of one of a hundred office buildings in the area. The receptionist shows me to Brigitte's office. As we walk down the hallway, we pass Gerard's office. The door is closed, the light off. It is a somber reminder of the brevity of life and a reminder of my own recent wake-up call.

Which, I remind myself, is why I'm here.

The receptionist seats me across from Brigitte's desk and tells me she'll be right with me.

"May I get you something while you wait? Coffee or tea?"

"Coffee. Black."

"Regular or decaf?"

I hesitate. I've got to get through this meeting. "Regular. Thank you."

I hear Brigitte talking to someone as she approaches her office and I stand to greet her. She stands at the open office door, her back to me, and instructs an admin on an assignment. I notice the cut of her dark suit, and see a flash of the red soles of her signature Louboutin pumps.

When she turns and enters the office, she smiles, but there is no warmth in her eyes, or in her manner.

"Andee, have a seat."

I've requested this meeting and she doesn't know why. It's her territory, but she's still at a disadvantage. Good.

"Nice to see you, Brigitte." Okay, so I'm bluffing, but I'm just warming up.

"And you." She seats herself in the chair behind the mahogany desk. "You mentioned a proposition."

The receptionist returns with my coffee and a cup of tea for

Brigitte. I reach for the cup and saucer she offers me and take a needed gulp. If I burn my mouth, oh well. Then I set the saucer on the desk and continue to hold the cup. Once the receptionist is gone, I respond. "Yes." I take another sip of the coffee and then set the cup down too and begin the story I've rehearsed. "I received a call on Monday from an investor I work with, an old friend, it seems, of Duke Whitmore. He said he heard, through the grapevine"—

I smile my most charming smile—"no pun intended, that Kelly sold a demand note for Azul."

I see Brigitte bristle.

"Where did he get that information? Kelly assured me the transaction would remain between us."

"He said he was at a bar, sitting next to her attorney. He was—in his words—flapping his lips about Kelly's business. He'd had too much to drink." I hold up my hand as I see the glint of anger in her eyes. "He didn't reveal who purchased the note. Just said another vintner paid a good price for it. He then went on to tell my investor what the note sold for."

She sets her cup and saucer on her desk and leans back in her chair. "And?"

"And he wondered if I could find out who made the purchase and make them an offer. It seems he has a soft spot for Azul." I shrug. "Who knows what his reasons are, but I asked what he's willing to pay and I thought you might find the offer intriguing."

"I'm not interested."

Her icy stare chills me and my heart begins to race. "Fine."

I bend to pick up my briefcase.

"Wait."

I set the briefcase back down and lean back in my chair.

"What's he willing to pay?"

"Double." My tone is cool, detached and, I hope, belies the panic I feel at the thought of putting out that much money for anything.

Her eyes narrow and her stare pins me to my seat. Of course, I don't let her know that.

"What will he do with the note? Will he demand Bill pay it?"

"I assume so, but I don't know."

She gets up from her desk, comes around to the front of it, and perches on the edge near me. She looks down at me. "Who is it? Who is the investor?"

I sit still and meet her gaze. "He wishes to remain anonymous."

She stands and walks back to her chair and sits behind the desk again. "I have a simple rule—one I'm sure you'll appreciate: know who you're dealing with. Wise, don't you agree?"

I shrug. "It's your business, Brigitte. As your financial advisor, it's my job to inform you when a deal like that comes across my desk. It is a lot of money—a fantastic return on your investment. Something worth considering, I'd think. But my hands are tied. As I do with you, I maintain a code of confidentiality with all my clients. I have to."

"My reasons for obtaining the note were personal. It wasn't a business transaction, per se. The note is not for sale. At any price. So, as I stated, I'm not interested in your investor's offer. But thank you for notifying me." She looks from me to her watch.

"If…you change your mind, you know where to find me."

"Oh, I never change my mind." She stands.

I reach for my briefcase again and as I grasp the handle my nails dig into the palm of my hand. I stand and turn for the door.

It's clear the meeting is over.

I don't let myself think as I leave her office and walk down the hall. But once I step into the elevator and the doors close, I lean against the back wall and bang my head against the wood paneling.

How could she turn down that much money? If money isn't her motivator, what is? How could I have been so wrong? I bang my head against the elevator wall again.

When the elevator stops at the lobby, I take a deep breath, step out, and walk out of the building, head held high, despite the anger, and despair, threatening to pull me under.

What now? If I can't buy the note back, how can I right my wrong? How can I fix things . . . for Jason, for Bill, and—who am I kidding—for myself?

I stand on the sidewalk, seeing nothing.

How do I redeem myself?

CHAPTER FORTY-EIGHT

For Christ to truly reign within you everything must be submitted to him without reservation.

JEANNE GUYON

*J*enna

I OPEN my e-mail and see, finally, a response from Andee. Has she decided to trust Lightseeker?

Lightseeker,

Okay, you win. But sell me out, and I'll make your life miserable. Not a threat, just a warning. You say you need to protect your identity in order to protect yourself. I know a little something about self-protection: It doesn't work. I've spent my life trying to protect myself and now, I face exactly what I've attempted to avoid. Ironic.

In your last post, you wrote about loneliness and having known perfect love. What's the deal with the perfect love? I know God is equated with love, and assume that's who you refer to, but how does one go about participating in a relationship with God?

And why would God want a love relationship with me? Believe me, I've done nothing to deserve anyone's love lately. In fact, I've driven everyone away and have betrayed those who cared at all.

So, Lightseeker, enlighten me...

A. Bell

I lean back in my desk chair and think of Andee. Not the Andee I've met, the Andee that dated Jason. But Andee Bell, financial advisor, author, radio personality. How much courage did it take for that Andee to expose herself to a complete stranger? To risk, as she wrote, being sold out?

How much is she hurting that she'd take such a risk?

Is the betrayal she mentions a reference to Jason? I hurt for him because I know he cared about Andee, but I don't resent her. It seemed evident that she gave what she could to Jason. She'd built a fortress around herself—anyone could see that. She was covering deep wounds—making sure nothing, or no one, wounded her again. At least, that was my sense after spending the weekend with her and Jason at the chateau.

I consider her warning—not about making my life miserable.

I smile. That's just Andee. I know I won't betray her confidence. No, I wonder about her warning about self-protection not working.

I think again of Brigitte and the blog and another wave of nausea rolls over me.

I reach for the steaming cup of peppermint herbal tea on my desk and take a small sip. After feeling so sick earlier in the week, I asked Hannah to replace my morning coffee with the tea, as it seemed to help the nausea.

Just the thought of Brigitte discovering my blog makes me sick to my stomach—and the tea does nothing to relieve that.

What have I gotten myself into?

And yet...

I look back at Andee's e-mail and my passion stirs. Would I forgo the opportunity to respond to Andee's question, to share the love and grace of Jesus with her, simply to protect myself from Brigitte?

I twist the band on my left ring finger and recall the vow I made: *I will have no other god before you.*

No, I will continue with the blog. I am honored, awed even, for the opportunity to share with Andee and others like her. I won't reveal my identity. And maybe my protection will fail, as Andee suggested, but if so, I'll trust God with the outcome.

I take another sip of tea and then begin my response to Andee.

Dear Andee,

I assure you, God wants a relationship with you. A deep, abiding, love relationship. He adores you. So much so that He gave up His only Son as payment for your sin—my sin. There is nothing you can do to separate yourself from His love. Nothing.

If you believe Jesus Christ is the Son of God, and is God Himself as part of the trinity, Father, Son, and Spirit, then you've already begun a relationship.

Like any other relationship, it is built by getting to know one another. But in this relationship, you are already fully known, fully loved, and fully accepted. Now it's your turn to get to know God—the lover of your soul. Spend time with Him. Read His Word—His love letter to you. Do you have a Bible? If so, begin in the New Testament, maybe with the book of John, and get to know Jesus.

I stop. Will Andee believe? Or will she doubt the truth of God's Word? *Oh Lord, open her eyes to Your truth, let her sense Your love for her, give her a picture of Your grace. Heal her wounds.* I feel my eyes well with tears. *Lord, let her fall so deeply in love with You that nothing else in her life matters.*

I think again of Brigitte. *And Lord, let me love You in that same way. Let nothing else, no one else, stand in the way of my relationship with You.* A ripple of fear threatens to unnerve me. But I take a deep breath and continue. *Lord, strengthen me to pick up my cross and follow You. I'm ready.*

Peace threads itself through my soul, stitching my fraying courage.

I return to my e-mail:

Andee, thank you for choosing to trust me. I will honor your trust. Thank you, too, for your words about self-protection—I will ponder your advice.

Blessings...

I sign off, close the laptop, and reach for my Bible. I turn to the passage in the Gospels that Matthew read to me a couple of weeks ago and read:

"I have come to turn a man against his father, a daughter

against her mother, a daughter-in-law against her mother-in-law—"

I skip down the page.

"Anyone who loves their father or mother more than me is not worthy of me: anyone who loves their son or daughter more than me is not worthy of me. Whoever does not take up their cross and follow me is not worthy of me. Whoever finds their life will lose it, and whoever loses their life for my sake will find it."

I smile. I'm great at losing things, so losing my life shouldn't be an issue. Although, I know I'm not clear on Jesus' meaning. So I look at the verses listed in the margin that reference other passages with a similar theme and see Luke 14 listed. I turn there and read Jesus words:

"If anyone comes to me and does not hate father and mother, wife and children, brothers and sisters—yes, even their own life—such a person cannot be my disciple. And whoever does not carry their cross and follow me cannot be my disciple."

Clarity comes. Picking up my cross—carrying my cross— means I'm willing to walk away from anyone, even loved ones, who stand between me and Jesus.

A scene from the Bible comes to mind—a conversation between Peter and Jesus. Does it apply?

I stand up and take my Bible to the sofa, sit, and then flip to the back of my Bible and search for that passage in the concordance. I find the verse in the concordance and turn to the referenced verses. I read Jesus' prediction of His death and then pick up His conversation with well-intentioned Peter in Matthew 16:22:

"Peter took him aside and began to rebuke him. 'Never, Lord!' he said. 'This shall never happen to you!' Jesus turned and said to Peter, 'Get behind me, Satan! You are a stumbling block to me; you do not have in mind the concerns of God, but merely human concerns.'"

That's it! Fascinated, I keep reading. And with the next verse, my heart skips a beat.

"Then Jesus said to his disciples, 'Whoever wants to be my disciple must deny themselves and take up their cross and follow me. For whoever wants to save their life will lose it, but whoever loses their life for me will find it.'"

The verses echo Jesus' words from the earlier chapter in Matthew—the wording is almost exact. One verse talks about seeking our lives, the other talks about saving our lives.

Andee's warning about self-protection comes to mind again. Is protecting myself the same as trying to save my life? I feel the fog of confusion roll in. But wouldn't walking away from Brigitte be a self-protective act? Isn't that saving myself?

I pose my questions to God, but the light of clarity dims, and soon I'm wandering, lost, in a dense fog.

I get up from the sofa, go to the desk, and make a note to talk this through with Matthew.

I sigh.

Why does it have to be so complicated?

CHAPTER FORTY-NINE

Do not regard the external, but the inward state of people.
JEANNE GUYON

rigitte

SHE PAYS the fare and then waits for the cab driver to get out and open the door for her. Once he does, she tips him. She steps onto the curb and opens her umbrella while cursing the rain. She'd rather have met at her home office, but no, this is better. Neutral territory.

She crosses the sidewalk, and steps into the lobby of the office building, shaking the water off her umbrella as she does. She waits at the elevator with a group of businessmen just returning from lunch, it appears. When she reaches the top floor, she steps out of the elevator into the reception area of Shultz, Shultz, and Gorman.

The receptionist greets her. "Mrs. Bouvier, please go back, Mr. Shultz is expecting you."

She heads for Max's office. As she passes the receptionist's desk she says, "I'd like a cup of tea. No sugar." She walks into Max's office without knocking. "Maxwell, I trust everything is in order?"

He stands. "Hello, Brigitte. I'm fine. Thank you for asking. Please, come in."

"Amusing, as always." She sets her briefcase down and comes around the desk and gives him a peck on the cheek, then straightens his tie and pats him on the shoulder. "Much better, oui?"

There's a tap on his door and the receptionist comes in with Brigitte's tea and hands it to her. "May I get you anything else?"

"This will do."

"Thank you, Rachel." Max gestures to the round table in front of the floor-to-ceiling window. "Brigitte, have a seat. Everything is in order, of course. As we discussed in Napa, I'll give you each a copy of the trust and I'll go through it with Jenna. Then you can present your...what shall we call it? Your offer?"

She sniffs. "Yes, Max, it is an offer, and a very generous one at that, n'est-ce pas?"

"I suppose it depends on your perspective. I don't think you can assume Jenna will agree to your stipulations."

"Don't be silly, Maxwell. They're hardly stipulations. Just a few requests."

"And if she doesn't abide by your requests?"

"She will. I've seen to that."

"Yes, I know." He smiles. "I'm glad we're friends, Brigitte, I'd hate to be your enemy."

"Wise man."

The intercom on Max's desk buzzes. He walks to the desk and picks up the phone receiver. "Thank you. Send her in." Then he walks to the office door, opens it, and steps into the hallway and waits. "Jenna, good to see you. Please come in. Brigitte just arrived."

Brigitte stands to welcome Jenna. "Hello, chérie, have a seat next to me and we'll get this distasteful business over with. I still can't believe"—she shakes her head—"Well, you know. It still seems impossible that he's really gone."

"Yes, I know."

The three of them sit around the table and Max opens the file folder and distributes copies of the trust.

"Jenna, I can read through all the legal jargon, if you'd like, or I can tell you in general terms what's stated in the trust. Which do you prefer?"

"General terms are fine, Max."

"Good. You have a copy of the trust, and I'd advise you, once we've gone through it, to have your own attorney look it over if you'd like. Though, I assure you, it's all in order. Any questions before we get started?" He looks from Jenna to Brigitte.

Brigitte shakes her head. "Just get on with it, Max."

"Fine." He puts on his glasses and looks at the trust sitting in front of him and then looks at Jenna. "When Gerard's father died, as you know, Gerard was still a minor, so everything was left to Brigitte. Much later, I prepared a trust for Gerard in the event and with the expectation that Brigitte would predecease Gerard and that the trust would hold whatever he accumulated and whatever he inherited. Following me?"

"So far."

"Good." He leans back in his chair, and takes off his glasses. "Now, Gerard was paid an annual salary from Domaine de la Bouvier, and any monies in your personal accounts, retirement accounts, personal investments, things of that nature, are of course, community property." He looks at Jenna again. "Understood?"

She hesitates. "So, you're saying nothing will come to me through the trust?"

"Right." Max looks to Brigitte. "Brigitte, would you like to take it from here?"

"Thank you, Max." She turns in her seat so she's facing Jenna.

"Now darling, unless there are accounts you're aware of that I am not, then I don't believe Gerard made many personal investments. In fact, on more than one occasion through the years, I've given him additional funds so he could maintain the lifestyle you seemed to want. And of course, you also received the generous allowance each month." She sits back in her chair and looks at Jenna and shakes her head. "Sadly, we both know Gerard wasn't much of a businessman. He seemed more interested in, shall we say, enjoying life."

Jenna looks at her clasped hands in her lap, then looks back to Brigitte. "His time and efforts were committed to Domaine de la Bouvier. He felt that was his best investment and believed it would provide for retirement and beyond. He worked hard."

"Well, I'm the better judge of his work habits, non?" She reaches over and places her hand on Jenna's arm. "But that aside, chérie, it should have been me, of course, who passed first. When Gerard wanted to change his trust, to add"—she clears her throat —"provisions, I discouraged him. Perhaps I was in denial—I couldn't face the thought of losing him. You understand, of course." She pulls back from Jenna and continues. "However, now we're faced with the unfortunate task of discussing life without Gerard."

Jenna sits, hands folded, and jaw clenched.

"Darling, you look quite upset, pale even. Are you all right?"

"Yes. I'm fine. Would it be possible to get a glass of water?" She looks to Max.

"Of course." Max goes to the credenza behind his desk, reaches for a glass, and pours water from the pitcher sitting on a tray on the cabinet. He returns to the table, hands the glass to Jenna, pats her on the back, and then sits back down. "These meetings are never easy, my dear."

"Thank you." She takes a sip of the water.

Brigitte scoots forward in her chair, "Max, hand me a copy of the agreement we drafted."

Max opens the file folder in front of him and hands a piece of paper to Brigitte.

She sits back and glances at the document and then says, "You know, Jenna, I love you as if you were my own daughter. And now, it is just the two of us. You stand to inherit all I have—the company and all its holdings and, of course, my personal estate." She leans over and pats Jenna on the shoulder. "So you see, you have nothing to worry about, chérie."

Jenna nods and then takes another sip of water.

"Before I change my trust, there are just a few things we'll need to agree upon. Max has drafted an agreement for you to sign."

"May I see it?"

"Of course, darling." Brigitte hands the document to her. "Please, read it and then if you have questions, though I don't know why you would, we can discuss them here." She sits back, folds her hands in her lap.

Marveilleux. All is going according to plan.

Jenna takes the document and begins to read, as she does, her hand, and the paper, begin to shake. She sets the paper on the table and folds her hands in her lap and then continues to read.

Brigitte watches, her gaze never leaving Jenna. When she thinks she's had plenty of time to read the agreement, she turns to Max. "Do you have a pen for Jenna?"

"Wait." Jenna's voice cracks. She takes a deep breath and looks at Brigitte. "My blog...how...how did you—"

"Are you surprised?" She doesn't even try to soften the hard, cold edge of her words. "No longer writing the blog won't be an issue, will it? We live in the public eye, Jenna, you know that—something like that leaves us open to criticism—makes us vulnerable. Surely you understand. It is time for you to re-involve yourself elsewhere. Now that the infection is gone, and once you've had the corrective surgery, you can immerse yourself in the charities you once enjoyed. Do something worthwhile again."

Jenna reaches for her water glass.

"Darling, you're shaking. Are you sure you're feeling well?"

She takes a drink of the water and sets the glass back down. Water sloshes over the edge of the glass onto the table.

"Here, let me get a napkin." Max starts to rise.

"Why not sign the agreement now, chérie, and then we can go enjoy a late lunch together. We'll go somewhere special."

"No."

Though Jenna whispers the word, it strikes Brigitte like a sledgehammer. "I beg your pardon?"

Jenna scoots away from the table and stands. "I said, no!" She turns and walks out of the office.

CHAPTER FIFTY

*You must walk with God with a total sense of abandonment and
uncertainty.*
JEANNE GUYON

enna

I STAGGER out of the building and onto the sidewalk. A cold wind
slaps me in the face. I pull my coat close, turn into the wind,
and walk.

And walk.

And walk.

I weave between people crowding the sidewalk, and step off
the curb to cross the street in an attempt to escape the masses.
Cars honk as I dodge them. And someone yells, telling me to
watch out.

I don't know where I'm going. I don't care. I just need to get
away—away from Brigitte. Away from her control.

My relentless pace matches my racing thoughts. *How did she find out about the blog? How long has she known? What has she read? How much did I reveal?* And the thought that repeats over and over: *Stop writing the blog and inherit millions.*

Does she really think she can buy me?

Of course she does. I've never given her reason to believe otherwise.

Stop writing the blog and inherit millions.

But that wasn't all. I stop on the sidewalk, close my eyes, and picture the agreement. There were three points, but I was so stunned by the fact that she knew about my blog that I just scanned the rest of the agreement. I try now to recall the second and third stipulations.

Ah, yes, of course.

The second stipulation was that I live with Brigitte for the remainder of her lifetime.

But what was the third stipulation? I continue walking, cutting through alleys and down side streets. It didn't register when I read it. My mind shuffles and again I picture the agreement and I see, in my mind, Matthew's name.

The wind whips my hair, the ends sting my face as they hit.

No further contact with Matthew MacGregor.

That was it.

Anger pummels me like a pounding fist.

I swallow the scream rising in my throat and wipe my face—rain mingles with my tears. When did it start raining? I slow my pace and look around. I have no idea where in the city I am. Heat from my exertion radiates from under my coat and I strip it off, drape it over my arm, and walk to the next corner where I can see the street signs.

Then I dig in my purse until I find my phone.

"Ahsan, I need a ride."

"Mrs. Jenna?"

"Yes."

"Are you all right?"

"No…no I'm not."

"Where are you?"

Still breathless, I give him the names of the streets.

"Mrs. Jenna, I will call another cab. I cannot be there soon. It will be at least twenty-five minutes."

"No, Ahsan. I want…I…need you to come. I'll wait."

"But Mrs. Jenna—"

"Please, please come." I choke back tears.

"I will be there, Mrs. Jenna. I will be there."

WHEN AHSAN ARRIVES, I'm soaking wet and shivering. I'd put my coat back on and waited under an awning, but I was wet to begin with. He pulls up to the curb, gets out, and leads me to the front passenger seat.

I slide into the cab and he closes the door for me. Then he goes around the back of the car, opens his trunk, slams it closed, and comes back and gets into the driver's seat. He hands me a towel. "It is clean."

"Thank you."

He reaches for the console, turns the heat up, and makes sure the vents are pointed in my direction. His simple acts of kindness cause my tears to flow again. I put the towel to my face and wipe my eyes.

Ahsan reaches over and places his hand on my shoulder. "Mrs. Jenna, what has happened?"

"Oh, Ahsan…" I tell him the whole story as we sit in the warmth of the cab, rain thrumming on the windshield as I talk. Ahsan is attentive, his turbaned head nodding as he listens.

Then I remember something he said, and the question it evoked. "Ahsan, what did you mean the other night when you said I've run the race well, but now the course changes?"

"The courses of our lives change, but if our focus remains on Jesus, then we remain steady. He makes our paths straight."

I stare out the window into the gray afternoon. "Has He done that for you?"

"Yes, Mrs. Jenna. My course changed when God led me to America. I had to leave my family, people I care for and who depend on me. And not all agreed that I should go. My father and my wife were very angry. But my eyes were on Jesus and this is where He led."

"Why? Why did He lead you away from your family?"

"He did not lead me away from my family, He led me closer to Him."

I take the towel Ahsan gave me and dry the ends of my hair as I ponder his words. "But how did you know? How did you know for sure that you were to come here?"

"I did not know for sure. We must walk in faith, Mrs. Jenna, which means being uncertain of where we go, but certain of He who goes with us."

His gaze holds mine, and I read compassion and understanding in his eyes.

"Now that I am here, I see more clearly. In America, I am free to worship my God, to live a life of dignity, to provide for my family. But the way is still uncertain. I do not know when God will bring my family here. I do not know many things. But I know Him." He points his finger heavenward.

As I listen, my soul settles and peace envelops me. I reach out and put my hand on Ahsan's arm. "Thank you, Ahsan. You offer God's mercy this afternoon."

He nods and smiles. "You are tired, Mrs. Jenna. I will take you home now?"

I look out the front windshield, through the pouring rain, and then nod my head. "Yes, take me back to the house."

It is not my home.

CHAPTER FIFTY-ONE

If entering into deep union with God were as easy as walking into a
room, many would gladly do it. The door that leads to life first leads to
many deaths.
JEANNE GUYON

ndee

I STARE at my computer screen, stare at Lightseeker's last e-mail,
until the letters on the screen blur into a jumbled mess—much
like the thoughts jumbled in my mind. I lean my elbows on my
desk, and my head in my hands. Then I rub my eyes, sigh, and lean
back in the chair again.

Since my failed meeting with Brigitte, agitation has gnawed at
me like a piranha, destroying my confidence in my own abilities.
As an adult, I've controlled my circumstances and often the
actions of those around me. Now, for the first time, I find myself
in a situation I can't control.

That realization both angers and scares me.

I'm consumed with that reality and in desperate need of help—hence, my return to Lightseeker's e-mail. Okay, I admit, I've read it multiple times a day since she sent it. Good grief. You'd think I have nothing better to do. Though, I haven't followed through on her suggestion to read the Bible. *Whatever.*

I swivel the chair and turn away from the computer. But before doing so, I reach for the remote control. I face the flat screen hanging on my office wall and turn the TV on and flip through channels, but nothing holds my attention. Nothing stops the nipping of the piranha.

I flip back to CNN and let it drone as background noise.

I concede and get up, go to the hall closet, and grab the box I dropped in there several days ago after it was delivered to my door. In the box is the Bible I ordered. Somewhere, I have a Bible from my childhood—a small book with a white leather cover. But I refuse to dig it out—too many reminders.

Anyway, that isn't the God I want to know.

Instead, I decided, if I was going to read the Bible, as Lightseeker suggested, I wanted a new Bible for a new God. Okay, so maybe He isn't new. But I need a new understanding of Him. That much I get.

I think back to the evening I ordered the Bible online. Who knew there were zillions of Bibles to choose from? And translations. Give me a break. I emailed Lightseeker back for a recommendation.

Now, I go to the kitchen, set the box on the counter, and then tear it open. I pull out the heavy book, take the wrapping off, and then hold it up to my nose and breathe in the rich scent of leather.

I take the Bible and head back to my desk where I sit, set the Bible on the desk, and fan through the fragile pages.

"Well, Sam, I guess there's no time like the present." Sam, who's laying under the lamp on my desktop, stretches his front legs out and then curls back around himself. I begin flipping through the pages again. I stop when something catches my eye, though most of it seems meaningless. I stop at the book of Ecclesiastes and read:

"Meaningless! Meaningless! Utterly meaningless!"

"Exactly."
I keep reading:

"What does man gain from all his labor at which he toils under the sun?"

I read to the end of the chapter. This, I get. It's what I've felt all week long. I inked a deal with a cable channel for the *Andee Bell Show*. I looked at buildings with Cass and the new broker and found two to choose from—both are perfect. I completed the first draft of my current manuscript. And I interviewed two potential publicists.

But so what?

None of it stirred anything in me.

The enjoyment I used to derive from my work seems lost to me.

I've done it all.

I have it all.

So what?

With the Bible still sitting on my desk, I close it, and then lean forward and rest my forehead on it. For the first time in my adult life, I have no idea what to do.

Everything seems pointless.

CHAPTER FIFTY-TWO

*Along the sightless path, you may begin to consider yourself separated
from God and feel that you are left to act for yourself.*
JEANNE GUYON

*J*enna

I WAKE to the same nausea and debilitating fatigue that followed
me home from the meeting with Brigitte and Max yesterday, but I
determine I'll push through it. Gerard's death, the uncertainties of
what his trust contained, and the continued stress of living under
Brigitte's rule have taken their toll. My body is reacting—telling
me what I haven't wanted to face.

Haven't had the courage to face.

It is time to leave.

Time to take care of myself, to be a good steward of the life
God's given me, as Jason suggested.

It is time to stand back from Brigitte.

To stand back from the life I've known and my own understanding.

Not only because I believe this is the meaning of God's message to me this last year, but also for my own well being. How can I follow God and His purpose for me if I can't function? If I spend more time sick than well?

It is time to pick up my cross and follow Him.

It all seems clear now.

I raise my head off my pillow, take a deep breath, and then sit up and put my legs over the side of the bed. I stand and determine, again, that I won't give in to my churning stomach. I walk to my closet, put on my robe, and decide I'll go to the kitchen and force myself to eat a piece of toast and drink some juice. It is early enough that I know I won't run into Brigitte, or even Hannah.

I hesitate at the elevator, but no, I'll make myself walk down the stairs. I take each step like a woman far beyond my thirty-three years. Winded as I reach the last step, I decide I'll call the doctor tomorrow just to make certain this isn't the infection. I haven't wanted, couldn't entertain that possibility. But it's time to face reality again.

Nicholetta, the cook, is alone in the kitchen when I poke my head in.

"Good morning, Jenna. May I get you something?"

"Good morning, Nicholetta. Just a piece of toast and some juice, please."

"Would you like it in your room?"

"No, don't bother bringing it up. I'll just have it here, if that's okay?"

"Of course."

I pull out one of the stools from under the island, and sit while Nicholetta drops a piece of sourdough bread into the toaster and pours me a glass of apple juice. When she sets the juice in front of me, she pauses.

"You're sick again."

I shrug my shoulders. "I'm okay."

"You don't look okay." Then she leans in and lowers her voice. "It is this house—the atmosphere—it is *her*. Pardon me for saying so, but you cannot stay here and be healthy. You are free now.

Mr. Bouvier is gone. You are free to leave. You must go. Otherwise, you will fall to depression. You will be sick forever."

I watch as she steps back from me, reaches for her gray bun, adjusts a bobby pin, and then goes to the sink, washes her hands, wipes them on a towel, and then butters my toast.

This is the first time in eleven years that one of the staff has said anything personal to me, or perhaps more surprising, anything against Brigitte. When Nicholetta sets a plate with my toast in front of me, I reach out and grab her hand. "Nicholetta, thank you. I think...I know you're right. Thank you."

She nods her head. "You need to take care of yourself." She smiles and gives my hand a squeeze then returns to her duties.

I take a small bite of the toast, chew it, and make myself swallow. Then I take a sip of the juice. I force myself to eat until the toast is gone. All the while thinking of Nicholetta's words. Depression. Yes, that's the gray cloud—the fog that's followed me. And I've read it can lead to physical ailments. Perhaps that is what plagues me.

It is time to go.

I knew it when I woke this morning.

And now that knowledge has been affirmed.

I stand, take my plate to the sink, and smile at Nicholetta before turning to go.

I don't have a plan, but I'll make one. I'll call my dad and Jason this morning. I leave the kitchen and climb the stairs while deciding what to do. I'll get Dad and Jason's advice. Maybe I'll stay with—

"Jenna, please come in for a moment."

Brigitte stands at the door of her suite and motions for me to step inside. She wears her robe and holds a cup of coffee. Her tone is cold, hard.

My stomach lurches and I long to turn and run, but there seems no way to avoid her, so I follow her into her suite and then into her office. I notice the file folder sitting on the desk. She goes behind her desk, sets her coffee cup down, and reaches for the folder and hands it across the desk to me.

"You left Max's office yesterday without signing the agreement. I thought you'd like to take care of that this morning so we can get on with things." She opens her desk drawer and takes out a pen and hands it to me.

I wasn't prepared to face her.

Not yet.

But maybe being unprepared is better.

I set the file and pen down on her desk, and put my hands in the pockets of my robe so she won't see them shaking. "I've"—I clear my throat—"I've made a decision." Her icy stare makes my skin crawl, but I must continue. "I won't... sign the agreement." As I speak the words it feels as though my lungs collapse. I take a shallow breath and feel my pulse pounding in my temples. My tongue threatens to stick to the roof of my mouth. I swallow. "I'll make arrangements to move."

Brigitte says nothing, but leans across the desk and picks up the file folder. She turns, opens the top drawer of her credenza, and replaces the file. Then she pulls out a different file and sets it on her desk. She turns back to me.

"That is a shame, chérie. I was hoping we could do this simply. But if that is the choice you've made, then I should share some additional information with you." She reaches for the new file, her acrylic nails claw-like as she pushes it across the desk.

"What is this?" I pick up the file and open it.

"That, my dear, is a little piece of business. Your father's business."

I read the sheet of paper in the file once. Twice. And break into a cold sweat. "I…don't understand."

"It's a demand note. Your father borrowed money against Azul and then never repaid the note. Not only does he owe the amount of the original loan, but also twenty-six years of interest."

"What?" I can't take in the information. It makes no sense. "Why…why do you have it?"

She reaches for her robe and pulls the top of it close to her neck. "I purchased the note from the original holder. I paid a great deal of money for it. So now, I hold the note and, if I so choose, will demand payment from your father for the entire amount."

I look at the note again and try to imagine what twenty-six years of interest alone would add up to. But the numbers are too big. Plus, I have no idea what Brigitte paid on top of that. I look at Brigitte, my earlier nausea replaced with roiling anger. "What are you saying?" My voice trembles now, but not from fear.

"You will sign the agreement presented yesterday, Jenna, and adhere, of course, to the stipulations. Or I will demand full payment from your father, which, as we both know, he won't be able to pay. Simply speaking, it will force him into bankruptcy."

"No." I gasp for breath. "No! You're lying!" I'm shouting, but I don't care. "I would have known." I gulp back angry tears. "He would have told me—told Jason."

"Evidently you don't know your father as well as you think you do."

Her calm infuriates me. I close the file and slap it onto her desk and turn to leave. I can't respond. I have to think—to call my dad. I can't—

"Jenna, there is one more thing."

Her tone sends a chill through me and I stop and turn. She hasn't moved—just crossed her arms across her chest. "You *will* end your relationship with Matthew MacGregor. If you don't—if you choose not to sign the agreement, not to abide by the stipulations—I will expose your affair with Mr. MacGregor in a very public and humiliating way. Humiliating, I'd imagine, for both of you."

I'm struck dumb by this outrageous claim. Me? Matthew? An affair?

She picks up the file folder, returns it to the credenza, and makes a show of locking the drawer. She drops the key in the pocket of her bathrobe. "Don't doubt that I have evidence to back my claims. I don't make false accusations. I have proof, of course."

The nausea returns and assaults me. I turn and run from her room.

I run down the hallway, through my room, and make it to the bathroom just in time. I lose the toast and juice I'd forced myself to eat. For more times than I care to count in recent weeks, I find myself on my knees on the bathroom floor—heaving and crying. I pound my fist on the floor and gasp for air.

It's too much, Lord. This is too much!

I heave, my stomach convulsing, until there is nothing left.

I lay on the floor—I have neither the strength nor the dignity to get myself up. Thoughts of Brigitte crowd my mind. I see her, finally, for what she is—a sick woman who cares about one thing, and one thing only: herself. Love me? She's never loved me or anyone else. She is incapable.

She lives life as a game, moving people as pawns at will, determined to win.

And won she has.

Checkmate.

Game over.

I think of the demand note and though I doubted its validity, I know Brigitte wouldn't threaten something she couldn't see through. I don't know why my father never spoke of it, but now it will destroy him. And Jason.

Unless I sign Brigitte's agreement.

What choice do I have?

Again, the anger boils and bubbles within. Not only toward

Brigitte, but this time also for myself. How stupid I was to think I could just walk away. Just pick up and leave. *What a fool I am!*

I roll to my back on the bathroom floor and tears pool around my ears.

Oh, Matthew, I'm so, so sorry.

What "proof" can Brigitte have when there was no affair? When, in fact, there was never *any*thing like that between Matthew and me? I don't know. But again, she doesn't make veiled threats. She will produce some trumped-up evidence. Something that will convince all concerned that her baseless accusations are true. And I don't doubt that the humiliation would be public and painful.

Too painful.

Defeat calls my name and I respond.

The fight is over.

I roll over, pull myself to my knees, and get up.

I reach for the box of tissue on the counter, wipe my eyes, and blow my nose again. And then I wobble my way from the bathroom back to my bed. I drop onto the edge of the bed and stare at the floor. I sit like that for a long time and consider what's to come. And consider my own failings.

I lift my left hand and look at the band on my ring finger—the symbol of my union with God . . . and now the symbol of my broken vow.

I shall have no other god before You...except Brigitte, it seems.

I slip the ring off, open the drawer of my nightstand, and drop the ring inside.

I shut the drawer.

Then I lie down, pull the covers up, and curl into myself.

CHAPTER FIFTY-THREE

*You may not practice what people consider to be obvious vices; but
inside, the essential self-nature is still very much alive.*
JEANNE GUYON

rigitte

JENNA HAS CONCEDED.

It's been two days since she shared the insurance policy with
Jenna. Two days since Jenna ran from her office. And now, two
days since Jenna's left her room. She smiles. Her plan has worked.
Bien sûr.

Hannah has taken meals to Jenna's room and reports that she
seems complacent, though perhaps depressed. She hasn't dressed
and is eating little. She is, however, checking her e-mail. This was
evident when Brigitte signed into Jenna's account. There were e-
mails from blog readers, as well as from both Matthew and
Andee, but she's responded to nothing. Matthew is concerned, as

she missed her "appointment" with him yesterday and neither called nor e-mailed him.

His concern was so great that he even showed up at the front door to check on Jenna. Ridiculous. Hannah relayed that Jenna is fine—just under the weather.

C'est la vie, Mr. MacGregor.

There have been no more blog posts either.

Though Jenna hasn't signed the agreement yet, she is abiding by its stipulations. It is just a matter of time. She will sign.

Brigitte taps her nails on her desktop as she thinks. She decides she'll give Jenna one more day to lie in bed feeling sorry for herself, then it will be time to move on. She'll get her up. Have her sign the agreement. And then they'll get on with life.

She reaches for a notepad and jots some notes. She'll call Dr. Bernard and get Jenna in to see him. She'll call Carolyn Harris and ask that she offer Jenna a role in fund-raising for the de Young Museum again—perhaps even a position on the board of trustees. It is time to get her re-involved with the right people and the right projects.

After she's had the reconstructive surgery on her jaw and after she's re-engaged with both society and Brigitte herself, then it will be time to discuss bringing her into the business. Give her a real sense of purpose. Train her. Prepare her. Give her a glimpse of all she stands to gain.

Yes, all is going according to her perfect plan.

CHAPTER FIFTY-FOUR

As you are made more Christlike, you begin to take on His qualities.
JEANNE GUYON

*M*atthew

I CLOSE the door behind my last client and then go straight to my desk. I pick up my cell phone, which I silenced during my sessions, and check to see if there's a message from Jenna. Nothing. Then I check my e-mail. Nothing there either.

"Dude, what is going on with you?"

Anxiety, a rare emotion for me, pesters. My stomach growls, reminding me that it's 4:00 p.m. and I've eaten nothing since dinner two nights ago. I reach for the box of matches I keep on my desk, and go to the cube between the two chairs and light the candle.

I drop the box of matches on the table next to the candle and plop myself down in one of the chairs.

I lean forward, elbows on my knees, and focus on the flame. Outside, a battering wind rattles the office door and hail peppers the windows. Forecasters predicted this would be one of the worst storms of the decade—and it isn't disappointing. Lightning flashes and the lights in the office flicker followed by the crashing of thunder that sounds like the sky is breaking apart and dropping onto the rooftops of the city. It's intense.

My growling stomach is my reminder to pray Jenna through her own storm. Man, I wish I knew what that entailed. But God hasn't made me privy to what's going on with her. Still, it's not like her to miss an appointment, or to not respond to calls and e-mails.

When I went to her house yesterday, the maid said she's sick. But as I stood at the doorstep of the Bouvier estate, I sensed there is more going around than the flu. Something is up. But God has made it clear. My part in all this is to fast and to pray. For how long, I don't know.

He hasn't shared that info with me either.

I bow my head and listen to the battering storm outside my door and, as has happened many times over the last few days, as I close my eyes I see the images from a battle scene. And the image I see today is Jenna, lying on the ground, bloodied.

Man, she's down for the count.

My heart feels like it splits wide open. "Dude, fight!" Then I begin to pray—letting the Spirit inform my prayers. It's one of those *repeat-after-me* prayers, where words whisper through my mind and heart, and I repeat them back to God.

"Courage, strength, perseverance—all these things I ask for Jenna, Lord. Provide—Your strength, Your stamina, Your wisdom. You through her. Surround her, sustain her, rescue her. Rescue her. Rescue her. Oh, Lord, send Your armies and rescue her."

I swallow the lump in my throat and wipe my wet cheeks.

I continue to pray.

I pray into the evening.
I pray until I'm exhausted.
I pray without ceasing.
"Fight, Jenna, fight!"

CHAPTER FIFTY-FIVE

Die to live.
JEANNE GUYON

enna

I ROLL over in bed and open my eyes. The room is almost dark. I glance at the bedside clock—4:00 p.m. Outside, I hear a storm raging. I lay my head back down. My legs are tangled in the sheets and my unwashed hair tangles on the pillow. I haven't changed out of the pajamas I put on . . . when? Two nights ago? Three nights ago? I sit up in bed and push my hair out of my eyes. The air in the room is stale. A long-cold cup of peppermint tea sits on the nightstand, specks of dust float on top of the murky liquid.

I can't stay in bed forever.

I can't hide from the choice I've made.

I get out of bed, reach for the robe draped across the stool at the vanity, put it on, and then amble out of the room and down the hall to Brigitte's suite. I tap on the door.

"Come in."

I take a deep breath, and then push the door open and walk in. Brigitte sits at her desk, glasses perched on the end of her nose. She looks at me, takes the glasses off, and then motions me to the chair opposite the desk.

I walk to her desk, but don't sit. A weak act of rebellion.

"Good to see you up, my dear. I thought I might have to come hoist you out of bed myself."

"I'll sign the agreement. Now." Lightheaded, I reach for the edge of her desk and steady myself.

Brigitte looks at me, her eyes narrowed. "Yes, I knew you would see reason, chérie." She turns to the credenza and looks for the file then pulls it out. As she does, my heart begins thundering in my chest and a film of sweat beads on my upper lip. Mouth dry, I swallow.

She opens her desk drawer, pulls out a pen, and then hands both the agreement and the pen to me.

I bend to sign the agreement but my hand begins to shake.

I shake my head to clear my mind. And then I stand straight, pen dangling in my hand at my side. I look at Brigitte and then think of my dad...of Jason...and Matthew.

"Sign it, Jenna. You have no choice." Her tone seeks to intimidate and, for the moment, it works.

I bend and place the tip of the pen on the signature line. But again, something stops me. And a new wave of nausea swells.

I stand, drop the pen, and cover my mouth with my hand. For the second time in less than a week, I run from Brigitte's office.

I stagger to my bathroom, gulping for air. I wait for the expected and now so-familiar result, but as I breathe in and out, in and out, the moment passes and my stomach stills. I slump against the bathroom counter.

Then I turn and look at myself in the mirror.

The woman who stares back is unknown to me. Her eyes are lifeless, her complexion gray. I hang my head and my hair falls forward.

I can't look at myself.

I pull off my robe and drop it on the floor. I check the bathroom door to make sure it's locked, then open the door of the large glass enclosure and turn the shower on. I reach for the small panel on the far wall and set the temperature and timer for the steamer as well. I get a bath sheet and place it on the towel warmer next to the shower, and then I step inside.

With the door closed and the glass fogged, I feel as though I've escaped—Brigitte...and myself—for a few minutes. I fill my lungs with hot, humid air, and let the water from the dual heads pulse against my taut neck and shoulders.

But the sense of escape flees as thoughts torment me. A thousand images crowd the screen of my mind, but like television static, nothing is clear. I see only flashes—flashes of Brigitte through the years.

I see her contempt. Her conniving. Her control.

I see her for who she is, but it does nothing to change my circumstances. I think, for the first time in days, of the blog and the readers who follow it. I think of Andee and the questions she's asked. Am I really willing to just shut the door on the blog—on the readers?

On God?

Lightseeker seems almost unknown to me now. Her purpose seemed clear, but my own has been thwarted.

Images war within.

I long to make a different choice, but how?

Confusion, a slithering serpent, wraps itself around my mind and constricts—suffocating the last of my hope. *You are crazy*, it hisses.

My tears, as hot as the water spouting from the showerheads, blur my vision. I turn toward the wall of the shower and lean my forehead against the glass tile.

Yes, I am crazy.

Crazy to have stayed all these years.

Crazy to have put up with Brigitte's abuse.

Crazy to fall to her final ploy.

That is crazy.

Hope gasps for breath.

For the first time in days, I pray. I beg God.

Show me another way. Show me, please.

I turn, lean my back against the tile, and slide down the wall to the floor of the shower. I pull my knees to my chest and wrap my arms around my knees. *Show me!* I scream the words to God. Not out loud but rather in the recesses of my soul—that place where faith tells me He still resides and hears my pleas. *Rescue me. Please...rescue me. I don't know what to do!*

I want to follow You.

Whatever the cost.

My sobs reverberate between the glass walls. I sob into my knees until my stomach aches. I lift my head and gulp the thick air. *Please, show me!*

Choose life!

I lift my head from my knees. "What?"

Will you choose death or will you choose life?

The question spoken to my soul is as clear as if it were audible. And the words are familiar. They are the words I was led to pray that dark night. Words I believed I was praying for another. Had they really been for me? My heart and mind still.

God has broken His silence.

This day I call heaven and earth as witnesses against you that I have set before you life and death, blessings and curses. Now choose life, so that you and your children may live and that you may love the Lord your God, listen to his voice, and hold fast to him.

All is still.

The only sound is the song of water droplets against glass.

But in my soul, God speaks. The words from Deuteronomy, run through my mind as though I'd read them just moments ago. Somehow God uses words meant for the Israelites so many generations ago, to inform my circumstances now. In this moment, they are His words for me.

I repeat the words: "'Now choose life, so that you and your children may live…'"

And repeat again, "'…so that you…and your children…may live.'"

I gasp.

Fresh tears flow.

"Oh…" I relax my hold on my knees and move my hand to my abdomen and rest it there. "Oh…"

Knowing comes like dawn.

His mercies are new every morning.

Just as He spoke creation into being, His words unfurl the serpent wrapped around my mind and soul and crush it. The static images are replaced with one, clear thought.

Choose life!

And to stay with Brigitte would be choosing death.

And so, in that heartbeat, I decide.

I choose life.

I don't know how. I don't have a plan. But I have a Rescuer.

I entered the shower lost.

I emerge found.

As I blow-dry my hair, I make a plan—though it doesn't extend beyond the next several hours. But certainty flows through me. God will lead, one step at a time. If I think ahead—or if I think of my dad, or Jason, or Matthew—fear threatens. Instead, each time those thoughts arrest me, I hand them to God.

I will trust Him.

I dress in jeans, a blouse, and a black wool sweater. Then I take a suitcase from the closet, lay it on the bed, and fill it with clothes, toiletries, and other necessities. I sit on the edge of the bed for a moment and open the drawer of the nightstand. I take the ring out that I'd dropped inside and slip it back on my left ring finger.

"Thank You for Your forgiveness. Thank You that nothing can separate me from Your love."

When Hannah knocks on my door with dinner, I open the door just a few inches and take the tray she holds. I tell her I need nothing else.

I set the tray on my desk and then sit and make myself eat the bowl of chicken soup and a piece of bread. My stomach recoils, but I take it slow and get most of the soup down.

I eat with new purpose.

When I'm done, I push the tray aside, and open my laptop. I log into my blog server, and begin a new entry:

Dear Readers,

My name is Jenna Durand Bouvier...

CHAPTER FIFTY-SIX

*This preoccupation with your accomplishments or your failures leaves
no room for you to be totally enamored with God alone.*
JEANNE GUYON

ndee

LIGHTNING FLASHES IN SHARP, jagged bolts above the city. Rain
beats against the panes of the floor-to-ceiling glass.

"Someone's ticked." I shiver and walk to the wall behind me
and turn up the thermostat. I was invited to attend a party hosted
by *Urbanity* this evening, but I declined. I've turned down every
invitation I've received lately. With this storm raging, I'm glad I've
adopted the hermit lifestyle.

I shake my head. "You're going to have to get a life, Andee."

I sigh.

Nothing holds any appeal.

I hear my computer *ding* in my office and walk in to check my e-mail. "Well, hello Lightseeker. Where've you been hiding yourself?"

I open the new post and read:

Dear Readers,

My name is Jenna Durand Bouvier…

"What the—?" I read those words again, but struggle to assimilate the information. Anger prods. "What an idiot." I'm not sure if it's myself or Lightseeker—no, *Jenna*—I'm speaking to.

I continue to read:

You have known me as Lightseeker because I've feared revealing my identity. But this evening, I'm choosing to crucify fear. And there will be no resurrection.

Illumination came as I fully surrendered my will and my ways to God.

For many weeks I've considered what it means to take up my cross and follow Jesus. It seemed like an impossibility. It means, for me, standing back from all I've known. Standing back from my life, hands open, and offering all to God. Standing back from my own understanding. Standing back from owning responsibility that wasn't mine to own. Standing back from enabling, encouraging even, the sins of another.

Stand back, Jenna. I have heard God's command for me, over and over.

Tonight, I also stand back from omission, and claim my God-given identity. I am Jenna Durand Bouvier. I am God's child. I am His unique creation. And I am standing back from everything and everyone who has something other than God's purpose in mind for me.

Tonight, I stand back from my life—which means I will walk away from my life.

I will walk into the unknown. Down a dark and winding path. But I will not walk alone. He will illuminate the path ahead, one step at at a time.

I finish reading and I want to stand and cheer for Lightseeker. "You go, girl!" But I want to strangle Jenna. How can they be one and the same?

How could she correspond with me, knowing it's me, and not reveal herself?

How could she betray me like that?

How could she betray—

The thought smacks me in the face. "Well, there's irony for you." Sam mews what I interpret as agreement. "Hey, whose side are you on?"

I wander around the penthouse trying to make sense of what I now know. Hadn't Jason told Jenna about the way I let him go— okay, the way I dumped him? Yet, she still responded to me. Still treated me with respect. Or maybe she didn't know. Maybe Jason kept that to himself, too embarrassed to let on that he'd been dumped.

But no, that's not Jason's style.

I make the circle through the living room, kitchen, and back through the office, ending up in the living room again. Then it hits me. The *who* of Jenna's posts—the person she is walking away from tonight is Brigitte.

I think back to the first encounter I witnessed between them that morning in the solarium at the Bouvier home. I recall Brigitte's anger and disrespect. But I also remember earlier, the moments before Brigitte made her debut as the wicked witch. Jenna's peace. My sense that she was somewhere else—something else—*ethereal* was the word that came to mind.

Now I understand. Okay, understand might be a little strong. I don't get it, but I know, having read her posts, that her peace that morning came from an encounter with God.

"I hope you can find that happy place tonight, Lightseeker. And stay there."

I assess her reality—and then feel sick.

The reality? She's walking away from the Bouvier estate—and that's a chunk of change. And where's she headed? Back to Daddy, I assume, who is now owned by Brigitte.

Thanks to me.

I sold you out, Lightseeker.

The same way I sold out Jason.

I sabotaged not just myself, but I also destroyed the Durand family. What will they do?

Somehow, I figured they'd always have Jenna—and all that Bouvier money—to fall back on. But no. They'll have nothing. Again, I clamor for a solution, a way to fix what I've destroyed.

A way to redeem the situation.

And myself.

Only one thing comes to mind, but the implications are…

I shake my head. I can't risk it. If I give Bill Durand the money to pay the note, Brigitte will figure it out. She'll know where the money came from. She's too smart. Too savvy.

And she'll destroy me.

My career.

Everything I've worked for.

"What's done is done, Andee. And boy, did you ever do it."

I land on the sofa, pull my knees to my chest, and sit with my self-contempt. I know God is supposed to be all about forgiveness, but how can He ever forgive me for this?

CHAPTER FIFTY-SEVEN

Seek to be clear and transparent, only what God wants. As you do His will you are made ever more pure and transparent.
JEANNE GUYON

*M*atthew

I THROW BACK the covers and climb into bed. Man, it's been a long day and it's time to put it to rest. "Hasta la vista, baby." I reach to turn off the lamp next to the bed just as Tess wanders in. She stops at the door and looks at me.

"You're in bed?"

"Nothing like stating the obvious, babe." I flip the light off.

"Hey, wait. You've got to read this."

I sigh and sit back up. My stomach growls, my head aches, and my patience is thinner than thin. I switch the lamp back on and take the piece of paper Tess hands me.

"Lightseeker?" *Finally.*

"No, Jenna Bouvier."

I look at Tess and then back at the blog she's printed. "What?"

"Read it."

I read the first line of the blog and my heart stops. "Whoa…"

"You didn't know?"

I look up and read pain in her eyes. Oh, man, not cool. "Yeah, I knew, but babe, I couldn't tell you."

She looks at the ground and seems to think. When she looks back at me, she nods. I reach over and pull back the covers on her side of the bed and pat the mattress. "Come here." She hesitates, but then comes and crawls in beside me. I put my arm around her shoulders and she settles in while I read the rest of the blog.

"Whoa, dude." This is what I've been praying for. I don't know what went on to get her to this point, but baby, she is depending on God and following Him. I lean over, kiss Tess on the cheek, and then lift my hand for a high five.

She gives me a half-hearted five. "So…did you know she was going to do this?"

"Nah, this is between her and God." I sit up straighter and turn so I'm facing Tess. "I knew something was up. Not because she told me, but because, well, I just knew."

"God told you?"

I look at her and see she's serious. She wants to know.

"Yeah, God told me. I mean, not in so many words, not like a booming voice from above. But I knew it here." I pat my chest. "That's why I've been fasting. I felt like God said Jenna was heading into a storm and that He wanted me to fast and pray for her."

I hold the blog up. "I'm guessing this is the storm." I look back at the blog and smile. "Looks like she's weathering it."

"Yeah, but what will she do?"

I shrug. "I don't know."

"Do you think she'll be okay?"

I look back at the blog post and read the last few sentences again. Then I look back at Tess and see compassion in her expression. I reach out and put my palm on the side of her face and then lean in and kiss her. When I pull back, I look her in the eyes. "Yeah, she'll be okay. God is with her, Tess. She's following Him. He'll lead. He'll provide. But that doesn't mean it will be easy."

She nods and is quiet for a minute. "I think we should pray for her. You know? Right now. Together."

I swallow the lump in my throat. "Okay, let's do that." I put my arm around Tess's shoulders again and pull her close and then we both bow our heads and I listen as my wife prays.

Dude, my wife *prays!*

When she finishes, with her head still bowed, she elbows me letting me know it's my turn. So I pray for Jenna—pray for continued strength. Pray for God's provision. Pray for her future.

After I say "Amen," Tess and I lift our heads and look at each other. Her emerald eyes glow. I suck in my breath and reach for her face. I hold her face in my hands.

"You've never looked more beautiful." I watch as a blush creeps over her freckled cheeks. "Your eyes…"

They're smoldering. Ignited by My Spirit, Matthew.

She puts her hand over mine. "Babe? Are you okay? Are you crying?"

I swallow. "Yeah, I'm okay. More than okay." Then my stomach rumbles in a big way and Tess giggles.

"Let's eat!"

"Really? Can you?"

I nod. "Yeah, I think I just got the green light. It's time to break my fast." I throw the covers back, leap out of bed, and race Tess to the kitchen. As she pulls leftovers out of the fridge and puts them on a plate, I stand and look out the kitchen window and see a full moon peeking through angry clouds.

There's a break in the storm.

But it hasn't passed.

CHAPTER FIFTY-EIGHT

My only desire is to completely give myself up into the hands of God without any idea of turning back or of fear of what may happen.
JEANNE GUYON

*J*enna

I POST my blog just before leaving. I pack up my laptop, close the suitcase, and lift it from the bed to the floor.

I wheel it to the door of the suite and open the door. I slip out and close the door, careful not to make any noise. Then I wheel my suitcase down the hallway, holding my breath as I pass Brigitte's rooms. I head for the elevator, certain that any sound I make is lost in the deep pile of the plush carpet. I reach the elevator and push the button and wait for the—

"Where do you think you're going?"

I jump. Every nerve in my body comes to attention. I take a deep breath, square my shoulders, then turn to face her in the dark hallway. "I'm leaving. I won't sign your agreement. I won't stay here."

She takes a step toward me, and my heart hammers.

But I don't back away.

"Who do you think you are? You're nothing! *Nothing!* Without *me!*" She spits her words at me, and droplets of her saliva spray my face. In that moment, a new realization becomes clear: not only is she battering me with her words, but she is also attacking the Spirit who lives within me.

Roiling anger bubbles within.

I take a step toward her and see her hesitate. "No, Brigitte. No. I am nothing without *God* and I will no longer allow you to stand in the way of His purposes for me. I'm leaving. You can't stop me." There is a calm control to my voice that I know is not my own.

As I turn to step into the elevator, she grabs my arm, her nails digging through my wool sweater. She raises her hand to slap me, but I dodge her and yank my arm out of her grasp. Rage is scrawled across her red face.

"I'll *ruin* you! And your family!"

There is no point in arguing with her. *Now* the game is officially over.

And, probably for the first time ever, she has lost.

But she won't accept defeat.

I turn, pull my suitcase into the elevator, and push the button to close the door. As I do, I see her reach for a vase. She lifts it above her head and, just as the elevator closes, it shatters against the door.

When the door opens on the bottom floor, I hear her footsteps on the stairs above, her rant continues. I pull the suitcase out and quickly head down the hallway leading to the garage. I walk out the door, punch the button to open the garage door, and then head to the back of the Range Rover Sport—Gerard's car. He bought it for himself. It's paid for—and now it's mine. I open the back latch, lift my suitcase inside, and then slam it closed. As I head for the driver's side, the door between the garage and the house opens.

Hannah stands there. "Go! *Go!*" she hisses at me.

Stunned, I stare at her. She turns back and looks at Brigitte charging down the hallway behind her and then blocks her from entering the garage.

"Go!" She hisses again over her shoulder.

I get into the car, shut the door, and turn the key in the ignition. And then I back out of the garage. My heart pounds in my chest and I struggle to catch my breath. My hands shake on the steering wheel.

I'm at peace, my body just doesn't know that yet.

I am following Him.

When I catch my breath, I press the button on the steering column that activates the phone and give it a voice command: "Call Bill Durand."

When my dad answers the phone, my sense of relief gives way to a fresh onslaught of tears.

"Bill Durand. Hello?"

"…Dad…"

"Jen?"

I gulp back tears and take a deep breath.

"Jen? What's wrong? Where are you?"

"Dad, I'm…coming home. I'm…leaving. I want to come home."

My dad is quiet for a moment and then his sigh whispers through the phone line. "It's about time. Does Brigitte know?"

"Yes."

"Where are you?"

The concern in his voice brings new tears. "I'm still in the city. I'm…I'm just leaving. Dad, I need to talk to you, and to Jason, tonight. Is Jason there?"

"He's here. We had a late meeting this evening and he decided to stay over."

"Okay. I need to make a quick stop and then I'll head that way."

"Jen, take it slow. Drive careful."

"I will. And Daddy...pray. Just pray."

"I already am. See you soon, baby."

I click the button, hanging up the phone, and lean back in my seat. It's been a dozen years or more since my dad's called me *baby*. Our relationship changed after I married Gerard. I got caught in Brigitte's web, and hiding the truth from my dad and Jason took more energy than I had. So I detached. Not completely, but more than I care to consider.

But my dad will welcome me home with open arms. He will understand, I know. I just pray he will also understand the choice I made and its ramifications for Azul. As I have all evening, I place it in God's hands again.

I make my way to the Golden Gate Bridge, cross it, and head for Marin County. Before I turn off and head for Napa, I pull off the freeway and pull into the parking lot of a drug store.

I dash inside, searching the aisles until I find what I need. I take it to the register, pay, and then ask for directions to the restroom.

I need to confirm what I already know to be true. I take the bag with the pregnancy test in it and head in the direction the cashier pointed. As I do, I count backwards in my mind to the last night Gerard and I spent together at the chateau.

And then, eyes still swollen from my tears, I smile.

As I walk back to the car, I have my first moment of doubt since leaving. I'm walking away from a vast fortune—from lifelong provision for my child. But then, I consider the alternative—raising my child under Brigitte's roof and rule.

No.

Oh, no.

This amazing gift, in God's perfect timing, is yet another affirmation.

Anticipation and awe fill my soul. *Oh, Lord, thank You. Thank You.* Tears slip down my cheeks as I climb back into the car. He will walk with me. And He will provide—not only for me, but also my dad and Jason.

And my unborn child.

IT'S JUST after 11:00 p.m. when I turn onto the gravel driveway that leads to the house. A full moon shines above a bank of clouds, casting shadows on the vines along one side of the driveway. I recall my sense that a season of pruning was ahead.

It has arrived.

God is pruning away all I've known and in its place He offers Himself.

When I pull up to the house of my childhood, the front door opens and my dad and Jason meet me at the car. Jason opens my door for me and as I get out, my dad wraps me in a hug.

"Welcome home, Jen."

Jason reaches over and kisses my cheek. "Do you have a bag?"

"It's in the back."

As Jason unloads my suitcase, I walk with my dad into the low-slung ranch house and feel the pangs of loss. I can't imagine my dad anywhere else. Or without Azul to run. Yet, I trust God has a plan.

I follow my dad into the living room and Jason follows behind us, leaving my suitcase in the entry hall. Dad and Jason spread out on the sofa and I take the easy chair across from them—the chair that used to be my mother's. I look at my dad and brother and realize they both look as tired as I feel.

"Sorry to keep you up late…"

Jason looks at my dad. "We'd have been up anyway, Jen." He hesitates. "It's been a long day here. So tell us what happened."

I lean forward in the chair. "I…it…well…" Then I sigh. "I don't know where to begin." Then I remember and I smile. "I'm pregnant."

My dad's and Jason's eyebrows rise in unison, and I laugh. "Not what you expected to hear?"

"I'll say!" My dad gets off the sofa and comes over and gives me another hug. "Wow! Jen, that's great." He shakes his head in disbelief and smiles. Then he runs his hand through his hair and even through his smile, I see his fatigue.

"So I'm finally going to be an uncle!"

I nod. "Finally."

"Congratulations, Jen. I'm so happy for you. I wish Gerard…"

"I know. Me too."

My dad studies me. "How have you felt?"

"Horrible." I smile again. "But I never suspected. I thought maybe it was the infection, then a virus, or just the trauma of Gerard's death, or maybe depression. Everything but this." I smile. "But this afternoon"—I shrug—"God made it clear and I confirmed it with a test."

My dad sits back down on the sofa and leans his elbows on his knees. "You know we're here for whatever you need."

"I know, Dad. Thank you." I hesitate. "Well, that's the good news …"

My dad and Jason grow serious again, and Jason says, "Okay, tell us the rest of it."

I sigh and begin with the meeting in Max's office regarding the trust and then tell them about the agreement Brigitte wanted me to sign. My dad shakes his head as he listens. Then he interrupts.

"I hope you told her in no uncertain terms that—"

I hold up my hand. "Wait. There's more."

He shakes his head again and anger etches his features.

Jason reaches over and pats him on the back. "Let her finish, Dad."

I start again. "I did finally tell Brigitte I wouldn't sign it. But that won't be the end of it." I pause and look at my dad and Jason. I feel my courage waiver. *Oh Lord, help me . . .*

"Dad... Brigitte says she purchased a demand note for Azul. She showed it to me. She said it was for a loan you took out twenty-six years ago and never repaid." I take a deep breath. "She said that if I didn't sign the agreement, she'd demand that you pay the note, plus interest and whatever she paid for it."

My dad and Jason look at each other.

"Well, that answers that question."

I look at Jason. "What question?"

My dad leans forward. "I told Jason about it this evening. We've been discussing it all night."

"It's true then?" My heart sinks.

"Well, yes, and no." He goes on to explain.

He tells me about Duke and the loan he offered my dad. And how he paid him back but Duke tore up the check and told him he'd tear up the note. He goes through what I'm sure he's already gone over with Jason many times. Then he tells me about Kelly Whitmore.

"I received a call from her attorney a couple of months back. Said Kelly had a note and was demanding payment." He shakes his head. "He wasn't interested in hearing the story of Duke saying he'd tear up the note. Anyway, I didn't want to burden you and Jason with all of it until I'd checked it out. So I gave Andee a call—"

"Andee?"

He nods. "Yeah, I sought her advice and she said she'd check into it for me. She called and spoke with Kelly Whitmore's attorney, but by the time she talked with him, she said they'd already sold the note."

"Did she know Kelly sold it to Brigitte?"

"No. She said she didn't know who they'd sold it to or what the buyer intended to do with it. She told me they could demand payment and that if I couldn't pay, then they could draw up an involuntary bankruptcy petition against Azul. And, well...that would be that." He runs his hand through his hair again and shakes his head. "I was going to tell both of you, but then Gerard..." He shrugs his shoulders. "It just didn't seem like the right time to burden you with more."

My mind reels back to Andee's e-mail—the one saying that she'd betrayed those closest to her. I assumed she meant she'd betrayed Jason by ending their relationship, but now I wonder if there was more. "Jason, would Andee..."

Jason's shoulders slump. And then he gets up from the sofa and paces the length of the living room and back. "I don't know, Jen."

"What are you two implying?"

"Dad, could Andee have gone behind your back—sold you out to Brigitte?"

His gaze widens. It's not something he's considered. He looks to Jason, who just shrugs.

"I don't know, Dad, I think it's possible. I hate to think the worst of her, but—"

I hold up my hand. "Let's not make assumptions. Let me finish telling you what I did, or rather, didn't do."

"You better not have signed that agreement, Jen." Now it's my dad's turn to stand. He towers over me and I think of the massive trees in the park—the overstory trees—protecting the growth below. And then I know. I've had a protector all along provided by God. My dad would have stood up to Brigitte or anyone for that matter, if only he'd known the truth. He sensed it, but I never confirmed it.

I never spoke truth.

Condemnation woos me. But I turn away.

For good.

Tears fill my already swollen eyes. "No, Daddy, I didn't sign it. At first, after she told me about the demand note, I told her I would. I just gave up. But then...I just couldn't do it. I begged God to show me another way. To"—I wipe the tears slipping down my cheeks—"to rescue me. I finally surrendered and told Him I'd follow Him, no matter what happened." I stand up next to my dad. "I lost myself to Brigitte. I cease to exist when I'm with her. I lose sight of God's purpose. I knew I had to leave—to walk away. I had to follow God." I place my hand on my abdomen. "Especially now."

My daddy's tears match my own. He wraps his arms around me again. "Azul has special meaning to us, but Jen, it's just a business. That's all it is. It isn't worth losing yourself. It isn't."

When my dad lets me go, I look at Jason and read the fury in his features. "How could she? How could she stoop so low?" He shakes his head. "Jen, I'm so glad you're out from under her. You made the right choice."

"She will do what she's threatened, Jason. She will. I have no doubt." Fatigue pushes me back down into the chair. "There's more too." I sigh. "I have a friend—he's my spiritual director—I've been seeing him for a few months. You met him and his wife at Gerard's service, Matthew and Tess MacGregor?"

Both Jason and my dad nod.

"We've had a special connection. From the beginning"—I slump in the chair, exhausted—"I felt it. Like God knit us together. It's spiritual. Nothing more. But Brigitte's accused me of having an affair with Matthew. She said she'll publicly humiliate us. And now...I'm pregnant... Gerard's gone. It may look like... What will Matthew's wife think? And what will that do to his career? It isn't true. Matthew's led me to God. He's shown me truth. But Brigitte says she has evidence. She has to be bluffing, but I don't doubt she'll produce whatever she needs to humiliate us. I'm not worried about myself, but Matthew..."

I cover my face with my hands.

Then I feel a hand on my shoulder. I look up and my dad stands next to my chair. He looks over to Jason. "Son, pull up a couple of chairs. It's time we commit this to God. It's time we pray. We're embarking on a new adventure and we don't dare go it alone."

Jason brings two chairs in from the kitchen and sets them in front of the easy chair. Both he and my dad take a seat and hold out their hands. We sit in a small circle, the three of us, hands clasped, hearts surrendered to God.

And we pray.

CHAPTER FIFTY-NINE

Remain in God's hands. He may cast down or build up. Let Him do whatever He pleases, both in you and through you.
JEANNE GUYON

*M*atthew

AT 6:30 A.M., just after our alarm goes off, my cell phone rings. I left it on the nightstand before going back to bed last night. I feel for it in the still dark room. When my hand lands on it, I grab it and look at the screen.

"Tess, it's Jenna."

"Take it!" She leans over and turns on the lamp on her nightstand.

"Jenna? Dude, where are you? Are you okay?" As I listen, I toss back the covers and sit on the edge of the bed. Tess gets out of bed, comes around to my side, and motions that she's going to take a shower. She's giving me time alone to talk to Jenna.

"What?" I continue to listen as Jenna pours out her story. "Oh man…" I lie back on the bed and stare at the ceiling. "Madame B strikes and lives up to all her name implies."

I close my eyes as anger heaves in my chest.

After I hang up the phone, I crash back on the bed and stare at the ceiling. How could anyone be so evil? Questions torment. Will people believe Brigitte's allegations? What will my clients think? How will this play out in my job?

Man, how will it play out in my marriage?

Anger burns. Righteous anger.

This is so not cool.

I shake my head and sit back up on the edge of the bed. I hear the shower turn off. "Lord, I need You to give me Your words. Prepare her heart. Let her see truth." As I pray, peace descends like a dove.

God has my back.

I get up, throw on a pair of sweats and my flannel shirt, and then I go to the kitchen to make a cup of coffee for my wife. I meet her with it as she comes out of the bathroom and hand it to her.

"Is everything okay? Is she okay?"

"She's okay. Hey, I'm going to brush my teeth, why don't you get dressed, and we'll meet in the kitchen. I need to talk to you."

I see the uncertainty in Tess's eyes and it breaks me. I put my palm on her cheek. "I love you—more than you know." I feel my eyes fill with tears, but man, I can't help it.

"Babe?"

"Get dressed. It's okay. It'll be okay." I step into the bathroom, close the door, and then lean against it. "Draw her close, Lord. Draw her close."

A few minutes later, we're standing in the kitchen together.

I pour myself a mug of coffee and tweak it with creamer. Then we sit together at the small bistro table at the end of the kitchen, where I lay the story out for her. "Remember what you told me about Jenna's mother-in-law? Brigitte Bouvier?"

Tess nods.

"Well, she's attempting to blackmail Jenna."

Tess shakes her head. "But Jenna didn't fall for it—she left. That's what the post was about last night, right?" She sets her coffee cup down. "Wait, this is why we prayed for her last night. God knew what was coming, so He had us pray?"

I nod. Even as righteous anger roils inside, I'm awed at what God is doing in Tess. I clear my throat. "Right on both counts. Jenna felt God leading her in one direction and Brigitte stood between her and God. So she had to choose. And her mother-in-law didn't like her choice."

"How did she blackmail her?" Tess stops. "Wait, what about client confidentiality? Why are you telling me this?"

I lean forward and reach for her hand. "Because it involves me. And you need to hear the truth from me."

I have to tell Tess the truth.

And it's a hard truth.

But dude, the truth sets you free.

I take a deep breath.

CHAPTER SIXTY

Your Father wipes away your faults as easily as an earthly father wipes mud off a child's face.
JEANNE GUYON

ndee

I SIT at my computer and read the comments on Lightseeker's blog post. It's been two days since she revealed her identity and her critics are making themselves known. But so are her loyal readers. There is a war of words taking place online—but Lightseeker, Jenna Bouvier, hasn't weighed back in.

I've busied myself with the mundane. Taping radio casts, writing blog posts, and meeting with the nation's top CEOs. Good times. But Jenna—the Durand family—have plagued my thoughts. Like the lyrics of a bad song I can't get out of mind, my betrayal of Jason, Bill, and Jenna plays over and over.

If Brigitte hasn't already betrayed my confidence, she will. Trusting her was just another facet of my sabotage. Word will be out soon enough and Jenna, Bill, and . . . Jason will know that I sold them out. The question is how far will the damage go? Brigitte could destroy my reputation in the financial world.

My act, while not illegal, was unethical. And ethics are important when you're dealing with people's money. She could ruin me.

And rightly so.

Though, I don't think I'm what she's after.

My intercom buzzes, letting me know someone is downstairs to see me. I glance at the time on my computer. 6:45 p.m. I'm not expecting anyone. I get up from my desk and head to the intercom by the front door.

"Yes."

"Ms. Bell, there's a Jenna Bouvier here to see you."

I feel the muscles in my neck and shoulders tense and I'm tempted to tell the doorman that I'm not accepting visitors.

"Ms. Bell?"

"Yes..." I make a quick decision. "Send her up."

I take a deep breath. I'll face her. See what she wants. My anger with her has dissipated. Who was I kidding? She's the one with the right to be angry. Now, I'm just curious. I'd like to know what she wants. And if she knows what I've done, I'd like a chance to apologize and make things right.

"Like an apology will do any good, Andee."

I'm such an idiot.

I open my door and wait for the elevator doors to slide open. When they do, Jenna emerges. She walks with purpose and confidence as she approaches me. The passive woman I met at the brunch has disappeared.

"Hello, Andee." Her tone is serious, but not cold. Perhaps she doesn't know.

"Hello. Come in." I step aside and motion for her to enter the penthouse. She stops in the entry hall and I lead her to the living room. "Please, have a seat."

She sits on one corner of the sofa and I sit just down from her. We turn so we're facing one another.

"Thank you for seeing me. I was going to call, but...well, I didn't know if you'd take the call."

I nod. And wait. What in the world does she want?

"I want to apologize. For hiding my identity. For not being truthful with you."

She's apologizing to *me*? Get a clue, lady. "Well, to each his own, right? I'm sure you had your reasons and I'm guessing, knowing your mother-in-law, that she was at the top of the list."

Jenna nods. "Yes, she was, but as you said, self-protection doesn't work. She discovered the blog anyway. I let fear drive me rather than surrendering to God." She shrugs one shoulder. "That didn't get me anywhere either." She smiles and her beautiful crooked features balance.

"Yeah, I get that." I look at her gorgeous eyes—the color of a twilight sky, Jason had said, and I think of Azul. I look at my hands resting in my lap. I can no longer hold her gaze.

"I also wanted to ask you something, Andee."

Her tone changes. I glance back up at her.

"Did you broker the sale of the demand note for Azul? Did you connect Kelly Whitmore and Brigitte?"

There is strength in her voice and her eyes seem to bore straight through me. I can see she already knows the truth. Odd, but I'm relieved. I glance back at my lap, take a deep breath, and then meet her stare. "Yes, I did. And . . . for what it's worth, which isn't much, I know, I'm sorry." I shake my head. "I am so sorry."

She turns from me and looks out the windows—looks out at the bay beyond the city. She is quiet. Says nothing. Her calm is unnerving. When she looks back at me, I see something in her eyes that I can't read.

"I forgive you."

"What?" Her words drive a stake through my heart. "Wait. Do you get the significance of what I did? Brigitte, for all intents and purposes, now owns Azul. She'll force the company into bankruptcy."

Jenna nods. "I understand. And I forgive you."

I shake my head. I can't…I don't…get it. Get her. "You can't just forgive me. I have to fix it. I will fix it. I want to give Bill the money to buy the note back. I would have offered sooner, but"—I shake my head, shamed again by my actions—"but like your family, Brigitte will ruin me. My career. My reputation. I had to come to terms with that. I get it. It's my penance. My conse-quence. And I'll take it. I *will* make things right."

Jenna leans forward. "We can't earn forgiveness, Andee. We can't right our wrongs or redeem ourselves. Grace is God's free gift." She looks back out across the city and stares at the bay.

I notice the dark circles under her eyes.

"Dad and Jason and I have discussed all the possibilities. Stayed up talking into the night. We've gone over everything. Jason wondered if you might offer to pay for the note. I think he hoped—"

I hold up my hand. I can't go there.

Jenna nods. "Anyway, we don't want your money, Andee. We don't want to buy the note from Brigitte. We want truth. Justice. We're going to fight for the truth."

"Fight Brigitte? But I did this. It would be so much easier to let me—"

"No." Jenna leans toward me again. "I forgive you, Andee. *We* forgive you."

I shake my head again. "I can't…"

"I can only offer forgiveness, I can't make you accept it. It's the same with God—He offers grace, but we have to decide whether or not we'll accept it."

I stand up and go to the windows and look out. I don't want her to see my tears. "Yeah, okay. Thanks." I glance back and see her stand to leave. She turns and heads for the front door.

"Wait…"

She stops and turns back.

"You wrote something in your blog the other night... You said you were standing back from everything and everyone who has something other than God's purpose in mind for you, right?"

She nods.

"I get that. I don't get much these days, but I get that kind of focus—that kind of choice. That's been part of my business philosophy—don't let anyone or anything stand in the way of your goals."

She takes a step toward me and smiles. "You probably have a deeper understanding of that kind of focus than I do. It's kind of new for me. The only difference I guess is the object of our focus."

"Right. I'm ready to change my focus. I'm ready for that relationship you talked about." My tears fall now and I look, I'm sure, like a big blubbering idiot. But Jenna doesn't seem to mind. "Sorry. I need to get a grip."

Jenna laughs. "Actually, I think you may need to loosen your grip. No offense."

Then it's my turn to laugh. I wipe my face with the sleeve of my blouse, staining the satin with my mascara. "Yeah, you might be right." Then I'm serious again. "I'm not ready for...for a relationship with...Jason. I wasn't ready, you know? And I hurt him. I mean, even more than destroying his livelihood. He's a good man and he deserved so much more. Will you tell him that?"

She nods.

"I realize I have some things to work through. I'm going to start with the whole God thing."

Jenna smiles. "That's a great place to start."

I nod. "Jenna, what will you and your family do?"

She shrugs. "My dad says we're on a new adventure with God. If we lose Azul, we know that God will provide in another way. We'll take it one day at a time and follow His lead."

"Well, I'd like to help in any way I can."

"Thank you, Andee."

She walks toward me and I take a step back.

"It's okay, Andee. I'm just going to give you a hug." She laughs. "It won't kill you, I promise." Her hug is quick, but sincere. "I'd like to keep in touch. To talk. If you want."

"I'd like that. Contrary to popular belief, my friendship pool is a little dry. I have your e-mail address. I'll drop you a note."

"I'll look forward to it. Take care, Andee."

I follow her to the front door, open it, and watch as she walks away. Then I go back to the living room and the view that's captivated me, in one way or another, all these years and I consider Jenna's words about forgiveness and grace. It's something I have to choose to accept. I look down as Sam saunters out of the office and comes and sits by my feet—his tail curls around my heels. She also said God's grace is free. "I like free. Free is a good deal." Sam mews. "I'm glad you agree."

But I still don't understand how Jenna, how the Durands, can just forgive me.

And I don't get how God can...

Wait a minute. "Don't over think it, Andee. Just let yourself accept it." I bend, pick up Sam, and heft him up to my chest and hold him close. He purrs in my ear. I pull back and look at him. "Sam, I think we're getting soft."

Finally.

CHAPTER SIXTY-ONE

Our fellowship is independent of external situations and what other people think. In Christ we cannot be separated from each other, for we are one with Him; and in Him and through Him we are one with each other.

JEANNE GUYON

$\mathcal{M}$atthew

SEVEN MONTHS LATER ...

I SIT at my desk looking out over the Hudson River. The neighborhood is a dive, the space expensive, but man, the view is happenin'. New York City. What a vibe! The city, people, traffic, noise, people. "This is life!"

Because life is all about people.

Dude, it's all about intimacy—I swivel my chair away from the view and stare at the flame of the candle I lit when I walked in this morning—but there are different kinds of intimacy. The dictionary defines intimacy as:

> close familiarity or friendship; closeness: the intimacy between a husband and wife.

> a private cozy atmosphere: the room had a peaceful sense of intimacy about it.

> an intimate act, especially sexual.

> an intimate remark: here she was sitting swapping intimacies with a stranger.

> closeness of observation or knowledge of a subject: he acquired an intimacy with Swahili literature.

But in my opinion, and yes, I usually have one, the dictionary leaves out an important example: spiritual intimacy.

Spiritual intimacy develops when two people share a common passion for the Object of their belief—I see Jenna's face as I stare at the candle—when they recognize the Spirit living within them, is the same Spirit living within another. When they stand side-by-side, arms linked, eyes focused on Jesus. Or when they share both the suffering and joy associated with living a life surrendered to Christ.

This intimacy is deep.

Rare.

And dude, it's beautiful.

It's like the relationship, I think, between Mary and her cousin Elizabeth, when the child in Elizabeth's womb leapt in recognition of the Messiah carried within Mary's womb. Or maybe like what David experienced with Jonathan—a knitting together of souls.

It is the type of intimacy that may develop between a spiritual director and a directee. Between two friends. Or between two people ministering together.

Some warn against such a thing, even cautioning opposite genders to steer clear of this type of intimacy. I understand the caution. Spiritual intimacy may be mistaken for or confused with romantic intimacy. But it's possible to be romantic without being intimate. And to be intimate without being romantic. There is sexual intimacy that occurs between a husband and wife. And there is sex without any sort of intimacy.

It isn't just one way or the other.

I think back to my conversation with Tess the morning Jenna called. I see again the look in Tess's eyes.

"It isn't true. You didn't...you aren't having an affair with Jenna, right?"

The doubt I saw flickering in her eyes pierced me. As did gratitude to God that I could answer without hesitation. "I am not and did not have an affair with Jenna. Or anyone. Ever." I reached across the kitchen table and took Tess's hand in my own. "You're it. Past. Present. Future. You, and you alone, babe. You and I both know my job requires trust. It's not always easy. I take precautions with my female clients and directees. Those boundaries are clear from the beginning."

She nodded and the doubt fled. "But Matthew, there was— there is—something special, or different, about your relationship with Jenna. I've seen it in you. What is it?" She shrugged.

"Yeah." I nodded. *Lord, speak to Tess. Open her heart. Teach her.* I leaned forward, elbows on the table. "It's like this—when two pilgrims journey together, there is an intimacy that may develop on the trail. Pretenses are dropped. Souls are bared. Agonies and triumphs are shared. That happens with my counseling clients sometimes too. But with Jenna, it was unique. I saw God in her. The same God who lives in me."

I put my hand on my chest, across my heart. "When we believe in God, when we accept that Christ is our Savior, the Spirit comes and lives inside each of us. Right?"

She nodded, emerald eyes wide.

"We each have an individual relationship with the same God and so we're all connected. It is a solitary dance, done together, in the presence of God."

"Wow. That's beautiful."

I smiled. "Yeah, I can be eloquent every now and then." I leaned back in my chair. "It ticks me off when those who don't understand it make it out to be something other than the pure love Christ calls us to for our brothers, sisters, and even our enemies. A love founded in Him, given by Him."

"We love, because He first loved us. Right? I remember learning that."

"Right. It's what I felt with Lightseeker when I read her posts. Two souls bound by a belief in and passion for the One True God. It is what I felt when I first sat across from Jenna in my office. It wasn't her I reacted to—it was the Spirit so evident within her. Tim helped me see that. I brought him into my direction relationship with Jenna. Asked for his accountability. That's one of those boundaries I set for myself."

Tess nodded. "Thanks for doing that."

I smiled. "I love you."

"I know you do."

"Anyway, with Jenna, or Lightseeker as I first knew her, it was a spiritual intimacy that grew beyond anything I'd known—because she, more than anyone else, reflected Christ. She taught me, as I sat with her week after week, what a romance with Jesus looks like. Her passion. Her courage. And her surrender. Stirred my own."

Those were deep waters to tread with Tess, who was just coming back to a relationship with Christ.

Tess's eyes filled with tears. "I saw that in you. I saw that passion and…I knew…I knew I was missing out on something."

"I want"—I cleared my throat—"I want that with you, Tess. I've wanted that all along. I want that spiritual intimacy with you."

"I want it too."

Man, what a day that was.

I bring my mind back to the present, swivel my chair around again, and notice a few clouds moving across the hazy horizon.

Spiritual intimacy *was* the missing ingredient in my marriage. The one thing I wanted more than anything with my wife. And it was through Jenna, or Lightseeker, actually, that I, that we, received that gift.

I'm rarely at a loss for words, but how do you express gratitude for the magnitude of that kind of gift? It changes everything. Now. And for eternity.

I look at my watch, grateful my first appointment of the day cancelled. It's been a crazy few months. And even I need to catch my breath once in awhile.

I continue staring out the window. Jenna is becoming a modern-day mystic. Someone who, by contemplation and self-surrender, seeks to obtain unity with God. Someone who apprehends spiritual truths beyond their intellect. Someone who is, as much as humanly possible, one with God.

What an honor. An honor, dude! To sit across from Jenna week after week. To let the Spirit move between us, illuminating, for both of us, truths we'd not known before. To watch the Spirit transform her before my eyes.

Hard to explain.

But then, it should be hard to explain because it goes beyond human understanding.

Brigitte did as she promised. She attempted to tarnish that intimacy—to make it lewd and betraying. She didn't care who she hurt in the process. She was out for her own gain. Anger still boils inside me when I think of what she did. What Tess and I stood to lose. What Jenna did lose.

Yet, I am called to love her.

What does loving an enemy look like?

Tess and I are learning this together.

Love and relationship are two different things. As are love and reconciliation. And sometimes, the most loving act is to break relationship with someone.

Jenna learned this as she walked away from Brigitte. And I continue to learn as I watch her.

But now, I watch from afar.

Shortly after Brigitte's scandal—the alleged affair between Jenna and me that broke in the local news—Tess was offered a job in New York City. That's a dream for a fashion plate like my wife. We didn't ditch San Fran to dodge the scandal. Truth be told, for the most part, people ignored it. Though it caused plenty of pain for those close to us. But we endured. In fact, Tess turned to God for strength amidst the gossip, and she stood by me. She knew the truth.

When we moved to New York, it was because we heard God's whisper—His invitation to dance. So, a few weeks ago, we took His hand and followed His lead.

And my fashion-plate wife has fallen deeply in love with her new Partner.

Yeah, I called her a fashion plate. The name cracks me up.

I picked it up from one of my new counseling clients. A woman working hard to overcome traumatic events from her childhood. Man, I respect her. She's surrendering one day at a time. She splits her time between San Francisco and New York now. She's here a couple weeks a month. She's making some transitions in her career—offering financial advice to nonprofit organizations here and on the West Coast. She was a well-known financial advisor to the rich and famous, but she made a mistake. And Brigitte capitalized on it.

When she's back in San Francisco, she spends time with Jenna, who is walking alongside her and showing her what it looks like to lose your life for Christ's sake. It's a road they're walking together.

Because of Brigitte.

Man, now there's some irony.

But it's also a choice they each made individually—with God —together.

How cool is that?

I glance at the calendar on my desk. Jenna's baby is due any day now. I can't wait to see that little guy. When Jenna found out she was having a son, she picked his name: Gerard Matthew Bouvier. "Bonus!"

Tess even told Jenna we'd babysit if she comes to the city.

Still twenty minutes before my next scheduled appointment. So I reach for the mouse on my desk and watch as the screen of my computer lights up. Then I open my e-mail and find what I'd hoped for.

Dear Matthew,

The sun has set on the life I've known and shadows loom, tempting me to once again languish in the fog of doubt. Loneliness beckons, wooing me to believe I will never again enjoy the intimacy we've shared. But I turn away knowing the truth. The intimacy we shared was but a whisper of what was —of what is. Here, in this gray landscape, goodness shines and my spirit stirs as I behold my Beloved.

All I've known is lost to me now: home, wealth, and the acceptance of those I once longed to please. The roles I once lived to fulfill are no longer. Though loss seems cause for grief, joy prevails, because what's found is a treasure beyond imagining. Within these earthly confines, I've found a spacious place where my soul is finally free to dance. Here I soar in Love's embrace. So, friend of my soul, grieve not. Lean not on your own understanding, as you so often exhorted me. Instead, rejoice! Our paths are straight.

What others suppose about me—about us—no longer matters. Their accusations were a piercing thorn, but truth is a soothing salve. Whenever a lingering concern reveals itself, it's evidence that a bit of me remains after all. What cause for celebration there will be when all of me is finally lost in Him.

In the meantime, my dear friend, let's dance…

Faithfully,

Jenna

ALSO BY GINNY L. YTTRUP

Words

Invisible

Flames

Home

Convergence

AFTERWORD

Dear Reader,

Lost and Found was written during one of the most difficult seasons of my life—a season where I, like Jenna, was learning what it meant to pick up my cross and follow Christ. It was a season of profound pain. A season of loss. Yet, as I surrendered to God, I found my life hid in Him and I found unexpected joy in His embrace.

During that year, I picked up the writings of Madame Jeanne Guyon. Born in 1648, Jeanne Guyon suffered more than I could imagine. Her autobiography was written from a cell in the Bastille at the command of her captors. Though she alluded to her suffering, it seemed almost an aside—an afterthought meant to simply highlight the delight she found in an intimate relationship with Jesus Christ. It was that very relationship, in fact, for which she was imprisoned.

Upon my first reading of her story, I was angered by her passivity in the face of emotional torment directed at her by her mother-in-law and her maid. I was exasperated by her husband's neglect of her. I was outraged that she didn't fight against the establishment that convicted her and stand up for herself and the Holy Spirit living within her. I judged her a weak example of stewardship of the life God granted her.

I put the book aside and intended to forget about Madame Jeanne Guyon.

But her story nagged.

And nagged.

Also, two of my favorite authors, women who've mentored me through their writing, had both written about Jeanne Guyon. Either I'd also misjudged them, or I was missing something in Madame Guyon's life. So, a few weeks later, I picked up her autobiography again.

This time, I saw her with different eyes. I saw her with eyes that see. Instead of passivity, I saw faith. Instead of weakness, I saw strength. Instead of a lack of stewardship, I saw a woman whose life and faith are still speaking three centuries later.

Jeanne Guyon was intimately acquainted with what it meant to give up one's life for Christ's sake. She knew what it was to share in the sufferings of Christ—to know harsh judgment founded on the fear and lies of others. She understood, like Christ, that she was called to listen for the will of the Father, and the Father alone.

After my second reading of Jeanne Guyon's autobiography, I knew God had provided a companion for me through my own suffering—another woman to lead me in the way of prayer and surrender to God. For many months, I felt as though Jeanne Guyon walked with me through my own hardships and I began to wonder what a contemporary Jeanne Guyon might look like. What would she suffer? How would she handle it? How would she relate to God? To others?

Thus, the story of *Lost and Found* was born. It is a picture, I pray, of what it looks like to lose our lives for Christ's sake today. It is also a picture of one woman's romance with Christ.

It is a romance, a dance, I'm also participating in—and it's beyond anything I've ever imagined. It is also a romance He's calling you to. Do you hear Him? Do you see Him holding out His hand?

Will you dance with Him?

I pray you will.

I'd love for you to share your thoughts on *Lost and Found* with me. You may e-mail me through my Web site: www.ginnyytrup.com.

Finally, if you related to Jenna's relationship with Brigitte in any way, if you find yourself in an emotionally destructive or abusive relationship, please, please, please pick up Leslie Vernick's book *The Emotionally Destructive Relationship* and allow God to lead you to a place of greater emotional health and strength found in Him (www.leslievernick.com).

Warmly,

Ginny L. Yttrup

DISCUSSION QUESTIONS

Discussion Questions

1. Like Jenna, victims of long-term emotional abuse often lose themselves in the abusive relationship. Are there relationships or circumstances in your life that threaten the core of who you are? How do you hold on to the person God created you to be?

2. How did you feel about the way Jenna handled her relationship with Brigitte in the beginning of the story? How might you have handled the relationship differently?

3. Jenna chronicled her suffering and her relationship with God through her blog. How do you handle suffering? Do you reach out for others as Jenna did? Or do you isolate yourself?

4. Due to the wounds of her past, Andee felt compelled to control her circumstances. Are there wounds from your past that affect your behavior?

5. After learning Andee's secret, did you feel more compassion for

her and less judgment of her? Are there people in your life you might extend that same compassion?

6. Both Jenna and Andee were faced with the choice of revealing truth or hiding behind their circumstances. How did the truth set them free? How does it set you free? (See John 8:32.)

7. At first, Jenna misinterpreted what it meant to pick up her cross and follow Christ, assuming it meant she had to stay in her place of suffering. What does it truly mean, based on Matthew 10:34–39, to pick up our cross and follow Christ?

8. Does anything about the verses in Matthew 10:34–39 surprise you? What?

9. Have you had to make the choice to walk away from people in your life who keep you from Christ? If so, was it a difficult decision and how did you handle it? If not, how would you deal with someone who came between you and your relationship with God?

10. Does the kind of relationship Jenna had with God seem extreme to you? Why or why not?

11. Jenna and Matthew shared a bond based on their mutual love for Christ. Do you have people in your life that you can share your spiritual journey with? If not, how might you establish such relationships and how would they benefit you?

12. Jenna seemed to have a romance with God. Does that type of relationship with God appeal to you? Why or why not?

13. Andee worked to redeem herself after she betrayed Jason and his family. Why did her efforts fail?

14. Have you ever struggled to accept God's forgiveness? Explain.

15. *Lost and Found* portrays God working simultaneously through the lives of Jenna and Andee. Unbeknownst to Jenna, God had her pray that Andee would "choose life," then He used that same passage of Scripture (Deut. 30:19) to encourage Jenna to do the same. Do you believe God works this way? Can you share an example from the Bible or from your own life?

16. Throughout *Lost and Found*, God seemed to speak to Jenna, Matthew, and even Andee. Do you believe God still speaks to His people? If so, how?

17. What did you take away from this story that you can apply to your own life?

ACKNOWLEDGMENTS

A novel is neither written nor published alone; instead, it takes a community of unselfish souls sharing their knowledge and gifts. During the writing of *Lost and Found* I was blessed with such a community.

Thank you to James Warrick, who quoted Madame Jean Guyon during one of our coaching conversations and set me on a road of discovery. Thank you, too, for your support as I learned what it meant to pick up my cross and follow Christ.

Leslie Vernick, your book, *The Emotionally Destructive Relationship*, offers hope and healing to many. It changed my life. Thank you for the many hours you graciously spent reading this manuscript and advising me on characters and plot. May those who recognize themselves in the pages of our books turn to God for healing and freedom.

Cretia Martinson, your training with the Meyers and Briggs' personality types and your willingness to share your knowledge with me as I created characters was both great fun and so helpful. Thank you.

Dr. Orville Easterly taught me the important principle that when we live to please others we will always fail and we will always lose ourselves. I used that principle to inform this story and also as a direct quote from one of the characters. Thank you, Dr. Easterly.

Thank you to Steve Burlingham, family law attorney, for your interest in my writing and your willingness to share your knowledge with me regarding family trusts. Your phone call with the exact answers I needed was invaluable. Your love for God is so evident and a gift to your clients.

Thank you to Dee Bright, Neil and Sharol Josephson, and Laurie Breining. You each provided a refuge and a home for me as I wrote. As I pressed toward the deadline, Laurie cooked, cleaned, and kept the dogs quiet (a major feat) so I could write.

Jan Johnson and Tricia Rhodes both shared their knowledge of Madame Guyon's life through their books and e-mails, answering my many questions and encouraging me. I am so grateful to both of you.

Glenna Salsbury, your teaching on Matthew 10:39 was invaluable, and your friendship is a blessing.

Thank you to Linda Sommerville for advising me on the scenes involving spiritual direction and for answering my many questions. I love calling you "friend."

I owe a debt of gratitude to Rick Acker, who helped me move forward with the story by brainstorming the business and financial fraud plot with me. I couldn't have done it without your expertise.

To my writers group and incredible friends who read early drafts of *Lost and Found*—you advised me (over and over), prayed for me, and cheered me on. I love you all!

Karen Ball, editor and friend—I love working with you. Thank you for your wise insights and your willingness to let the story go where I wanted it to go. And thank you for talking me off the ledge a time or two when I was sure I wouldn't make my deadline.

Steve Laube, as always, I value your expertise and advice as my agent. I also highly value your patience with my unending stream of questions.

To my B&H Publishing family—you are a group of gifted souls who works hard each day for the glory of God. I am blessed by each of you.

And finally, to my sons, Justin and Jared—Justin, you advised me on cars and always willingly answered my e-mails or texts about what cars are cool. Thank you. Jared, thank you for listening to me over lunch one day and offering insight into the business plot I was struggling with. Thank you both for your interest and enthusiasm in what God is doing through my books. Thank you, too, for your understanding when I had to say no to lunch or dinner dates because I was working. More than anything in the world, I LOVE being your mom!

ABOUT THE AUTHOR

Ginny L. Yttrup is the Christy, *RT Book Reviews*, and *ForeWord Reviews* award winning author of six novels. Ginny is also a sought after writing coach and speaker. She loves spending time with her two adult sons, her daughter-in-law, and the small group of close friends who add depth and laughter to her life. She lives in Northern California with her rescue pup, Henry Higgins.

If you'd like to receive updates on Ginny's work, sales, frequent giveaways, and glimpses behind the scenes, subscribe to her newsletter: http://ginnyyttrup.com/contact/

facebook.com/GinnyYttrup

twitter.com/GinnyYttrup

instagram.com/ginnyyttrup

CPSIA information can be obtained
at www.ICGtesting.com
Printed in the USA
LVHW111729130521
687356LV00006B/617

9 780996 144780